Critical Acclaim for Bret Lott's
New York Times Bestseller
JEWEL

"Lott is one of the most important and imaginative writers in America today. His eye for detail is unparalleled; his vision—*where* he looks—is like no one else's in this country."

—*The Los Angeles Times*

"Bret Lott's *JEWEL* is a beautifully crafted first-person epic of one poor Southern woman's personal duel with God. . . . This is a voice we don't want to stop hearing. . . . Some of the tenderest scenes of family love since those in Dickens."

—*The Chicago Tribune*

"*JEWEL* is a reminder of one of the chief reasons to read: for the experience, for the story. *JEWEL* is a simple first-person tale of a family that faces life with courage, if not always insight, and grows wiser for the doing. The work has the solid characterizations of Steinbeck or Harper Lee—and the corollary scope and universality of three-dimensional people doing believable things. . . . Bret Lott's creation of full humanity in Jewel, both in voice and spirit, is near-perfect. His dialogue is solid and real, his prose hard, lucid, and seamless. . . . Mr. Lott's pivotal scenes are likewise beautifully written and are both plain and profound. In Jewel's crude but generous understanding, we find not only the human condition, but compassion for the human condition—and the redemptive power of love."

—*The Dallas Morning News*

Also by Bret Lott

The Man Who Owned Vermont

A Stranger's House

A Dream of Old Leaves

Reed's Beach

How to Get Home

Fathers, Sons, and Brothers

The Hunt Club

JEWEL

A NOVEL BY

BRET LOTT

POCKET BOOKS

New York   London   Toronto   Sydney   Singapore

This book is a work of fiction. Names, characters, places and incidents are products of the author's imagination or are used fictitiously. Any resemblance to actual events or locales or persons, living or dead, is entirely coincidental.

POCKET BOOKS, a division of Simon & Schuster Inc.
1230 Avenue of the Americas, New York, NY 10020

Copyright © 1991 by Bret Lott

Originally published in hardcover in 1991 by Pocket Books

ISBN: 0-671-04257-2

First Pocket Books paperback printing December 1999

10 9 8 7 6 5 4 3 2 1

POCKET and colophon are registered trademarks of Simon & Schuster Inc.

Cover art by Bradley Clark

Printed in the U.S.A.

For the true jewel,
Myrtis Jewel Purvis Lott

And this is the father's will which hath sent me, that of all which he hath given me I should lose nothing, but should raise it up again at the last day.

JOHN 6:39

How unsearchable are his judgments, and his ways past finding out.

ROMANS 11:33

BOOK ONE

BOOK ONE

1943

Chapter 1

I was born in 1904, so that when I was pregnant in 1943 I was near enough to be past the rightful age to bear children. This would be my sixth, and on that morning in February, the first morning I'd known I was with child, I'd simply turned to Leston in bed next to me, the room gray from a winter sky outside the one window, that sky not yet lit with the sun, and I'd said, "There'll be no more after this one."

He rolled onto his back, his eyes still shut, the little hair he still had wild and loose on his head. He put his hands behind his head, and gave a sort of smile, one I'd seen enough times before this. Five times before, to be exact.

He said, "Another one," and kept the smile. Then he said, "What makes you think so?"

I said, "Doesn't take divining, not after five," and I paused. I reached a hand up from beneath the quilts, felt the chill of the morning on my skin, that skin the same color gray as the small strip of sky I could see above the box pine and live oak outside the window. I touched Leston's cheek, did the best I could to smooth out his hair. He was still smiling.

I said, "I just know."

Then came the morning sounds, sounds of the everyday of our lives: first the slam shut of the front door as

James, our oldest, started on his way to work at
Crampton's Lumber; then the scrape of our other two
boys, Burton and Wilman, from their room above us, the
first sounds of tussling and fooling that started now and
ended only after dark, the boys back in bed. Those two,
I thought as I lay there, my hand back under the quilts
to keep warm as long as I could, we'd had too close
together, Burton seven, Wilman almost six. Billie Jean,
my second child, would not be up for as long as I would
let her sleep, around her on the bunched and rumpled
blankets of her bed the movie magazines she lived for,
fanned around her like leaves off a tree. And Anne, my
baby, would be stirring soon, then following Burton and
Wilman around like a lost dog, wanting only to be one
of them, blessed by the rough and tumble of pinecone
wars and whittling knives.

I heard Wilman say, "That's not yours," then Burton
putting in, "But it was," and then the pop and crack of the
heart pine floor above us as the two started in on each
other.

"Boys," Leston called out, his voice as deep and solid as
every morning.

The fighting stopped, the room upstairs as quiet now as
when they were asleep.

"Sir?" they called out together.

Leston smiled, though on my boys' voices was the certain sound of fear. He said, "Chunk up the stove. The two
of you."

"Yes sir," they gave back to him, and then their whispering started, and I knew whatever they were fighting
over wouldn't be settled until sometime late in the day, if
at all.

Leston sat up in bed, turned so that his back was to me,

his feet on the floor. He looked to the window, then down to the floor. He brought a hand to his face, rubbed it, ran that hand back through his hair. Wisps of it still hung in the cold air, copper going gray, the line of his shoulders still the same hard and broad line I'd seen the first time I met him, the same shoulders I'd held while we'd conceived each of our children this far. But now, his head hung forward, his hands holding tight the edge of the mattress, I thought I could see for the first time the weight of age upon him, those shoulders with the burden of our years and our five children, one of them already set to working his way through the world, and me with a brand-new one now on the way.

Leston had left the quilts pulled back, my face and shoulders and arms out there to the cold. He lifted his face to the gray window again, gave out a heavy breath that shone in a small cloud before him, the room so cold. Leston said, "No more after this will set fine with me."

Then I shivered, felt it through my whole body, a shiver so deep whatever warmth I'd had beneath the quilts disappeared entirely, and I knew my sleep was over, that day and all the days left to me until this next child was born now begun. I let out a deep breath, too, saw the cloud it made in the room, and in that breath I saw what I'd known all along, known all the days until this one when I'd been thinking maybe, just maybe I was going to have another child: it was me, too, that age was weighing down on hard.

I sat up in bed, put my feet on the cold pine floor, my back to Leston. I stood, called out, "Boys," heard Wilman and Burton holler, "Yes ma'am!" The floor above us filled up with the scrabbling of two boys trying to get their clothes on, then the rattle of them both on the stairs.

I was on my way to the door and breakfast when Leston, behind me and still on the bed, said, "Jewel Hilburn, you take care."

I turned to him, my hand already on the doorknob. He'd gotten the smile back, his eyes the same deepwater green I'd known for what felt all my life.

I said, "You know I will," and held my eyes on him.

He said, "That I do," and nodded, and then I was out the door and on into the kitchen.

I'd taken care of myself most all my days, though things had eased up once I met Leston. Before that, though, before Leston and the stop and start of our having children and trying to feed our own selves, there was a world sometimes I would like to sooner forget than think about at all. But it's history that matters, what keeps you together in the tight ball of nerves and flesh you are and makes you you and not someone else.

I was an orphan at age eleven, my mother dead of a fever, my father not two months before she passed on having broke his neck on a log just under the water at the bend in the Black River, the bend nearest town where the post oak lay low to the water, and where, in spring, light through the leaves breaks across the river so that nothing can be seen beneath. He broke his neck right then, right there, with the quick and simple dare of diving into water, and when I was a little girl of eleven with both my mother and father gone, and me living suddenly with a grandmother I'd only met three times before, I used to imagine it wasn't a fever that killed my mother, but a broken heart at the death of her beloved.

But the truth was he'd moved into a logging shack a year before he'd broke his neck, and only showed up to our house at twilight on Saturday nights to have at my mother, then to attend church the next morning, his black hair slicked back and shiny with pomade. It was the thick and sweet smell of his hair that woke me up Sunday mornings, me staying up just as late as the two of them the night before, listening through the walls to the mystery they tended to each Saturday night, sounds I'd hear again only when Leston and I were together, so that on our wedding night twelve years later the low moan he made and the pitch and twirl of sounds I heard coming from me were like the ghosts of my long dead parents, sounds I knew but had forgotten in the cloud of years filled with taking care of me and me alone.

Sunday mornings we would go to church, where we'd sit in the pew, me between my momma and daddy, their only child. I'd had a brother, who only now comes to me as part shadow, part light, a baby born when I was three and who died when I was four, and there are times before I go to bed when I will stop in at Burton and Wilman's room, sometimes even James', though he has fast become a man and lost the look of a child, and I will see in their faces the faintest trace of my brother, the thin baby line of an eyebrow I believe may have belonged to him, the open mouth and pale lips soft with air in and out which perhaps I am remembering, perhaps imagining. No real memories do I have of him, except for the idea somewhere of my daddy holding Joseph Jr. on one knee and playing buggety-buggety, and the picture in my head of a baby asleep. But that's all I remember of my brother, and even calling that a memory is giving the image in my head more credit than is due.

After church we would file out of the sanctuary into air even hotter than inside, live oaks thick with gray moss like

clumps of a dead man's hair fairly lit up with the noise of
cicadas, everyone everywhere fanning themselves with
bamboo and paper fans printed with the words to
"Amazing Grace" on one side, Psalm 23 on the other.
Daddy would shake hands with Pastor, pass time with
whoever might want to, all the time his one arm round my
mother's shoulder, his hair still just as shiny, little runnels
of sweat slipping down his sideburns. He acted the part of
my daddy, would even on occasion hunch down and kiss
me on the cheek, pat my hair, smile at me, though everyone in the entire congregation, and even those heathens
not in attendance, knew we no longer lived together.

Once we were home, he would simply see us to the
door, give me that pat on the head good-bye I hated even
more than his showing up at sundown the night before,
and kiss my momma full on the lips. Then he would turn,
step down off the porch. Without so much as a backward
glance or the smallest of waves, he would head off down
our dirt road, back to the logging shack not two miles
away.

Momma and I watched him go each time, watched
until the road took him deep into pine and cypress, the
green of wild grape vines everywhere that swallowed him
up. I wished each Sunday afternoon that green would
never let him go, wished he'd never make it back to whatever pleasures he found during the week, pleasures he
wanted to pursue more than plant himself at home with
us, his own. We watched him go, and only once we could
see no more movement, no more slips of white shirt
through the shield of green forest, did we go in. My
momma always went in first, though it had been her he'd
given his kiss to, her who'd given her whole self to him.
She turned, her eyes down to the porch floor, and moved

on inside. I was always that last one out on the porch, just watching that green, hoping he would not find his way out.

The day he broke his neck was a Tuesday. I was already home from school, out on the porch with my tablet and thick red pencil, doing my figuring for the next day. I knew even then I wanted to be a teacher, something in me with the need to lead and stand before people and explain in a plain and simple voice bits of the world they could not know were it not for me. I was only eleven, but knew already, too, that my wanting to teach had to do with my momma and how she acted once Daddy had gone, how our trips into Purvis had become ordeals for her, her standing at the dry goods store and touching a bolt of gingham, a tin of baking powder, looking at them as though they were troubling bits of her own history, things she knew she needed but hated all the same. I ended up taking her by the hand to Mr. Robineau at the register, where she'd give her feeble smile to him as I placed our items on the glass counter, him never meeting our eyes but smiling all the same.

So that on that Tuesday, when I saw four men through the green of the forest, I was the one to go into the house and take her hand and lead her up from her cane rocker, the one she spent most hours of the day in, and out onto the porch. The men had cleared the trees by then, and I could see them, hair wet, faces white, jaws set with the weight of whatever lay in the doubled-up gray wool blanket they toted, one man to a corner, the middle sagging, nearly touching ground with each step they took. They wore only undershirts and blue jeans, all of them barefooted, their feet red with the dust of the road they'd walked.

I wasn't afraid, not even when Momma, behind me, whispered, "Oh," then, louder, "Oh, oh." I heard her take one step back, then another, but there she stopped. The men were off the road and onto our yard now, their eyes never yet looking up to us; men I couldn't place from anywhere. I looked behind me to Momma, saw her there with a hand to her face, covering her eyes, the other hand at her throat and holding on to the collar of her dress.

I turned to the sound of the men on the porch steps, felt myself backing up too. The four of them moved toward me, struggling with the burden they bore, the wool blanket seeming heavier than anything I'd seen before. Yet they were gentle with it, eased it up and onto the porch itself and inched toward us, finally letting it down onto the wood with a grace I would never see again.

They stood back from it, four men with hands on their hips, eyes on the heap before us. Then one of them, a man with hair as black as my daddy's hair flat and wet with strands of it long down and into his eyes, squatted, his elbows on his knees, eyes still on the blanket. He put out a hand, held it a moment above the wool, then reached down, took hold of the blanket, and pulled it back to reveal to us my dead and naked father.

His head was bent back from us, so that what I saw first was his throat, already swelled and purple. His face was gone from me, twisted up and away, and for a moment I had no genuine idea in my head who this was, or why he had been brought here. The blanket had been pulled back far enough to bare his chest and arms and stomach and one leg, the edge of the blanket left just below his waist, so that next I saw the pencil-thin line of hair that started at his navel and traced its way beneath the gray wool, disappearing there. He had no hair anywhere else, his skin already turning the milk-white of the dead, his arms and the one leg I could see bent at the joints, him all movement and peace.

"We was swimming," the man with the black hair said. He still held the edge of the blanket, and my eyes went to his fingers, watched as he slowly rubbed his index finger and thumb together. "We was swimming, and then he just didn't come up. He was jumping off—"

"Benjamin," my momma let out, her word choked and hard in the air. "Stop."

The man, this Benjamin, looked up. His fingers stopped moving, his eyes on my momma.

I looked up to her. She still had a hand to her eyes, the other at her throat, and then I moved toward the blanket, toward the body I still didn't know as my daddy. I wanted to see the face, know who it was, and as I made my way toward where I would see him, two of the men who'd carried him here moved out of my way, their hands still on their hips.

I stood next to this Benjamin, and looked down at my daddy's face. His lips had gone blue, his eyelids gray, his hair matted and snarled.

Benjamin let go the blanket. I didn't move, not yet certain what any of this meant.

Then he put his hand to my back, held it just below my shoulder blades. The touch was near nothing, only contact.

He said, "Your daddy and me was brothers."

But the words didn't mean anything to me. I was thinking of Sunday mornings and the smell of pomade, and of me sitting between the two of them while Pastor gave up to God our congregation's prayers, and how my God had finally answered the prayer I'd been whispering to myself while Pastor pleaded for everyone else: I wanted him never to come back.

Here was my reward for righteous, heartfelt prayer, for asking in Jesus' name what I knew would make my momma and me better off in the long run, no matter what those sounds I heard from their room meant.

Which is why I reached down and picked up the edge of the blanket my uncle had let fall, and pulled it back over my daddy, covered him up. The four men were watching me now, waiting, I figured, for whatever might happen next.

I said, "Bring him on inside." I paused, then said, "Somebody go find Pastor, too."

It would be lifetimes later before I knew what'd really kept me out there on the porch Sunday afternoons long after my momma, kept my eyes on the green and searching for signs of his life. Only after the lifetime between my daddy's death and my momma dying, two months that couldn't be measured by any means of a calendar or the movement of the moon; then the lifetime spent on the little piece of childhood I had left, spent with Missy Cook, my grandma, in a house more dead than my parents would ever be. Then the lifetime of school I spent away in Picayune, lifetimes that ended, all of them, with my first night with Leston and hearing the ghosts of my momma and daddy there in the room with me. And since then have come countless nights spent with those ghost sounds surrounding us, the strength and power and quiet warmth of Leston's hardworked body the surest comfort I have ever known. My silent husband's language grew to be my own body and how he touched me, the miracle of a callused hand placed gently to my cheek, my neck, my breast word enough of the love he held for me.

But on that first night, our wedding night, those sounds of my momma and daddy rose up around us like the resurrected dead: I knew love then, the doom and joy of it, the pain of Leston inside me and the pleasure of knowing the promise of a future. I knew only then that I'd stayed out on the porch because I loved them both enough to wish my daddy dead, but loved them both enough to wish him back.

I have taken care of myself since the moment I pulled the blanket over him, a fact Leston already knew before he'd even let out his words to the cold morning of our room. I knew what loss was, knew what it was God could take away from you, His answers to prayer sometimes the greatest curse you could call down. But even so, I prayed right then and there, my husband sitting on the edge of our bed and growing old in what seemed only the few moments we'd been awake, myself going the same way, too, I knew, that the baby inside me would be born alive and breathing, with ten fingers and ten toes. That was all I sought, what I figured couldn't be too much to ask.

Chapter 2

We'd buried my daddy the next day, him lying out in the room off our kitchen just overnight, time enough for Pastor to have his hand at trying to comfort us, and time enough for my momma to dress Daddy in a bundle of fine clothes I'd never known we had. Time enough, too, for the men who'd brought him, my uncle Benjamin one of them, to get back to the logging camp and settle up his monies with the foreman, then pack up his belongings, all of them fitting into one yellowed pillowcase.

When the four of them showed up on our porch the next morning, they were all cleaned up and wearing what I figured were their best clothes: new jeans and white shirts buttoned up to the throat, boots rubbed with a daub of oil. Each of them's hair was thick with pomade, and for a moment I wondered if they'd used my Daddy's own tin of it, greased up their hair with the toiletries of a dead man.

I'd been the one to answer the door, and Benjamin led them in, the pillowcase slung over his shoulder. Once they'd filed in, Benjamin let it fall off his back, held it in front of him. He started to smile at me, the corners of his mouth just turning up, but before he could finish I'd brought my eyes down to the floor, closed the door quiet as I could. I didn't want to see him smile, didn't want to

run the risk, I knew even then, of seeing in his face any bit
of my daddy's.

I turned from the door, watched what would happen
next. If I had my way, I thought, if I could fix all this, I
would have them out of here and back at camp, my
momma and me the only ones waiting for Pastor and for
Mr. Reeves, the coffin-builder in Purvis and the man who
would be digging the grave not fifty feet behind our
house.

It was what Momma asked for as soon as Pastor had
arrived in his wagon the afternoon before, as soon as he'd
made his way in the door. She'd looked Pastor square in
the eye, her chin higher than I'd ever seen it, and said,
"Bring a coffin tomorrow at noon. Mr. Reeves can bury
him out back."

Pastor had only nodded, took off his hat, held it with
both hands. For some reason I thought I could see fear in
his face, as though her merely meeting his eyes were
enough to destroy him, or as though she'd suddenly
become someone else, a woman with standing, bearing, a
voice he knew he had to listen to.

She said nothing else to him, though he stayed until
after dark, reading to her from the Psalms and Ecclesiastes
and the Gospels of Luke and John, first by the light from
the failing sun outside the windows, then by the fire. All
that time she only sat in the rocker, her chin still high,
Pastor hunched with the work of recognizing words in a
room too dark for reading.

Then he left, his Bible tucked under one arm, the hat
in both hands as he backed his way to the door, me standing there and holding it open for him. When he made it
to the threshold he paused, glanced down at me. He
reached out a hand, touched my head, and I twisted away

from under his palm, the move now instinct in me. I wanted no one, ever to pay my head again.

"Jewel," he said, smiling. "You'll be fine." He looked at my momma, still in the rocker. "The two of y'all will be just fine. Given time, and the Lord willing."

My momma gave him a small nod, let her eyes fall back to the fireplace, the dying light there, and he was gone.

As soon as I heard the sound of his wagon moving away into the night, Momma stood, her chin now low on her chest, hands limp at her sides, eyes nearly closed. She stared at the fire a moment, then turned, and I followed her back into her room, listened in the dark to the low groan the bottom dresser drawer made as she pulled it out, heard her move hands through whatever clothes were in there. Then came the sound of the drawer pushed closed, a small, high scream of wood on wood, and I turned, not certain where she was behind me, but knowing we were headed for the room off the kitchen, where the men had laid my daddy on the table.

We moved through the darkened kitchen, the only light the small bits of flickering red that made their way from the fireplace in the front room. Before me was the room my daddy lay in, but I could see nothing in there, only black, a black so black it seemed to crawl into me, a darkness that came in through my eyes and ears and skin, and I remember closing my eyes, holding my breath, afraid the darkness would swallow me up. I moved into the room, my hand in front of me, feeling the air, and then I touched rough wool. I stopped.

Behind me came the sound of a match strike, the sudden and awful smell of sulfur in the air, and I opened my eyes.

Momma had lit a candle she'd gotten from somewhere,

before me now the heap that was my daddy, covered with the blanket. Across the gray folds and contours danced my own shadow, Momma with the candle held high behind me. My head and shoulders were huge, moved across him, bobbed and jumped with the light from the candle, and I knew I would never be that big, knew I could never move in such fanciful ways, my daddy now dead.

"You go on into the front room," Momma whispered behind me. "You leave us two alone." She was beside me, my shadow trailing off the blanket and, I could see out the corner of my eye, taken up by the wall. I was even bigger now.

I stood there a moment, reached to the wool again, took a piece of it in my hand and fingered it the way Benjamin had. Then I let it drop, looked at Momma.

She had a bundle of clothes under one arm, the candle in the other. She swallowed hard, her chin down, her eyes never leaving the blanket.

I couldn't recognize her. I'd never seen her before, never seen the hair pulled back and tucked above her neck, the soft curve of her nose, the line of her chin. A lady stood next to me, one whose beauty I'd never felt nor could lay claim to, and I knew already she was on her way to dying, something inside me, maybe the Holy Spirit, maybe God Himself letting me know what was ahead, the word *orphan* suddenly too close, loud in my ear.

She lifted her chin, blinked. "Go," she whispered, but there'd been no need for the word. I was already backing away from the two of them and toward the kitchen, then toward the fireplace. Once there I poked up the flame, the spring night outside still holding close some last shard of winter, and as I felt the warmth and comfort of the fire rise up to me, I heard the hard, cold weeping my momma gave

out, the give and pull of the blanket as she revealed him
to herself, and began dressing him.

Benjamin and the others—I would never know their
names, never even see any of them, my uncle included,
again—stood a few feet from my mother, her rocker still set
near the hearth, the flames and embers and heat long gone.

He still had the pillowcase in front of him, then gently
set it on the floor. He said, "Ma'am," and paused. I was
next to the rocker now, my hands at my sides, though
some part of me wanted to place my hand on Momma's
shoulder, feel whatever life might be in her after she'd
stayed up the entire night with my daddy. Her eyes were
puffed up and full, her hands white as she worked her fingers, clutching them, letting go.

Then, quieter, Benjamin said, "Patricia," and looked
down.

"Ma'am will do just fine," she shot at him, her voice
iron. I nearly flinched, her words so quick. Her chin was
up, and the same feeling I'd had, the feeling she was no
one I knew, came on me again.

"Ma'am," Benjamin said right back at her. He looked
up, and despite myself I saw in his face pieces of my
daddy: his cheeks high and shiny, his skin a deep tan,
black hair with the same smell as Sunday mornings. And
there were his eyes, the irises nearly black, the whites all
the brighter for it. Of course he was my father's brother.

He knelt, the pillowcase on the floor blossoming with
the move so that what lay inside suddenly spilled out.
"This here's his things," he said.

I leaned forward, looked down at the small pile. No
one else moved, not even Momma, and for a moment I felt
I'd somehow betrayed her by giving in to what lay here.

But then I knelt, too, and began to take things up, examine them for what they might tell me about the man I'd wished dead.

The first thing I picked up was a cigar box. I shook it, the sound like rocks inside. I opened it, found only one rock, a chunk of fool's gold the size of my first three fingers, the gold specks in it bright enough to give good reason, I figured, to keep it. Next were two cuff links, cheap things rusted where the gold paint had chipped off; in there, too, were three small arrowheads, nothing special, one of them even with the tip broken off. I'd seen enough of them before at school, boys bringing them in from the ground their fathers worked. There was nothing else in the box.

No one spoke while I pawed through my daddy's souvenirs, what he'd deemed keepable from his life, this pile his legacy to me and my momma. There were a few picture postcards from New Orleans: a steamboat; Jackson Square; another of a smiling black mammy, a little burrhead next to her, the two of them grinning and holding huge pieces of watermelon. Scrolled across the bottom of the picture were the words *Greetings from New Orleans.* On the backs of the cards were no words, no stamps. Only blank space and the small words telling who'd printed up the cards. I held them in my hand, just looking at the empty space.

"He couldn't write," Benjamin said. "Nor read, of course, neither."

I put them down, then pushed around an old comb, a coil of rope, a belt. I said, "When was he there? In New Orleans?"

No one answered, and I didn't look up, didn't want them to believe I might truly be interested. But I was.

Momma was the one to speak. She said, "That's where your daddy and I had our honeymoon, right down in the French Quarter. That's where he got those."

"Oh," I said.

Benjamin took up the cards, held them out to Momma. "You want to keep these?" he asked.

"I—" she started, and I held my breath. She stopped rocking, then slowly put out a hand to him, took the cards. Benjamin put his hand down as soon as she'd taken them, and Momma let the cards rest on her lap, her hands holding one another again. She didn't look at them.

Then I found the tin of pomade, there beneath a shirt with three buttons missing. I opened up the can, saw inside the dull pink swirls, evidence of his fingertips. I brought the tin close to my nose, took in the sweet smell, but this time it was too much for me, so that I gagged a moment, brought the tin down and snapped back on the lid as quick as I could.

Benjamin must have thought I'd begun to cry, because he put his hand to my back again, the same touch he'd given yesterday when we'd stood looking at my newly dead father, and said, "Now, honey, you go on ahead and cry."

But I got my voice from somewhere, tried my best to make it the same iron my momma had. I said, "Don't worry about me," and reached down to the bottom of the sack where a photograph lay face down, all I could see of it the curlicued edges of the paper, the white back faded to brown.

I picked it up, turned it over. It was a picture of a man, the photograph soft and worn, as though it'd been crumpled and rolled flat any number of times. He stood next to a big wingback chair, his elbow resting on top, the other hand on his hip. His chin was hard, the bones in his cheeks high, his skin even darker than my daddy's. His eyes were black, turned from the camera to something far off. He had on a white hat, the crease in the crown perfect, the vest he wore black and white stripes, gray pants. His boots shone in the picture, one foot crossed over the other so that the toe pointed down and rested on the Persian rug beneath him. Even through the wrinkles and folds of the photograph I could feel the attitude he bore, the one that kept the eyes focused somewhere else, the hand at the hip, his head tipped just a hair to the left, as if daring the photographer to tell him to hold it up straight.

Before I could think of what I might be asking, I said, "Who is this?"

Again no one answered, and I waited, the photograph in my hand.

I looked up from it after a few moments, saw Benjamin eyeing my momma. I turned to her. Her eyes were on the window, searching for something I couldn't imagine, and she nodded.

Benjamin said, "That's his daddy. Our daddy. Your grandpa." He paused. "Jacob Chetauga. Then Jacob Chandler. Choctaw. Was. He been dead twenty-one years."

I looked up to Momma. Her eyes were closed now.

I turned to the photograph, tried to figure what this might mean, my grandpa an Indian.

But it only took a moment before I felt my fingers go hot, felt my face flush at the sudden knowledge that things tumbled down from this photograph, down to me and who I was and the part of me that gave me the same black, fine hair my daddy had, the same thin nose and skin that stayed more tan than any child I knew, even through dead winter, while my momma's skin turned red after twenty minutes outside.

I held it with both hands, ran a finger across the soft

paper, and I saw for the first time that no matter how much I'd wished my daddy gone, he would always be with me, here in me, just as he was here in his own daddy. This was me I saw in the photograph.

I stood. I could feel everyone's eyes on me now, even Momma's. I said, "This is what I'll keep," and I turned, headed into the kitchen.

Once in there I didn't know what to do, where else I could go. From where I stood at the sink-pump I could see into the room to the table my daddy lay on, could see, in fact, his legs from the knee down, boots stiff and shiny, pantlegs black. I knew I didn't want in there, but outside, right out the back door, was the coop and the garden, beyond that the tree he'd be buried under not long from now.

Then Cathedral stood in the doorway. She was holding a huge blue cookpot, her thin, black arms straining with the weight, the muscles there shiny with sweat. I moved to the screen door, the photograph in one hand, and pushed it open.

She moved in, and already I could smell the food. Chicken, I knew. And sweet potatoes, and collards and biscuits. Her teeth were clenched, and I wondered how far she'd carried the pot, as she made her way through the kitchen and toward the room my daddy was in.

"You can't——" I started, but by that time she was in the doorway. She froze.

"Lord have mercy," she whispered, and turned, her eyes shut, teeth still clenched, sweat across her forehead. She made it to the stove, and set the pot down. She opened her eyes, looked at me only a moment, her eyes never meeting mine, before she brought them to the floor. She'd never looked at me any longer than that.

Her hands were at her sides, and she shook them a little, loosing up the muscles, her arms still glistening. I'd always imagined she was a couple of years older than me, her hips still narrow but her face with a grimace I figured could only come with a little more age, more knowledge about the world as she moved through it. But all I knew of her was that a nigger girl had showed up at our house not a week after my daddy'd left, and had been here three times a week since to weed out in the garden or to clean out the coop, take eggs into town, chop off the heads and pluck the chickens we would eat, while my momma sat on the porch and I practiced my multiplications. One evening a few weeks after she'd started I asked Momma where she'd come from, how she'd gotten her name. Cathedral never spoke to me any more words than she had to, our language a series of nods and glances defining which rows of tomatoes she would work, whether the rhubarb was ready or not, each jerk of a chin or half-word freighted with what we wanted to give it. I knew her name only because I'd asked her after she'd been working for us a week.

Momma'd answered that Cathedral's family'd been owned by Catholics in Bogaloosa, and that she'd hired her on now Daddy was gone, that she'd been paying her a nickel a week. I believed her about the name, but I knew that the money paid out wasn't true; I'd never even seen the two of them talk to each other, much less exchange any money between them. She was only here, standing at the back screen door each Monday, Wednesday and Friday once I was home from school, or there just at sunup during the summer, waiting for me to signal her what to do.

She gave her arms one last shake, and stopped. The room was choked with the smells of food now, and I realized I hadn't eaten since the day before.

Then Cathedral spoke, and for an instant I didn't know where the voice came from, or whose it was, my mind on chicken and collards and sitting down to eat.

She said, "Missy Cook, she say bring this here to you."

I hadn't seen her mouth move, her eyes still on the floor. She put her hands together in front of her, held her fingers.

"Cathedral?" I said.

She looked up. "Yes'm?" she said, her eyes on my chin, then on my chest, my shoulder.

I said nothing, only felt my stomach moving, hungry for what lay in the pot. But I was thinking about her, and about this look between us, and about the full sentence that'd come from her lips.

"I sorry about yo' papa," she said, and finally let down her eyes.

I heard myself say, "Thank you," though I hadn't felt the words form.

She looked up at me again. "Missy Cook, she say tell you one more thing. She say tell you she the one be paying me to work for y'all. And she say she want you come live with her now yo' papa gone." She paused, looked back to the floor. "I mean, now yo' papa pass on."

Missy Cook. My mother's mother and suddenly I recognized the line in my mother's chin, and how she'd held it high, and why, perhaps, Pastor had cowered in whatever small way he had last night: the three times I'd met Missy Cook she'd held her chin the same way, up and above us all, her mouth in a frown that let me know no matter what happened that she was here and would always be here. She was here to stay. She was the woman of standing, of bearing. And my mother was her daughter.

She lived in Purvis proper, on Willow Street in a big

house with windows and drapes and fine china plates we actually ate off of, my momma and me. The last time we were there was just before Daddy'd left; the other two times I'd been too small to recognize an occasion. But I'd seen the furniture, and'd been told to stay off of it by the woman who now wanted me to come live with her.

I said nothing, kept my head as level as I could make it, my eyes cold and steady and focused on Cathedral, her twisted knots of hair, her thin, cotton dress and bare, black feet.

"And be one more thing," she whispered. She glanced toward the door into the front room, where my momma and Benjamin and three other men were, none of them making a sound. "She say she going raise you up right," she whispered, her eyes on the floor again, her voice so quiet I wasn't even certain she'd spoken. "She not be making the same mistakes she make with yo' mama. She say you her last chance in this world."

She stood with her hands still at her sides, glanced up at me.

I whispered, "She told you to tell me that?"

She shrugged. "Yes'm. Except the last part. The part about raising you up right, and about the mistakes and all."

Though my stomach felt as though it might die on me right then, the smell of cornbread and milk gravy now making its way into me, I held on, thinking instead of my momma marrying some half-breed Choctaw who couldn't read or write, me being born to the two of them, so that in Missy Cook's eyes I was the biggest mistake her daughter could ever make. And now I was her personal mission, what she wanted to save from the horrors of low-living in this world.

I looked at the photograph in my hand, wondered at

the man there, my grandpa, and what it took to hold your head just that way, who you had to be.

I looked at Cathedral. I said, "Why did you tell me?"

She shrugged again. "Don't need no reason." She paused. "Just figured to warn you."

Then I wasn't hungry anymore, and I turned, went into the front room and past them all, nothing any different than when I had left, my daddy's belongings still spread on the floor. I went to my room, got from under my bed one of my tablets, a pencil. I took one more look at the photograph, then slipped it between pages in the back of the tablet.

When I came back into the kitchen, Cathedral had already pulled out the food from the pot: heaps of chicken and cornbread, bowls of collards and gravy, a sweet potato pie, all of it in serving dishes from the same fine china we'd eaten from in a three-story house in downtown Purvis.

She turned from the food, glanced at me.

I said, "Cathedral, you know how to write?"

She have her head a quick shake, put her hands behind her.

I said, "Come with me," and I moved to the screen door, pushed it open.

She glanced up again, then looked to the doorway into the front room, as though we were betraying those in there by abandoning this food and who it came from, the woman Cathedral worked for, the woman who wanted my life.

She stood still a moment, then said, "Yes'm," and moved toward me.

Chapter 3

I taught her to write, and she taught the man she ended up marrying, then taught her own children as well, so that the four niggers outside our back door, all of them employed by my Leston, could read and write, and as I stood at the stove and carved off pieces of bone bacon into the skillet, I held some small piece of pride in me, thought that maybe I'd been a good teacher after all.

The four of them—Nelson, her husband, and their three boys, Sepulcher, Temple and Creche—worked for Leston cutting down pines, then blasting up the stumps and hauling them down to Pascugoula where they'd be turned to turpentine for the war effort. It was my part to feed them all. Each morning I awoke to fry up eggs and bacon, boil grits and bake biscuits for my family, Cathedral's boys, and the rest of Leston's crew: Garland and JE, cousins of Leston's, and Toxie, Leston's nephew, the three of them the supervisors over the crew; then six more niggers, boys and old men from up and down the woods. We had four trucks in all, plus the Caterpillar, none of it in anywheres near good shape, Toxie and Sepulcher working on one or another of them from the time they put their breakfast plates down until they disappeared up the road, headed home. But we had vehicles, Leston'd say time and again, ones that gave us this roof over our heads, let our children wear clothes, and gave us food to eat.

Food, I'd decided three years ago when he'd started in with but one lonesome truck and Nelson only, would be part of their pay. We were comfortable in this house, the second one Leston had built for us since we'd married eighteen years ago, and we had the steady work this World War provided, a twisted sort of blessing, I knew. We could give them food.

Burton banged in to the room, behind him Wilman, the two of them in their bib overalls and still fighting. But rather than holler at them to quiet down this first morning new life was in me, I took a second to look at them, at how they'd grown, Wilman with the sprinkle of Leston's freckles across his nose, Burton's skin taking my complexion, the tan and my black hair. Wilman's front teeth were out, and when he gave a sneer to whatever it was they were arguing over, I could see all the way into his mouth, the child-red gums, the perfect white teeth. Then he shoved Burton's shoulder, knocked him into the table. One of the chairs fell over.

"Momma?" Burton cried out, turned to me. "You saw that, Momma?"

"Yes, I did," I said, and sliced the last two pieces of bacon into the skillet, the fragrant steam off the meat already making its way up and into our morning. I wiped my hands on the towel hung on the oven door, then put both hands on my hips. I said, "Wilman, pick up the chair before your daddy gets in here, and straighten up, the two of you."

"Yes ma'am," Wilman whispered, and looked at Burton, in his eyes the hate brothers can only have for each other. Burton, of course, stood with his arms crossed, his head tilted just the same way his great-grandpa's had in the photograph framed and hung in the front room of this house.

It wasn't the first time I saw Burton in that pose, a stance I knew he'd picked up studying that picture, and each time he struck it I wondered if there weren't some danger to it, some invitation buried deep to lead the wrongheaded life Jacob Chandler had led. My momma'd been the one who'd finally told me what I wanted to know about him, and told me, too, what I shouldn't have heard.

On the last day she was alive, my momma about to die in the luxury of a house in downtown Purvis, she told me of the man in the photograph, though I hadn't asked her straight about him. Instead, I'd been spending days beside her bed trying best to avoid Missy Cook and the books she'd already laid out for me to read—*Middlemarch* and *Pride and Prejudice* and *Wuthering Heights,* all of them books I just as soon would read on my own. But Missy Cook's view of me and the world was angled so that the only thing I could do with her was be what she wanted me to be, read what she wanted me to read, answer the questions she wanted answered. And I had done so the first week because there had been nothing else for me to do. I simply came home from school, a new one where most of the children wore the same frills I did, frills given to me and my mother the evening we moved in, just the day after Daddy'd been buried.

Missy Cook—that's all any of us were ever allowed to call her—was a tall woman, her hair coiled up in a huge gray bun that sat atop her head. She wore eyeglasses with silver rims, behind the glass brown eyes like bits of broken glass sunk deep into her sockets. Many's the night I have had dreams of those eyes and how, after my momma was dead, she bore into me with them like a red-hot poker, an old woman aware of her powers.

That first evening we'd arrived a little after sunset, and'd climbed down off Pastor's wagon, the three of us having sat together on the seat, behind us only Momma's rocking chair, our clothes wrapped in bedsheets. A frail nigger-woman met us at the door, her hips not much wider than Cathedral's, and I knew right off this was her momma.

Once inside and the door closed behind us—another nigger had appeared from around the side of the house and'd started untying the rocking chair, Pastor all the while still seated up at the reins, his eyes straight ahead—Momma turned to the niggerwoman, said, "Molly, how are you?"

Molly paused a moment, as if this pleasantry might be some test, her answer either right or wrong. She tried to smile, gave a small curtsy, and said, "I fine, Miss Patricia." She swallowed, glanced up to me, said, "It be nice having you back to home here. The two of you," and curtsied again.

"This is true," came a voice from behind us, and we all three turned to it. Then Molly was gone.

Missy Cook was coming down the stairs, one hand on the polished banister, the other at her chest. The frown I'd always seen her with was still there, chin held high, her deep and frightening eyes shrouded even more so by the thin light from the gas-lit chandelier above us. She had on a beige dress with a high, stiff collar that encircled her throat, and I remember touching my own throat, wondering how she might breathe. Her waist was pinched down near to nothing, and I tried to imagine, too, the corset she wore, and how that might cut out breath altogether. She seemed to float down the staircase, the hem of her dress simply dancing about her hidden feet, so that for a moment I thought maybe she *had* died, was in fact a ghost before me.

I looked down at myself, at what I had on: a pale yellow cotton dress with a row of buttons up the front, my school shoes with no socks, and suddenly I felt I looked no different than Cathedral of a summer morning, peering in at the screen door.

I looked at my momma, who wore a dress much like my own, but long enough so that her ankles didn't show, the dress waist pinched in some. I knew she wore no corset, her shape a young woman's, not the filled and forced shape of the woman who now moved off the stairs and toward us, her hands low and open in front of her, coming to take ours. My momma's chin was high, too, and I saw the muscles in her jaw begin to work, her teeth clenched.

Momma put out a hand first, and I followed. Missy Cook hadn't yet looked at Momma, but at me, her hand warm in mine, softer than I had imagined it would be. She said, "I am deeply saddened at your daddy's passing," and I let myself believe her for an instant.

Then Momma said, "No, you are not." She let go Missy Cook's hand, moved past her and to the staircase. She put a hand on the banister, placed one foot on the first step, and stopped. She looked up the staircase, and said, "Jewel."

I was still holding Missy Cook's hand, felt her fingers going tight around mine. Her eyes had never left my face.

I looked at the polished wood floor, the gleam of the chandelier there. I said, "Yes ma'am," and she let go my hand. I walked around her and toward Momma, who held out her own hand to me, and the two of us started up the stairs.

At the landing I looked back downstairs, saw Missy Cook hadn't moved. My momma didn't even look.

*   *   *

Later, after we'd gone through the boxes of new dresses
stacked in the room we were to sleep in, all of them made
of lace and fine linen and pearl buttons, and after we'd
eaten the pork chops and cheese grits and okra and biscuits Molly'd bought up to us on that same fine china,
Momma and I climbed into bed together, the two of us
wearing matching white nightgowns with thin, pink ribbons at the wrists and neck. Then Momma climbed back
out, went to the gas key at the doorjamb.

But as she reached for it, Missy Cook opened the door,
held her hand over the key. Momma and I both jumped,
me taking in a breath, Momma bringing a hand to her face
as though Missy Cook might hit her.

"No one in this house," Missy Cook said, smiling at
me, though nowhere in her face was there any bit of joy,
any piece of happiness, "touches the gas. This is my
responsibility, and no one else's. Please remember this."
She twisted the key, the room slowly going dark until the
gas gave a small *pop*. She pulled the door closed behind
her. She hadn't even glanced at Momma.

Momma stood in the darkness a few moments, then
came back to bed. Once she was settled, I could hear
nothing, the absence of sound deafening somehow after
living where we had. I wanted words from my momma in
the room, wanted night sounds, something familiar to
help put me to sleep, and for a moment I even wished I
might hear the sounds Momma and Daddy made Saturday
nights, anything to fill the dead air in here.

As though she'd felt what I wanted, she whispered,
"This is a dangerous place. We have to be careful, or we'll
be swallowed alive here."

I knew what she meant, had seen already the power in

her momma, in her hands and eyes, in the warm food, the
fine clothes; but some part of me, even after seeing whatever darkness lay in Missy Cook's brown eyes, wanted to
give over to it, to nestle down into the warm bed we were
in, to get up tomorrow morning and find a meal already
cooked for us, put on crisp, clean dresses and live this way.

"But—" Momma started again, and there was a soft
knock at the door. A crack of light pierced the room, then
filled it as the door opened just wide enough to let in
Molly.

She whispered, "It's just Molly, Miss Patricia, Miss
Jewel. Come to get yo' old clothes, take care of them for
you."

"In the corner," Momma said, and we watched as Molly
made her way to the end of the dresser and leaned over,
took the pile of clothing up in her arms.

"We see you in the morning," she whispered.

I said, "Good night," Momma silent beside me. Molly
pulled the door closed, and here was the silence again, the
dark. I whispered, "What were you going to say?"

But then I saw the color at the window, the faint dance
of orange and red across the black glass.

Momma was out of the bed before me, made it to the
window first, her black silhouette there against the growing
color, her hands to the window. Each finger was outlined in
an orange that grew brighter even in the seconds it took me
to get to the window, stand next to her, place my hands
against the cool glass too.

I looked down at the yard behind the house, where a
fire burned some twenty yards back into the rows of pecan
trees. The nigger who'd unloaded Pastor's wagon for us
stood next to it, a hoe in one hand, the other on his hip.
He was just looking into the fire, his head down.

Molly appeared beneath us, coming from inside the house and down the back steps to the yard. She was carrying something, and I knew before she was halfway to the fire that it was our clothes, the clothes she'd just gathered up in our room.

The nigger at the fire looked up, stood taller, his hoe at the ready while Molly came toward him. She stopped at the edge of the fire, her back to us, and started in to peeling off piece by piece our clothes, tossing each garment into the fire. I watched, silent, as she peeled off what I knew was my dress, the one with the buttons up the front. Molly held it up, looked at it a moment, the material illuminated, and dropped it on the fire. Thin wisps of flame shot out beneath it, then swallowed it up.

"That nigger," I said out loud.

But Momma said, "She's a good nigger. She's only doing what she's been told."

I turned to my momma, saw her face flicker with the movement of the fire, the color almost lost on her. I said, "Why?"

She nodded at the fire, and I turned back to it. Molly held up Momma's dress now, then dropped it on the fire, this time the flames out from beneath it bigger, thicker. The nigger reached in his hoe to the fire, stirred it up. Sparks lifted into the air, bits of light that melted before they even cleared the trees.

Momma said, "She's doing what she's been told. You watch this, because this is for you and me. You and me are supposed to be seeing this, supposed to be standing right here and watching it all." She paused, and Molly dropped in the last piece, one of Momma's old, thin petticoats. "Somewhere in this house Missy Cook's watching this, too. There's not anybody in this house, maybe not on the whole street, who's not watching this. But it's for you and me."

Then the nigger dropped the hoe and headed away from the fire, disappeared somewhere near the house and to our left. I glanced up at Momma. She hadn't moved, but when I turned back to the fire, I heard her swallow hard, say, "I know what Marcus has gone for."

He reappeared, this time carrying something high and over his head: Momma's cane chair. Molly edged back from the fire as he came closer. He stopped, eased the chair down from his shoulders, and laid it on the fire. For a few moments nothing happened, the frame of the chair like some strange and twisted skeleton, but then the seat caught, and the wood of it, and the flames grew until the sparks it gave off drifted high and above the tops of the trees before giving up.

"This is for us," she whispered, and I didn't look at her, afraid of what I might see.

The day she died, two months later, began with me sitting with a pencil and tablet in an overstuffed chair I'd had Marcus pull close to her bed. She'd taken ill two weeks before, and hadn't eaten in four days, taking in nothing more than sips of cool water Molly gave her. Missy Cook had nagged me enough times about being in a sickroom, but I didn't care. I'd even gotten Cathedral to stand watch for me at the door, warn of Missy Cook coming up. But she never did.

I hadn't shown Momma the picture of Jacob, had kept it hidden since the day I'd gotten it, but for some reason that morning I pulled it out from where I'd wedged it deep between pages.

The room was kept dark all day, summer beginning to

rise around us in thick walls of heat. My legs kicked beneath me as I studied the picture, and though it would be years before I would realize it, the room seemed cooler that morning than any of the last fifteen. Perhaps, I would later think, it was due to the rain that would arrive late that night, after Pastor had come to tend to the dead once again, and after he would once again try to pat my head in some gesture he figured must be comforting. Or perhaps it was due to the heat my momma gave off, the fever I could feel even from the chair. Or maybe, just maybe, it was her soul already departing even as she spoke there that morning.

She whispered, "Your Grandpa Jacob," and my legs stopped kicking. I turned to her. I'd thought her still asleep, but her eyes were open, and she was looking at me, her eyes full and small in her face. Her hair, unbraided and fanned out on the pillow, was wet at the temples and hairline. She swallowed, closed her eyes and opened them again.

I said, "Momma, don't talk. Don't—"

"You listen," she said, and looked at the ceiling. She brought a hand from her chest to her forehead, let it rest there. "You need to know what stock you're from. I'm telling you." She paused, let her eyes close. "Your daddy's daddy was long dead before I met Joseph. But people knew about him. People knew Jacob Chandler was a horse stealer. He was." She took slow, deep breaths, and for a moment I wondered if she was awake at all or if she might be in some haze, maybe even talking in her sleep. But it didn't matter. She was giving me what I wanted, some history of me so I would know my place here, no matter how fine the dresses, no matter how fine the china. Since the night of the fire I hadn't let Missy Cook look me straight in the eye, and at breakfast the next morning, during which my guidelines were laid out—no skipping school, no playing with the niggers, no turning down the gas by myself before going to bed—Momma and I sat silent, our eyes on the food before us. We never mentioned the fire in the back yard. Ever.

"Your daddy's momma was just a cracker, left Jacob Chetauga with two boys, Benjamin and Joseph, when Joseph was only two," Momma whispered. "And Jacob left those two with his sisters, Choctaws living in shanties up near Columbus. That's how your daddy was raised. I thought he would be different from his daddy." She paused. "He wasn't. But it wasn't stealing horses he was bad about. It was me." She swallowed again, and I looked at the picture, rubbed my finger across his face.

"Your grandpa," she went on, "was caught stealing horses, and they brought him in to Columbus, run him through court and had him up to a tree just north of town, him sitting on one of the horses he'd stolen, a rope round his neck. All this before sundown the same day. They were going to hang him. And your daddy was there. Him and Benjamin both, sitting on the shoulders of those squaws. They were there to watch their own daddy get hanged for horse stealing."

All this time I was staring at the picture, at how he held his head and the hand there at his hip. She was talking more clearly than I'd heard her in the last two weeks, but that was nothing I cared to think about. Maybe she was getting better, I figured, but I only wanted to look at the picture, imagine this man with the invincible pose on a horse and ready to be strung up. This man I was blood kin to.

"They gave the horse a swat, and the thing was gone, your grandpa hanging and swinging from the tree. The

way your daddy told it, the only sound he could hear was
the heavy creak of the rope. He says he watched his own
daddy's feet stepping on air, trying to find something firm
to stand on. But there was nothing." She took a deep
breath, as though thinking about him hanging there was
taking her own air from her, then she went quiet, and I
had to look at her to see if she hadn't gone back to sleep.

Her eyes were open wide, her mouth closed. One hand
was at her throat, moving slowly back and forth. Her eyes,
it seemed, were focused on nothing. "And then," she whispered, "the rope broke. It snapped up near the limb, your
daddy tells me, and Jacob fell to the earth. He didn't move
for a while. Neither did anybody watching. But then he sat
up, looked around. And he was smiling. And then they let
him go, because it was God's will. The sheriff just bent over
him sitting there on the ground, loosed the rope round his
neck and the one round his hands. It was God's will."

I was looking at the picture, and here came my
momma's hand, reaching for it. Her hand was white, as
white, I thought, as my daddy's body'd been when they'd
pulled back that wool blanket.

I let her have the photograph, watched as she brought
it close to her face. Her hands started to trembling with
the effort, and I thought I could see tears in her eyes, her
mouth only a thin line now, no color. She said, "This here
picture was taken not a week or two after that. That's why
your daddy kept this with him. It's a picture of a man
who's lived through death. That's what it is. But I wish he'd
been killed. I do." She closed her eyes, and a tear squeezed
out, slipped down her cheek and into her hair. "Lord forgive me," she whispered, "but I do. I wonder how
Joseph'd been different if he'd seen his daddy die. I think
he might have been a good man if his daddy'd died before

his eyes. But he didn't, and he kept this picture of a man who couldn't be killed, and that's how come he turned out like he did."

Her hands were on her chest now, the picture face down, and I whispered, "Why'd you marry him then?"

"Love," she said right out, the word quick and soft from her. And, just as quiet, she said, "Hate." She paused. "I knew I loved him. I knew I hated my momma. Those two things are why I married him."

She shot open her eyes. She was smiling, the look on her face as strange as any I'd ever seen her give, and I thought that maybe the fever'd gone through her brain, ravaged her such that she'd gone mad. She reached the picture over to me without looking at me, and I took it, then scooted a little deeper into my chair, away from her.

She said, "But you have to know about this family, too, and what your stock is from here. From my momma. You got to know that, too." Her eyes were still to the ceiling, as if the painted tin up there with its rows and rows of circles in squares was giving something important to her. "There's things about my family you need to know, things Missy Cook won't ever tell you." She was still smiling, and I could feel myself pushing even deeper into the chair.

"This one you won't ever hear her tell, because she knows it's true. The reason we've got all this," she said, and though she made no moves of her hands or eyes to show me what she meant by *this*, I knew she meant the house, the clothes, the food, the niggers. What else was there? "The reason we got all this," she said again, "is because she married a Yankee carpetbagger. A man from Pittsburgh, the man who was my daddy. And her daddy and this Yankee carpetbagger were in cahoots together, buying up land and houses and banks after the war with money Missy Cook's daddy'd been able to lay his hands on through my daddy. Don't ask me how, but that's true."

She closed her eyes, the smile grown even wider. There was joy in her now, pleasure found in telling me all this.

"But that's not the story. That's not the one I want you to keep, because plenty of women, plenty of old would-be spinsters like Missy Cook married Northerners like my daddy." She swallowed hard, opened her mouth and took in hollow, quick breaths, as though she'd just climbed a set of stairs. I wanted to reach toward her, to touch her, to stroke her forehead and tell her to stop, to save herself. But I didn't, because I wanted the story.

"No," she whispered now, "no, what I want you to take is this: Before the War, the town of Columbus was known as Coogan's Bluff. That's Missy Cook's maiden name, Coogan. Her daddy was who the town was named for, and that's because he owned the most niggers. He owned the most niggers in that part of the state, and he wasn't even in the Confederate forces because he owned so much land, and so many niggers." She stopped again, and suddenly she seemed to disappear with her whispered words, her breaths only shallow gulps. I remember the room going even colder a moment, remember gooseflesh all up and down my legs and arms, remember holding myself in the near-dark of the room, the photograph in my lap. My momma was still smiling, her eyes still closed, fingers clutched and drawing the sheet taut up to her neck. "So when the Columbus, Ohio, militia march into town," she whispered even more quietly now, her words only ghosts in the room, "they liberate the niggers, they rename the place, and they burn down every last piece of property they know belongs to the man named Coogan. Missy Cook's daddy. But they can't find the man, and do you know why?" She stopped. Slowly she turned to me, and before I realized what she'd asked, she was staring at me.

But she wasn't looking at me, I could see. Her eyes were on me, but passed through me, so that my momma was already gone, and I thought again of her profile in the light of a candle held above my dead daddy, and how God had planted in me the knowledge she would die even back then. This was what my momma was leaving to me, the only legacy she knew to give: stories of who I was from, however failed their lives.

I looked down, said, "Why couldn't they find him?"

She laughed, the sound in her like dead leaves underfoot. She turned to the ceiling again. Cathedral or Molly or Marcus couldn't do any help now. She wasn't of this world anymore.

She stopped laughing, tears drifting down her cheeks. She whispered, "I watched my daddy get slapped across the face by Missy Cook the first time he told me this story, and I watched him laugh in her face, Missy Cook standing above him, him in his favorite chair in the parlor, her with her hand back to hit him again. But he'd only laughed, and then, because she didn't know what to do with that hand held high, palm open, she came straight to me sitting on the divan, and slapped my face. And my daddy only laughed harder at that, brushed back tears from his eyes. Missy Cook just left the room."

She paused, reached up a pale hand to her face, and gently touched her cheek, the look on her face surprise, her eyebrows knotted, her mouth open. "She hit me right here on this cheek, right near my eye, because I'd only listened while my daddy told me why they never found my grandpa." She paused, swallowed. "Missy Cook's daddy'd dressed as a woman, and hid out in a nigger shanty. And when those Ohio militia came through to liberate all them niggers, let them know about what Mr. Lincoln'd given them, the niggers still hid him, put him into a barrel and let him hide. Dressed as a woman and hiding in a barrel, right there in front of all them niggers he owned, every one of them laughing their nigger hearts out, I'm certain, and then when the militia'd gone, and they're all freed slaves, they just brought him out of the barrel, and stayed with him the rest of their lives, them and their children and their children's children. Molly, Marcus, all the field niggers. They're all sons and daughters of the ones hid my grandpa when he was dressed as a woman and balled up in a barrel. And don't think they don't remember it, neither."

My hands were together in my lap, beneath them the photograph of Jacob Chandler, Jacob Chetauga.

She whispered, "So you take those two stories now, and you decide. Two stories of people who lived through their own deaths. You take them both, and you decide why I'd marry your daddy." She paused, and I hadn't the courage to look at her, simply stared at my hands in my lap, at the photograph. "You choose which of the two you want to take: one who'd lived because it was the will of God, no matter how bad the life he led. Or one who saved himself, God be damned, and passed on to this daughter a shame so fierce only hate could cover it up." She gave a small laugh, the sound only thin air forced from inside her. "Or you could do the smart thing, and pass all this up. Make your own story. Maybe, God willing, going out into this world with these stories like stones in your pockets won't make a bit of difference. The Lord knows it wasn't that way for me."

I swallowed, closed my eyes. I said, "And now you're going to leave me here." I held my hands even tighter, felt the grip of bone against bone.

She whispered, "It happens to all of us one day," he words so quiet I had to hold my breath to hear. "Your momma and daddy leave you at some point, and then you are on your own. Everyone ends up an orphan. Even me. I been an orphan since I was born."

I let out my breath, opened my eyes. I looked at her. Her eyes were closed, a smile on her face, her fingers holding tight the sheet.

She died late that afternoon, when I was downstairs in the kitchen, Cathedral and I drinking cold buttermilk Molly'd poured for us. It was Marcus who'd been there when she died, him to come into the kitchen, eyes down to the floor only because I was in the room. He said, "Miss Patricia, she passed on now." Molly gave out a quick breath, Cathedral only looking from me to Marcus and back to me, her eyes never really meeting mine.

That night, once Pastor was gone, my momma's body taken to the mortician's to prepare her for a proper burial, I climbed into bed with the same nightgown on I'd worn our first night here, when we'd watched our old clothes burn like pine straw in the night air. The gas light above me was still on, and out of habit I sat there, smooth, cool sheets around me, and waited for Missy Cook to push open the door, give me the same practiced and dead smile she gave each night, then turn off the gas.

I was alone, finally. Cathedral had seen me into my room, followed by Molly, who'd touched me with the gentlest hands I could remember. But now I was alone, sitting in my bed, waiting for the woman who'd struck my momma for no good reason but that she'd been a witness to the truth of her family.

So I waited no longer. I climbed out of bed, went to the

door, and reached up, slowly twisted the gas key. The room grew dark around me, the furniture—the dresser, the bed, the armoire in which hung my and my momma's fine new clothing—all changing into huge and ugly shapes, drowning in the darkness I was giving. Then the room was black, and I heard the faint *pop* of the gas shutting off.

My turning off that gas was a move, I knew, just as logical, just as inevitable as me pulling the blanket over my dead daddy barely two months before, further evidence I knew how to take care of myself, even if Missy Cook chose to strike me for it. She couldn't have me, I knew. I wouldn't let her take into me, wouldn't give up to her.

I had the photograph, and the hard and sure memory of two stories my momma'd told. That was what would keep me alive here. That, and Cathedral, and Molly. These were all with me.

I climbed back into bed, drew the sheets up around me, and settled in. I thought of pretending sleep, waiting for Missy Cook to open the door to find I'd broken the first rule she'd put on me the night we'd moved in, but there was no reason to pretend. It didn't matter what she thought or did. If she chose to beat me in my sleep, I'd awaken. If she chose to do nothing, I'd be asleep already, moving all that much faster toward the day I would leave here.

Chapter 4

My baby Annie toddled into the kitchen a little after Leston and the men had finished breakfast, Wilman and Burton just starting in to theirs. The niggers, who ate outside, had already finished, too, and'd stacked their plates beneath the steps down from the back porch, the same place they'd find them when they headed for home tonight.

Annie held on tight to the scrap rag that'd once been a blanket, what now she called her nye-nye. She had the blanket over one shoulder, her red hair tangled with sleep, a hand to one eye and rubbing it.

Wilman and Burton, the two of them shoveling in grits and biscuits with syrup and fried eggs as quick as I could turn it out, sang together, "Annie, fannie, baby with a blankie." They looked at each other, laughed, started back in with the food.

Annie turned to them, and from where I stood at the stove I could see her eyes squinch down to nothing, then she swung out at empty air with the hand she'd had to her eye. Burton imitated her, Wilman doing the same as soon as he'd seen what his older brother'd done. They laughed even more.

From where I stood, too, I could see out the kitchen window to Leston, Toxie, Garland and JE, the four of them standing outside with hands in their jacket pockets, shoul-

ders up against the cold morning, each with a cigarette to
his lips. Beyond them, back near the trees, were the niggers, the ten of them forming a jumbled circle. The sun
still wasn't up, and I could see the bright red spark of a
cigarette tip pass from nigger to nigger, each taking one
small pull, then passing it to his neighbor.

Then Leston raised a hand in the air, gave a quick wave,
and they were all of them off, led by my husband. He was
first to disappear from my view, followed by JE and
Garland and all the niggers except Sepulcher, a tall, thin
boy whose pantlegs stopped a good four inches above his
ankles. He and Toxie went off in the opposite direction, to
my left, back to where one of the trucks had been parked
since they'd towed it from the woods last Thursday.

Annie was hitting Burton's leg with her free hand, the
other still holding on to the blanket. The boys were
leaning over, poking a finger in her hair, another in her
ribs, another under her chin, them laughing at each
twist away their baby sister made, her giving only half-
hearted squeals, enjoying the attention. It's what children did together, I'd realize only after James and Billie
Jean'd been at each other's throat their first years or so.
A game: see who could poke who the most until one or
the other cried, got Momma mad.

But I wasn't going that way this morning, not even after
the age I'd seen in Leston's shoulders earlier, not even after
knowing there'd be another whole stretch of time in my
life when another child would fall party to this game of
attention and tears.

Annie, as always, broke first, finally gave up slapping
at Burton's leg. She backed up a foot or so from the boys,
and sat down on the floor. Her eyes were closed, tears
spouting out now, her mouth open in a loud cry.

In walked Billie Jean, still in her nightshirt and socks, one hand scratching at her head, a creased and wrinkled *Photoplay* in the other hand. She stopped in the middle of the kitchen, yawned, then opened her eyes, and said just loud enough to where she knew I'd have to make remark, "Why can't a woman get enough sleep in this place?" She put her hands on her hips, gave a look as grown-up and hard as she could muster at her brothers and sister.

"Momma, we didn't make her cry," Burton hollered, and Wilman put in, "Momma, she did it herself."

Annie still cried.

But all I could see my way to doing was to stand there at the stove, cross my arms, and smile. The bellyaching and crying still went on, even Billie Jean looking up at me, saying, "Well? Why can't a woman?" They all wanted *me* to break, I knew; they all wanted in their own way nothing more than what they'd lost when the next child had been born: just a hug and a soft word from me. My full and undivided attention, what I knew I would never be able to give any of them again. That was the sorrowful part of being a mother: each of your children had to move up a notch toward some end of childhood with the birth of the next child. And so I wouldn't get mad at any of them, wouldn't holler and carry on about getting a switch or holding back the quarter for a movie and popcorn in town Saturday if they didn't straighten up, all of them. No, this morning, I would only love them. Soon enough they would know what was coming.

That evening, supper spread across the table in steaming bowls and plates of hot food, we gave thanks, Leston at the head of the table, me next to him. The children, starting with Annie next to me, were seated around the table by age, so that James was sitting next to Leston, all of us holding hands. "Dear Lord," Leston said, his voice as low and even and empty of fear as every other night, "hear our prayer: we give You thanks for the many blessings You bestow on us each and every day, and ask that You bless this food to the nourishment of our bodies. Amen."

The children let go each other's hands quick as they could, but Leston still held mine. I looked up at him, saw him smiling at me.

"Almost forgot," he said. He closed his eyes, still smiling, and held his empty hand out to James, who looked at me. His face was his father's: the same spray of freckles Wilman had gotten, the broad forehead and giving eyes the same green as my husband's. I smiled at him, but it didn't change the puzzled look he'd taken on, mouth slightly open. He said, "Momma?" and slowly moved to take his daddy's hand. My eyes fell to his hand as he placed it in Leston's, and I saw the calluses and cuts, evidence of the hard work he'd been doing for over a year now at the lumber mill. But even those scars were only pale imitations of the ones Leston'd had for years, his big, red hand now, swallowing up James'. And I remembered for a moment James' soft, white hands when he was a child, remembered my firstborn at my breast, suckling to keep himself alive, drawing deep my milk with the same mighty purpose each one after that'd had.

James'd dropped out of the high school last January when the first men left for the armed services, back when Roosevelt was making the big pleas for all able-bodied men to join up, and many a job needed doing around here went begging. He was only fifteen, but neither Leston nor I minded much his quitting; he'd learned to read and write and figure quicker than any of my children so far, had enough common sense about him to pick his way through whatever this life would give him.

But he and Leston hadn't spoke much to each other since then, and I knew it was because James'd chosen to take on at Crampton's, and not follow his father out to the woods, not bore holes into tree stumps with a hand auger, then shove in pieces of dynamite and light fuses, scatter like scared bats. A piece of me was glad for that, too: Toxie'd already lost three fingers on one hand and the hearing in his right ear, this the result of a fuse too short and too fast. James'd chosen instead to head out each morning to the mill, to walk the two and a half miles there and tend saw, shove in boards at one end all day long.

I knew the reason they didn't speak other than to ask for the salt or comment upon the weather, though, had more to do with Leston than James. Something in Leston made him want the family with him, wanted his sons to be there to take up what he'd grown to consider a firm income, an honest trade. Many's the night we would lie awake and dream out loud for what we wanted, and though my own desires had more to do with seeing my children grow up with their parents alive and well, loving brothers and sisters surrounding them—just those things I never had—Leston's was always about his own company, run by him and his boys. He imagined them all in old age, marching into the woods each morning, a battalion of niggers behind them, until every stubborn stump of heart pine'd been boiled down in Pascagoula. To him, James'd already abandoned the family, though I knew that for James, Crampton's was only his first chance at trying out himself on the world.

"Momma?" James said, still looking at me. "What's this about?"

At least the two of them were still holding hands, I thought this time of prayer what we had left to unite us. I whispered, "Just let's pray." I smiled at him, gave a small shrug. Leston's head was already bowed, waiting for us all.

The children were looking at me, and I reached to Annie's hand, took it in mine, her hand bigger than even this morning, her growing up with every second that went through us all. I bowed my head, knew the children would follow.

Leston said, "Dear Lord, please make certain to take care of the new life in Momma. Amen."

When I opened my eyes, every one of my family was watching me, all except Annie, who reached a hand to her plate for a piece of honey cornbread.

Now it was over. They all knew, and we'd begin the accommodations each had to make from here on out. Annie would be the hardest hit, I knew; her not looking at me was sign enough she didn't yet know what any of this meant.

Billie Jean was first to speak. "What will I tell all my friends at school?" she said, on her face some kind of pure horror, eyebrows twisted into each other, mouth fallen open. Her hair was pulled back in a tight ponytail, and she had on one of Leston's old shirts, the sleeves cuffed up to her elbows. She held a fork in one hand, her knife in the other, forearms resting on the table. "What am I supposed to say? Am I supposed to just say, 'Hey, y'all, my momma's having yet another baby'?"

"Yes, you are," Leston said. "And you listen to how you're talking to us. You listen." He'd leveled his eyes at her. That would be his last words to her about the whole matter, I knew.

Billie Jean closed her eyes, nodded. "Yes, sir," she managed to get out. She held them closed longer than need be, just to make to us some kind of point, one lost on Leston, who looked down to his plate, forked up collards.

"A baby?" Annie said, looking up at me. She'd already eaten half the slab of cornbread she'd been given, the crumbs dusting her chin and hands. Nye-nye, like at every meal, was draped across the back of her chair, a thin and forlorn comfort, though Annie couldn't see it unless she turned all the way around in her seat.

"Another baby," Burton said. "A baby, a baby. There's too many of them here already," and he turned to Wilman, gave a push at his shoulder.

Wilman said, "You're the only baby, the only burrhead pickaninny around here I know of," and pushed Burton just as hard, the two of them suddenly arms and hands.

"Wilman," Leston said. "Burton." They stopped quick as they'd started, and seemed to draw down on themselves, the threat of Leston's belt across their bottoms unspoken in this household, but always present. He'd done it enough, just stood up from the table and carted them out the house to behind the repair shed, where off would come his belt. A few minutes later there they'd march, the three of them in a line headed back toward the house, Wilman first, Burton next, the two of them with red eyes and wet cheeks and not making a sound, Leston behind them and rebuckling the belt.

My heart broke each time that went on, but there wasn't much I could do. Once, a little over a year ago, he'd taken Billie Jean back there for painting on thick, red lipstick she'd been given by a friend at school. I'd followed them out, certain I wouldn't interfere. Leston was the daddy, the one whose job this was, but when I'd seen her bend over with her hands at her knees, Leston with his

arm raised, belt in hand, I'd let out a small cry, sound
enough to give him cause to stop, glance at me.

"Go on inside," he'd said, his mouth barely opening
with the words.

I'd had to turn, give up to him my child, my first girl,
and head back to the house. I'd never struck any of them,
always in my head the clear and polished picture of Missy
Cook slapping my momma for no reason at all. The punishment was up to Leston, and I was glad for it.

The boys started in on dinner as though nothing happened, the moment of Leston's silent warning and the news
they'd have another child to terrorize either lost on them or
of no matter. I wasn't sure how hard Burton and Wilman'd
fall when the next one finally came on. They were too close
together, but maybe that was better for them: they had
each other, and if they chose to kill each other or to be best
friends—both of which they were willing to do at any
moment of a day—at least they'd have their own company.

No, it was Annie, my baby Annie, I was worried most
about. She was still looking up at me, only nibbled at the
cornbread now, more crumbs than bread into her mouth.
She held the bread with both hands, then let go with one,
slowly reached above her shoulder and behind her, took
hold of the blanket on the back of the chair, her eyes still
on me. She blinked.

I leaned toward her, brought my face down close to
hers. I whispered, "Now don't you go to worrying, Annie.
You're my baby girl. You know that." I swallowed, the hurt
of the possible lie I was about to tell her thick in my
throat, the memory of my momma dying pushed too close
to me so that I thought I might never breathe again, not
after giving to her the same comfort I'd had to give each
child when they found out they wouldn't be the center of

my world anymore: "Momma will always be here," I said. "Just you don't worry about me not ever taking care of you." I reached a hand to her face, traced the perfect curve of her cheek, touched a finger to her thin eyebrow. "Momma will be here to take good care of you."

She smiled, slowly pushed a corner of the cornbread in her mouth, took a bite too big to handle. She let go the blanket, and brought that hand to her mouth, covered it while she chewed, her eyes on me the whole time.

I sat back up, a hand still to her shoulder, and saw James staring at me, a smile on his face, too. His hands were flat on the table. He hadn't touched the ham on his plate, nor the collards or cornbread.

"James?" I said, and Leston looked at me, then to James. Their eyes met for a long moment before Leston said, "Son?"

"Today is a fine day," he said, and looked down at his hands. He closed his eyes, shook his head. Then he looked at me again. "It's a good day because you're having a baby." He paused. "It's a good day because there's a new one on the way to take the place of this old one heading out."

He quick looked from me to Leston to me. "Today's a fine day because I signed up today. That's why it's a fine day."

Leston turned back to his food. He leaned forward, his forearm on the table, and forked up a piece of ham. He said, "You aren't old enough."

Slowly James lost the smile. "I signed up to sign up today," he said. "It's a new program the enlistment officer downtown let me in on. So when I turn seventeen next month, I'll be in the Armed Forces." He smiled again, this time even wider. He lifted one hand a little above the table, slapped it down. "Imagine that."

But I'd imagined this day all too much already, his news

nothing of the surprise he'd figured on it being. Leston and I'd both known a day like this one would be coming, a war we'd taken our sustenance from all along now laying claim to our son like a bad debt we owed.

Billie Jean sighed, let out, "I can't wait to see you in a uniform. It'll be so glamorous," and James laughed, shook his head again.

I hadn't moved, one hand on the small shoulder of my baby Anne, thankful she still had years I couldn't imagine before she'd be out of this house, and suddenly I saw all my children lined up and waiting for a meal like this one, when each in turn would give up the love and care we had for them to a future no one could count on, and for some reason I thought of Missy Cook dead and gone for near on twenty years, every moment she was alive filled with the bitter taste of a daughter who'd left her for a Choctaw half-breed. You could take your child's leaving, I saw, with either hate or love, no matter what doom or good luck they seemed headed for. Only hate or love; there wasn't any ground between.

I reached a hand across the table to James, held it out for him. Leston, still with his arm on the table, still not having looked at his son, only took in another bite of ham.

James took my hand, held it tight, his smile only growing. There was no spite here, no malice aimed at his daddy, what I knew Leston believed moved his son to work at a mill instead of for him, and now made him want to join up and fight in a war we made our living from. Here was only our son, our oldest child.

I said, "God will bless you," and I felt my eyes begin to fill. All the children were listening, this moment none of us ready for. Though Leston's eyes were to his plate and nowhere else, I was still glad for my oldest's hand in mine, for my youngest next to me, the rest of my children quiet and watching; glad, too, for the baby inside me, already growing.

And just as my eyes brimmed, one smooth warm tear slipping down my cheek, there came a knock at the kitchen door. It was a quick sound, three crisp knocks and nothing else, and I stood, let go James' hand and smiled down at my children, all of them watching me, mouths open. Their mother was crying, and I tried for a moment to think of another time I'd cried in front of them. There was nothing I could recall.

I knew the knock, that strange authority Cathedral'd taken on the older she got, and when I opened the door, there she stood, across her shoulders an ancient and frayed wedding ring quilt against the cold. Light from the kitchen fell down at her at the bottom of the steps, filled her eyes. She was looking right at me, staring at me. I swallowed, touched the back of one hand to the tear of my eye. I smiled.

"Cathedral," I said, and took a breath.

Her eyes glistened in the light, her mouth closed tight.

I heard a noise behind her, the scrape of boots on hard ground out there. A small orange ember rose, grew, died down. Nelson was with her, smoking a cigarette some ten or fifteen feet behind her.

"Go on, Cathedral," he whispered, and the night air came into me, and I shivered, the same huge and awful shiver I'd begun my day with when Leston'd pulled back the sheet.

Still she stared at me, this ability of hers to look me in the face for as long as she wished something she'd found, I knew, when she was born again, baptized in the Pearl River when she was fourteen. She'd found Christ, she'd told me the next day, a little past two years after my momma'd died, Missy Cook trying to hold me by the throat every day of it. Each night after my momma died I'd been the one to turn off my gas light, and I'd taken to playing with Cathedral as often as I could, even let Missy Cook know I was teaching her to read and write. For these transgressions, Missy Cook'd had Molly take a switch to Cathedral, had spent three months straight coming into my room at night and turning up the gas, then turning it down again, even had Pastor come to the house each Thursday afternoon for a year, the two of us sitting in the parlor as though he were holding some kind of court. He asked me time and again if I knew disobeying Missy Cook was a sin, and if I knew teaching Cathedral to read and write was almost nearly as bad. Then he'd go on to ask me how I felt about my momma perishing, and about whether or not I thought she might be in Heaven. Pastor never took his eyes off me, the two of us certain Missy Cook stood just outside the room, listening to all that went on. I never broke, never surrendered to him that I did all of this to give some sort of honor to my momma's memory, what I thought she'd want me to do.

It wasn't but a month after Cathedral'd found Christ that I'd been baptized in the Pearl myself, the same Pastor working on me whatever magic the Holy Spirit had given him to save my soul from the ravages of sin. When I came up from under water, Pastor's hand at my back and lifting me, I'd expected to see a new world, one somehow clearer and more delightful, leaves on trees brighter, greener, the sky some miraculous shade of blue. Instead, I'd only rubbed my eyes, then opened them to the same trees, their dull green branches heavy with late summer air, the sky a pale and hazy blue, the river itself the same thin wash of brown.

I was thirteen, and the Sunday before had made the decision to come forward after Pastor's invitation, and make my public confession of Jesus Christ as my Almighty Savior. The sermon over, the congregation standing and moaning out "Nearer My God to Thee," I'd simply made my way along the pew and past Missy Cook without looking at her, afraid that if I caught her eye she'd give some genuine smile, the possibility of that happening a dire threat to any peace I planned to find in Jesus. Once in the aisle, it was easy: I only walked forward the few feet to the pulpit—Missy Cook always sat in the second row on the center aisle—and waited for Pastor to come down, ask me what I wanted, then present me to the congregation.

But once his hand was on my shoulder, I saw this wouldn't be as simple as I'd thought: somewhere inside his eyes was love, I could see, easy and pure, a shine I hadn't expected, his hand on my shoulder not nearly as heavy as I'd figured it would be. He said, "What is it, Miss Jewel?"

I closed my eyes, not wanting this man's hand on my shoulder, the same one that'd tried to pat my head twice before. Not wanting to see in his smile that he was only a man, one who loved God the best way he knew how. My teeth clenched, I'd had to push the words from me: "I want to accept Jesus Christ as my Lord and Savior."

"Praise God," he said just loud enough for me to hear above the roll of verses being sung behind me, people all with their eyes on me, Missy Cook chief among them.

The hymn ended, the long last *Amen* dragged out for days before the organ went quiet. The only sound left was the whisper of a hundred bamboo fans. Pastor held my shoulders, and turned me to face the congregation. My eyes were still closed.

"Through the powerful grace of God our Heavenly Father," he began, and I could feel his fingers tense with the words, as though by squeezing my bones he might instill the Holy Spirit in me, "Miss Jewel Chandler has come humbly before our congregation to declare publicly her acceptance of Jesus Christ as her Personal Lord and Savior on this day. She will be baptized into the glory and righteousness of God our Father next Sunday afternoon, and I am sure it is her wish that everyone here be present to welcome her into God's precious fold."

That was when I opened my eyes, only to see Missy Cook, a lace hankie to her broken-glass eyes. She was crying, her shoulders heaving with some divine relief, as if she'd had the largest part in my coming to the Lord.

But of course it hadn't been her. It hadn't been Pastor, either, the sermon he gave that morning lost to the great abyss most every sermon I've ever heard has fallen into. It wasn't the congregation, which had doubled by the time it'd made its way to the bank of the Pearl to watch Pastor and me, the two of us in white robes that took up the river brown as soon as our hems touched water. None of them, I knew, were there to see Jewel Chandler be baptized, but were there to see Missy Cook's granddaughter be baptized. They were there more to give respect to the rich old lady in town than to witness the Holy Spirit descending upon me.

No, what I'd expected I'd see when I came up from the water was a new world in which the quiet and practical God I knew had become the strange and moonstruck one Cathedral'd found: on the Wednesday after she'd been baptized, the two of us were out back of Missy Cook's, her hanging up wash, me reading out loud to her from one of my old McGuffey Readers. Then I heard the wet swish of material dropped to the ground. I looked first at Cathedral's feet, where one of Missy Cook's finest white sheets lay in the dirt. Then I looked at Cathedral. She stood with her shoulders up, fingers stiff at her sides. Her face had gone slack, her eyes back in her head.

She spoke, and the words from her mouth all rolled out in a ball, syllables and throat sounds and hard breaths I recognized from nowhere. She was speaking in tongues, I knew, and my knowing that seemed a miracle of my own.

I dropped the book, stood with my hands clasped together in prayer. Still she went on, the song moving up and down some scale only angels knew for certain. I felt myself begin to cry, the sound so beautiful, so filled with a god who'd love you enough to bestow on you a freedom from the same old words that chained us all.

Then Molly was there with us, moving toward Cathedral still speaking. She took Cathedral by the shoulders and gently shook her, said, "No, no, no, child, you can't be doing no speaking now."

Cathedral's words began to thin down, the sounds broken and tired, until finally she closed her eyes, let her shoulders fall.

My hands were still clasped. Neither Molly nor Cathedral had even looked at me yet. I took a breath, said, "Why does she have to stop?" I swallowed, my tongue dry and thick.

Molly put an arm around her daughter's shoulder, Cathedral's face wet with sweat, her arms limp at her sides. "Because," Molly said, her eyes on Cathedral, "that what the Apostle Paul say. He say, 'Wherefore let him that speaketh in a unknown tongue pray that he may interpret.' They ain't no one to interpret here." Cathedral, eyes still closed, leaned into her momma's shoulder. Molly whispered, "We got to wait for Sunday, that's what we got to do," her words not meant for me, but for her daughter, words suddenly earthbound and the same as always.

That freedom Cathedral'd found was what I wanted, a freedom, too, that let her look me straight in the eye for the first time since I'd known her. Since that day in the back yard she'd searched out my eyes, hung onto them with her own. That was the freedom I was after, what I figured God must have given her, freedom from this earth and its words and what you knew your only role here would ever be. That would be my triumph over Missy Cook, the abounding grace of God. All I need do was to confess Christ and be baptized, the only two things required to enter the new Jerusalem.

Ushered to the shore, though, after Pastor had held me under, I felt no different. There was a God, I knew, and he dwelt in me, took care of me. He was a God who so loved the world that He gave His only begotten Son, so that I might not perish, but have everlasting life. This much I knew was true.

When Missy Cook took my hand and pulled me to her, and I heard the slow murmur of Hallelujahs around me, a sound like the vague roll of summer thunder it might have been, I realized it was all information I'd had before. I'd believed all along, my standing before the congregation and immersion in dirty river water only thin symbols of what had first to be in the heart. Cathedral and I were of the same God, I knew; but the face of Him she'd seen would never be the face I would come to know. The piece of God I'd gotten wasn't the flamboyant and exotic one she'd found. The God I'd found was the same one who'd answered my fervent prayer with the death of both my daddy and momma, blessed me with Missy Cook and a

crowd come to see what the next generation of Cook
looked like sopping wet and crying.

"Cathedral," I said again, and now I was wringing my
hands on my apron. "You want to come in?"

She shook her head. Behind her, Nelson dropped the
cigarette, and I saw in the darkness the failing orange light
disappear beneath his foot.

She said, "First Corinthians fifteen five say, 'I would
that ye all speaketh with tongues, but rather that ye
prophesieth, for greater is he that prophesieth than he that
speaketh with tongues.' "

She looked down, the same old Cathedral, the only difference I could see being in her face and the skin drawn
taut over bones, her mouth grown thinner. She looked up
at me. "Nelson tell me you with child again."

I nodded, smiled, though I felt certain she couldn't see
me for the kitchen light behind me. "I guess Leston told
y'all," I said, and looked past her to Nelson, quick disappearing in the growing dark.

He said, "Yes'm."

"I come to prophesieth unto you," Cathedral said, her
eyes still on me. She moved her shoulders beneath the
quilt, pulled it tighter around her. "I come to prophesieth
unto you about coming hardship you or nobody ain't ever
be ready to bear."

I tilted my head, stopped with my hands in the apron. I
lost my smile, though I'd wanted to show Cathedral how
pleased I could be at my age with a baby on the way. But I
figured it wasn't the baby she was talking about. I said, "You
know about my James heading off to the War?" I dropped
the apron, put my hands together in front of me. The night
was growing colder as we stood there. "Because even

though I love my James," I said, "God will bless him and us both, and his being gone one way or the other will be a hardship we can live through. At least that's my prayer."

"I don't know nothing about James," she said, and blinked. Nelson said, "We don't know nothing about that." His voice curled through the black around him, the words coming to me like an echo.

She looked down again, moved her foot on the ground. The light from the kitchen grew stronger the darker the world became, until now she stood in a hard rectangle of light from the doorway behind me, my shadow on the ground her only interruption.

She poked her heel in the dirt, tapped it twice, took in a deep breath. She lifted her head to me, swallowed. "I say unto you that the baby you be carrying be yo' hardship, be yo' test in this world. This be my prophesying unto you, Miss Jewel."

Nelson leaned into the light, reached toward her. All I could see of him was his arm and shoulder and head in the light from my kitchen. His hand touched her elbow, and he glanced up at me, then at the porch steps. "Come on, now," he whispered.

Cathedral didn't move.

Slowly I shook my head, made myself smile. "What are you saying?" I said. "Why do you say this?"

Cathedral smiled, let the quilt loosen, slip an inch or so off of her neck. "The Lord say to tell you, Miss Jewel," she said. "You and me both know He work in mysterious ways. But this not any mystery. He telling you right out. He letting you know. He smiling on you this way."

I felt my palms begin to sweat out there in the cold. I went to the edge of the porch, moved down one step.

"Momma," Billie Jean called out, on her voice the

whine she'd perfected in the last year or so, "close the door or come back inside. It's cold!"

"Momma?" Annie said.

Nelson gently pulled at her elbow. "Come let's go," he whispered.

But Cathedral and I were still looking at each other. I moved down another step, then another, until I was only a foot or so from her, her eyes on mine, her smile still there.

I put out a hand, cold with sweat, held it in front of me. I wasn't smiling anymore.

From beneath the quilt one of her hands appeared, took hold of mine. She squeezed down with some unknown might.

"We sorry, Miss Jewel," Nelson said, and now he tugged at her arm. "We going on home now. We don't mean to burden you."

"The Lord smiling down on you this way," she said again, and then Cathedral let go, her hand disappearing into the quilt. She moved out of the light.

I tried to watch them go, but they were lost to me even before they made it past the repair shed. There was no moon out, not enough stars to do any good. Just God above with some plan for us all.

I didn't know what to think, whether to believe her or not, and I tried to imagine how news like this could be of help, and whether that unaccountable piece of God Cathedral had hold of could be trusted to figure into the stone wedge of Him I knew.

The light I stood in broke to pieces, shadows falling about me, and I turned, looked up to the doorway. There stood James and Wilman and Burton, the three of them, all my boys, crowded into the doorway. Wilman and

Burton pushed at each other for room, while James, a boy suddenly taller than I ever imagined he might become, stood still, one hand to the doorjamb. "Momma," he said, "what's going on out here?"

I shrugged, uncertain myself. I only knew I was cold out here, and that somewhere along the road headed away from Purvis walked Nelson and Cathedral, the dark of no consequence to them. And I knew there was a baby in me. "Nothing," I said, and I shrugged again.

"Jewel," Leston called, the word neither question nor demand. Only my name.

"I'm here," I said, and started up the steps.

1944

Chapter 5

Our headlights cut through the black woods before us, the road into Purvis unfolding like some mystery, a place I'd never been before. The baby'd been trying to make its way out for the last fifteen hours, my mind long past battling with making sense of this world. There was only movement, darkness, light, an old, oiled road, and Leston hunched up over the steering wheel, a cigarette at his lips.

"Just hold on, Sugar," he whispered, and I thought I might have seen the tip of the cigarette bobbing with the words. "Sug, you just hold on."

"Sug," I managed to get out, and closed my eyes, the work of keeping my lids open too much to bear. "Sug," I whispered again, and thought of how I hadn't heard him call me that in years, not since we were newly married and still in the years when whatever future—a future that would account for five children bore in these Mississippi woods—seemed somebody else's life, not our own.

But then we must have hit a pothole or someplace where rains had dug into the road, because the world sank beneath me, and I fell what felt two feet deep into the seat, my ears filled with the roar of our slamming on through it, and I let out a yelp through no choice of my own, both hands on my belly.

"Son of a bitch," Leston whispered. "Son of a bitch, Sug."

The other five had been born at home, all of them so quick that with Wilman there hadn't been time enough for Cathedral to make her way over to deliver him. James'd taken the longest with his six hours, Cathedral's presence each time as much a comfort to me for her friendship as for her skill at midwifing.

This time she'd been to my door faster than any time before, showing up not an hour after I'd sent Burton for her, Cathedral all puffing, the washed-out blue dress that hung on her sweat through, her hair pulled back and knotted. Her eyes were right on mine as she came into the bedroom, Annie sitting in bed beside me.

"Now you move on out of here, baby-doll," she'd said to Anne, though her eyes were still on mine. "Our Lord be blessing you soon enough with another brother or sister, but right now you go play with the ones you got."

Annie had looked to me, and I'd turned to her, smiled, though I could feel another wave moving into me. "Go on," I said.

She slid away from me and off the quilt, dropped to the floor, her nye-nye tight in one hand. She backed out the room, and I heard Wilman say from just outside the door, "Annie, let's go out and we'll play kick the can, hey?" then the shuffle of feet down the stairs.

"This one be the quickest yet, you think?" Cathedral'd said, smiling now.

I'd started to nod, but the pain swept into me, mindless pain that wouldn't even let me answer her, and she'd taken my hand, squeezed it hard. I closed my eyes, felt her settle herself next to me on the bed.

I'd sent Burton first to Cathedral's, then to find his father, the crew working its way through the woods out past Jacob's Ferry Road, a good four miles from Cathedral's. I hadn't counted on them showing up for quite a while, maybe even after this baby was born, new life in here a giant surprise for Leston when he drove in. Then I heard the engine on one of the trucks moving up the road outside, the slam shut of doors, the hurried banging upstairs.

I opened my eyes, saw the two of them moving into the room, Leston, hat in hand, eyebrows furrowed, Burton just behind him, his hair wet, cheeks flushed. Cathedral stood, moved away and to the washstand beneath the one window, her back to us, and Leston came toward me. He let go the hat with one hand, and touched my cheek. He smiled, and I could smell gunpowder and pine tar and engine oil all at once.

I said, "What time is it?" and heard how weak my voice had become, a clouded whisper in the room.

Cathedral looked over her shoulder at Burton, who hesitated only a moment after he'd net her eyes.

"Momma," he said, "I'll be outside if you need anything else." He crossed his arms, held them tight to his chest. I nodded, said, "My big man."

He looked down, embarrassed, but then smiled, said, "Take care, Momma," and he was gone.

"It's five-thirty," Leston said, both hands at his hat again, and the old pictures of bearing my other children started coming in: Leston awkward and delicate when Cathedral came, as if he were a guest come to visit the near-dead in his own home; the shapes in the hard stucco of the ceiling in this room, shapes I turned into mountains and foreign countries and the grown-up faces of the children I was bearing as I lay here; my fingernails digging into the pine headboard above me until blood came from beneath my nails with the last few pushes; each child I had—James and Billie Jean in the cabin on Rosehill Road, Wilman and Burton and Annie right here—as Cathedral surrendered them to me, wiped clean and swaddled, ready for my breast.

"You be passed out for a time, Miss Jewel," Cathedral said, still at the washstand, and then I realized what Leston had said: Five-thirty. I'd sent Burton a little past one to Cathedral's.

"Five-thirty?" I whispered, and Leston seemed to move back from me, still smiling.

"We would have been here a touch earlier, but Burton lost himself in the woods for a time." He paused, swallowed. "How soon before this one?" he said, and he touched my cheek again, this time his fingers there for only an instant before he brought them back to the hat.

"Only the Lord know," Cathedral said. She came back to the bed, touched her wrist to my forehead. "Right now, Mr. Hilburn, you be a better help to God and his mercies you head on downstairs. I let you know what going on up here."

"Oh," he said, then, "Fine." He almost seemed to bow, and backed out the room. "Take care," he said.

I smiled, nodded as he pulled the door closed behind him.

Cathedral took her hand away from me. I said, "I never passed out before."

Her eyes wouldn't meet mine as she sat down next to me again. She said, "Every birthing different, Miss Jewel. You know that."

By nine, nothing had changed: every five minutes or so huge gusts of pain pushed through me, my belly separate from me then, some white-hot curse and blessing at once, me wanting it out more each time that pain came. But each time there was Cathedral at the foot of the bed, her saying, "You just breathe now. Go on and breathe," her eyes focused between my legs, my knees up, the thin sheets wet with my sweat and heavy as wool blankets. It was only October; the day had been as warm as any the last month, trees and vines and kudzu only in the last few days losing the deep and sturdy green they'd held all summer to the dull wax sheen that signaled fall was coming on. Annie'd spent the morning and early afternoon beside me, while I made breakfast for the crew, dinner for the boys and Billie Jean once they came home from school. And then I'd felt the first one come, the first pain that started at the top, just below my breasts, and shivered slowly down me, that first small push telling me God'd already decided this would be the day. And I'd sent Burton.

But now was the time, I told myself, those pains on me for eight hours straight, the word *Push* heavy in my head. I closed my eyes, bit down hard on my bottom lip, the pain and blood taste there only a small and welcome distraction to what I felt below my heart. I let go my belly, reached for the headboard, held on tight.

"Oh no, no, Miss Jewel," Cathedral said, and I heard her move from where she sat, felt her rough hands touch my cheek, my chin, brush back my hair. "You can't do this now. Yo' body ain't be ready for this now. All in the Lord's good time." She paused, and I felt her hand in my hair, her touch comfort. Slowly the pain eased, and I pictured in my head a lone tree somewhere, a young sycamore bent to a heavy wind, that wind easing, green branches lifting up to blue sky.

"This baby just be borning different from the others," she whispered, and I opened my eyes. She was looking at her hand, her eyes wet, half-closed. "I will stand upon my watch," she said, "and set me upon the tower, and will watch to see what he will say unto me, and what I shall answer when I am reproved." Her forehead, I could see even through the haze of this long in labor, was wet with sweat, and I wondered what she knew and wouldn't say.

I opened my mouth, formed the words my head stirred up, wanted spoken, but my eyes closed, and I felt the room begin to tumble, felt the center of it, my belly, become some fire wouldn't go out. I dug my nails deeper, trying to hold on, keep the bed from spinning me off the face of the earth, but I disappeared.

I came to at the sound of whispers, voices swimming up: my mother whispering in another room, and my grandfather whispering, too, and my father and his father, Jacob Chandler as well, all of them whispering words I couldn't make out, verses from the Bible that seemed somehow to fit. Someone held my eyes closed, a heavy hand tight on my lids, but I managed them open, blinked at the light from the lamp next to the bed.

I tried to move my arms but couldn't, the weight of our quilts now on me, pressing on my chest, my legs, my belly—and I remembered I was here to bear a child still in me, the mound below me no smaller, no wails through the room of a child letting the world know it was here, ready to start in on the fight every life becomes. There was only me here, the door to the bedroom shut, behind it those whispers.

"Cathedral," I called out, my voice far away from me, not even of me but mine for the name it called out.

The door opened, and Cathedral, silhouetted by the light from the hall, moved toward me. Here was her hand on my head again, in my hair, that familiar comfort, and I closed my eyes.

She whispered, "Now, Miss Jewel, it near on to four o'clock in the morning, and you still not ready to have this baby be born." She touched the backs of her cool fingers to my cheek. "So we been at this for too long now, and Mr. Leston and me, we both think you best be taken into the hospital now."

I opened my eyes to her. "The hospital?" I whispered. "What's wrong here?"

Leston came into the room, at first silhouetted by the hall light, then lit with the lamp. It was as if he'd only been gone a moment: the hat was still in his hand, the brim moving round, and for an instant I wondered if those useless hands could possibly be the same hands I'd let fill me up with the same pleasures I'd known for so many years now. Hands I'd given up to, only to be ushered into this moment, and the pain of bearing our next and last child.

He leaned close to me, Cathedral moving away to give him room, and I could see that, though maybe they were the same hands, something else had changed in him: his eyes had become even older, fear dug into the lines below them, into the creases beside them, the green gone now to a color I couldn't name for the trouble they seemed to see, and I knew this change signaled from God I was lined up to die, the birth of this child my own death.

"Leston," I whispered, and he held up a finger to his mouth to quiet me. He tried to smile, then reached that finger to me, touched it to my lips.

"We got Sepulcher and Temple right here, too good, strong bucks, they're going to carry you on downstairs and out to the truck. We're going to take care of you, Jewel. You just hold on." He paused, blinked. "I already got a call over to the hospital, and they should be ready for us when we get on up there. So don't you worry none. That's all I want you to do for me: just don't you worry none."

"The hospital," I said again, and Cathedral edged in front of Leston, touched a cold cloth to my face. "Now hush," she whispered, "now hush."

She looked from me to the door. Leston backed away, looked there, too. Cathedral nodded, and in came two of her sons, boys with mouths closed too tight, eyes turned from me, foreheads glistening though the room was cold now, ice cold, and I knew that, yes, I was going to die.

I prayed, the words rising up in me suddenly, a small and perfect and horrible prayer: *If it's a death You want,* I gave up to God, the words in my head shiny and polished and black, *let it be the child's.*

Sepulcher came round to my right, Temple to my left, so that they faced each other across the bed, Cathedral tucking the quilts around my legs, my arms. Then the boys looked to Cathedral. She nodded, and they bent to me, moved their hands beneath me until they met, and lifted, carried me over the footboard and toward the hall, where Leston was already moving backward, glancing over his shoulder to the stairs, to me, the boys, over his shoulder.

I held on tight to Cathedral's boys, my arms round their shoulders, my eyes wide open as we moved down the stairs. They took each step slow and deliberate, eyes on each other as though that might give them some greater balance.

But it wasn't fear of falling that kept my eyes open. It was my prayer, and how it'd come to me so easily, so clearly, the words swelling in my head, my heart thick with them: *Let it be the child's, let it be the child's.* They made perfect sense, and though I tried to stop them, another part of me held tighter to them, and to the purpose I finally saw for them: I wanted none of my children to know the sorrow of a lost parent, a sorrow I'd known too close my whole life.

We were at the bottom of the stairs now, Leston with his hat on, holding open the door. "Annie," I said, and closed my eyes a moment, conjured a picture of her on the bed next to me.

"She be sleeping," Cathedral whispered, and I felt the cloth at my forehead.

"Burton," I said. "Wilman, Billie Jean." I saw my oldest in uniform, somewhere in the South Pacific right now, blue water, beaches the color of bone. "James," I said.

"Now you be hushing up, Miss Jewel," Cathedral whispered, "because you know all yo' children be asleep. They all asleep. Even James, he be asleep right now wherever he be."

I opened my eyes to the truck parked before the house, the yard a white fire in the light cast by the headlights, and now other words came to me, the words I'd formed to ask Cathedral, the ones I'd put together and readied to give her before I'd passed out in my room.

"Cathedral," I said as the boys eased me into the cab, Temple moving aside, Sepulcher settling me in the seat.

She was there with the cloth again. "You save yo' words, Miss Jewel. You save yo' strength."

"Cathedral," I whispered, the words old, ancient, though I'd not yet spoken them. I whispered, "Is this the hardship? Is this how He smiles?"

Her eyes met mine for an instant, hung there only as long as she used to let them, before she came to know her God. Then they were away from me, settled on the cloth she still held to my cheek. "You just pray," she whispered, "you just pray."

She closed the door, looked through the glass to

Leston, nodded. He gave it the gas, and we were gone, and
I was certain she hadn't heard me answer her, hadn't heard
me say "I am" before she'd pulled the cloth from my
cheek, my black prayer already resumed: *Let it be the child.*

"Push!" the doctor yelled, and it was as if the word were a
birth itself, welcome and painful at once, me holding back
as long as I had. There was no telling how long I'd been in
the hospital, my mind gone now, all I knew the white of a
room, the first hospital I'd ever been in, my legs apart and
high in the air, strapped to metal bars poking out the end
of the bed, sheets hiding everything everywhere. That was
all I knew, and the faces of the last people I'd know on this
earth: the doctor, all I could see of him above the sheets
below me a flat forehead and thick spectacles low on his
nose, eyes all careful concentration and focused between
my legs; next to him a nurse, a woman older than me and
smiling, a tooth or two missing in front, loose folds of skin
beneath her chin; and one other nurse, a girl who seemed
no older than my Billie Jean, hands the color of porcelain
as she held on to one of my own.

"Now push, darling," the younger one whispered, all of
them here and ministering to me, I saw, as if I had no idea
what to do.

"Push," the older woman said. She nodded in what I
figured was a motherly way, though I'd no idea how my
mother might have urged me had she been here, me fast
approaching her and the hereafter, if the Lord chose not to
honor my steadfast prayer.

I surrendered to the notion I was going to die here and
now, the feeling in me some white wave, a peace that took
on whatever might happen, me heading to meet my God.
I finally pushed, pushed with everything I had in me, and

then with even more. I pushed, not because they'd told me to, but because it was what my body'd led me to believe was right, what it knew to do.

"Dammit, push!" the doctor yelled, and the young nurse squeezed my hand harder. "Push," she whispered again.

I pushed, my eyes squeezed tight to where I could see only swirling red circles and squares whirl and pop before me, a red quick going to white, and I thought I was at the gates of Heaven, readying for entrance, round my neck the millstone of my prayer for the death of this child.

I pushed, and pushed, felt something, a power greater than me, pushing, too, the help of some force not of me at all, and I drove open my eyes, my teeth clenched, my jaw tight as it would ever be.

It was the doctor, there beside me. He was pushing on me, mashing down on me, the fingers of his hands locked together, the palms at the top of my belly. He was mashing down on me, his moves quick and tough, as if he were kneading dough, and with each push down I felt air leaving me, felt the tear below me.

"Now is the time," I heard him whisper, then yell again, "Push."

The older nurse was below the sheets now, her eyes the same iron as the doctor's had been when he was down there. She licked her lips, ran the back of a hand across her forehead. She blinked twice, said, "Here it is."

I pushed, felt his pressing on me, forcing my baby out, all these at once, the moment in front of me the one between life and death, but both of them just past my touch. I was only watching, distant observer at the birth of my sixth child.

Then the pushing stopped, the white wave cresting in me, falling, the mashing on me gone, and I opened my eyes, looked below me to the foot of the bed, where the doctor held blue-pink feet chest high. He raised a hand, held the baby a little higher, and slapped its bottom once, twice, three times before it gave a startled cough, and cried.

No one except me—not the doctor, not the mother nurse, not even the girl who'd called me Darling—took notice of the small cleft between my baby's legs, that certain proof to the world that she was a girl, so that, finally, it was me who called out in a voice as clear as if I'd just been out for a walk in the woods, "She's a girl."

The doctor took her into his arms, said, "Why, you're right. So she is," and I saw him smile despite the sweat on his face, despite the thick glasses, despite the blood up to this wrists, his white gown all the more white for it.

"Count them up," I whispered, and already I was feeling the loss of blood and strength, the loss of the will that brought her here. I was cold, my arms and legs jittery with that loss. "Count them up," I whispered again. "Count up her fingers and her toes."

"There's ten of each," the girl said, her voice a warm whisper in my ear, words mixed with the small cry of my baby. "Stubby little fingers and toes, ma'am. But there's ten of each."

I was shivering, my body lost to me, and I cried, cried out of joy for the two of us alive and here, God in Heaven choosing to honor not the prayer for the death of my child, but the one I'd uttered the first day I knew I was pregnant, the one that she'd be alive, toes and fingers all present and accounted for.

"Then go tell Leston," I said, and I felt a warm blanket laid upon me, listened to my baby's cry a moment longer before I gave in to sleep.

Chapter 6

"Jewel," Leston whispered. "Jewel, it's me."

I opened my eyes. I was in a room with gray walls and one window. Light tumbled from the window, the shade up, and I blinked, turned from it to see Leston next to me in a chair. His face was near mine, him leaning forward, clean-shaven, hair combed back. He had on one of his Sunday shirts, the yellow one, buttoned up to his neck, over that his good Sunday jacket. He was smiling.

I whispered, "Sug," and put a hand up to his cheek.

His smile turned into a grin at that word, and he brought his eyes down a moment, lifted them again.

He leaned even closer, kissed my own cheek, and pulled back, his green eyes working on me, digging deep into mine in a way they hadn't in longer than I could remember.

He said, "She looks like all the rest of them. Just as perfect as all the rest of them."

I swallowed, let my eyes close a moment.

He said, "You been out a whole day. You been asleep for a whole day, you and the baby both. Pretty tough work for the two of you, I imagine." He touched my cheek again, and I could feel myself smile.

I heard footsteps into the room, hard and quick. Leston's hand moved from me, and I opened my eyes. A nurse, this one round and pink-faced with a paper hat folded in some odd shape atop her coal-black hair, stood at the foot of the bed, a clipboard cradled in one arm. She had bright red lipstick on, cheeks rouged up. She was looking at the clipboard, flipped back a page, then brought that page to the front again.

I said, "When do I see my baby?"

I glanced at Leston sitting up straight in his chair. On the low dresser behind him was his hat, next to it a bunch of flowers in a glass: a few ragged daisies, a stalk of geraniums, some greenery.

Leston looked at the dresser, back to me. "The children," he said, and smiled. "They send their love." He paused, glanced at the nurse, still looking at the clipboard. "Anne wanted to send her blanket," he nearly whispered. He leaned an inch or so toward me and no more, afraid, I knew, the nurse might catch him showing too much affection. "Cathedral said no, you had plenty of them here." He gave a quick smile, glanced at the nurse again, sat up straight.

He cleared his throat, looked at the nurse full on. He said, "My wife would like to know when she might be seeing her child."

She still didn't look away from the clipboard. She said, "That, sir, will be the doctor's decision. He will inform y'all when the moment has come. Not before that."

She turned, never having met our eyes, and left the room, her same hard steps ricocheting round the bare walls.

"A hospital," I said. "So this is what I've been missing my whole life." I moved to sit up, tried to reach behind me to push down a pillow, and the same old pains ground through me, what'd been white fire now a bank of sharp embers settled low in my belly, between my legs.

I grimaced, my eyes twisted closed, and heard the scrape of Leston's chair on the floor as he quick stood up, jammed the pillows down himself.

"Easy now," he said. "Easy. Took you twenty-two hours to have that baby. Don't expect to get up and at 'em too quick."

Twenty-two hours, I thought, *twenty-two,* and when I opened my eyes again, there was the doctor at the foot of the bed, the same doctor with the wide forehead and spectacles. But now he had on a red bow tie and blue button-down shirt, his hair combed wet across his head from the top of one ear to the top of the other. He had the same clipboard in his hand, eyes hard on whatever piece of my life was on that paper.

He looked up from the clipboard, still without a word of warning or congratulations, and faced the doorway, where in came the nurse with the rouged face, lips drop-dead red.

In her arms was the bundle I'd waited nine months to hold, had battled against my body more hours than I could have imagined I would. The nurse was smiling now, and as she neared me, her arms reaching my child out to me, she became my friend, the best one I would ever know next to Cathedral, and I smiled back at her, our eyes meeting in the same way they always did with Cathedral each time she handed me my new life.

I peeled back the corner of the blanket that lay across her face, and saw my daughter for the first time. Leston was right: she was as perfect as all the rest of them, a thin copper halo of hair, eyelids a frail blue as she slept, one hand in a fist nestled next to her cheek. She was beautiful, even more beautiful than any of the others, I couldn't help but feel, Leston and I never able to do better than the newest baby in my arms.

"She's still sleeping it off herself," the doctor said. "Seems she's even more wrung out by the whole thing than you. But that's fine. It's what her body's telling her she needs."

Just then her pale pink lips quivered, set to sucking at nothing, and I whispered, "There's something else this little body needs," and I looked up at the doctor, the nurse, back to my baby. I said, "And if you will excuse us, we'll be getting to it."

"Why certainly," the doctor said, and I glanced up to see him and the nurse already turned, moving toward the door.

I turned back to the baby, but heard next to me the scrape of the chair again. Leston stood next to the bed, and I looked at him. He'd already grabbed his hat from the dresser, was leaning over to kiss me good-bye.

"You can't go," I said. "You've got to stay here with me. With our baby."

He stopped, stood straight. He tried to smile, opened his mouth to speak. He didn't want in here, I knew, not with a new mother ready to start nursing. This moment had always been between Cathedral and me, Leston's only role in all this him standing outside the door and grinning at the birth of a new child.

But we were in a hospital now, my child just handed over to me by two strangers as if she were a gift from them, their property, real estate deeded to me. She'd been out of my hands the whole first day of her life, and now Leston wanted out.

I said, "You stay put now. We don't know anybody here from Adam, and I'm not about to nurse my baby in a cold room with nobody here."

Leston smiled. He glanced at me, then the baby. He

shrugged, said, "Be glad to stay," and sat down. He tapped the crease in the crown of his hat once, then said, "This is my first time in a hospital, too, don't forget." He paused. "Feel like I'm being bullied, all these educated doctors." He smiled again. "That dolled-up nurse."

I nodded, smiled. Here was my husband, the king of all he surveyed, made to bow down to a pink-faced doctor in a bow tie.

"But," he said, and looked at me. "It's my baby daughter here what matters. And you."

I wanted to reach a hand out to him, wanted to touch his clean-shaven face again, but just then the baby in my arms let out the smallest of cries, and I looked to her, shifted so she sat lower on me. I peeled back the hospital gown I had on, showed my shoulder, then my nipple, my breasts filled, already a day late at this.

Her eyes were still closed, her lips still quivering, and I snuggled her close, my nipple hard and ready, a drop of clear wet poised at the tip, and then my baby took me in, started life, taking from me what I was glad I could give.

I smiled, though there was pain in my milk coming down. But it was a pain I took with my whole heart, a pain I wanted with me for as long as my baby wanted my milk. I could fix things, could bear up in whatever came my way. If I could live through this birth by the grace of God, and come through it with the sweetness of my milk just as ready as it was with every other child I'd bore, then I could do anything.

And I saw that I'd done the right thing in taking hold of my own life and setting it straight, my momma and her stories of who I was and where I came from—*like stones in your pocket,* she'd said—better provision for me than the warning of burning clothes in a nighttime orchard, or the threat in the cold, brown eyes of Missy Cook. I'd gone on from that life into this one, to a husband providing for me better than most women I knew of, children healthy and fit. The stories of my father's father and of Missy Cook's father had been stones in my pocket, all right, but not the kind to weigh you down, not the sort you pile in before jumping off a bridge. They'd been the polished and smooth ones, stones cool to the touch, tough and foreign and necessary all the same.

"You are a beautiful woman, Jewel," Leston said, and I turned from the baby to him. He was leaned forward in his seat, watching the two of us.

"What makes you say that?" I said.

"Your being beautiful," he said. "And that baby you got there. Plenty reason enough."

My newest baby still pulled down my milk, and Leston eased back in the seat, reached a hand to the inside pocket of his jacket.

"Got something for you," he said, and brought his hand out, held in it a piece of polished wood.

It was a piece off a dogwood branch, I could see right away, a slender piece, crooked in its own graceful way, and fit my husband's hand perfectly, from the tip of his thumb to the tip of his pinkie finger.

It was a beautiful piece of wood, not so much for the gnarled knots along the big end of it, nor for the thin point it came to at the other, not even for the gray-brown color of the wood.

What made it beautiful was how it shone in the light from the one window, and the care I knew he'd taken with it to make that shine come up, make the grain glisten, those knots whorls of smooth color. It was beautiful because of what he'd done to it with his hands.

"Found it last week," he said. "Just saw it on the

ground. Picked it up." With his other hand he turned it over, revealed to me new twists in the grain, more new ways the light could shine off it. "Knew I could do something with it."

I looked at him, smiled. I said, "It's beautiful. Like all the rest of the gifts you've made me."

The baby safe in the crook of my arms, still sucking away, I reached to the wood, touched it. This was his gift to me, his own small tradition, one he'd started on his own at the birth of James, back when we lived in the cabin on Rosehill Road, and I remembered then the shutters he made for me at the birth of his firstborn.

They were shutters not for closing up when a storm came or cold weather, but shutters purely for the beauty of them, and how fine they made the house look. They were white, solid, and in the center of each was a raised cutout silhouette of a pinetree painted a dark forest green, and I remembered right then lying in bed one morning only days after James was born, him there next to me and nursing away just like the baby in my arms right now. I'd heard some small scratch of sound come through the walls of the cabin, a sound more like a squirrel working away than Leston with a screwdriver outside my window. Then'd come Cathedral's voice out there, her talking and laughing, Leston giving out a word or three now and again. Once the scratching'd stopped, Cathedral came into the house, James asleep, and helped me struggle up out of bed. She'd smiled, her eyes on mine all the while as she led me through the doorway and out front of the house.

There had stood Leston, hands on his hips, grinning away. He looked at me, then to the house. Slowly I walked to him, then turned, faced the house to see his perfect gift, a gift of his hands and hard work: shutters a crisp white, pine silhouettes a cool green, our cabin now filled with the promise of new life—a *son*—and I'd turned to Leston, smiled, kissed him full on the lips. I whispered, "Thank you."

I picked up the piece of wood from the palm of his hand, felt how warm it was, how soft and clean. He'd sanded it just enough to give it this feel, this touch.

"Wish I could've done more," he said. "But the work. Too much of it." He shrugged, wouldn't let his eyes meet mine, him embarrassed at how small this gift was.

Since the shutters, the other gifts had grown smaller in size as our lives took off, time swallowed up even more with each new child. After Billie Jean was born, he built me a small cedar chest; after Burton, three window boxes for geraniums. After Wilman, it was a jewelry box, though I had only a couple necklaces, one set of earrings. Before the piece of wood in my hand right now, after Annie'd been born, I'd found on the kitchen table two cherrywood candlesticks.

"I'll make something better, once things ease up," he said.

"No," I said right away, the wood in my hand still warm from where he'd carried it in his jacket, still warm from the palm of his hand. "This will do fine," I said. "It's beautiful."

He shrugged once more, grinned. Then he did something strange and wonderful: he stood, leaned over to me, and kissed me on the lips, and I thought again of him calling me Sug, and how long ago it'd seemed we'd abandoned those love names.

"Leston," I whispered. "Sug. I love you."

He was already sitting in his chair again, his face gone red, him smiling away at his hat.

"I love you, too," he said.

I looked to the baby again, touched a finger to her fine, pink cheek. I said, "This child needs a name. She's got her whole life ahead of her, one day of it already gone."

She let go my nipple, her eyes never opening, and I lifted her, amazed like always how little a baby weighed, and brought her to my other breast, let her start in there.

"I got the name this time," Leston said. He was smiling. "The way I figure it is," he said, and looked at the baby, fixed his eyes on her, "this is the last baby. Last but not least. So I get to name her."

"Depends," I said, "on what you name her." My milk was coming down on this side, the same deep and dull pain in me. I felt my jaw tighten a little, blinked it away.

He took a breath, sat up straighter in the chair. He put his hat on one knee, fingers touching the crown. He let out a little breath, closed his eyes. He said, "Brenda Kay."

Slowly I looked from him to the child in my arms, this newborn with the beautiful hair, suckling in her sleep. I said, "After your sister," and thought of Brenda Kay, a girl born ten years before Leston, and of the stories he'd given of her, her auburn hair and green eyes, her beaus. I thought too of her dying giving birth to her first child, Toxie, and how Leston had grown up with that boy, himself a kind of older brother to him. I placed no faith in namesakes and how some people thought it bad luck, doom wished upon a new soul on earth if the name of someone who'd died in a bad way were given. Brenda Kay was my husband's sister, a woman he had loved, family. His own blood, and for a moment I envied him those memories he had of her, evidence she'd lived and had loved him.

I touched my daughter's hair, her ear, her fingers pink

and small, smaller than they would ever be from this day forward, my child already growing right before my eyes, right in this room. "It's a beautiful name," I said. "The perfect name."

I looked up at Leston, and held out the same hand I'd touched our daughter with, held it out for him.

He lifted his hand up, and our fingers touched. "That's her name," I said, and we held hands that way for the longest time.

Chapter 7

Brenda Kay slept. She slept those four days I spent in the hospital in Purvis, no one to visit but Leston; slept the ride home on the same road we'd driven in darkness, the trees lining the road now alive with a fall breeze that moved the high limbs; slept through meeting her brothers and sisters the first day home.

Billie Jean seemed to forget she was a teenager with friends who'd be appalled at this new proof her parents still actually touched each other. She'd leaned in close to the cradle next to my bed and touched Brenda Kay's cheek with one finger, gave a small kiss to her forehead. Billie Jean turned to me, on her face a smile I'd never seen before, proof to *me* she was becoming a woman, her face suddenly thinner, lips fuller, eyes deeper. Without a word she leaned over and kissed me on the forehead, too, and hugged me. I thought I could smell on her the faint trace of rosewater, and hugged her the closer for it.

Next came Burton, who stood at the foot of the bed and said, "Momma, I helped with this, you know." I nodded, said, "Without you your daddy'd probably still be out in the woods taking out stumps," and Burton gave a short, stiff nod, acknowledgment of the truth I'd uttered. He looked into the cradle, the same one he and each of the others had rocked in, at his new sister, gave the same nod at her, and turned, left the room.

Wilman'd been leaning against the wall near the door, hands still in his pockets, head down. Once Burton was gone, he looked up, pushed himself from the wall, and made his way toward the cradle. He looked in, blinked, turned his head first one way, then another. He looked at me.

He said, "It hurt, didn't it?"

I smiled, shrugged. I laced my fingers together on top of the quilt. "Yes," I said. "But the hurt doesn't matter, not when you see all the love your children bring you."

He looked at Brenda Kay, brought his hands from his pockets and reached down, fingered the blanket that lay over her. He stooped, hesitated, and brought his face to hers, kissed her. He pulled away a moment, then kissed her again, whispered, "Brenda Kay."

That was when I lifted my arms, held them out to him. He smiled, finally, and came to me, his shoulders in my arms a soft dream, one coming to an end every day he grew up, every day each of them grew up. He patted me on the back, his small hands giving the finest comfort any human being could give.

He pulled away, looked at me. He said, "Don't cry, Momma," and reached a hand to my eye, touched at tears I hadn't known were coming. "Don't cry," he said.

I nodded, took in a small breath, said, "Now send in Annie."

He smiled. "I been taking good care of her, me and Cathedral both," he said, and turned, ran from the room.

"Don't run," I called after him, afraid for a moment of the sound his steps made on the floor, my baby still asleep. But she hadn't woken yet except for her small cries at feeding. Maybe waking her would be the thing to do.

I leaned over, pulled back the blanket so I could see her, hands in fists near her face, fingers curled into her palms so tight they nearly disappeared.

Then Annie stood next to the cradle. I hadn't heard her come in, saw only her tiny feet next to the cradle, the ragged bottom edge of her nye-nye on the floor.

I looked up. Her eyes were on me, third and fourth fingers in her mouth, nye-nye held to her shoulder.

"Annie," I whispered, "this is your new sister, Brenda Kay."

She didn't move, only swallowed, reached up with her free hand and rubbed an eye.

"Aren't you going to say hello?" I said, and eased back into the bed.

She shook her head once, fingers still in her mouth.

"Come here," I whispered, and held out my hands to her.

She rubbed her eye again, then looked at the floor. Slowly she edged round the cradle and to the bed. She still hadn't looked at me by the time I could reach her, and I took hold of her hands, squeezed them.

I said, "You climb up here in bed and take a nap with Momma."

She wasn't smiling, her mouth open, the whites of her eyes the clean and unbroken white of childhood, the brown irises filled with some wonder at what all this was about, and who that baby in the cradle was, and why everyone was so quiet in a house usually filled with noise. All of that was in her eyes, and as she climbed up the quilt and then under it, nye-nye still clutched in one hand, her body nestling in to mine, I gave her no answers, simply decided that this time of quiet and sleep was the best I could hope for.

And while she settled in next to me I thought of James in the South Pacific, and of the only things I knew of that place: black and white pictures in ancient issues of *National Geographic* I used to read when I was in college. Black water and black trees and gray dust, above it all a white sun that burned away any color I might have been able to imagine, though James'd sent home letters describing flowers he'd never thought could be, shades of green deeper and brighter than any summer in Mississippi, water the blue of a cold and cloudless November noon here. He was with the Seabees, him and his fellow sailors making barracks and airstrips and offices on each new island we won down there, but in my thoughts of him all that was gone. There was nothing, only the knowledge as sharp as a knife in my heart that James was there, me here.

But even in the face of that knowledge cutting deep, even in the face of my firstborn not yet knowing the beauty of his newest sister, I was still grandly grateful for the God up in Heaven and His ignoring my prayer to let this child die. He was a merciful God, I knew, this fact bore witness by the kiss Wilman'd given, the sweet nod of the head Burton'd made. His mercy was there in Billie Jean's eyes and how she'd looked at me, in the warmth of my Annie in bed beside me, and I wondered how I'd survived the sort of God I'd had inflicted on me when I was a girl, a single child, no brothers or sisters to usher me through this life, back when it was only me to stand before the world and watch what it could give you and just as easily take away.

When it came clear to Missy Cook I wasn't going to change, wasn't going to become the woman of taste and bearing and gentility—everything her daughter had killed when she'd gone for that half-breed Choctaw—I was sent away to the Mississippi Industrial School for Girls, a place for wayward trash and delinquents, certainly what I must have become in her eyes. Cathedral was reading away by that time, the two of us trading chapters in the Bible to read to one another while I worked at my figuring, her doing her chores. She'd already met Nelson by then, too, him a short, thick buck working on the county road crew, the two of them meeting at the Ebenezer AME where Molly attended.

It had been a day like every other in late winter, the overcast sky, I could see outside the dining room window, heavy and dark. Missy Cook and I were seated at the table, and Molly came from the kitchen, sat before us food in the same fine china I'd known for five years.

Missy Cook cleared her throat and, like always, took my hand in hers for the blessing.

But instead of going right to her same old words over the food, she smiled at me, her head tilted to one side.

Molly was gone from the room, and I looked down at my plate, gold-rimmed with yellow flowers circled with cobalt ribbons, china as fine, I imagined, as when her daddy had given it to her and her new Yankee husband.

She said, "Beginning Monday the next, you will be attending a new school. The Mississippi Industrial School for Girls. It will be a place for you to grow up, to learn to become a lady of manners and heart." She paused, gave a small squeeze of my hand. "A place where you can build upon your walk with the Almighty, and where you can learn how we are placed upon this earth and to what ends that placement will serve us, if we only serve Him first and best."

I swallowed hard, did my best to let my hand go loose, but nothing happened. The muscles in my arm were tight, on fire. I hadn't looked up at her yet, my eyes on a single cobalt ribbon and how it glided, danced about the perfect flowers. I said, "Does this have to do with teaching Cathedral to read?" not certain if she would know what I was talking about, but testing all the same.

She let go my hand, and suddenly my hand was cold, her flesh having warmed me somehow. I could see steam up from the plate of food before me, and I thought of Molly sampling the lima beans, her small laugh.

Missy Cook said, "I watch for you from upstairs simply because I feel it my God-given duty to keep an eye out for you, to watch for your welfare." She brought her hands to her lap, her signal I should do the same for our blessing.

I held my hands together in my lap, tried to warm them up, but couldn't, and I suddenly felt I was dying here, and just as quick this Mississippi Industrial School for Girls became some garden to me, an escape, lodging in a night that'd started with the death of my momma and daddy, the School one more minute closer to a dawn I hoped I would recognize when it came. Sometime.

"Our Father," Missy Cook started, and I bowed my head, her voice the high-pitched, pious whisper it always was. "Bless this food, as You have been so kind to bless this household and all its inhabitants. We thank Thee for the blessings of the future, the blessings of the present, and the blessings of the past that have made so abundant this table before us."

That was where she usually stopped, and I was already lifting my head, ready to eat this abundance before it grew cold, before I'd be booted on my way to whatever next new life was to come. But Missy Cook's eyes were still drawn tight and closed, her hands still in her lap, and for a moment I wondered whether she might be ready to burst into tongues herself.

What I did was wrong, I knew. But there was nothing for it. I simply laughed, not loud or on purpose, but a laugh that left me, the picture in me of Missy Cook's eyes rolling back, words from another world leaving her, and that image was what made me give way to the freedom suddenly in my heart: I was on my way from this place, from fine china, the dead gray sky outside the window, from food blamed on a God who would keep the niggers back in the kitchen from reading.

I laughed for only an instant, but loud enough for Missy Cook to hear me, for her to crack open one eye, and I snapped my head down, held my hands tighter together.

She said, "And bless my granddaughter on her imminent journey, on her passage from child into adult, from ignorance into wisdom, from the abyss of great darkness into the gates of Heaven. Bless her, dear Lord, with the knowledge of Christ's grace and love and tender mercy." She paused, breathed out in a heavy whisper, "Amen."

I had only a moment to look up before her open palm came down upon my cheek. A blast of white pain seemed to split open my face, the shock of it enough to keep back tears, even to keep me from looking away from her own face, her teeth clenched, hand up and ready to slap me again.

"You chose a path when you were baptized, and that path is not one from which you can fall," she said. "Laughing in Christ's face. 'For the wages of sin is death,' saith the Lord. To laugh in Christ's face is sin."

Her hand was still up high, the fingers beginning now

to shiver with what I figured must have been anticipation, more sin from me.

But I turned toward her, faced her. I could feel the welt rising in my cheek, the rush of blood there, but I looked at her, let her eyes enter me, let mine, as best I could, enter hers. I held her look for a few moments, then closed my eyes.

I wasn't certain now how many Christs there were at work in this world, how many Gods, from Cathedral's and Molly's to whatever god had driven my father and my mother toward and then away from each other, to the one that operated somehow in the woman before me, but I did the only thing I knew the Christ in me would have done: I gave her my other cheek, offered up the side of my face that was still smooth and white, untouched by the hand of her Christ in rebuke of me laughing.

I was frightened, but not of her hand, the coming blow. What filled me with fear was the sudden certainty of what I saw that gesture meant: it was a dare, a line drawn in the dirt. Christ knew that, knew the shape of that moment when the accused would stand innocent. And I wasn't certain which was worse: me aligning myself with Christ, doing what He'd instructed, or the hate that seemed to guide me into daring her to strike her again. There were two sides to the gesture. Two sides to everything, I saw.

I held my eyes closed, waiting, waiting, but she only yelled, "Insolence," the thick and silent and cold air of the room shattered.

On Saturday morning a wagon came for me, driven by a white man in overalls and wearing a cap tipped to the left, almost covering one eye. Next to him sat a white woman in a gray dress, around her shoulders a heavy black wool coat, a gray wool bonnet tied tight around her face. She seemed not to have any lips at all, her mouth a hard slit, and I knew that this was the end of one life, the start of the next, Molly's eyes as she stood on the old porchy shiny, her hands in front of her, fingers laced. Cathedral stood next to her, her face holding nothing, no smile, no frown, as she lifted one hand to me and waved.

I waved to her, me in the back of the wagon, in my lap the Bible Pastor had given me after my baptism, next to me a tired and beaten leather valise, inside it everything I needed: two dresses with petticoats, two pairs of shoes, three tablets of paper, three red pencils, and, wedged between sheets of the newest tablet, the photograph of my grandfather, Jacob Chandler. And somewhere above me, looking out a window down on us all, was Missy Cook.

The driver gave the reins a shake, and we started off.

"Ezekiel thirty-seven," Cathedral called out, and brought her hand down. She stood with her arms at her sides, calling out the chapter I would have read to her this afternoon had I not been sent away from here by my grandmother.

"Ezekiel thirty-eight," I called back, the wagon now at the foot of the drive and pulling out into the street, where one last cold snap the night before had near-frozen the mud ruts. "Just you make sure you keep on with your reading," I nearly shouted, and I smiled, waved even harder, my words meant not only as encouragement to Cathedral, but as a signal to Missy Cook, the same sort of signal a burning high-back rocker had meant a night so many years ago.

Cathedral nodded. Molly hadn't moved. Then the two were gone, the porch now hidden behind trees on the street, and I was alone again in the world.

I felt a hand on my shoulder, turned, looked up at the

woman. She was smiling at me, said, "Now let's just be quiet back there."

I did my best to smile back at her, but the ruts in the road took over, and I bounced hard, the only cushion beneath me a wool blanket. The woman turned forward again, her gloved hands gripping the edge of the seat.

"Hold on," the driver said.

But I'd already let go, had my Bible open, was turning in it to Ezekiel 37, and I started reading: "The hand of the Lord was upon me, and carried me out in the spirit of the Lord, and set me down in the midst of the valley which was full of bones, and caused me to pass by them round about: and, behold, there were very many in the open valley; and lo, they were very dry. And he said unto me, Son of man, can these bones live? And I answered, O Lord God, thou knowest."

I shut the book right then, closed my eyes. I knew this story by heart, knew about the dry bones coming up from the ground and forming an army for the whole house of Israel. I was out of that valley now, those dry bones, the savable ones, already up and walking: Cathedral and her boyfriend, Nelson, and in a way Molly, too, her knowing all along I'd been teaching her daughter.

"You all right, child?" the woman asked, and I opened my eyes. She wasn't smiling, on her face concern, her eyebrows together.

I said, "No ma'am." I paused, watched my old street and the trees and the other homes all falling away behind the wagon, places and things and people I counted on never seeing again. I said, "Just scared."

She nodded. "You've every right to be," she said, and I knew she meant it, the way she'd nodded, kept her eyes right on mine. What was ahead was anybody's guess, so I did the only thing I could do: I sat in the back of the wagon, started the long ride to the Mississippi Industrial School for Girls in Picayune, hours away. Things after that would come clear, I knew, and I settled in, held myself against the cold, against the banging wheels on frozen ground, against the lives I was leaving behind.

Late that day, me sleeping on and off, the roads never seeming any less bumpy than my old street, I climbed down from the wagon, finally, there in Picayune. The driver helped me, his hands cold in the evening air, clouds low and near-black above us all, the woman smiling down at me no different than before, as if there were plenty she knew about what would happen to me here. I followed her into the building, huge and ugly, yellow brick with windows no larger than shoeboxes. She led me up to the third floor to my room, inside it six beds all with iron headboards like bars from a jail cell door, walls the same ugly yellow brick as outside, quilts as thin as paper. The room had its own sink, a mirror, beneath the sink a bucket and mop and can of Bon Ami.

Within a week or so I had a best friend, one Cleopatra Sinclair, a tall girl with strawberry blond hair she kept in two ponytails, one on top of the other at the back of her head. She was from a town called Bobo, Mississippi, placed here because she'd thrown a brick through a storefront window in town two days after her father'd shot himself in the head in the outhouse behind her old home. Her mother'd died four years before, and the town fathers figured on her best being served by sending her down to Picayune. "Where I could find a useful and redemptive life," were the words she used when she told me the story of how she was sent here.

Cleopatra had brought with her the same brick she threw through that window, slept with it under her pillow every night. Another girl, Mavis Petrie, a short girl with black hair to her waist, legs like tree trunks, kept with her a mother-of-pearl inlaid brush and comb, gifts to her from her aunt, who'd sent her here for no other reason than that she'd caught her smoking rabbit tobacco out behind their wagon one evening. "It was the only thing wrong I ever done," Mavis said each night as she brought the brush through her hair a hundred times, "the only thing I ever done wrong, the only thing," though Cleopatra had it on good measure that the real reason she'd been sent here was because the aunt had found Mavis in bed with the uncle one Sunday morning, and that the brush and comb were in fact gifts from the *uncle*, him thankful for the good time she'd shown him. Of course I never questioned Cleopatra, never asked her where she'd gotten her information, but only stared at Mavis each night as she brushed her hair and muttered about what she'd done wrong, Cleopatra and I exchanging glances now and again, amazed at what she might know about men, what neither of us had any idea about.

And I'd secretly thrilled at the intimacy of our glances, Cleopatra's and mine, and at how there were secrets we knew of others, and how we'd nod our heads at each other when some other girl was around, the both of us knowing precisely what we meant. I thrilled at that, because I'd never known such closeness, not even when I'd been reading to Cathedral. This was a friendship, the kind, I figured, maybe only sisters could know, and I was happy.

Another girl, this one about my height though a year younger, brought nothing with her, only showed up one day in late July, my first summer there, wearing only a pale blue dress stained with dirt and grease and who knew what

all, her hair matted and filled with burrs, her fingernails bit
to the quick, several of them bleeding. She'd been brought
in by one of the hall mistresses, Mrs. Archibald, who'd simply said, "Ladies, this is Bessy Swansea," all the introduction
she ever gave. She turned, left the room, at which point
Bessy Swansea backed into a corner, slowly slid down the
wall. She crouched there, elbows on her knees, hands open,
palms down, sizing us all up, her eyes catching on each one
of us a moment, then moving on to the next.

"Hey," Cleopatra said. She was lying on her bed, just as
the rest of us were, all of us at work on the summer course
homework we had to finish before dinner, courses during
the summer simple things like Proper Care of the Home
and Farming Chores and Preparing Vegetables; the rest of
the year was spent with the real courses: Latin, Geometry,
Grammar.

But she said nothing, only stared at each of us in turn,
Mavis, a finger already wrapped in a lock of hair, glanced
from me to Cleopatra to Beaulah—another girl in our
room, famous for her nightmares every Wednesday night,
her waking us all up like clockwork with loud screaming
about horses and rifles—then to the last girl in our room,
Duchess, a big-bosomed girl with blond hair like broom-
straw and brown eyes as dull as mud. We all waited.

Finally, Cleopatra rolled onto her tummy, turned her
back to the new girl. She said, "It's only hey," and let out a
sigh, shook her head.

We all did the same, turned our backs on the new
intruder, me the last, all of us waiting now for the dinner
bell.

It was a week solid before Bessy finally spoke to any of us,
and then it'd been to Mavis, and it'd been to ask if she

could touch Mavis' brush. By this time Bessy'd been soaped down enough to where the grime and burrs and all else had disappeared, leaving behind a girl prettier than any of us could've imagined the night she'd come and sat in the corner, though her nails were still bitten all to pieces, two or three on each hand bright red and sometimes fairly dripping blood. We all wore the same uniform, a gray cotton blouse and black cotton jumper with black leggings, but there'd been something in how the clothes wore on Bessy that made all of us look at her more, see her differently than the rest of us. Her skin was soft, begged you to touch it, and her hair, worn now in a single ponytail low on her neck, caught early morning light when we took the mandatory four-times-around-the-school walk, all 165 of us in one big chain encircling the school grounds, Bessy in front of Cleopatra and me bringing up the rear. Her eyes were always on the ground before her, her arms crossed and held tight to her chest like this were dead winter, though we were still in July.

The night she first spoke, she'd only whispered to Mavis, "May I hold your brush?"

All of us turned from our homework. Mavis clutched the brush to her chest, all of us up off our beds now, wanting in on whatever was happening. "No!" Mavis whispered, then reached quick to the comb that lay next to her, afraid, I figured, Bessy might take that up instead. "You can't," Mavis cried, "you can't."

My eyes were on Bessy. She opened her mouth, showed for the first time a line of perfect teeth, white and shining and straight. She leaned her head back, her mouth open wide, and let out a laugh that shot through all of us, made me blink and shiver at once, her ponytail quivering with that long laugh.

"You," Bessy said, and pointed a finger at Mavis, the tip blood-red, the nail sheered off. She pointed at each of us, one at a time. "All y'all," she said, smiling, perfect teeth, perfect skin, perfect hair. "All y'all, you're all nothing but scared, that's all." She paused, let out a chuckle, but nothing to compare with that laugh of a moment ago. "You're all just a gang of scared, mewly, snot-nosed burrhead babies," she said.

It was Cleopatra to answer. She said, "And who the hell are you?" Her hands were already in fists at her sides, ready for whatever this new girl could muster, her head cocked, her hair out of the ponytails and falling off her shoulders.

Cleopatra said, "Little Miss Pretty Fingers."

Bessy lit into her with a shriek that brought girls from the two floors below heading for our room, the two of them falling backwards onto the floor with a heavy sound that seemed to shake the beds. Bessy was on Cleopatra's chest, her knees holding her down, and she was pulling at Cleopatra's hair, held two fistfuls of it, shook and shook and shook so that Cleopatra's head seemed almost pulled off her neck. Neither of them made any sounds, though; Bessy's shriek was gone, replaced by the echoes of girls running in the hall toward us, and with Duchess and Beaulah and Mavis, all three of them sobbing.

Then, in a move so quick I couldn't even figure how it happened, Cleopatra was on top of Bessy, though Bessy still had hold of her hair, still shook. But Cleopatra's hands were free now, no longer pinned down by Bessy's knee, and Cleopatra started slapping Bessy's face, one hand after the other, first the left then the right then the left again, each hit a solid strike, and I could see the welts already rising on Bessy's skin, that perfect skin all welling up red. Still she shook Cleopatra's head, and when I took my eyes off that beautiful skin Bessy'd once had, I saw on the back of Cleopatra's head a bloody spot the size of a peach.

Girls flooded the room, all of them surging in and around and hollering, choking me off from what I'd finally realized had been on its way since Bessy'd come in here, and since Cleopatra'd said Hey. They were fighting, trying to figure who'd be boss around here.

I didn't move, let the girls who didn't belong in the room take over and fill the room with more noise than the entire school'd heard since as long as I'd been there.

Finally Mrs. Archibald and Mrs. Winthrop, the other hall mistress, and Tory, the nigger janitor, made it to the doorway, pushed their way through the girls, no one moving out of the way on her own.

Above it all I could hear Mrs. Archibald, the older of the two, hair gone to gray, eyes heavy with wrinkles we called carpetbags. "Girls," she was hollering, "girls, girls," though no one was quieting down, in front of her and doing the most work through the crowd Mrs. Winthrop, silent, only holding on to girls and pushing them aside. Tory, a sad-faced nigger with red eyes that always looked like they were ready to bust out in tears, only pushed along behind Mrs. Archibald, eyes as much on the ground as they always were.

Mrs. Winthrop stopped, disappeared below the heads of all the girls, all of them suddenly gone quiet, as though they'd never even noticed her coming up.

Then she had a girl in each hand, held them by the collars of their blouses. Both of them were taking in quick, shallow breaths, hair down in their faces, the two of them so alike in how they breathed, how their hair fell down and across their eyes, mouths open, they could have been sisters. Both had bloody noses, both looked at each other, both did nothing, only held there by Mrs. Winthrop.

Mrs. Archibald stood before them now, looked first at Bessy, then at Cleopatra. Then she turned to Tory, who stood off a few feet, the girls finally having cleared space for all that was going on.

She said, "Tory, bring the belt."

"Yes'm," Tory said, and bowed his head, turned and headed for the door, the girls he'd had to push through a moment before making clear a path for him. He was out in a second.

Girls were leaving almost as quick as they'd come in, all silent, all heads down and looking at the floor, some even with hands folded in front of them. In less than a minute the room was empty save for we six girls, and Mrs. Winthrop and Mrs. Archibald.

Tory came in, held the thick leather belt reserved for occasions just such as this, though I'd never seen it before, only heard tell of it in legends that went round the school. It shone with the gas light above us, glistened for having been oiled Tory only knew how many times. It was four or five inches wide, maybe a fingernail thick. And, I saw, it wasn't a belt at all, but only a long piece of leather, fashioned just for this use; no buckles, no holes, nothing. Only leather.

Mrs. Winthrop let go the two girls, and without another word they all turned, headed out the door. Once there, Mrs. Winthrop, the last one out, turned, leaned into our room. The girls behind me were still crying, their sounds no different one from the next, just three girls crying.

She whispered, "Lights out," and reached with her hand to the gas key, twisted till the gas popped. She closed the door, then yelled, "Lights out," her voice as deep and heavy as any man's.

In the darkness I could hear their footsteps down the hall, the slam shut behind them of the stairwell door. We all knew what was next, the sounds up and down the hall of everyone in the school crowding now to get to the windows. Though lights were out in every room, I knew there wasn't a single girl in bed; the ones in the rooms across the hall from our side were sneaking out and into rooms on this side, though none were making their way into ours, this room cursed by what'd happened here.

The four of us stood at the window, heads almost touching, faces pressed up to the glass, and we waited, watched the dark down there.

Tory came out of the building carrying a lantern, the shadows dancing and moving all about him as he walked on the sidewalk below us, behind him first Mrs. Archibald, then the two girls, I couldn't decide which was which, then Mrs. Winthrop.

No one spoke, either in our room or down there in the courtyard, but the moves they made were all perfect, as if they'd rehearsed it all: Tory stopped at the flagpole, set down the lantern, backed off a few feet, and stood with his hands at his sides, his head down. Next Mrs. Archibald went to the far side of the pole, followed by one of the girls. Mrs. Archibald stopped, the belt still in her hand. She turned around, and all I could see of her was her white face in the lantern light, her white hands holding the belt in front of her.

The girl with her turned around. It was Cleopatra, her hair tucked behind her ears now. She bent over, wrapped her arms around the flagpole, and I couldn't see her face anymore.

Across from her stood Mrs. Winthrop, and then Bessy went to the flagpole, bent down and wrapped her arms around it, too. They were on opposite sides of the pole, arms touching, heads close enough to one another that they could have whispered to each other and neither Mrs. Winthrop nor Archibald'd ever know.

Mrs. Archibald folded the belt in half, held the ends with one hand. With the other hand she reached to Cleopatra's jumper, pulled it up over her hips. Then she stepped back, held the belt with both hands, reared back her arms, and brought the belt down hard on Cleopatra.

I could feel the sting inside the crack of sound the belt made through the summer night air, crisp and clean and cold. But then came the terrible surprise I'd had no way to prepare for: Cleopatra howled, let loose a sound from deep inside her that turned the crack of the belt into nothing, just punishment for a fight in a room. Her howl took out my breath, brought sweat to my forehead and neck and down the small of my back.

The sound stopped, and Mrs. Archibald stepped back, held the belt out to Tory. He took it, and went to Mrs. Winthrop, gave it to her.

This was how they were going to do it, I saw, one whipping after another, each girl given her turn, each hall mistress administering the whipping, Tory the middleman, his the task of handing the belt back and forth, back and forth.

Mrs. Winthrop lifted Bessy's jumper over her hips, brought the belt back with two hands, just as Mrs. Archibald had, and for a moment I wondered if they hadn't been given lessons in all this, some summer course in Proper Whipping of Delinquent Girls.

But before she brought the belt down and onto Bessy, she paused, looked up to the building, up at all of us girls hidden away in the dark windows of Lights Out. I knew she couldn't see any of us for the dark, but still I flinched, pulled away an inch or so from the window, just as Mavis and Beaulah and Duchess did, just as every girl in the Mississippi Industrial School for Girls did, I was certain, and it came to me what was going on in all of this: they were doing the same thing to all of us as Missy Cook'd done when she'd burned our clothes, my dead momma's words now floating up to me like ghosts themselves. *This is for us,* came my momma's whispered words, *You and me are supposed to be seeing this, supposed to be standing right here and watching it all.*

Mrs. Winthrop turned back to Bessy and the task at hand, and brought down the belt.

I closed my eyes. The crack of leather split the night, and then came Bessy's cry, one not at all different than Cleopatra's, and I thought again of the two of them after the fight, and how they'd looked so like kin, sisters maybe a year apart.

I turned from the window, made my way through the dark. Before I got to the bed another crack came, another howl, Cleopatra again. I touched the iron footboard, felt the cold metal, heard the next crack, Bessy's cry. I undressed with my eyes closed, slipped over my head the sleeveless cotton nightshirt we all wore. Then I climbed into my bed, pulled the sheet up to my chin, turned my back to the window.

I wasn't going to watch, wasn't going to do precisely what they wanted me to do. They couldn't make me see what they wanted, couldn't control me that way. That was why I'd taught Cathedral to read, why I'd kept close the stories my mother'd given me, why the photo of Jacob was still with me, jammed into my tablet and shoved beneath my mattress.

But I could still hear the crack of the belt, the howls,

heard them go on and on, finally losing track of who was who crying out in the dark.

The next morning, there on her bed lay Cleopatra, her face toward me, eyes shut deep in sleep, her mouth open. She had on her nightshirt, her sheets bunched up around her feet, her hands tight together at her chest.

I looked to Bessy's bed, saw her there, her face away from me, blanket and sheet pulled up tight to her neck. The blanket moved up and down with her slow breaths in and out.

Although I'd listened what seemed all night long for them to come in, I'd heard nothing, and for a moment I wondered if everything I'd seen last night had really happened.

Then the two of them rolled over in their sleep, and I saw the truth: Bessy rolled over toward me, and here came her face, the welts from last night given over to blue bruises, eyes swelled slits, her lips puffed up and near-black, cheeks not cheeks at all anymore, only fat skin bruised and bruised.

I looked at Cleopatra, already struggling in her sleep to roll over away from me, her eyes still closed, her mouth still open. She lifted her head an inch or so from the pillow, turned, and I saw the back of her head, a huge gauze bandage taped on to bare skin there. They'd shaved off her ponytails.

When they awoke, the world was different: Bessy and Cleopatra were suddenly best friends, the two of them never apart, though it took three or four weeks for Bessy's face to come back to normal, and though there was a place on her left eyebrow where it's split in two and that kept her forever touching a wetted finger there to try and get the hairs to fall together; Cleopatra's hair was months in growing back, the square of shaved head hid as best she could by piling and pinning the top and sides back.

But I'd been given the role of follower, me the one behind on the morning walks round campus, Cleopatra and Bessy ahead of me and laughing and giggling along.

Cleopatra Sinclair was the only person could even come close to my calling a sister, and she'd been stolen away from me with the slap of fists, the mixing of their blood as they fought. There'd come out of their being whipped a new bond, something I knew I'd never formed yet with anyone, never would unless I surrendered to whatever passion it was the two of them set free in that fight. My days from then on were spent even more alone, me buried deep in the same kind of solitude I'd carried since my brother'd died, an unrecognizable solitude, as much a part of me as the color of my hair, the shape of my lips, my brother always and only the memory of a baby on a daddy's knee, and of him sleeping away in a cradle, breathing in and breathing out.

That was my only history of the love of a brother—that vague picture in my head—or the love of a sister—the picture of Cleopatra there with Bessy Swansea. The two of them always walked ahead of me, me there with my arms crossed against my chest, my eyes to the ground, while the two of them set about making themselves their own sisters.

It was blood to forge that bond, I finally knew, my baby Annie here asleep next to me now, blood coursing through her as she breathed in and out herself, the light outside the window gone, night on us. It was blood that brought us all alive, as alive as the soft memory of my baby brother, his blood and mine what kept him alive in my head. Blood, too, as red as the blood on the hands of the doctor who'd held up my newest baby, asleep in the cradle next to me, and slapped her into this world. Blood part me, part Leston flowing through the bodies of all our children. It was that blood that made us all whole, made us this family, the Hilburns, these six children, and my husband, and me.

Cathedral came into the bedroom then, touched my shoulder in the dark, whispered, "Miss Jewel, wake up. Time for supper."

"I'm awake," I whispered, and suddenly the world came crystal clear to me, everything around me and everything that'd ever happened to me solid and worth keeping.

"Cathedral," I whispered, and she gave my shoulder a gentle squeeze. "Twenty-two hours," I whispered. "And now God's smiling."

I thought I could see her smile in the dark. She whispered, "You put in the work, and now God given you a beautiful child."

I nodded, whispered, "Six of them," touched Annie's warm body next to me, but still on my heart the stone of James being gone.

She held her hand on my shoulder a moment longer before she stood, slowly moved to the door. "Yo' supper be up in a minute. Meantime you be keeping it quiet like you been."

"Six of them," I whispered loud enough for her to hear, and she stopped in the doorway. She looked back, one hand on the doorjamb.

I heard from downstairs Burton say, "First dibs on the legs," then Wilman whine, "Me first," and Leston: "Boys."

"Smiling," she whispered.

Annie moved in her sleep, an arm onto my lap, and I touched her hair, smiled myself.

Chapter 8

Still Brenda Kay slept, on through the rest of October, and then into November, me by that time thanking even more my God for the blessing of a child who took so little tending. And she was a blessing, certainly: four children all growing bigger, calling for more of me with each next morning, Cathedral slowly disappearing from us, her help around the place falling away as it did after the birth of each new child. By early December, I was only seeing her every now and again, word of her and her boys and how they were all doing coming to me through Leston through Nelson, and there were days when I wondered if I might even see her again, this new sleepy child my last baby.

So that the blessing of Brenda Kay sleeping was only magnified: I had time for mending, time for tutoring the boys and Billie Jean with their homework, time for Annie, who'd taken to napping with me each afternoon, the three of us—Brenda Kay, Annie, me—a sort of girls' club for sleep. None of my other children'd slept through until at least five months, Wilman not until he was eleven months, and there were cold mornings now when I would wake and realize I'd forgotten about the baby in the cradle next to me. But then my breasts would start to filling, and I would roust Brenda Kay out, her eyes opening for a few minutes, eyes the closest to Leston's green of any of the children, and she would start to feed. She was healthy, ate just as much as any of them had. She was a little small, and those fingers curled into her hands seldom unfolded, but I counted all this a blessing. She was a different child was all, maybe my change of life baby, and I wondered how delicate her skin might be when she grew up, if she would be as beautiful as her namesake, have as many boys following her home as Leston told me his sister had.

By late December she was awake an hour or two a day, and on Christmas morning I dressed Brenda Kay up in the silliest thing I'd ever paid for: a red flannel outfit, more a sack with arms, around the collar and at the wrists puffs of white cotton; along with it came a little red flannel nightcap, a cotton puff at the end. Before I let anyone downstairs to see what Santa'd brought, I laid Brenda Kay on the bed, Leston already down in the front room and stoking the fire, the children stamping like horses, ready to run. But I took my time with Brenda Kay, this her first Christmas ever, and once I'd gotten her dolled up I couldn't help but laugh at this little elf on my bed.

I picked her up, held her with her head at my shoulder, and opened the door.

"Go ahead," I said, and all four of them tore off down the stairs.

Leston was the only one dressed, him in his overalls and a red corduroy shirt. The tree was set up in the far corner, before the front window, on it the strings of popcorn we'd made the day after school got out, here and there ornaments we'd gotten over the years. Nothing like what I saw in the magazines, not in *Saturday Evening Post* or the ads in the *Reader's Digest* or the occasional *Life* I'd pick up when we took the children into Purvis Saturday afternoons for the matinee. In all those magazines the trees were lost in too much glitter and light and tinsel. But our tree, I knew, looked as trees ought: something clean and different in the house, a guest here, rooms filled more than ever with the smell of pine.

The children went at their presents, each lost for a while in them: Wilman and Burton both got shiny new pocketknives, Billie Jean a hairbrush and mirror, Annie a store-bought doll with two outfits. Next they took in to the stockings above the fireplace, Burton first to upend his on the floor, treasure spread before him: a pack of Beeman's, chocolate candy coins, three new red pencils, a gum eraser, a tangerine. Then Wilman dumped his, got instead of the Beemans a pack of Juicy Fruit, instead of the gum eraser a rule, and though I knew the differences in their gifts would start a fight, I didn't care. Juicy Fruit was for my baby boy, Beeman's for my little man.

And I thought of James, wondered if this morning somewhere south of the equator where, he'd written last week, it was dead summer, he were opening the package we'd sent him: a new razor and strop, a Whitman's Sampler, and pictures of home drawn by the boys, Annie choosing instead to draw a picture of the three of us asleep of an afternoon, no difference in our sizes, just two stick bodies lying on a stick bedframe, another stick body in a stick cradle next to it, all of it drawn with a green crayon. Billie Jean had written him a long letter, and I was proud of her for that, for taking four nights to write it. I'd wanted to look over it before I sent it, but she'd already sealed it in an envelope, across the front the word PERSONAL written in her teenage curlicues. She'd smiled when she gave it to me, and though I knew Leston wouldn't have approved— what, he'd wonder, did a sister have to say to her brother the rest of the family couldn't hear?—I'd only nodded, tucked it in with the rest of the package.

I imagined him there in a barrack or whatever it was they lived in, and opening the box, getting all those presents, sharing the chocolates. Maybe he thumbtacked the pictures against a wall near where he slept, or maybe folded them up, placed them in his shirt pocket, him touching those pictures two or three times a day, making certain we were there with him.

I was sitting in my rocker now, Brenda Kay still against my shoulder. Billie Jean took her stocking from its nail, knelt with it. "Momma," she said, "I'm too old for this here," but she wasn't even looking at me, only dumped the stocking out near as fast as the boys had. In hers was a roll of cherry Lifesavers, a little note from me saying I'd resubscribed to *Photoplay* for the next year, and a small compact of corn-silk powder, a tangerine.

She looked up at me when she saw the compact, then held it in her hand, opened it. She took out the little powder puff inside, lifted it to her face, held the mirror up, eyed herself. The movements were too quick, I saw, almost routine for her, and I hoped Leston hadn't picked up on what I figured must be the fact she'd done this a hundred times already.

She stopped, looked to me again, then to Leston.

He was sitting in the chair next to the fireplace close enough to where he could lay in wood as he saw fit. But now he was looking at Billie Jean, his elbows on his knees and leaning forward a bit.

He looked at me. I'd bought it for her, hadn't told him about it. I smiled, gently shrugged, Brenda Kay stirring a moment. I said, "Who can blame Santa Claus?"

He stared a minute more, then let his head fall, slowly

shook it. When he looked up again, he was smiling, though I could see, too, he was trying to hold it back with a half-hearted grimace. He said, "You women."

"Yes," I said, "we are."

Billie Jean still held the puff near her face. Her eyes were huge, her mouth open.

"You'll catch more flies than boys with your mouth hung open like that," Leston said.

Billie Jean's cheeks went red. She stood, my oldest daughter, and I could see beneath the flannel the swell of her new breasts, the curve there. She'd begun her month-lies two years ago, but nothing had gone on up top for so long I hadn't paid any attention. Now here she was on a Christmas morning, full on her way to the beautiful woman I knew she would turn out to be.

She came to me, gave a small kiss to my cheek, and smiled at me, at her daddy, then moved quick to the top of the stairs and for the privacy of her bedroom to try out her new toy. I'd have to show her sometime this afternoon the trick of how wet cherry Lifesavers worked near as well as lipstick if you did it right.

"Don't you worry," I said to Leston. "She'll grow up whether you forbid her to or not, so you might as well not worry yourself over it. It'll happen."

He looked up at me, smiling, and nodded. He said, "Now what about presents for Momma?"

Wilman and Burton had their knives open, Burton with his cradled in both hands, Wilman with his in one hand, turning it this way and that.

Annie'd dressed the doll, held her naked in her arms, gently rocked her.

Leston looked up. "Well?"

Both boys snapped shut their knives. They'd heard

him, of course, but only played out the moment, what all children did: act as though you hadn't heard, then go for as long as you could ignoring whatever command you'd been given, what was in your hand the center of the world at any given moment.

They crawled across the floor to the tree, and both pulled out presents for me, two small boxes wrapped in plain blue paper. The presents looked exactly alike. They always bought the same things for me: one year two sets of stationery with the exact same yellow lily design at the top, another year two tortoiseshell headbands, and I wondered what it might be this year, what Billie Jean had helped them pick out at the five and dime.

They crawled over to me, each with his closed knife tight in a fist. Burton held his present out to me first, but Wilman pushed his arm aside, held out his.

"Wilman," I said, and he let out a heavy breath, pouted, sat back on his legs.

Burton held his present out to me, grinned.

"Thank you," I said, "but will you open it for me?" I motioned with one hand at Brenda Kay. "My arms are a bit busy now." I smiled.

"Sure," he said, and tore at the paper, had it off in a second. He held the white box, opened the lid, and reached in with two fingers, brought out a small red change purse with a gold clasp. He held it up to me, his grin gone to a true smile, lips together, head tipped to one side.

"It's beautiful," I said. "Thank you, Burton."

"For you," he said. Then he opened the clasp, turned the purse over, and a shiny gray penny fell out. He held it up, said, "For good luck," and dropped it back in, snapped closed the purse. He looked up at me again, his face the serious one of an eight-year-old bent on instruction. "Now don't you ever spend that, you here? That will bring on bad luck. And you don't want that."

"Not at all," I said, and solemnly shook my head.

He scooted back, made way for Wilman, who moved closer, and I wondered what I could say about a second change purse.

He paused a moment before he opened the lid, two fingers tapping the white cardboard. Then he opened it. He reached in, pulled out one end of a piece of red yarn, pulled it higher and higher until out came a pinecone tied at the other end. On each leaf of the cone was a dab of gold glitter, and as he held it up, the pinecone slowly turned on its own, first one way and then the other. He held it away from him, and I could see behind it the fire in the fireplace, that pinecone slowly moving, surrounded by the soft orange light.

"It's beautiful," I said, and my heart filled up with the pride and sorrow and joy only a mother can feel for her children.

"He made it himself," Burton said, and reached a finger over to touch it. I thought Wilman would have pulled it away, but he didn't, just let his brother touch it, watched it swing to the left and right, still twirling.

"It's beautiful," I said again, those the only words coming to me.

Wilman nodded, satisfied.

Annie sat next to the tree, the naked doll still in her arms. She looked at the pinecone, then turned her eyes to me.

Nye-nye lay on the floor next to her, and she took a fistful of it. She stood, and the four of us—my husband, my two boys, and me—watched as she came toward me, dragging the blanket behind her.

She made it to me, and held out the hand with the blanket. "This is a present," she said, and I glanced at Leston. He shrugged, shook his head.

"This is a present," she said again. "This is for you when we sleep. You can use nye-nye when we help Brenda Kay sleep. She needs our help."

Slowly I reached for the blanket, certain that was all I could do: take the gift from my child, thank her.

My fingers touched the blanket, and I held it there a moment, the two of us touching, her eyes on me. I said, "Thank you, Annie," and she let go. I nodded, felt my chin about to give way, felt my eyes filling up.

"You're welcome, Momma," Annie said, and if the feeling I'd had looking at the pinecone on a string, the change purse in my lap, had been a mixture of joy and sorrow and pride, the blanket I held up to my chest and covered my last baby with now let in a new feeling, one that'd been somewhere inside my head and heart and wanting in for a long time: fear.

Fear, because now it was clear and strong even to my Annie, my youngest until three months ago, that something was wrong here, and that Brenda Kay sleeping this much had something—everything—to do with it. That fear I'd put off believing in for the last month or so walked right in Christmas morning, three of my children smiling up at me, my oldest in a war somewheres and carrying in his shirt pocket a picture of green crayon stick figures sleeping away, Billie Jean practicing how to be a woman in an upstairs room right now, the gift of a compact and cherry Lifesavers suddenly a nail in her coffin and mine both, me pushing her to grow up when there was nothing for it really, growing up: family here and around and always with you is what mattered, I knew, especially now, when I'd finally recognized in the small gift of a ragged blanket that my baby Brenda Kay was wrong somehow, that something in her was wrong.

Still my children smiled, and I looked at Leston, saw him smile, too, then lean toward the heap of wood on the hearth, toss into the fire another chunk. I watched as sparks flew up, disappeared into the chimney, Wilman still holding high the pinecone.

Chapter 9

But I let that fear hole up inside me until February, praying each day something might happen: that my baby would smile up at me when she came to, that she would roll over, that the sound of a baby's laugh might escape her and make its way into the house.

Nothing came. Now she was five months old.

I told Leston after the children were in bed that we needed to take Brenda Kay to the doctor.

"Why?" he said. He looked up from the cigarette paper he held at his fingertips. He looked back to the paper, pulled from his shirt pocket the small sack of tobacco he kept there. He pulled the drawstrings loose with his teeth and free hand, tipped in the tobacco. He licked the edge of the paper, rolled it with just his thumb and those two fingers. I'd seen him do it a hundred thousand times, his moves so smooth and quick.

When he was finished he didn't put it to his lips, only held it there in his fingers. He was waiting for me.

"I don't know," I said, giving him the easy lie, the one I wanted to believe myself, the one would absolve me from taking her in earlier, me hoping for some miracle to turn things round, God's big hand changing the world. I knew what was wrong, though I couldn't say exactly what: My baby sleeps too much, my baby can't roll over at five months.

I swallowed, whispered, "Something's wrong, Leston."

Dr. Beaudry's office was above the hardware store in Purvis, the door into the place at the top of a steep set of stairs on the outside of the building. Leston went up first, me behind him, carrying Brenda Kay wrapped tight in blankets against the damp cold, the sky bruise blue, rain coming.

We hardly ever saw a doctor, living as far out as we did and having children up until then who'd remained fairly healthy. We'd been here before to set a broken arm James got when he was eight, jumping out of a haymow playing cowboys and Indians one Saturday afternoon; Wilman was here for a nail he'd stepped on while making his way to the outhouse one summer night, him the one who'd left the board and nail on the ground late that afternoon after giving up on a tree fort he and Burton were building.

But Dr. Beaudry acted as though he knew us all the same, ushered us into his office after Leston had knocked but once. He offered us cups of hot coffee, his smiling eyes all the while working over what little he could see of Brenda Kay, still in my arms. "No thank you, sir," Leston said, and I knew he meant no coffee for the both of us.

We took seats in hard straight-backed chairs, Dr. Beaudry on a stool. He was a few years younger than us, though his hair was gone except for a brown fringe just above his ears and collar and a tuft above his forehead. He had on a white coat buttoned up almost to his neck, black pants and shiny black boots, and sat with his hands laced in front of him.

"So," he said, still smiling. He looked at me. "What might be the problem here?"

"She's been sleeping—" I started, but then Leston cleared his throat, and I glanced at him.

His eyes were on mine a moment, then turned to the doctor. He seemed to square his shoulders, sat straighter in the chair. He said, "She's sleeping all the time. My wife says there's something wrong with the baby, seeing as how she's sleeping so much. Can't roll over yet, either."

He looked back to me, and I thought for an instant I'd seen something in his face, maybe in his eyes. There was something, I was certain, but then the look was gone, his eyes back to the doctor. He was only my husband again, a man who figured he had to be in charge of this strange and ugly visit, whatever the reason.

But I wanted to say to him right then, right there, *This is my baby*. I wanted to say to my husband it was me to tote the child day in, day out, to nurse it, let it sleep with me every day all day long.

And it was me who'd put off finally coming here so long, whatever guilt accrued for that waiting all mine.

So I turned from Leston, looked straight at the doctor. I said, "My baby is not well," me full aware I'd used that word *my*, as though the child in my arms belonged to me and me alone. I said, "She's nowhere near being as far along as the rest of my children were at her age. That's why we're here."

I paused, looked at Leston, still sitting up straight in the chair, his bottom on the very edge of the seat, his back not even touching the back of the chair. He held that same old hat with both hands, his jaw set, eyes hard on the doctor, and I wondered if he'd even recognized what my words'd tried to say: *This is my baby*.

"Well," Dr. Beaudry said, and lost the smile. He let go

his fingers, reached out to me and the baby. "Just let me take a good look-see at this baby," he said.

I hesitated a moment, not certain of what was going on inside Leston's head, not certain what was going on inside mine: my baby and whatever was wrong with her, whatever I'd kept to myself these long months, was about to be revealed. Then I gave her up to him.

He held her in his arms, jostled her a little, said, "Baby Brenda?"

"Brenda Kay," Leston said. He hadn't moved, hadn't even blinked yet. "Her name is Brenda Kay."

Dr. Beaudry glanced at him, tried to smile. "Brenda Kay it is," he said, and looked back at the baby. "Baby Brenda Kay? Baby Brenda Kay?"

I said, "She was up for a while not long ago. She was up two hours ago, so she'll probably not come awake for you." My voice seemed frail in the room, too small for the importance of this place.

Still he jostled her, though he was looking at me. "How long was she awake?"

I looked at my lap, afraid again of giving the wrong answer, the one that would show to him I'd been a poor momma to this child. But it was the truth he was after, I knew; the truth, too, what I was looking for. I wanted to know what was wrong with my child.

I swallowed, said, "Twenty minutes."

He said nothing, and I looked up at him, saw him tickling her chin. "Brenda Kay," he said, "pretty baby Brenda Kay."

"Tickling her seems to do nothing," I said.

"Doctor," Leston said, his voice low and flat. He still hadn't moved. "We didn't bring her here to be tickled. We want to know what is wrong with her."

"Leston," I said, tried to make my voice sound as reproachful as I could muster. Still his eyes didn't move from the doctor.

"Well," Dr. Beaudry said again, but now he stood, made his way from the office toward the door that opened into his examining room, the room where James' arm'd been set in plaster.

He reached the door, opened it. White light fell into the room, and I could see beyond him those white walls and white cupboards.

He stopped, turned to us, Brenda Kay held in one arm. He smiled at the both of us, said, "Who'd like to come in and supervise this little hoedown?"

I looked at Leston. Though I knew it could only be one, something made me turn, look.

He nodded once, as though the decision were his to make. He let his eyes fall to his lap.

I stood, followed the doctor in.

Naked and on her back on the examining table, Brenda Kay looked like a different child, though I'd seen her this way as many times as a mother would. But here it had to do with the lights: severe and bright to show off whatever might be wrong. Her legs seemed shorter, thicker, her forearms smaller somehow. She lay with her arms held against her chest, her hands just beneath her chin, her legs out straight, eyes closed, mouth open. Her hair had started coming in now after she'd lost it early on, hair the same copper Leston's had been the day I first saw him, and she was putting on weight, though I knew she was truly small for what five months ought to be.

Dr. Beaudry first pulled her fingers out straight, bent her arms at the elbows, then examined her toes,

bunched up and curled, too, like her fingers. But Billie
Jean'd been born sucking at her first finger, kept it there
for near on till she was two. Who was to say, I figured,
that toes and fingers curled down and held tight wasn't
just how this baby was formed inside me, what she
would outgrow?

He bent her legs at the knees, pushed and poked her
tummy and sides and underarms and chest. He opened
her mouth wide, peered inside. He looked at her ears,
peeled back an eyelid, covered the eyeball with the palm
of his hand and quick took it away, then did the same with
the other eye. He propped her up, listened to her heart in
front and back.

He lay her down again, and went back to her eyes,
opened them again, let the lids close. Finally he stopped,
held her head with both hands, Brenda Kay still sound
asleep. He stood there in the hard light of the room, and
looked at her face, looked and looked. Then with one
thumb he gently touched an eyelid, let the thumb trace its
outline.

He wouldn't look at me after that, and I knew whatever
was wrong was real. Softly he rubbed a hand on her chest,
said, "I hope this doll-baby isn't getting cold in here." He
touched her forehead with his fingertips, said, "You can go
ahead and bundle her up."

"What's wrong?" I said, that word *wrong* a dull ham-
mering in my ears. *What's wrong? What's wrong?*

"You just bundle her up good and warm, and I'll be out
with you in a minute." His eyes nearly met mine, but
didn't as he touched me on the arm, fiddled with the pile
of clothes and blankets. He turned away from me, went to
the counter on the other side of the table, started writing
down whatever words he was keeping secret from me.

I dressed Brenda Kay, my bottom lip between my teeth the whole time, my baby limp as I struggled with first one arm, then the other.

Dr. Beaudry came out holding a piece of paper, looking down at it. Leston and I hadn't spoken yet, in my eyes when I came out of the examination room enough fear, enough tears ready to go, to signal him no words were needed. I'd only come back to my seat, Brenda Kay in my arms. He'd reached over one hand, placed it on my knee. Next had come Dr. Beaudry's voice as he spoke on the telephone, the sound of words behind a closed door, even the pauses between them as he listened to words I would never know, all as dark and heavy as the sky outside, Leston's hand the only comfort I knew.

But as soon as the doctor was back in the room, Leston's hand was gone, back to helping hold his hat. It was gone, and the doctor spoke.

"I've just spoken to a doctor in New Orleans," he said, and looked at me, at Leston. Then he looked down at Brenda Kay, reached a hand toward her and touched her cheek. Her mouth quivered. She was getting ready for feeding.

He sat on the stool, said, "I'm sending you to the South's best baby specialist. Dr. Floyd Basket." His eyes finally met ours full on, and for a moment I wasn't ready for them, blinked and swallowed. This was the news, what mattered enough to sit down, look us in the eye. "He's down in New Orleans, and he's a very busy man." He laced his fingers together in front of him again. "My telephone call to him was to set up a day for you. I took the liberty of going ahead and confirming a date." He paused, looked at Leston now. "He's the very best there is."

I swallowed again, whispered, "Best at what?"

He glanced at me, and looked back to his hands. Whatever power, whatever strength he'd started with a moment ago was gone now. He took a breath. "I don't want you to think I'm ducking your question. I'm not. But I don't want to say. I don't want to guess at it, so—"

"Then guess at it," Leston said. "Sir."

I looked at him. His jaw was still tight, eyes square on the doctor, but behind those eyes was that same look I'd seen before, that look I didn't know.

"I will not," Dr. Beaudry said a moment later, and sat up straight, tall, his hands on his thighs now. "My job here is to give you the best advice possible. This is a small town, and I am a small-town doctor. I will not guess at something I am not genuinely prepared to understand." He stared at Leston, who stared back at him, as if this were some sort of contest. "This is why I have set up an appointment with Dr. Basket, in New Orleans. Because he is prepared to say what is wrong here, and I am not."

He stopped, the two of them in whatever man's game staring at each other entailed, and I whispered the only words in my head, the only thing that mattered in this world: "Will she die?"

His shoulders held up for a moment, but then fell, his head down again. He was silent, we were all of us silent, the only sound I could hear the steady breaths in and out of Brenda Kay sleeping. I looked at her, saw no movement in her, bundled so tight.

"I'm not sending you out of here," he said, and stopped. "I'm not sending you out of here," he started again, "thinking your little girl is going to die. I won't. She's not. But she's got to see someone—Dr. Basket—soon as she can, see someone best qualified to tell exactly what is the problem with your daughter."

Her mouth quivered again, and she turned her head an inch or so, readying.

"When?" I whispered.

I could see from the corner of my eye him look at the paper again. "A week and a half. Ten-thirty Thursday after next."

He folded the paper in half, held it out to Leston, who took it only after letting him hold it there in the silence of the room for what seemed a full minute. Then Leston lifted his own hand, that hand shaking, I could see, and took the piece of paper.

"On that," Dr. Beaudry went on as though Leston hadn't made him wait an instant, as though Leston's hand had been sturdy and still, "is Dr. Basket's address, the date, the time. All the necessary information."

Leston stood, and I looked up at him. He put the paper into his coat pocket without looking at it, said, "How much do we owe you?" His eyes were on the wall behind the doctor.

"Nothing," Dr. Beaudry said, and waved away the question with one hand. He stood. "You don't owe me a penny."

Leston, eyes still on the wall, nodded. He said nothing, then turned, went for the door, stood with it open before I was even up from the chair.

Then I was at the door, the cold air outside already surrounding me and Brenda Kay, and I turned back to the doctor, tried to smile, to say Thank you out of whatever respect I had for him and the way he'd touched my baby's forehead, traced the outline of her eyes. I tried to say those two small words, but nothing came.

* * *

The sky opened up, let fall cold rain before we could make it to the truck, so that once inside it the smell was awful, wet wool and old cigarette smoke.

Leston started up the truck, switched the heater on high, turned on the wipers. Then he pulled out papers from inside his coat, the bag of tobacco from his shirt pocket, started rolling. But when he got it to his lips I said, "Don't."

He stopped, a match already out of the box, ready to strike. His hands were shaking even more now. He looked at me, hands still in midair, for the first time since I'd come out of the examination room.

I said, "The baby," and turned from him to Brenda Kay. Her eyes had come open, her mouth moving quick now, ready.

Slowly I pulled open my coat, unbuttoned my blouse, brought my breast to my baby's mouth.

Leston brought his hands down to his lap, and watched, on his face that same look I didn't recognize, but then it came to me: it was fear in him, dark and simple. Fear, what I'd not thought possible in this man, the same man who built homes for us with his own two hands, the one who'd built shutters, and'd polished a bit of dogwood until it shone with the love and power of those two hands. Now his hands shook, and shook with fear.

We'd hit something, I knew, something neither of us knew what to do with, whatever hope I'd had now a distant, dead friend, my prayers only words on a cold wind.

The cab was warming up, though the rain fell harder, the wipers barely able to make clear the world outside the window.

Chapter 10

Soldiers and sailors. That was what I saw in New Orleans, from the moment we made it on into the city, buildings, people, cars and colors all over. But it was the soldiers and sailors everywhere that struck me: men in uniforms everything khaki or white, everywhere twos and threes and fours, laughing and slapping each other on their backs, or stumbling blind drunk along sidewalks, an occasional woman in tow, skirt hiked up above her knees and make-up smeared.

"Now where again did y'all want to be let out?" the taxi driver called over his shoulder to us in the back seat, a thin store-bought cigarette wedged tight into the corner of his mouth, only one hand on the wheel. The other hung out the window, and he waved now and again at other taxis, other cars, even some of those soldiers, as if he knew the whole world here.

"The office of Dr. Floyd Basket," Leston said. "Twelve Beaufain Court." He'd memorized the address, most likely burned into his mind the first moment he'd looked at the slip of paper Dr. Beaudry'd given us back in Purvis.

Neither of us had ever even been to New Orleans before, though we'd talked of it often enough once we were alone in bed, the children down and the house silent, that the only time we ever had alone, when we would whisper to each other of what'd happened that day. When we got around to talking about New Orleans, it was with some sort of glee: our honeymoon had been only two nights up to Hattiesburg in a hotel looking out on the town square and the statue to the Confederate dead; I'd had to be back to teaching Monday morning, and ever since then we'd talked of dinner at some fancy restaurant in the French Quarter, of walks through Jackson Square, of sitting on the bank of the Mississippi with oyster po'boys. Of just being alone and able not to worry.

But we didn't speak of it after coming home from Dr. Beaudry's, hadn't mentioned word one of the three-hour drive we knew was coming up, didn't even wake the children at dawn this morning, Cathedral showing up at the doorstep with Nelson and the rest of the niggers and Toxie and JE, Toxie now in charge for the day, I knew, Cathedral just walking in, starting up the bacon in the pan. I hadn't even told her to come, hadn't bothered, because I knew she'd be here.

Then we drove, down through Tolowa and Lumberton, then through the two stoplights in Poplarville, even through Derby and Carriere and Ozona, all of them the small towns I'd ridden through in the back of a wagon of a March day colder and darker than this, the next town Picayune, Mississippi, home of the Mississippi Industrial School for Girls and Pearl River Junior College, and the life I'd led before I met Leston.

But as we moved through Picayune, along the same green square all these towns had, past cars and trucks parked on the main street, people all walking on the sidewalks, people with lives to lead on a Thursday morning in a town where I'd spent six years of my life and where no one here would even recognize my name, I couldn't help but feel that this life I knew, the comfortable one with five healthy children, food on the table, clothing to wear, was coming to its own end, shuttering quick to a stop, its dead end another hour or so away in New Orleans.

Then we were out of Picayune, back on the blacktop and headed next for Nicholson, Slidell, then across Pontchartrain, the north shore as far south as I'd ever been. Picayune was gone, around us only more of the same old trees, some of it giving way every so often to marsh and scrub pine, more and more water.

I looked down at Brenda Kay, who hadn't come awake since her feeding outside Lumberton. She was the reason we were here, the reason we were going to head across that lake, do what we'd only imagined doing before. She was the reason this life I knew was about to end.

Brenda Kay only slept, and slept, and then my eyes became heavy, too, and I lay my head against the window, held on tight to my baby, and fell asleep.

I opened my eyes, and we were stopped. I blinked, swallowed, squinted out the glass beside me to see a street, sidewalk. Not much different than Picayune. Not what I figured New Orleans to look like.

I turned to Leston. He had both hands on the wheel, his eyes straight ahead. Slowly he turned to me.

"Where are we?" I said, and let my eyes close a moment, opened them.

"Outside town," he said. "I don't know. Here, at this grocer's. Ernest Tulley over to the plant said to park here." He was looking at Brenda Kay, still asleep. "I am not driving in to that place. Ernest Tulley said a taxi can take us in easier than driving myself."

He let go the steering wheel with one hand, pointed at a wrought-iron gate a few yards ahead. "Highway's behind us. This is where Ernest said to park. Said we can get a taxi from here."

"Fine," I said, and opened my door, climbed out.

I heard Leston's door slam behind me, and then he was beside me. We were both of us silent, our heads too full with what was coming, whatever surprise God was ready to serve up to us under a blue morning sky already going hot. The breeze in off an ocean still miles away made the air along this street of storefronts even wetter than home, and I wondered what it had looked like, Lake Pontchartrain, as we crossed it.

The driver stopped the taxi in what looked like an alley, said over his shoulder, "This be the place," and laughed, his shoulders shaking with whatever joke he'd figured was in his words.

Leston already had two dollar bills out, held them over the top of the front seat. Without looking back, the driver reached up, took the money, shook his head at something else I couldn't figure. He reached in his pocket, handed Leston back the change.

Leston looked at the money—a quarter and a dime—and picked out the dime, held it out to the driver.

He took the dime, looked at it just as he had the bills, shook his head again. He said, "Gee, thanks, Pops," but by then we were already moving out of the taxi, and I couldn't see Leston's face, whatever red anger or humiliation might be there at our being a small joke to that driver.

The taxi pulled away, and we were left standing before a brick and mortar wall a little taller than me, in the center of it a wrought-iron gate. A brass plate black with tarnish was mounted next to the gate, on it the words *Dr. Floyd E. Basket, M.D.*

I turned to Leston, looked up at him, but his eyes were on the building behind the walls, sizing up, I knew, what we were heading in to meet.

He looked down at me, gave a smile that meant nothing, only a movement of muscles in his face. He touched the gate, pushed it open for Brenda Kay and me.

Here was a little courtyard, the ground old bricks covered in green mold like a thin layer of velvet, in one corner a small fountain with just a dribble of clouded water falling into a brick trough. Along the opposite wall were the skeletons of geraniums in a brick planter box.

I stopped a moment, looked at the courtyard, at the cracked white paint of the door before us. I turned, tried to smile up at Leston.

"New Orleans," I said.

He looked at me, the same smile there on his face. He said, "New Orleans," and leaned past me to the door, knocked hard three times.

We waited, and waited, certain, I figured, we couldn't just walk into the man's house, if that's what it was. Leston knocked again, harder, but as soon as his hand was down the door opened, and an old woman not much taller than Burton stood there, a white paper hat on her head, white dress down to her ankles. She smiled, held out a hand as if we were neighbors she'd known for years.

"Come on in," she said. "There's no need to knock. Just come in and have a seat."

Her hand was wrapped around mine, her fingers longer, stronger than I could have imagined. She didn't let go, but gently pulled me into the front room, a parlor of sorts with old oak chairs lined up against each wall. Oak paneling went waist-high on the walls, above it white and green striped wallpaper. A hallway right across from the

door led back into the house, back into examination
rooms, I imagined.

Five or six mothers each with a child were seated round
the room, and right then I knew who Leston and I were,
knew we were foreigners in the midst of people who probably figured us ignorant or half-addled crackers, the taxi
driver's joke clear now: all the mothers had on makeup,
hair down and bobbed at the shoulder, atop their foreheads hair curled up in furious heaps, and I couldn't help
but think every one of them subscribed to Billie Jean's
Photoplay, had spent too many nights in moviehouses.

My hair was just back in a bun, the same way I wore it
every day, and I wore no makeup, my dress down to just
below my shins, almost ankle-cut. These women's knees
were all but naked, every one of them with hose on, shiny
shoes.

They looked at me, sized up both me and my husband,
him closing the door behind us. I didn't want to sit here,
didn't want to be the object of their attention, whatever
ridicule they might want to hand out.

But in only the passing of a moment each of them's eyes
fell from mine to my baby, then to their own baby. Then
my eyes, too, fell to the baby I held in my arms. We were
all of us looking at our sick children, all of us, I knew,
wondering what would happen next.

One of the children sneezed, this one about a year old
and propped on its momma's lap, its nose crusted and red,
eyes watery. This child's momma wiped its nose with a
handkerchief, the movement quick and simple, rote for
her. Then another baby, this one only a few months old
and wrapped in a thick, pink blanket, gave out a big
whoop cough, the mother blinking at the sound, touching
the baby's cheek with the back of her first finger.

"You must be the Hilburns," the old nurse said. I looked at her. She was smiling, trying to give me the comfort she must have thought it her job to give. "You go on right ahead and take a seat anywheres in here, and the doctor will see you in just a few minutes." She nodded once, a quick and sharp move, as if we'd settled something between us. She turned to the room. "Mrs. Darby?" she said, and a woman with red hair done up the same as the others stood, in her arms a baby that hadn't made a sound since we'd been in here. The nurse slowly moved toward the hallway, mother and child behind her.

I sat at the chair nearest me, Leston next to me. He was the only man here, and I wondered what that might mean to him, wondered if it meant he'd never come back here.

If we had to come back, I thought.

An hour later, we were the only ones left in the room. Leston hadn't spoken yet, but'd looked at his pocket watch and'd walked to one of the windows that looked out onto the courtyard and stood with his hands in his back pockets enough times for me to know how he felt, and for me to worry what he might say about waiting this long.

But when the nurse came into the room, held out her hand and said, "The doctor will see you now," all I could see from Leston, what anger he had in him, was a huge sigh he let out, then the deep breath back in. He turned from the window, ran his hand back through his hair, picked his hat up off the chair next to me.

I stood, moved toward her, took her hand. She hadn't held the hand of any of the others she'd led back here, and I wondered if that weren't some measure of the situation, of how sick my baby really was.

"The doctor has surgery this afternoon, but he wanted

to make certain to see you," the nurse said as we passed one door and then another. She stopped at the third door, took my hand in both hers. Then she let go one hand, reached to touch Brenda Kay's face, her pale white fingers even whiter against my baby's pink skin.

"There, there, little baby," she said, and smiled. "It's just fine, it is."

She turned from us, opened the door. "If there's anything I can get you or do for you, please let the doctor know, and I'd be tickled to take care of it."

"Thank you," I said, and nodded. The door was open, ready for us to walk through, but I wanted to look at this woman, wanted to take in her face. I wanted to stay here and look at this lady, a nurse ready to care for us no matter what. That's what I wanted.

Leston nudged me from behind, whispered, "Let's go," and I could only smile at her, move on into the room.

Books lined the walls, at the center of the room a huge desk, the top littered with papers and more books. Behind it sat the doctor, an old man, older than the nurse, white hair thick on his head, wire glasses low on his nose. He had a book open on his lap, and looked at us over the rim of those glasses.

He snapped the book closed, lifted his head so that now he was looking at us through the glasses. He smiled. Slowly he stood, as if the act were some long journey, one hand with the book, the other holding hard to the chair arm, him pushing himself up and up, until he was standing. He was taller than Leston, and finally let go the chair to put out his hand, first to Leston, who shook it once, then to me. His hand was soft, a doctor's hand, the flesh of his palm thick and warm.

He motioned for us to sit in the two chairs in front of

his desk. I glanced behind me as I took my seat, hoping for one more smile from the old nurse, but the door was already closed.

"Now," the doctor said, and sat back down. He leaned forward, put his elbows on the edge of the desk, laced his fingers together. "Dr. Beaudry tells me I need to have a look-see at this baby." His eyes were on Brenda Kay.

I tried again to smile, said, "*Look-see* must be one of these new doctor terms. That's the same thing Dr. Beaudry said he wanted to do." They were words of no use to any of us, spoken more to hear my own voice in here than for anything else.

He laughed, leaned back in the chair at the same time, his hands still laced together. "Dr. Beaudry's an old student of mine. I imagine he's taken some of my own terminology with him."

"Doctor," Leston said, and for a moment I wondered if, again, he would try his best to take over here. He hadn't even looked at me this time, had even done away with the pretense of clearing his throat. He said, "We came all the way from Purvis this morning. We waited more than an hour in your office." He paused. "All due respect, sir, we want to talk about Brenda Kay."

Dr. Basket looked at Leston, his smile there for a moment, but then gone.

Leston said nothing else, but I was thankful for his words this time, for his having spoken. He'd given us entry into the terrible truth we were facing right now. His words had opened the door I wanted kept closed, but knew needed opening all the same.

The doctor moved to the edge of the desk, his elbows there again. He said, "You'll have to let me examine her, of course. Then we can talk."

He stood again, held out his arms to me as he came slowly around the edge of the desk, and without a thought I held up my baby to him, Brenda Kay so much smaller in his arms than mine, a baby so small it didn't seem possible that in her could be anything so awful we had to come to a city hours from home. But still here she was, and I felt myself standing, felt my legs carrying my body along behind the doctor as we went in to another examination room, the same equipment hanging from the wall and laid out in trays as in Dr. Beaudry's room, only more of it in here, all of it glistening with what looked like some clean idea of death, my naked baby on the table, white light pouring down on all three of us. Brenda Kay was awake this time, her arms and legs moving like she was under water, slow and deliberate and without effect. She still couldn't yet roll over.

He gave her the same examination, but spent longer on each push of an arm, each stretching out of fingers, each look in her eyes. His movement was slow, but perfect somehow, his long and thin fingers holding out Brenda Kay's in a way that seemed softer than was possible, the touch simple and distant and warm all at once. I don't know how long we were in there, didn't care. Leston was back in the office, readying himself in his silence, and I was readying myself in here, just standing near, though the doctor didn't even look at me. He didn't ask a single question of me, didn't even ask for my help as he finally pinned up the diaper, ran his fingertips across her forehead one last time, traced her eyes just as Dr. Beaudry had. He even dressed her, slipped back on the green flannel gown I'd dressed her in in the dark of a morning that seemed a thousand miles from here.

He handed her to me. I was looking for him to hide his eyes from me, too, just as Dr. Beaudry'd done, but he looked at me as he gave her over, a small smile on his face, his head dipped down, his eyes taking me in over the top of his glasses. "Let's go and have a seat," he whispered, and pulled open the door into his office. He let me go first, and as I passed from the white light into the dark wood office, I felt his hand on my shoulder, felt it pat me once, twice, then rest there a moment as we came near his desk.

I felt my mouth go dry, felt my heart go to stone. I didn't even look at Leston, or if I had, didn't see him. I only sat, Brenda Kay in my arms.

The doctor sat back in the chair, his eyes on the desktop a moment. But he gave up on that idea, and looked first to Leston, then to me. He glanced at Brenda Kay, did his best to look at the two of us, tried hard to hold us each for a second or two.

He said, "What I will tell you is not easy to hear. But what I have to tell you, these words, are necessary." He paused. His hands were flat on the desk, and he lifted them, held them in front of him, looked at them. "Hands," he said, and stopped. He took a breath. "Our hands tell us much," he said, "and Brenda Kay's hands tell us much, too. They tell us that she is a child given to us by powers none of us can understand. They tell us we can't always depend on nature. That things go wrong."

My arms were stiff with straining, locked into place around what I carried, my child.

"Brenda Kay is a Mongolian Idiot," he said. He brought his hands down, let them settle into his lap. He was looking at me.

I swallowed, felt my palms sweating, clutched on the blanket my baby was wrapped in. I felt minutes pressing down on me, felt time and air and everything pressing down.

I whispered, "What does that mean?" the words ground glass in my throat.

"It means," he said, "she is mentally and physically retarded. She will never progress much more than this, than what she is right now." He paused again. He held up his hand, pointed to his palm, gently ran his finger along the lines there. "The evidence is in her hands, and her feet. Flat, broad hands, abnormally short fingers, little fingers curved in as drastically as they are, and the two smaller toes as well. And an abnormal line pattern." He stopped, adjusted his glasses. "And there is her face as well. Her eyes, their slanting upward, her broad forehead, her features smaller than a normal child's." He stopped again, brought his hands together on the desktop. "What I must say is quite difficult, but as I said, I need to let you know." He folded his fingers together. He said, "Because of this condition, chances are small that she will live past two years."

I'd waited since Christmas to find why she slept as much as she did, afraid all the while of an answer. And I'd waited eleven days since the doctor back in Purvis wouldn't tell us what was wrong. I'd waited for this moment.

Now here it was, and there was nothing in me. I was hollow, dead wood. The only thing I saw in that moment, the doctor's own hands on the desktop again, his mouth drawn closed, eyes fixed on me and the baby I held—a Mongolian Idiot, two words already weighing down my arms, my chest heavy with them, my breath now short and as hollow as the rest of me—the only thing I saw in that moment was that I'd spent my whole life waiting for news like this to come, not just the time since Christmas, not even just since near a year ago when Cathedral'd stood in light from my kitchen and told me it was coming, all of it was coming, all of it from God up in his heaven.

No. I'd been waiting for this since the moment my Momma'd died in an upstairs room in a mansion, because there'd been too much good come to me since then: Leston, my children, food on the table, a roof above our heads.

All this in a moment, before I even thought to look down at my baby in my arms, her squirming; before I thought to look at Leston, see where he was, see who he would be now. All this even before I thought to breathe again.

Then I remembered the birth, remembered the doctor pushing, pressing down on me with all the might a small-town doctor like him could give, but strength enough to hurt my baby. It was blame I was after then, blame and responsibility and someone to look at and spit in the face of. It was the doctor: him and his hospital, when I'd bore every one of my children at home and'd done fine.

"It was the doctor," I said. "It was when Brenda Kay was born, and how he pushed me, pushed my baby. He pressed down on me to get her out. That's why her face is that way, why her hands are that way. That's why she's not right." The words left me in one string, all of them chained together and falling from me without any thought. But it was true: it was his fault, the blame square on him. I knew that.

"Mrs. Hilburn," the doctor said. He closed his eyes, opened them. He let out a breath. "This condition is present at conception. That much we know about it."

He bowed his head a moment, and suddenly I thought of him, of what it must take for him to deliver news like this; saw, too, that Dr. Beaudry'd known all along, knew she'd die in two years and'd told us otherwise just so he could pass us on to his old teacher for the filthy work this was. I saw that there was pain in it for him, too, for Dr. Basket. But my heart didn't go out to him. He hadn't borne my child, or any of the others he'd ever given this speech to. He could go home from here, have his dinner, tend to surgery later today while we drove on home, poor crackers he felt sorry for, a Mongolian Idiot there in the front seat of an old pickup truck they'd left outside town, afraid of driving in the big city.

He looked up. He said, "The best thing for you, the best measure to be taken, in my considered opinion, is to give her up to an institution. There she will be cared for, tended to. The burden she could be to you for however long she lives is immeasurable. Institutionalized, she will be away from you and your household, and cared for."

"Institution," Leston whispered, his first word.

I didn't look at him. I only stared at the doctor, my eyes dry, no tears for him or for Leston or for anyone, not even for me.

I stood. I said, "Good-bye, Doctor," and I turned, moved for the door.

I heard from behind me the squeak of Doctor Basket's chair as he stood, heard steps on the hardwood floor behind me.

The nurse opened the door before I was even there, light from the hallway spilling onto me and my baby, the old woman standing to one side, no smile anywhere, only her eyes on me, her forehead a field of wrinkles, trying again for that comfort she wanted to give.

I didn't look at her, and turned, went down the hall into the front room, headed for the door.

"Mr. Hilburn," the doctor said, "we will need to meet again. We will need to talk together." His words were calm, smooth. There was care in them, I knew. But I didn't want his care right now. I didn't want him to be in on this, whatever it was. I reached the door, pulled it open to sunlight outside flooding the courtyard, no shadows anywhere. The bricks, the mold, the dirty water in the trough and those dead geraniums were washed out in white light, and I couldn't wait to get past them and through that gate and into another taxi and out of this place and home, where I might be able to make sense of how this world was crashing to its end, me unable even to imagine there might be another to come.

I heard Leston say, "Sir," imagined him just touching the brim of his hat, giving the smallest nod to the doctor, then turning, following me out onto the street, where I was already waiting for a taxi.

Lake Pontchartrain was nothing, only a dull green body of water we passed over, the bridge low and flat and gray. Picayune was just another town, and I didn't give a care as to whether I'd ever lived there or not. The soldiers and whores in New Orleans were long behind us. The only thing that mattered was the baby in my arms.

We passed through those towns again, the ones we passed through this morning, no difference in them at all. I'd expected something different, expected people to walk slower, their faces to wear some cold and clouded look after the news from New Orleans. But there was nothing different: people still smiled, talked, held their hats against the afternoon breeze, bent down to tie shoes, double-parked outside the drugstore. The same pine and crepe myrtle and high thick roadside weeds swallowed us up each time we left a town, broke up each time we entered a new one.

But on that ride, certain things came to me, most clearly me and that blanket and how I'd pulled it back to show my dead daddy. I thought of New Orleans, the city that'd existed in my head before this day, the place my parents'd had their honeymoon, and I wondered, too, whatever happened to the postcard of Jackson Square my momma had taken out of the pillowcase the morning Benjamin brought over my daddy's belongings. I thought of my momma telling me her last stories so I'd know what I could of who I was, and there was the picture in my head, too, of Molly and Cathedral and that chapter in Ezekiel. These pictures came to me, stories of my own life, and how I'd taken hold of it by the throat, made it come around to what I could make it, how I'd fixed things on my own. I still had the picture of my grandfather, Jacob Chandler, *Jacob Chetauga*, framed and in the front room of the house, Burton still taking his leads on how to stand, how to act, how to take care of himself from how his great-grandpa stood in that picture.

What all those pictures told me, what all the stories in my life said to me there in the cab of a truck, my baby in my arms, was that I could fix things, though the world was falling down on itself, crumbling beneath us.

I could fix things. I knew I could. All the child in my arms, all Brenda Kay—I decided then, there, that no one would ever use those two words, use *Mongolian Idiot*, to describe her in my presence, unless they wanted my full wrath down on them—needed was my love, not my abandonment. I had lived that loss myself, no matter my baby wasn't normal as I'd been, was sick in some way I couldn't understand; no matter, too, she was what the doctor figured on being only a burden. No matter he was already figuring on her dying. He didn't know me, didn't know what

I could live through. I could do it. I could fix things: my life, my children's lives, my husband's life. Brenda Kay's.

And so on that drive home, me losing track of what town was which as we moved along the old road, Leston not having lit up a cigarette yet, both hands tight on the steering wheel, his knuckles white as the skin my dead daddy's'd been, I tried out my words, said to the cab, "We'll keep her." I said, "She'll be loved, no matter how long she lives." I said, "God will fix her," though I knew I was putting faith into a god I hadn't yet been able to count on for anything other than what I didn't want. But the words sounded right, seemed full of some promise I was ready to grab hold of. I said, "We can fix this, if everyone in this household gives her the love they've got, and all of it." I said, "We can fix this. We can."

Leston finally turned to me. I hadn't been looking at him, but out the front window to the blacktop cutting through the green.

I looked at him. His eyes were wet, red, his mouth open, the hair on this man, this man even older now, tousled by the wind from his open window. Fear was on him now, fear like an open wound, fresh and raw.

He swallowed, said, "Can we, Jewel?"

I nodded, quick and sharp, and thought of the same move the old nurse had made before we'd entered the doctor's office, only a few minutes before my last life ended, and this new one'd begun.

I turned from him, my eyes back on the road. I said, "You just get us on home."

Chapter 11

The days after New Orleans were days clouded over with grief, the house empty save for Brenda Kay and me, Annie out back and digging at sweet potatoes, the chore I gave her so that I could sit in an empty house with only my baby. Each and every day I sat in my rocker before the fireplace, holding tight to Brenda Kay, letting her nurse whenever she wanted to, my breast about the only gift I could give her, the curtains pulled closed since the afternoon we made it back from New Orleans. I wanted no light in here, wanted nothing, only the dark. They were terrible days, days filled with nothing other than the weight of the baby in my arms, me waiting for her to die.

Not one of those days went by without the idea in me of putting her away, of giving up whatever gift from God she was. That thought was with me every day, even after the resolve to face this new and ugly world had come to me in the cab of the truck on the way home. I thought of giving her up each day, that word *institution* a curse and a means of escape at once, so that those two notions—the chains of a blessing from God, and the means to escape that blessing—were like two huge and awful birds circling me, just waiting for my baby either to live or to die.

And more times than I wanted during those days filled with the idea of *escape* there came to me the memory of the one time I tried to leave the world God'd deemed the just and correct one for me. Too many times, the house closed up around me, Brenda Kay asleep in my arms, there came to me the one night in late fall, only a few months after Bessy Swansea'd stolen away from me Cleopatra Sinclair, a night like any other, me wide awake in my bed, wondering exactly what I was doing there, which God— Missy Cook's or my own—whose plan for my life I was wandering through.

We were in our courses then, taking arithmetic, Latin, grammar, music, all of us in our uniforms and in our assigned chairs and calling out "Present" to each teacher no matter if our minds were there or not. So far the only class I'd really cared for was Latin, in the maze of conjugations and forms and history of the language some deep comfort, refuge from what kept going on every day here: me not being in charge of who I was and where I was going. Suddenly I started in to missing Missy Cook and how it'd really been me in charge there, and in charge of Cathedral, and in charge of Molly, too. Now look where I was: at any given moment a hall mistress could come in here and lift my nightshirt up and beat whatever Hell out of me she felt certain was there.

At that moment Cleopatra touched my shoulder, whispered close in my ear, "Take what you want with you in your pillowcase," and neither her touch nor her words surprised me, all of it only the next logical thing could happen in my life. Here'd come another chance to take charge of it, fix it, the notion big in me that I could grab my life and mend it in ways unimaginable in other people's heads.

I sat straight up, quietly slipped off my pillowcase,

pulled from between the mattress and the springs my
tablet and pencil and my photograph, put them into the
pillowcase, then reached under the bed and, without
thinking of it, picked up my Bible. I hadn't cracked it open
in months, had given up reading every day along about
the early part of Daniel, when at Belshazzar's feast the
handwriting appears on the wall. Last April that'd seemed
as right a spot to stop as any, the handwriting on the walls
before me here at the school indicating that, like King
Belshazzar, I'd been weighed and balanced and'd been
found by God to be wanting. Still, I didn't hesitate, only
picked up the Bible, dropped it in. I eased out of bed and
over to the pine dresser, pulled out the dress I'd worn in
here that day in March, put it in the pillowcase, put on my
jumper, then my coat. I slipped on the shoes I kept
beneath the dresser, and a moment later stood at the door,
just behind the two of them.

Bessy was first, and opened the door, which gave a
small creak that seemed big as a boulder in the empty hall.
We tippy-toed out, and I pulled the door to behind me
without letting it click shut. None of us looked at each
other, but instead at the darkened leaded glass window at
the end of the hall, where Mrs. Archibald and Mrs.
Winthrop roomed together.

We turned, headed off down the hall, and I saw that the
girls didn't have shoes on, and I worried a moment at what
they knew and I didn't, them having planned down to
accounting for the sounds shoes made in an empty hall,
their shoes, I figured, hidden away in their pillowcases.

I stopped, leaned against the wall and, the pillowcase
in one hand, reached down with the other and worked off
my shoes.

Cleopatra and Bessy were already at the end of the hall,

stood at the doorway into the stairwell. Not five feet from
them was another door with a glass window, this the small
anteroom, more a large closet, where Tory slept, and as I
pushed myself away from the wall, my shoes in hand, a
light came on inside.

Cleopatra saw it first, and turned to me. Bessy shoul-
dered into the stairwell, left Cleopatra there and staring at
me, but then she, too, disappeared inside, and I was left
running toward the stairwell door, hoping to get there
before it fell shut, and before Tory opened his door to
whatever he'd heard to set him off in the first place.

And I made it, planted my bare foot inside the doorjamb just as the door came to. If I hadn't been out of
breath and scared and angry all at the same time I would
have hollered at the pain of the heavy door on my foot,
but I only leaned into it, pushed it open.

I turned. Tory stood in his doorway, watching me. His
eyes were full and wet, no white to be seen, and he reeked
of whiskey. He had on the same clothes he wore every day:
the overalls and red workshirt, the workboots scuffed and
muddy.

I froze, remembered him handing back and forth the
belt, back and forth, back and forth.

He did nothing, only met my eyes with his, slowly
shook his head. We looked at each other that way for
what seemed an hour, him and his face and the gray
flecks in the nappy hair. And for a moment I pictured
what he must have seen: a scared white girl with her
shoes in one hand, everything she owned in a pillowcase
in the other, in her eyes the stunned fear every girl in here
must have carried in her eyes, fear he'd seen every day
he'd worked here.

Then that moment was gone, and he stopped shaking

his head, pushed closed his door. A few seconds later the light inside went out.

I breathed again, slipped into the stairwell, eased the door closed.

Bessy and Cleopatra were at the small service door at the bottom of the stairs, Bessy working something in the keyhole.

Cleopatra turned to me, whispered, "What happened?"

"Nothing," I said, and found the lie easy, something in how Tory'd shook his head and in how quick that light'd gone out that made me say it. "Nothing at all," I said, and knew, too, that I wasn't a part of them; they'd asked me along for pity's sake, perhaps, or because I could offer them something they couldn't get on their own.

Bessy got the door unlocked, pulled it open, and October night air filled the stairwell. I shivered, pulled the coat closer to my neck, and followed them out.

By daylight we were a few miles from Picayune, the two of them together a few steps ahead of me, the sun coming up behind us. Already my shins'd started to hurting, the step onto hard ties awkward, every tie too close together, ever other tie too far apart.

I was hungry, and my arm hurt from carrying the pillowcase, and my heart hurt, too, for not being in the midst of the two of them up there, in on whatever secrets they knew about the world and about each other, until, finally, I just stopped, moved off to the gravel beside the tracks and sat down.

They kept on walking, kept on talking and giggling, the sun shining brighter on us as it hit the tops of trees, spilled out over everything. I caught on the air the smell of bacon frying up somewhere, and my stomach seemed to catch fire.

I hollered, "Hey," waited for them to turn.

They didn't.

Then I hollered, "Why'd we escape in the first place?" just loud enough for them to be afraid I'd said it too loud.

Bessy was first to turn around. She stared at me, pillowcase in hand, and then Cleopatra turned. Neither was smiling. Cleopatra only looked at me a moment or two before her eyes started scanning the woods that tunneled us in here.

I looked down at the gravel, took a handful of it in my hand, felt how cold it was, felt how hungry I was, felt how far we'd walked only to end up here. Nowhere I knew.

A minute later they stood next to me, their black leggings and shoes right next to me, Cleopatra a few inches behind and to the side of Bessy.

I said, "I'm hungry." I let a few pieces of the gravel slip between my fingers, disappear into all the rest of the gravel. I said, "Or did you forget about that part of things?"

"Didn't," Bessy said, her word dead, as though she wished, maybe, I was too. "Not at all."

Cleopatra gave a little laugh. With one foot she twisted a small circle in the gravel.

Bessy didn't move. I said, "And?"

"There's a house ahead," she said. "Not more than a mile. We'll eat there."

She turned, moved ahead. Cleopatra stood next to me a moment more, her toe twisting another quick circle in the gravel. She whispered, "Come on, girl," and before I could look up to see whose side she may have been on in all this, she'd turned, was already headed up the tracks.

And there was a house up the tracks, just as Bessy'd said there'd be; we'd come around a wide bend, crossed a small trestle over a black backwater creek, and'd come upon a small blue house, the roof all battered tin, the chimney puffing out smoke thick as gray cotton.

As soon as we saw it, Bessy put up a hand to us, then turned, moved right past Cleopatra and me and back along the tracks. We looked at each other.

Cleopatra said, "What's going on?"

Bessy said nothing, only walked, and of course we followed.

When we got back to the trestle, only a hundred yards or so from where we'd seen the house, Bessy stepped off the tracks and down the creek bank. She set down her pillowcase, reached in and brought out the blue dress she'd worn her first day in at the school, and we knew what to do. Cleopatra and I moved down the bank, too, opened our pillowcases, brought out our clothes. By then Bessy'd already taken off her jumper and underdrawers and leggings and blouse, so that she stood before us naked. I saw for the first time her breasts, how full and rounded they were, the nipples up and hard in the cool morning, and I saw the dark hair she had between her legs, the wisps of it thicker than mine.

Then my eyes went to her belly, and to two long scars there. They ran from just below her belly button up to her ribs, her skin all goose-pimpled up, the two scars parallel to each other and purple and the width of a fingernail, and I couldn't help but shiver at what I saw, at what I didn't know. She stood before us naked without a single breath of embarrassment or humility, and I felt my breasts shrink into themselves as I took off my blouse, my back to the two of them; felt, too, a cold, sharp twist of pain across my own belly.

I dropped my jumper, quick put on my old dress, hurried into my coat.

I glanced over my shoulder once to see what Cleopatra was doing, saw her there in just her underdrawers and leggings, her back to us, too, as she shimmied into a dress I recognized from nowhere, then remembered she'd been brought in before me. When she turned around, she'd become someone else altogether: the dress, a pink one with a white satin ribbon round the waist tied off in a bow, was a little small on her, but every inch beautiful, from the bit of lace at the neck to the pink ribbon at the hem, and I imagined all the town fathers buying that dress for her as some sort of farewell gift, feeling sorry and pitying her and at the same time glad to rid their fair town of a hellion with a brick. She was beautiful in the dress.

Our eyes met a moment, then hers broke from mine to look down at the dress. She smiled, said, "I haven't had this on since the day I was brought in," words which didn't mean a thing, just the only ones she could muster at this moment, the three of us suddenly who we were before we'd been pushed into the Mississippi Industrial School for Girls. Just three girls, and I wondered if Cleopatra knew of the scar on Bessy's belly; wondered if she'd heard Bessy's story about it, envied her if she knew and at the same time wanted none of it.

Bessy was down on her knees now, and Cleopatra and I watched as she stuffed into her pillowcase the blouse, then the jumper, leggings and underdrawers. She stood, went down to the water, brought back a big rock, moss-covered on top and muddy on the bottom, and dropped it into the pillowcase, then twisted the open end into a knot, lifted the handle.

She looked at us, and smiled. There were her teeth, all perfect and simple and white, and I thought again of what you could not see: the scars, the deep purple and chill of them.

She laughed, the sound dry and hard in her throat. She looked from me to Cleopatra. Then she turned, went down to the water. She said, "Won't ever be needing these again, that's for goddamned certain." She swung the bundle back, brought it forward, and let it sail out into the middle of the creek, where it hit with a loud splash, and disappeared.

She turned to us, still smiling, and walked right between us, up the bank. Then she was up on the tracks.

Cleopatra wouldn't look at me, and though she was first to follow Bessy, this time she hung back a few extra feet, the three of us spread out along the track, only two of us with pillowcases now, headed for that blue house with the tin roof.

We squatted behind bushes next to the house. Bessy reached into them and pulled back a few branches, peered through. From where I sat all I could see was smoke lift into clear blue air, disappear with the wind up there.

Bessy whispered, "Nothing to this one," and let the branches fall back into place. She turned to me, no smile now. She whispered, "Now you find out why we took you on in this here little venture," and she reached a hand over near my face.

I flinched, pulled away quick, afraid she might lay fists on me for whatever reason she had in mind.

But her hand reached my face all the same, and she touched my cheek with the back of her fingers before I could do anything else. The touch was soft, and for a moment I wondered if she weren't thinking of her own face, her own skin, her breasts. Her face still bore the marks of the fight she'd had with Cleopatra months ago:

the split eyebrow; a bruise high on her left cheekbone
that'd never wholly disappeared, now a red spot the size
of a pea; a small scar at the base of her chin. And as she
touched her fingers to my cheek once again, reached up to
my hair, tucked a lock of it behind my ear, I wondered,
too, how long she'd been trading on her face, that skin,
her breasts and the hair between her legs. Long enough, I
realized, to let her stand as she had with no clothes on,
and long enough, too, to end up with scars like she had.

"Yes ma'am, you little sugartit you, you're right along
with us here because you come from money, you do." Her
eyes met mine now, and she brought her hand to my cheek
again, let it rest there. Then slowly she took hold of my
chin. "You come from money, ain't nobody in that shithole
school don't know that." She was smiling, and I cut my eyes
over at Cleopatra, squatting right next to us. Her mouth
was open, her own eyes going from Bessy to me and back.

Bessy whispered, "Now you're going down round to the
front door of that shanty, and you going to knock on that
door, and when whoever it is lives there comes, you going
to engage them in some sorrowful story." She started
holding tighter to my jaw, pressing hard on my chin, on my
teeth, my mouth." And they going to believe you, they are.
Because you come from money, and folks with none,
whether niggers or crackers, can smell it on those that do,
and they'll believe whatever it is you have to say, because
they can smell that money on you. They always do, and
you telling your little story will divert their sorry-ass attention for a while. So you lie your sweet little virgin ass off at
that door to whoever it is comes." She paused, held tight
my chin a moment longer, then let it go. I took in a breath,
looked at her. She smiled again, tucked a lock of hair
behind my other ear. "Now you go."

I did. I didn't even look to Cleopatra again, didn't think of her, only thought of those scars and the sound that rock and her clothes made into the black water beneath the trestle, and before I knew what was happening I was coming round the front of the house—the blue clapboards, I could see up close, were ancient, the paint blistered and cracked and falling off—and I was heading to the door, gray wood with only a small hole where a knob should have been.

I knocked, and the door opened a moment later. There stood an old niggerwoman, her hair white, skin black as any nigger's I'd ever seen before, her eyes set deep in her head and even blacker than her skin. She had on a filthy apron, was wiping her thin hands with it.

Before I could even open my mouth, she was smiling, and I knew what Bessy'd said was true: people without money believed the ones who had it, and I didn't even let her say one word to me as I started in on a story about how I was a little girl whose mother had died recently, and whose grandmama, who owned a mansion up in Purvis, had sent me down to New Orleans for a new dress, and how a swindler, a good-looking young man named Rutledge, had stolen all my money from me, and how I had no other choice of getting back to Purvis than to walk.

The niggerwoman frowned, drew her eyebrows up, gave her face a tilt to one side, listening to it all, and when I got to the part about my satchel and all my belongings in it being stolen by that swindler Rutledge, the niggerwoman reached out a hand and touched my cheek. This time I didn't pull away, though; I only let her touch me, and for a moment as I went on with my story about how I needed help back in the right direction and how I would be able to give her a reward from my grandmama's cash-

box, I let my eyes close. This niggerwoman's hard and callused fingers touched my cheek even more gently than
Bessy'd done when she'd started giving my instructions,
and suddenly I fell back into my own place in Purvis, pictured in my mind Molly touching me, pictured the old
kitchen, the walls, the cupboards, the butcherblock
stained black with years of blood. I pictured all of that
while I heard myself tell the story of a girl's mother dying
of a fever in an upstairs bedroom, and I found myself
telling her, too, of a father who was a logger and who'd
broken his neck, and heard, too, of the soft memory of a
brother, a small baby who'd died when the girl was only a
young child herself. All this time my eyes were closed, the
niggerwoman's hand on my cheek, and I felt tears coming,
felt them spill out my eyes and down the cheeks of a girl
telling her story as a lie, none of it the truth but the truth
all the same, my story only to divert her sorry-ass attention for a while, while Bessy and Cleopatra did whatever
it was they were going to do here.

That was when I opened my eyes, the story of my life
cut short by the sound of a pan knocked to the floor inside
the shack, and the niggerwoman brought her hand down
from my face, turned to the inside of her house.

There stood Cleopatra, holding a skillet with the hem
of her pink dress, in the skillet bacon frying up, eggs in
there with it. Inside the room was only a fireplace, a metal
grate of some kind hooked in there, on it a battered and
steaming black kettle. A busted-up chair leaned against
one wall, a quilt heaped in one corner. The back door of
the place stood open behind Cleopatra, and the light silhouetted her in a way that made her seem bigger than she
already was. I saw all this in an instant, the time it took
the niggerwoman to turn from me to her home. She

turned back to me, and I saw in her puzzlement at what was going on here, her old eyes taking everything in and trying to piece it all out. Still Cleopatra only stood there, looking at the two of us, her mouth still open.

From behind her stepped Bessy, who looked first at the woman, then at me. "For god's sakes," she said, "this here's just some old nigger shanty. We didn't even have to send you out on your story," and she moved to the fireplace, with the hem of her own dress took hold of the kettle. "Grits," she said, and looked at the niggerwoman, smiled, nodded. "Much obliged," she said. She turned, was gone out the back door.

Cleopatra backed toward the door, disappeared.

The niggerwoman took a step toward the back door, but turned to me, looked at me, her face no longer filled with the puzzle of this all, but with the stunned and milky look of a dead animal's eyes. She just stood there, looked at me a long moment.

I ran, took off round the back of her house, saw a pillowcase up on the rise where the tracks lay. When I got to it, I caught sight of the last bit of Cleopatra, saw her running into the woods on the other side of the tracks, the pan in hand. She'd already disappeared from the waist down for the brush back there; Bessy, I figured, was already buried.

Cleopatra stopped, turned. She called out, "Come on, girl," and waited an instant before she turned back to the woods, started off again. The last thing I saw of her before she was swallowed up entirely was the back of her head, the short growth of hair there, long tendrils of hair on either side of it trailing back with what small wind she made running.

I held my pillowcase with both hands, turned to the

shanty. The niggerwoman stood just inside the back door, her hands at her sides, dead, useless. Because what, I thought, could she do? There was nothing: three white girls'd swooped in like chicken hawks and'd taken what they wanted at will. There was nothing she could do, her life in our hands.

But it was my own life in my hands, I saw, and I felt how sorrowful my own story really was; not the story of my family all dying around me, not the story of being sent here by a grandmother who didn't give a damn about me. No, the sorrowful story, I knew, was that this was where I'd brought myself when I'd taken my own life into my hands. Come here to this moment, robbing a nigger-woman of her food, then tearing off into woods. Which seemed like no way to fix a life at all.

So I ran. I ran back in the direction we'd come, ran along the tracks and over the trestle and the black creek where, at the bottom, lay remnants of somebody else's life, a life, I knew, would end in disaster, those scars on her belly a good headstart on that road. I ran, and ran, and ran, all the while holding on to my pillowcase, wanting to protect what was inside it—my tablet and the photograph, my Bible—from whatever might come out of the woods to lay into me in whatever way a man or a woman had done to Bessy. I ran.

I made it to Picayune by noon, stopped and slipped back into my jumper in somebody's privy not far from school. I walked right on to campus, walked right past the big live oak at the east end, strolled right into the dining hall, took my place in line for the food we all were given each day, the girls all around me silent, staring at me, at the pillowcase I carried, my mouth shut tight with what small piece I knew now of the world.

Then came Mrs. Archibald's hand on my shoulder, fingers digging into my skin like talons, and I knew it was over.

Mrs. Archibald, still behind me, pulled me out of line, pushed me through the girls swarming now, their words quiet murmurs, each whisper building one on another until the sound in the dining hall roared in my ears. She pushed me to the door onto the courtyard, and I reached to the knob, opened it. Then she pushed me on out to the courtyard, across the lawn to the flagpole in front of the main building.

I let go the pillowcase, let it settle next to my feet, and I bent at the waist. I hugged the flagpole, felt the cold steel of it press into my face, burn into my cheek.

Tory came from inside the main building and down the steps, in his hand the belt, and when he came close enough I let my eyes look up at him.

He didn't look at me, but handed the belt to Mrs. Archibald. I couldn't see her take it, only saw Tory step behind me with the belt, step back without it. He put his hands together in front of him, looked at the ground, him the last one here to see me before I'd tried to escape my life.

Mrs. Archibald lifted my jumper over my hips, and I pictured each girl at the school pressing her face to the glass windows of the dining hall, imagined I could hear the talk they gave, though the only sound was the fall wind in the tops of trees, the whirr and hiss of it.

My eyes went to the blue sky above me, a deep blue and still and cutting. I kept my eyes open as long as I could, focused on that frightening cold blue, until they blinked shut of their own when the belt finally came down on me.

The snap of it was louder than I could have imagined, the pain of it shuddering up through the backs of my legs and into my stomach and my lungs and on into my face and out to my fingertips. But I kept my eyes on that blue the whole time, through each shock of the belt, through each wave of pain.

It was that memory in my head to come back and haunt me each day I spent waiting, a haunting that kept me from the escape handing Brenda Kay over to an institution would be, and I found myself whispering out into the cold dark of the room, into the closed eyes of my baby daughter, whispering to myself and to all the ghosts that seemed to stay with me wherever this life led me words I'd heard most all my life, yet'd never truly known until then precisely what they meant: *Whither shall I go from Thy Spirit?* I whispered, *Or whither shall I flee from Thy presence? If I ascend up into Heaven, Thou art there: if I make my bed in Hell, behold Thou art there.*

There was more to that psalm, that presence. But this was where my words stopped: *Behold, Thou art there* and I saw only then that perhaps those two great and ugly birds circling over us, those notions of *escape* and *no escape*, might actually be one and the same, one great and all-powerful being: my own God in Heaven, waiting up there on high.

But then one morning three weeks after we came home from New Orleans, there came a knock on the door. I did nothing, only opened my eyes. I'd fallen near asleep in the rocker, and the sound of the first knock, then the next, gave me a second's dream of my Uncle Benjamin, come to knock on my door to take my baby away, so when there came still one more knock I'd shot open my eyes, hollered, "No!"

Dr. Beaudry pushed open the door, poked his head in. He squinted into the darkened room, smiled. He said, "Mrs. Hilburn, you all right in there?"

I said nothing, didn't even rock the chair.

"Mrs. Hilburn?" he said again, and came in. The door stood open behind him, light falling in.

"Close the door," I said. "Just close it."

"Not too good for you, neither you nor your baby. This dark." He turned, slowly pushed it closed.

"If you're here to try and take away my baby," I said, "then you just might as well head out right now." I paused, gave myself a push in the rocker, started us in motion again. Brenda Kay stirred, reached up, touched nothing.

He stood with his black bag in one hand, his jacket in the other. He had on a black vest and pants, the jacket the same color, and a white shirt gone gray in the dark. He looked at me a few moments, then turned, looked for a place to sit.

Against the far wall we had an old divan, a quilt thrown over it, but he didn't seem satisfied with that, only set his bag and jacket on it, then looked past me toward the kitchen. He walked in there, pulled out one of the chairs from the table, set it in front of me, not three feet away. He sat, looked right at me.

He said, "We don't want you to give up your baby, not if you don't want to."

"What do you mean 'we'?" I whispered. Brenda Kay's hand dropped, lay flat on the blanket.

He looked down to the small patch of floor between us. He had his elbows on his knees, his fingers together in a fist in front of him. He said, "I think you know."

"I do," I gave right back to him. "And you didn't have the guts to tell us, neither." I paused, let him have hold of that for a moment. Then I said, "So why ought I believe you right now, that you don't want me to commit my child?"

He looked a few moments longer at the floor, then up to me. In the darkness I could see him blink once, twice. "You don't have any good reason to believe me, I guess. And I'm sorry about how you found out. But I thought it best for Dr. Basket to make the diagnosis, the evaluation." He stopped, let out a sigh. He sat up, his back to the chair now, his hands loose in front of him. His head was to one side, his eyes on Brenda Kay. "But the truth is—"

"That's all I'm after," I cut in on him. "The truth."

He paused a moment, took in my words, measured them in some way that made his shoulders seem to fall, as though he'd surrendered finally to whatever it was in me that wanted him to squirm.

He said, "Dr. Basket and I both want you to know that if you want to keep her, we will help in what ways we can."

I was quiet a while, the only sound my chair rocking on the hardwood floor. I said, "And what ways might those be?"

"For one," he said without a moment's pause, "I'd like to see her at least once a month. And every three months Dr. Basket wants to take a good look at her. That's for starters." He leaned forward again, the fist in front of him. He brought his hands up, let his chin rest on them. "And there is a form of medication. Calcium glucanate, a bone strengthener. One of the problems with Mongolian Idiots—"

"Don't you ever say those words in front of me again," I said. I'd stopped the rocker without knowing I had, felt myself holding Brenda Kay even tighter to me. I whispered, "Don't you dare."

He stared at me, his chin still on his hands. He nodded,

let his eyes fall from mine. He whispered, "I understand," then took a breath. "The injections," he went on, his eyes still away from us, "help strengthen bones. Soft bones are one of the problems with . . ." He paused, touched one ear with a hand, brought it back to his chin. "With children of this special nature," he said.

"Thank you," I said, and I closed my eyes.

After a long moment, he said, "Soft bones can be helped along, we believe, with calcium glucanate injections every six weeks. That way we can help her grow as well as she can. It's quite a modern process. We're fortunate to have access to such a medication."

"Injections," I whispered.

"Yes," he said quietly. "I wish they could be administered in some other way, but that's all we can do. Dr. Basket's already instructed me on proper dosage, and precisely where the injections are to be made. And he's ready to send up the first prescription."

"Where?" I said, my eyes still closed. I wanted as much dark as I could get hold of.

"Why, to my office," he said.

"No," I said, "where on my baby's body will she receive the shots?" I paused. "You said there's a precise place."

"Oh," he said, his voice, like his shoulders, fallen somehow. "She would receive two shots, one in each hip. That's where the bones need the most strength."

I said nothing, only pictured in my head that great bird circling higher and higher, up and away from us, disappearing high into a cold blue sky.

"We need to talk about how much this entire procedure will cost," he said, his voice almost a whisper.

I opened my eyes. "No we do not," I said.

1949

Chapter 12

Leston spent his days combing the woods for lightered knots from all the splintered wood they'd blown up years ago, occasionally blowing up a stump on his own with old sticks of dynamite he'd find somewhere in the shed. But even then it'd be only for the splinters that he'd light fuses, that business of hauling stumps for turpentine down to Pascagoula long dried up, the end of the war the end of our money. Once the boys were home from school, the three of them—Leston, Burton and Wilman—drove along dirt roads out to nigger shanties to sell them bundles of the kindling, just trying to make enough money for us to get by. There was no way on this earth he'd be caught selling to the whites in town. Just no way.

Billie Jean, a year out of Purvis High, worked as a teller at First Mississippi downtown; she hated the work, and there'd been days beyond number over the last year when I'd had to roll her out of bed, feed her biscuits and gravy in her sleep, plug her under the shower before she'd awake. Then she'd dog it while getting dressed and into the pickup, where Leston waited, silent, eyes straight ahead, coffee and cigarette in hand. But she was faithful to give up her paycheck to us, save for a dollar or two allowance we gave right back to her.

My job was in the cafeteria at Bailey Grammar School,

where I served up sweet potatoes and fried okra and on
good days a thin sliver of ham to all the children. At the
end of the day I was allowed to bring home a few servings
of what little food was left. I was the only white woman at
work there in the cafeteria, but that didn't bother me.

It was the money we were after.

Billie Jean hadn't subscribed to her magazines in two
years; the last piece of new clothing I'd bought for myself
was a scarf three years ago for when we went into New
Orleans, the wind down there whipping sometimes too
hard for me to stand. Toxie and JE and Garland and all the
niggers were on their own now, playing pickup at whatever
work they could find. Leston'd sold off the equipment four
years ago.

But this morning, this May Saturday, we were headed
for a picnic in celebration.

Thursday night Brenda Kay took her first step.

She was five years, six months and four days old
Thursday, and'd finally taken her first step, my baby with
the copper hair leaving Billie Jean's arms and slowly dod-
dering over the braided rug toward me across the front
room from her, her feet heavy in shiny white orthopedic
shoes laced up to her ankles. The dress she had on, a
faded blue thing with embroidered yellow ducks around
the hem and sleeves, was one Anne'd worn when she was
three, and as Brenda Kay came close, I thought I could see
in her face a trace of Annie, somewhere in her eyes a hint
of her sister, though the baby's eyes did slant up in a way
at times made her look like some of the children in the
World Book Encyclopedia. It'd taken me three years to work
up the nerve to search out exactly what Mongolians
looked like, and I remember swallowing hard, taking in a

deep breath at seeing the photographs there in the library, women and children and men from the country called Mongolia, with their fine straight hair and thick, heavy eyes and broad, flat foreheads.

But then the trace of Annie was gone, and she was Brenda Kay again, my baby, those green eyes wide open in surprise at being on her own as she moved, her short arms out to either side, dimpled knees, pink skin; and there was her smile, the one she held right then and that showed all her teeth, small and thin and distanced one from another, her heavy cheeks puffed out even more for that smile.

The night outside the open windows was filled with the whirr of cicadas, treefrogs, all else that lived in the darkness and away from what was happening inside. The only other sound was the radio turned low and playing some big band from the top of a hotel in New Orleans, rich people dancing to music in clothes I could only imagine, colors I'd never see in this life. The boys were up in their room and, I hoped, embarked on the nightly torture they believed homework only good for. Leston was at the kitchen table, quiet as always, hunched over a cup of coffee I knew had lone gone cold. Anne lay before the empty fireplace on her tummy—like every night, she'd finished her homework hours before dark, fed up with following her brothers around, the two of them still fighting as much and as hard as always—her legs crossed at the ankles, feet up in the air and swinging away to the dance music. In her hand was a thick red pencil, on the floor in front of her a tablet of paper so like the one I had when I was a child I'd thought for a moment that indeed it was mine, misplaced ages ago and now miraculously appeared.

But the miracle here was Brenda Kay, and how she

came toward me and away from Billie Jean while all else in the world shuffled along, dead to the six feet my daughter moved across.

Brenda Kay fell into my arms, and I held her to me, heard her say, "Momma, Momma," her only word so far, heard her say it again and again.

Then other sounds came to me: Billie Jean, still seated on the floor on the other side of the rug, was clapping; next came the rush and pounding that could only be my boys on the stairs down. "Momma, Momma," they shouted, and once they reached the bottom, Wilman said, "What's going on?"

Anne was up and coming toward Brenda Kay and me, her arms out, the red pencil still in one hand. She hugged the two of us as best she could, Annie growing up and eight now, older suddenly than I wanted her to be. "I saw it," she said, "I saw it," and I felt her hold us tighter, Brenda Kay tucked between us.

"Momma?" Burton said, still one step up, his hand on the railing, Wilman in front of him.

Billie Jean turned to them. "She walked," she said, "she walked."

That was when I heard Leston's chair push back, heard his steps across the floor and toward us all, the boys now down with the rest of us, though they were too manly, I could see, to feel the need to hug as Billie Jean and Anne did. But they were with us, and I felt them pat my shoulders, saw them touch Brenda Kay's head and arms and back. "Good job," Wilman said to Brenda Kay, whose eyes were on him now, her mouth open in that smile, and Burton said, "Good job, Brenda Kay."

I looked behind me, saw Leston in the doorway, hands wrapped around the coffee cup.

Finally, he smiled. He nodded, the move slow and measured, his mouth never opening. Then he knelt next to me, and he kissed my cheek, moved his face into my hair.

He said nothing, but what he'd given was more than he'd offered in longer than I cared to recall: a kiss, his face close to mine. Only that, but I was happy with it.

I said, "Saturday we're going on a picnic, out to Ashe Lake." I paused, looked at my children's faces. They'd gone quiet, mouths open. "A picnic. Fried chicken? Potato salad?" I said. "Any takers?"

The boys and Annie started in to laughing, Wilman and Burton still touching Brenda Kay. Billie Jean started to give excuses why she wanted to go to town, said something about having lunch with her friend Ruby Sitwell. Then it must've come to her: a picnic, something I couldn't remember our doing, not since before Brenda Kay, and Billie Jean smiled again.

Leston stood. I watched him move back to the doorway, where he stopped, turned around, and leaned against the doorjamb, the coffee cup still in his hands. His eyes were on Brenda Kay. He was smiling, and brought the cup to his lips.

Brenda Kay started churning in my arms, excited at all these goings on: walking, clapping, laughing. Her mouth was open and taking in too many breaths, and she tried to clap, her eyes on the children; her hands came together twice, then missed, came together again.

Walking at five years and six months, her word *Momma* coming at four and one month, out of diapers only five months ago. She lifted her head at one year, rolled over at two.

To say things were hard on us is to do us all wrong, and Leston's kiss to me, his face in my hair, signaled to me what all we'd sacrificed so that I could tend to my baby. His heart'd been gone for some time now, and I can't say as I blame him for it. When the war was over, Pascagoula seemed to shut down altogether, like there was a gate into the place and nobody'd open it for him, and that good, clear money we'd had for so long might as well have been only a dream we'd all carried on for years.

Because we woke one morning in September of 1945, and looked at each other while the sounds of the house started up like every morning. But the look we'd given each other wasn't anything like the one we'd had the morning I told him I was pregnant with Brenda Kay.

This look was one of bewilderment, neither of us certain what was going to happen to the baby in the cradle next to us.

That morning in September I was to bring Brenda Kay to Dr. Beaudry's office for another set of shots, her needing them every six weeks, as per Dr. Basket's direction. The routine of each visit had been in motion since April of the year before, when the war was in full swing, and we were winning, and James' letters home were filled with more and more good news of how they were all squashing the great Empire of the Sun with each push of their bulldozers, each hammer driving home a nail.

But that morning there was no money, and no prospect of it, other than what Leston said to the empty room, to the air in there that seemed suddenly too close, too thick: "We'll sell off two of the steers. See where that puts us."

"Leston," I said. I didn't move, didn't touch him.

He pushed back the sheets, got up.

The shots cost money—twenty-three dollars each time—and the doctor visits cost money—two dollars each time—and the trips into New Orleans every three months cost money. And now we had no money. We had five steers and three cows by that time, what money we'd been able to squirrel away and not put back into the stump business invested in them.

"How much longer will she have to keep up with the shots?" I said to the room, to Leston's back, though I knew the answer to that better than he did: for as long as she needed them, Dr. Basket'd said, which I took to mean, For as long as she lives. Back then she wasn't yet two years old, the age Dr. Basket'd said she wouldn't live past, and I couldn't help but imagine sometime the shots would stop, and we might see ourselves clear of this. But I'd hoped at the same time for a trainload of shots for her, her visits every six weeks for the rest of all time and eternity, for us marching up and down those stairs to Beaudry's office above the hardware store until we were all so old we had to be carried. I'd only asked my question to hear it, as if with my words Leston'd know I felt as scared as he did about what the future would give.

But he was the one lost his job, the one who'd already let go everybody. In September of 1945, only Toxie and JE came over, where they would stand outside in the early morning dark, lean against the truck and smoke while I made breakfast, portions so much smaller then that I had to remember how to cook little batches of grits, remember to crack open only six or seven eggs and not three dozen. They smoked and smoked, and after breakfast the three of them would just drive off, Leston in the lead in the pick-up, JE and Toxie following in the flatbed. They showed up in the early afternoons, maybe only one stump on the flatbed one day a week.

We sold off the two steers, then the rest of the cattle, one by one, while nothing like a real job came close to Leston. Finally JE and Toxie stopped showing up, and I'd taken the job at the grammar school, and the boys and Annie took to selling vegetables from our garden out front of the house, all to pay for what I'd committed us to with my words to Dr. Beaudry on a morning what seemed decades ago.

It was Cathedral to tell me of the job opening up over to the grammar school, one of her cousins leaving, moving north to the city of Detroit. After supper the day she told me of it, the children all bathed and in bed, I finally worked up the nerve to inform Leston of my plan to go over to Bailey the next day, and ask for the work.

Leston was in the kitchen, leaned against the countertop, and I came up next to him, put my hands together. I said, "Leston, I'm going to ask for work in the cafeteria at Bailey." They were the words I'd rehearsed all day on my own, and I thought my voice'd seemed honest enough, sincere enough. They'd come out as clear and strong as I'd intended them to.

Because it was nigger work, serving up food at the cafeteria. It was nigger work, plain and simple, and I figured my words would need to be as strong as I could make them for my husband. I'd figured he'd rage on at me and this news, my husband a man who'd been the boss over nearly a dozen niggers himself at one time. Now here was his wife, readying herself to go join their ranks, serve up food to white kids who, he and I both knew, would rush home to their own mommas with the news of Mrs. Hilburn ladling up food for them.

He turned to me, his mouth straight, eyes blank. He said, "Guess you figured there's no sense in asking me. Figured you'd just tell me what you were going to do, whether I wanted you to or not."

I looked away from him. He was right; I hadn't asked him a question, but'd only told him. I'd already decided I was going down there to Bailey bright and early tomorrow, whether he said yes or no. I knew I'd be down there at the cafeteria door, Brenda Kay in my arms.

Because it was a life we were saving. It was Brenda Kay we were saving, and it didn't matter where the money came from, because we were saving our daughter's life.

He looked at me a long moment, opened his mouth and closed it like he was gasping for air, or was drowning at the bottom of some deep well. But he made no sound, until finally he whispered, "You do what you think best."

He turned from me, dumped his cold coffee in the sink, then stepped out the back door, where I knew he'd stay for a while, smoking away.

He left me there in the kitchen, alone with the decision I'd made, a decision that was no decision. I'd wanted him to approve, wanted him to at least nod his head, or touch my cheek, or even put his arms around me, something to let me see he knew what I had to do. I needed that touch from him.

But it was a life we were saving, I told myself enough nights after that, when Leston started staying up with his coffee, just staring out the window above the kitchen sink, where I found him every time I came downstairs and begged him back to bed. And it was a life we were saving, I told myself enough days the children went on to school in clothes mended and patched so many times there was no telling what was the original material and what I'd been able to pick up at the piece goods store.

It was a life we were after, I thought enough times we got checks from James, me feeling guilty for the gift of the money from a son trying to put himself through college, him a married man now. Guilty, because each time I got a check from him I felt relief, as though the only good thing I felt for my firstborn and his wife was thanks for the money they sent. But it was a life we were after.

One morning in 1946 James'd simply showed up at the house with a girl on his arm, a brassy blonde who chewed gum and wore high heels so tall she staggered like she was blind drunk while walking up the ruts in our dirt drive, the two of them dropped off like visiting dignitaries by one of the three taxis Purvis had to offer.

We all smothered James, who looked as much like a man as I knew he ever would, him in his uniform, and then we hugged him separately, first Annie, then Wilman, Burton, and finally Billie Jean, the two of them exchanging looks like they'd thought they'd never see each other again. Then I gave over Brenda Kay to James, his sister a little over two years then and with the startled, dazed look her green eyes almost always held, her small hand touching his chin, his nose, his cheek.

That was when he finally turned to the girl beside him, said, "Y'all, this is Eudine, my wife."

She stopped chewing her gum, swallowed it, and put out her hand to me. "Eudine Hilburn," she said, smiling and parting her red lips to show big white teeth. "Formerly Eudine Trahern, late of Dumas, Texas," and she laughed, put a hand up to her mouth to make like she was being modest. She had on a bright blue skirt that stopped right at her knees, a jacket the same color, a white blouse with an open collar, and just as much makeup as any one of those girls we'd seen in New Orleans. "I guess I'm just a ding-dong daddy from Dumas, Texas," she said, still laughing, her hand still out to me.

I paused a moment, looked at her, then at my oldest son. Here was another of those moments a mother doesn't want so much to see, evidence of her children growing up and away, and I thought again of the dinner when he'd been only sixteen and told us of his heading off to war. I hadn't thought heavily on what exactly I'd expected him to do once he was out of the service, but nothing I ever imagine'd come even close to this: a gum-swallowing Texas girl with hair no natural color on earth.

I took her hand because it was the polite thing to do, and shook it. As soon as we'd let go, she reached to James, took Brenda Kay out of his arms, and held her. "Now this here's the one I want to take ahold of," she said, and started to bobbing with Brenda Kay, jostling her just the smallest way. This Eudine took one of Brenda Kay's hands to her lips, gave her the littlest kiss, said, "This here's the one I've heard so much about, this here little baby-cake," and she held Brenda Kay close. Eudine never looked at me to see if I was taking any of this in, measuring her to see if she was worthy or not of my oldest boy. She was only holding Brenda Kay, and holding her close, not afraid at all.

I looked to James, wanted to tell him with my eyes that she was welcome here, that as far as I could see she would make him a good wife, all this just from the touch she'd given his baby sister.

But he was looking toward the house behind me, his chin set and high. I turned.

Leston stood on the porch. His hands were on his hips, his feet spread shoulder width.

"Leston," I called, already trying to settle myself

between the two of them. We'd seen James only twice since he'd joined up, both leaves ending with Leston inside the house, me driving James back into town so he could catch his bus. Now James was out of the service altogether, who knew what would come.

"Congratulations," Leston said. "I don't suppose you'll be moving back in."

James took off his hat, held it in both hands. Eudine, next to him, whispered baby talk into Brenda Kay's ear. Burton and Wilman and Annie stood around James, and I watched my oldest son, looking for what he would do to follow up taking off his hat, whether he'd put his arm around his new wife, move toward his daddy, what.

But it was in his eyes I saw what he was up to, how he wasn't afraid to let them meet Leston's any longer, how they'd seen enough of this world and all it contained, had worked and sweat with enough men to make certain this moment wouldn't be anything he couldn't handle. I could see in his eyes and how they just rested on his daddy's that he was already gone from this place.

"Moving to Texas, Daddy," he said. "Going to college, Texas A&M." He paused, swallowed, though his eyes were steel, heavy on Leston. "Not sure what I'm going to study, but I'm going to study all the same."

Leston crossed his arms, seemed to stand even taller. He said, "Don't be expecting any money out of this household to be helping you on your way."

"College," Billie Jean whispered, and I turned, saw her standing next to Eudine, Eudine smiling her big-teeth smile at her.

"Don't need any money, Daddy," James went on. "Uncle Sam's seeing to that, for the most part."

He finally looked down, let his eyes fall on the hat in

his hands, ran the brim round once, twice. In the move was so much of his daddy that there shouldn't have been any doubt in anyone's mind, no sorrow lost, no grief over his moving out. James' leaving us now was the only real thing that could take place.

We'd all gone silent for one long terrible moment, a silence that seemed to shout out to us all that Leston, my children's father, my husband, had nothing left to offer: no business his children could take over, no money even to lend out. The only thing left was wandering through woods to old haunts, where stumps'd been exploded years before, so he could pick up from the forest floor the remains of those days, and sell them in bundles to niggers. Only that.

Now James belonged to one Eudine Hilburn, late of Dumas, Texas, and so the only thing I could do, the only thing anyone on the face of this earth with any ability to see the obvious could do, was to go to James, hold him as close as I could ever hope to hold my child, and with that hold say good-bye the best way I knew to do.

It was a life we were saving, and with the checks James managed to squeeze out to us, with the money from Billie Jean, with the money from the kindling and the grammar school, even the change from the vegetable stand outside, we'd managed to get here, to this day, a Saturday picnic to celebrate Brenda Kay's first steps. Five years, when they said she'd live two. Six feet across the front room floor, when they said she'd never walk.

But there was something else I was looking for, too, something I wanted to try out on Leston, and as I packed into the picnic hamper the fried chicken I'd made up the night before, Sunday's dinner already cooked and ready to eat, I couldn't help but feel myself a sinner at having on my mind anything other than that picture of Brenda Kay walking across the rug. So we would have beans and rice for dinner tomorrow. We were celebrating, and I was ready to talk to Leston about something I figured on changing our world all for the better. I wanted to talk to my husband, the man who, it seemed for all intents and purposes, had pulled up stakes in this family, given up in the face of his baby daughter and the fact of no jobs.

I stood in the quiet of a Saturday morning kitchen, watched through the window Burton and Wilman throw into the pickup two old inner tubes, patched and repatched, leftovers from when we had the big trucks, while inside I folded cloth napkins so thin you could see right through them, put them in the hamper. Next I set in a jar of pickled okra I'd put up late last year, then bowls filled with potato salad and black-eyed peas and cold cheese grits, each of them covered with sheets of wax paper I'd used at least a half-dozen times apiece and tied off with old bits of twine.

I looked back out the window, the morning sun outside shining through me, and I decided right then I'd try out the word I wanted to use on Leston, even though we'd be out there to celebrate my baby's walking. I'd offer him the word, one I hadn't yet uttered aloud, too afraid of the sound it'd make, at maybe how far off and ridiculous the idea might seem. I decided I'd try the word out on him, because he was my husband, no matter how deep that well he'd fallen into, no matter how hard he was gasping for air inside God's will for his life. He was still my husband, and I was still his wife.

"California," I whispered, then tried it again, a little louder, but still so quiet I knew I was the only one could hear: "California."

"Momma," Brenda Kay cried, her voice coming to me from her bedroom upstairs, the room Anne'd had to move from, the room that'd been James' so long ago. The word came out in the same taut, high pitch it did every time, as though it might be lodged in her throat, her choking every time on the only word she knew, my name.

Burton threw a coil of rope and an old wooden crate into the bed of the pickup, for what I couldn't say, and Brenda Kay cried out again, "Momma!"

"Jewel," Leston said from somewhere in the house. "She's calling."

But I let myself say the word once more, felt it there in my mouth, soft and foreign and clear.

Chapter 13

It was in the *Reader's Digest* I found out about it. That was the only magazine I let come into the house, and I'd kept it a secret, that money I spent on it. Cathedral was the only one who knew about it, her taking care of Brenda Kay when I was out to the grammar school, us paying her a quarter a week to see after her, watch she didn't crawl off somewhere we couldn't get her, spoon-feed her lunch. Oatmeal was Brenda Kay's favorite.

And there were weeks, too, especially around when we were getting ready to take Brenda Kay for her shots, when we couldn't even pay her the quarter. But she didn't complain, never spoke one word out of line about our situation. She'd always quote the same verse to me when those weeks came up: "And if ye lend to them of whom ye hope to receive, what thank have ye? For sinners also lend to sinners, to receive as much again," she'd say to me, and smile. "Luke chapter six, verse thirty-four," she'd say, "the words of our Lord Jesus Christ," and she'd turn, head off for home.

The mail came near one-thirty each day, and I was usually home by that time to get it. Cathedral my only witness as I tore off the crisp brown wrapper, my *Reader's Digest* the highlight of the month. Even James' checks coming to us couldn't compare, because there was always surrounding those bits of paper the feeling of dread at how hard it was for them to give it, the obligation they had to feel to help save James' little sister. On occasion there'd be a letter with the check, always written by Eudine, whose handwriting was the fanciest I'd ever seen, her capital letters big and swirly, her dots big circles floating about the i or j. In the letter she would talk about James' grades, about her job as a secretary for the athletic director and how her typing capabilities fared, her word per minute rate creeping up slowly, on into the fifties now. But beyond that there was nothing in her letters, just the simple everyday things Eudine must have thought might comfort us.

Even more seldom came photographs: one was of James in his full uniform, standing before a barracks of white corrugated metal. The photo was slightly blurred, and you couldn't quite make out the look on his face, whether he were smiling or just squinting into the Texas sun full in his face. In another photo stood Eudine and another girl, the two of them as good as twins, grinning at the camera and standing before what seemed the same barracks building. On the back Eudine had written *Clarenda and I, out front of the apartment.* It was in this way I found out that they were living in a barracks. She'd never made mention of that before, and the check that accompanied it, ten dollars made out to Mrs. Leston Hilburn, seemed even harder to surrender to Billie Jean at the bank.

The *Reader's Digest,* though, took me elsewhere, let me think of myself as someone still able to learn a thing or three about the world. I kept the newest issue between the mattresses in my bedroom, and when I went to bed, Leston always staying downstairs to ponder over what all it was we'd lost these few years, I pulled out my magazine, read it by the lamplight, and went to Geneva, Switzerland, or into the childhood of one of our Presidents, or onto the flight deck of an aircraft carrier right before Guadalcanal. When my eyes started to get heavier than I could keep open, I'd tuck the magazine back where it belonged, go downstairs, and touch Leston on the shoulder.

Every night he was at the kitchen sink, staring out the window at the black out there, or at his own reflection cast by the light in the kitchen, I was never able to tell which. And every night he jumped at my touch, whether I called out his name before I let my hand rest on his shoulder or not.

When I was through with the magazines I gave them to Cathedral, who seemed genuinely to want them, her thin hands holding each issue as if it were a precious photograph, only touching the edges, holding it back and away from her, admiring the paintings on the back.

But the last two issues I hadn't given up to her, each of them containing an article about what was called "Mongoloids," and I was thankful right from the start that someone somewhere'd finally taken out the second word, that the word *Idiot* and all it carried'd been cut off.

The first story was about an American woman who was born and raised in China by her missionary parents, and how she ended up having a Mongoloid child, and about her moving to the United States with this child. The upshot of the story was that she finally decided to give up the child to a special home in a place called Vineland, New Jersey, and how it was the hardest decision she ever made, but that it was all for the best of the child.

I didn't much care for the article, because it went against everything I'd tried to make for Brenda Kay—a loving household, proper medical treatment, good care while I was out of the house and making money for that treatment. And the woman's child didn't seem nearly as bad off as Brenda Kay: nobody said her son would die at two, nobody said he'd never walk.

What made me keep hold of that issue, though, was the note at the end of the article, set off in a little box: "In the next issue, *Reader's Digest* reports on a new miracle drug that helps increase IQ in 'Brain Food for the Backward Child.' Don't miss it!"

I wouldn't. I didn't have an idea what made for a backward child, whether that was a Mongoloid or simply a slow child, but I waited, read the article each night, felt more and more apart from that mother while hoping more and more for some deliverance with the next issue. I read the box and its message a hundred times, and when finally the 20th came around, the day my magazine came each month, I made certain I was out of the cafeteria by one, waiting by the mailbox in front of the house by one-twenty.

Mr. Boone, our mailman, drove up in his truck, leaned over and handed me the only piece of mail we got that day: *Reader's Digest.* I smiled for him, nodded, and had the wrapper off even before he'd pulled away.

I sat on the steps, Brenda Kay, I knew, already down for her nap—she still slept four or five hours a day—when Cathedral came out.

She stopped, said, "The new one here already," but I said nothing, ran my finger down the table of contents on the front, found the page, turned to it.

She left, called out, "Good-bye, Miss Jewel," and it was only then I looked up, saw her already out on the road, the thin cotton dress she had on wrinkling in the small spring breeze. "Oh," I said, then called out, "Good-bye, Cathedral."

She didn't turn, only lifted one hand above her head, waved, brought it back down.

I looked back to the magazine, found right after an article about the starving people in India what I'd waited for: "Brain Food for the Backward Child."

I stood, turning to the house and went upstairs to Brenda Kay's room, slowly opened the door, though I knew I wouldn't wake her, and closed it behind me. My rocker was in this room now, and I sat in it. I read the article, moving through it slowly, word for word, knowing that once I'd ended it the wait for this news, whatever it was, would be over.

The article was a short one, and only ran onto two pages. It was the story of a Mongoloid boy named David who'd tested in with an IQ of 49, but, after taking medicine from doctors at the Columbia School of Medicine, had it shoot up to 61, and he was reading now, and he was improving.

I had no idea what IQ Brenda Kay would have, didn't know anything about the Columbia School of Medicine other than that it was in New York City, didn't have any idea how much more than calcium glucanate shots this whole procedure cost. But what I knew was that something out there was holding hope, and so when I got to the end of the article and saw the boxed message there, I read it with a new and different kind of hope. Hope that maybe there was something out there could help me fix what was going on in our lives, the burden here.

"*Reader's Digest* suggests," the message read, "that if you would like more information about care for the retarded child, clip out the coupon below and mail it to: The National Association for Retarded Children, P.O. Box 1712, Los Angeles, California."

Below the box was a small form, lines for our address, the name of our child, how old she was.

Of course I stood, left the room for Annie and Billie

Jean's room, went through the top drawer of their dresser, what Billie Jean called the trash drawer, and got one of Annie's red pencils. I sat on her bed, filled out the form. The next morning, as soon as Cathedral got there, I left, headed for the five and dime for an envelope, then to the post office, had that coupon on its way to California and whoever it was would have to hand out help from that far away.

Brenda now called out "Momma!" one more time before I made it up to her room, pushed open the door to see her sitting up in bed, still trying to clap hands.

"My baby," I said, and she turned to me, on her face nothing for a moment, then the smile that always started these days out. She was happy, always happy, and for at least that much I was glad. There'd been more than enough ear infections, me pouring warm oil down into her ear and trying my best to make her lie still for a while, this going on every other month or so. And there were the shots, and how since she was seven months old she would let out a wail when the needle broke skin, her voice thick and dark coming up from her throat, her eyes squeezed shut in the pain of it. There was no difference in how she took them even to this day, always that cry, me having to turn my head, unable to watch while Dr. Beaudry and I both held her down. And there were still plenty of mornings when I'd come in here to find she'd wet or messed in the bed, and there'd be that extra chore to start out with, the weight of having an infant these five years, what I'd never counted on: feeding by hand, carrying her wherever we went, my baby drooling for years on end. But she was happy no matter what, it seemed; once she'd been given the shots she seemed to forget they ever existed; once the ear infections were gone, she'd slowly

crawl out the door if we didn't stop her. This morning she
was dry.

"Now let's go on to the toilet," I said, and I took her by
the hands, sort of half-lifted, half-dragged her to the edge
of the bed. She put her bare feet down, toes still twisted
up and bunched together in a way Dr. Basket'd informed
us they'd be for the rest of her life.

But she was walking now, and with her holding tight to
both my hands, she stepped across the floor, me behind
and above her, making certain she didn't fall.

She knew the way to the toilet, out her bedroom door
and to the left and the end of the hall, though if I were to
say to her Go left, or Go to the end of the hall, it'd mean
nothing. She only knew where to go, how to get there, fine
enough with me. "Momma," she said as we went,
"Momma, Momma."

When we reached the door into the bathroom, Leston
came out of our bedroom. He had on one of his old work-
shirts, a pair of blue jeans and suspenders on, what he
wore every day. But he'd combed his hair wet, slicked
back on the top and sides. He smelled of Old Spice, the
bottle he had in his dresser years old. He hadn't opened it
in maybe two or three years, since back when he went to
church with us all Sunday mornings.

He smiled, bent down and touched Brenda Kay's head,
then leaned and kissed her forehead.

"My baby girl," he said. Without his eyes meeting mine,
he stood, leaned into my neck and kissed me. Then he
turned, headed off down the stairs.

There was nothing to say, and I only stood there,
watching him as he took the stairs quicker than any
morning in recent history.

I looked down at Brenda Kay. She was half-turned to

him, watching him, too. Her eyes were open wide, her mouth open, as if this person were a stranger, someone she'd never seen before, even after five and a half years inside this house. And maybe, I thought, that's exactly what he was to her, why she looked at him this way every time she saw him.

Then something came clear to me, and I knew what he'd already planned for our outing. And just as clear I knew, too, how I'd introduce him to the notion of California.

We were on the road east toward Ashe Lake by nine-thirty, Leston, Brenda Kay and me in the front seat, the children in the bed of the pickup. On occasion I'd glance back through the rear window to see Billie Jean with one hand holding down her hair, the other on the edge of the bed, her eyes always ahead of us, watching what was coming up next; or Wilman reaching out a fist to Burton, Burton dodging, moving just so, Wilman's swing lost to air. Annie never moved, only huddled next to Billie Jean, her legs pulled up close to her chin, her hands holding on to her shins. She only stared across the bed to the opposite wall, her red hair in pigtails that bounced with each dip in the road.

Leston put his arm on top of the seat back, let his fingers just touch my shoulder. He tilted his head to one side, his eyes on the road, said, "Figured we'd rent us a canoe. From that old nigger up there, Jason." He paused. "What do you think?"

Brenda Kay started rocking forward and back right then, her hands tight together in her lap. Her mouth was open, her jaw pushed forward so that all you could see of her mouth were her bottom teeth, her chin way out. Then she started clicking her teeth together, her jaw just barely moving, going to some rhythm only she knew about.

I touched a hand to her back, and she only kept with the slow, smooth rocking.

I said, "What about money?"

He laughed, short and clean, like he was tossing aside the whole idea of what things cost.

He said, "I got a few cents saved up." He paused, looked at me for the first time today. "No big bankroll," he said, smiling. "But a few cents."

I turned, looked to the road. My hand was still on Brenda Kay's back, making slow circles now, never certain what it was she thought me doing by touching her: sometimes she'd be startled, turn quick as she could to give me the cold-eyes and empty stare she gave Leston each time she saw him; other times she'd turn, smile at me, her thin red lips nearly gone for the smile, the row of bottom baby teeth right there. This time she did nothing, still rocked, as though I weren't even there.

"The children'd like that," I said. "We haven't done that since before Brenda Kay was born."

I looked at him. I wanted to see how he'd take that, my words right out in the open. We never spoke about Before, that word gone from the ones we always used, ones that usually dealt with money.

But he didn't flinch, didn't even move. His fingers still lay on my shoulder. His eyes were on the road, and he said, "Figured you—" and he stopped. He looked at me, one hand on the steering wheel, his elbow out his window, the air cool and dew-wet air out there. "Figured you and me, we could take a little ride ourselves." He paused, swallowed. "You and me."

I took my eyes from his, looked back to Brenda Kay.

She'd started in to rocking too far forward, too far back, the slow arc her body made too big for the cab, her back hitting the seat a little harder each time.

Leston took his arm from the seat top, put both hands on the wheel. He glanced at Brenda Kay, then to the road, then to her again.

I reached my other hand to Brenda Kay's chest, tried to hold her. But she was strong, and it took me a minute or so before I could get her to stop, until she was sitting up straight again, breathing hard, cheeks flushed, her small fingers still clasped in her lap.

"With Brenda Kay, of course," I said then, one arm around her shoulder. With my other hand I touched her cheek, felt her smooth skin damp with sweat.

"No," he said. He was smiling at me again. "Just what I said. You and me. Billie Jean can take care of her, does it often enough already."

I knew what he wanted, there was no doubt. And he was right: Brenda Kay'd be fine with Billie Jean. Still, I had to play this out the best I could, wanted him to feel what was coming was all his idea.

I said, "Leston, are you certain?" I tilted my head, drew up my eyebrows in a way I knew he'd believe the rest of his life.

He said, "Positive." He let go the steering wheel with one hand, placed that hand on Brenda Kay's head, patted it as though he'd never had any children of his own, his fingers flat and stiff, afraid to touch her. "She'll be fine," he said.

"I don't know," I said, and crossed my arms to show him how worried I was, then settled back in my seat, already figuring on what I'd say once we were out on the water.

Chapter 14

Leston parked the truck out front the nigger Jason's shanty. Not a hundred yards behind the place was Ashe Lake, his shanty looking like every other shanty I'd ever seen: clapboards weathered to nothing, a huge flat stone for a front step, smoke from a chimney.

He and Leston stood out front, Jason's eyes on the ground before him, Leston with his hands in his blue jeans pockets and rocking ever so slowly forward and back on his heels. He looked directly at Jason, just talking to him.

I leaned out the window, hollered, "Leston, let's get going."

He only glanced at me, turned his head the smallest bit, then back to Jason, who, suddenly, looked too much like Tory to me: hair the same flecked gray, eyes down on the ground the same way, raggedy clothes.

The engine rumbled beneath me. Brenda Kay'd started giving in to rocking forward and back again, and the boys were standing in the bed of the truck, chucking rocks they'd gotten from somewhere off into the woods. Then Leston pulled one hand out of a pocket, looked into his palm, held it out to Jason. Money for the canoe.

Jason lifted a hand, waved off Leston, shook his head. Still he wouldn't look up.

But Leston wouldn't let it pass at that, instead stood with his hand and the money out.

"Momma!" Brenda Kay screamed then, my name choked off in her throat, high-pitched and piercing, making me jump at it. She was going full tilt again, her head almost smashing into the scratched green metal of the dash as she swung forward, the back of her head hitting the seat as she slammed backward.

I took hold of her, and for a few moments I, too, was swinging with her, lost for an instant in the cold rhythm she carried through her body, made her move as hard as she did, and I held her even tighter, afraid I might lose control, though I already had. Her getting to this moment, this abandon, was my fault, me watching what was happening out the window instead of what was going on in my child right next to me.

Because that was what being her mother was about: watching, every second, waiting and watching and waiting. Every moment, every breath of my life was taken up with care for her, and how best to keep control of her life, then my children's lives, and, finally, my husband's. When Brenda Kay screamed, when she pulled a chair over on herself, when she wet her underdrawers, when she crawled too close to the fireplace, when she banged her chin on a kitchen drawer she pulled out too fast, when she threw up, when she had a hair in her eye, when she found a sharpened pencil, when she slept, when she ate, when she drank and breathed and breathed, I was protecting her, stopping her, carrying her, helping her. That was who I was, and as I struggled yet again to slow her down, to stop this wild movement—she'd done this more and more of late, the movement what Dr. Basket'd informed me was merely her own way of learning to coordinate her muscles, her body trying to take charge over itself as she grew older—I wondered when this all would stop, or if it would, or if I really hoped it would never stop at all. This purpose, this mission I had now was the giant center of everything I did, and I thought again of what I was here to do, what that canoe meant to me and what it meant to Leston, and how it was Brenda Kay and her welfare, her life, I was after fixing.

I had her tight in my arms, had her stopped, finally, the both of us breathing hard this time, my eyes closed with the effort.

When I opened them, there out front of the shanty stood Leston and Jason, Leston's hand and the money still held out to him. But Leston was turned to us. The morning light played across his face to make even deeper the wrinkles of his forehead, even more severe the lines beside his eyes as he strained to see what exactly was going on in the cab of his truck.

I glanced over my shoulder and out the rear window. Billie Jean was staring in at us, Wilman standing up and with his arm cocked back and ready to throw the rock in his hand, Burton standing with his hands in his pockets. Only Annie wasn't looking, simply stared off into the woods.

I turned to the front window, hollered, "We're fine, Leston. Let's just get on."

He turned back to Jason, reached to Jason's shirt pocket, dropped the few bits of change in.

Jason nodded a quick couple of times, pointed off to his left, all without looking up. Then Leston looked back to the truck, snapped his fingers once and pointed to where Jason had.

The boys jumped out of the bed and disappeared around the back of the shanty. A minute later, here they

came, the scarred and dull blue canoe they carried hiding
their heads.

I looked down at Brenda Kay, my arms still around her
shoulders, and marveled at how strong she could be, the
power in her muscle and bone. And I wondered what she
saw as the boys came nearer the truck, the canoe upside
down and on their heads. But her eyes were filled with the
same empty thickness they always were, only staring, my
baby quiet and still.

Leston slowly drove the truck down a two-track dirt road,
the center of it high with weeds that disappeared from
before the hood as we moved over them, vines and
branches off magnolias and low pines and water oak all
coming down from above. I'd looked again out the rear
window, saw the boys, one on each side of the canoe and
with a hand holding tight to an edge, the other hand
pushing back the branches.

We parked at the end of the road, and let the boys take
the canoe out first, watched from shore as they made like
Red Indians, war-whooping and screaming, the two of
them working the paddles in good time, disappearing to
the north where the lake bent and wandered off. The only
thing left of them was the slice of empty water where'd
been a thick carpet of lily pads before they'd launched,
and the sound every once in a while of their yells carried
across the water to us.

They were getting on now, it hit me as the last of their
hollering came to me. Burton was already fifteen, Wilman
thirteen, though he had a few pounds on his older brother,
stood only an inch or so shorter. Billie Jean was already
nineteen. Annie, nine, and as Billie Jean and I spread out
the old red wool blanket we'd always used just for picnics

like this one, these sorts of occasions commonplace before
Brenda Kay'd come along, I wondered what had happened
to that time. But I knew even before my next breath that
the answer was right in front of me, already crawling
across the blankets, bringing on the soles of her heavy
white shoes sand and grass and mud, my five-and-a-half-
year-old infant.

"Brenda Kay," I said, and she looked up at me, first the
empty eyes, then the smile. She was on her hands and
knees, but lifted a hand up, fingers spread wide. I couldn't
tell if she was trying to wave at me, or if the move was
something she'd had no choice over, only her body doing
more of what the doctor in New Orleans said she'd do.
There was no way to tell.

Once I'd gotten her sitting up and brushed off as best I
could, and after I'd given Annie the job of going back to
the truck for the food and Billie Jean the task of seeing if
she couldn't head up the lake aways, call the boys back in,
I sat on the blanket. Brenda Kay was in front of me, trying
again to clap her hands. She made sounds all the while,
the same sounds she always made: open-mouthed hums
that wandered all over, up and down, soft to loud to soft
again. I put my arms around her from behind, pulled her
close to me, and held her hands with mine, clapped with
her to my own rhythm, something we did every day. I
thought there might be in the words I sang and in the feel
of my arms around her a healing power; love, like I'd said
to Leston in the cab of the truck on the way home from
New Orleans that first time, was the biggest power we
could any of us give her. I sang in her ear the first verse to
"Love Lifted Me," a song that seemed to calm her down,
and that made her hum all the more. I couldn't help but

think of her humming as her own trying to sing with me, more evidence we were on the road to some recovery from the blow we'd been getting these five and a half years.

"Listen," I said out loud to Leston, who leaned back on his elbows beneath the live oak we'd laid the blanket under. He had his feet crossed at the ankles, his eyes on the lake. His eyes creased closed with the smoke off the cigarette at his lips. He reached up with one hand, took out the cigarette, shot out smoke. He looked at us.

"Love lifted me," I sang quietly, clapping Brenda Kay's hands together as I did, "love lifted me, when nothing else would help, love lifted me."

Brenda Kay hummed and hummed along, now and again moving her mouth in some way that changed the sounds she gave out, made them near-words, all of them choked and stiff, but sounds all the same.

Leston smiled, looked back to the lake. He put the cigarette to his lips, leaned back on both elbows again. He said, "Ought to put you both in the church choir," and looked at me.

I smiled at him, hoping he'd see the joy his baby daughter was capable of, the happiness she held in her heart, the two of us clapping away to words that meant nothing to her, me smiling away at her own words, ones I knew I'd never understand, either.

But then Leston turned from us, his eyes back out to the water, and I knew his mind was on the canoe, and what we'd do once we were out there.

And though I was smiling at him, at his boyish try to keep hidden from me precisely what he wanted to do, a piece of me kept tearing inside, sharp with the knowledge that, of all my family, he might have been the biggest casualty of all, the one most laden with the weight of what God had dealt: no job, a retarded daughter, children growing up and away. A wife working in a grammar school cafeteria. His might've been the biggest burden of all, though when I'd first met him he was untouchable, a strong boy, me a brand-new schoolteacher in a two-teacher school in East Columbia, him just moved from home with his eyes on owning his own lumberyard.

Once I'd recovered from the whipping I'd received from Mrs. Archibald, things around and in me started to changing, and I finally surrendered myself to the work at hand: my classes. I saw that there was no means of escape except to take the years handed you, make them your own by holding them tight, wringing from them all you could.

It'd worked: by the time I was to graduate, somewhere in my mind had been planted the idea of college. Though I can't remember for certain when it happened, I know the notion was put there by Mrs. Esther Faulk, my Latin teacher, an aged woman with whom I'd met the last two years. The two of us and four other girls met in her class-room Tuesday and Thursday afternoons to work not only on Latin, but on our other coursework as well. That room became a friend of mine, so much more giving and filled with light than where I slept at night.

But there came a day a week or so before graduation when the topic came up, the word "college" uttered by me for the first time, the two of us there in her room and going over I can't remember what. The other girls'd already left.

"What is it you plan to do once you leave here?" she'd said out of nowhere, maybe in the middle of one last geometry problem, perhaps at the end of a bit of Latin I'd done my best to translate on the spot for her. She was old, older even than Missy Cook, and wore her hair wrapped tight in a bun that sat at the very top of her head.

"College," was all I'd said, and suddenly the idea sounded ridiculous, a place I'd never end up because I knew it cost money, something I had none of at all: Missy Cook's house had burned down in March, and she'd died not three weeks later, living in the Pastor and his wife's home.

I'd been told of the funeral by Mrs. Winthrop, informed by her I could be brought there and back if I so desired.

But I hadn't desired that at all, not out of hate for Missy Cook—that was over, I knew, since I'd turned and run back to school on railroad tracks two years before, over and done with in the whipping I'd gotten, over and done with in the cold metal of the flagpole on my face.

Over, too, with each letter Missy Cook'd sent me starting some six months after I'd been there. The letters came like clockwork each first Monday of the month, and were written on delicate, perfumed stationery, her handwriting always elegant and billowing and beautiful. In each letter she suggested I come back home—home her word, not mine—for a short visit, during which we could chat, that being her word as well.

And at the end of each letter was written a Bible verse, divine signals of how I was to act, her never wanting to surrender control over me: "The Lord rewarded me according to my righteousness; according to the cleanness of my hands, hath he recompensed me. Psalm 18:20," she once wrote; another time, she wrote, "I have taught thee in the way of wisdom; I have led thee in right paths. Proverbs 4:11."

But with each letter she sent I sent one back, mine written on the coarse and heavy paper I received from Mrs.

Winthrop, and in each letter back I politely declined, citing any number of homework assignments and class activities as my reason. And I finished each letter with a verse of my own, my own signals from the same book she drew hers from: "For thou wilt save the afflicted people; but wilt bring down high looks. Psalm 18:27," I wrote, and, "A high look, and a proud heart, and the plowing of the wicked, is sin. Proverbs 21:4." And still her letters had come.

No, I hadn't gone back for her funeral, because that part of me was over, long dead, and the self-pity I knew Missy Cook had wanted me to feel, pity for the sad and ugly life she knew I must be leading at this girl's school, would only have been magnified were I ever to lay eyes on her again. What she didn't know, though, and what she'd never know now, was that there'd been no room in my life for the kind of self-pity I'd been stripped of there in front of all the girls, in front of the hall mistresses, in front of Tory. Just no more room for that luxury: feeling sorry for myself.

I'd chosen not to go back because this was my home now, where I lived, worked, ate and slept. Here.

"College," I said again, only this time in a whisper, a word to myself I wasn't sure I wanted divulged even to Mrs. Faulk.

"Then go," she said, and I remember looking up at her from where I sat in the front row desk, her eyes above her half-glasses right on mine.

"How?" I said. "I don't have any money."

"What if," she started, and leaned back in her chair, a move she'd never made in front of us before, her back always straight as a board, her hands always holding her glasses or papers or both. She took off the glasses, and I watched as she placed them on her desk. Then she turned, looked out the window. It was hot that day, June already and all those windows open, air in the room, warm and thick. All you could see out there was the green of trees, the haze-blue sky.

I looked at her, saw a drop of sweat slip down her cheek, disappear into the high collar of her dress, and I saw again my mother in a fever, sheets soaked, her near on to death.

"What if," she said again, "the school were to help you out in this situation. If the school were to contribute in its way to your furthering your education?"

She hadn't taken her eyes off whatever she saw out the window. I said nothing.

"You have performed here exceptionally well, even in the face of your, shall we say, indiscretions early on." She looked at me, smiled, but not a smile that took glee in the memory of my being whipped. Rather, it was almost a conspiratorial grin, and I remember being startled at that, at the warmth of a smile brought on by my sad attempt at escape.

She looked back out the window, said, "We are prepared to pay for your tuition at Pearl River Junior College, provided you do there the best work you are capable of producing."

She turned her eyes to me again. She smiled, said, "What is it you wish to do as a career?"

I hadn't even the need to blink, to take in a breath, before the old answer came to me, what had been with me even before my daddy'd died. I said, "A teacher."

I wrote her letters from school, made the hour walk to the Mississippi Industrial School for Girls at least once a month, sat in on some of her classes, even taught a few sessions myself over the two years I was at Pearl River, furthering my education. I took courses in literature, courses in mathematics, courses in Latin, courses in drawing, courses in physical education. And, after two years of studying and listening and talking and reading, I found myself with a job at a two-teacher school in Columbia, Mississippi, the superintendent of schools for Marion County a friend of Mrs. Esther Faulk's.

My class was the first through fourth grade, and that first morning I wore a new blue dress I'd paid for with money I'd earned over the summer working as a typist for Pearl River, no lace on that dress anywhere, no ribbons, only a blue dress that spoke nothing but *teacher.* I entered the room, saw before me the faces of thirty-three children, all of them seated in desks, inkwells dry, desktops scarred and carved. Some of the bigger kids in the back rows wouldn't look my way, some sneered at me. A girl, red hair in pigtails, picked at her nose; another girl, this one with fine blond hair and seated in the front row, had her hands flat on the desktop, smiling, no front teeth. Another student, this one a boy in the third row back, had a black eye, a bruised chin, his hair filthy and mussed.

But how these children looked didn't matter, nor did the fact I'd be three weeks in getting ink, two more in getting pens, two months in scraping together from castoffs at schools around the county enough McGuffey Readers to start in on.

None of that mattered, not even the fact I was making only twenty dollars a month, because I was a teacher now. Because I'd gotten here, had survived and in fact had fixed in the best way I could everything God'd seen fit to throw me for whatever reasons He'd had, reasons that wouldn't come clear to me until years later, when I'd gotten from him the giant blessing and curse of a retarded child, the one I held in my arms right now, and to whom I sang hymns in His honor. He, my God, wanted to see how I could fix this huge piece of all our lives.

Billie Jean was coming back toward us now along the old trail that circled the lake, a trail the children'd all explored at one time or another before Brenda Kay was born, that word *before* pushing in on me again. She pushed back branches and vines as she came, waved a hand in front of her face at the gnats that'd started in on us.

And I saw the boys coming round the cypress out to the end of the point, the two of them still hollering, still paddling that canoe with the same mighty grace only young men could have, each stroke of their paddles reaching deep into the water and into themselves for whatever new strength they could find.

Annie set the basket next to Brenda Kay and me, then sat down, held her knees to her chest, stared out to the lake. Somewhere, too, James was breathing, taking in air and letting it out just as we all were here, him in Texas, a place so foreign, so unimaginable all I could see of it was a barracks painted white, two girls standing before it, one named Eudine, the other Clarenda.

And I asked myself—I had to—what I had done wrong, what I'd done to God in heaven, to have been given these fine five other children, and my good husband, each of them slipping out of my hands, it was simple to see, the older the baby grew. And I had no answer, no voice in me like'd come to Cathedral when she'd been hanging clothes, God's mystery rising in her heart until those words burst in miraculous sounds from her own mouth. There was nothing, no word from Him up above. Only me here, and the knowledge that what I had to do today, here, on this picnic, was my best chance to fix our lives.

Chapter 15

Wilman and Burton gave the canoe a hard push, and we glided out onto the water. I sat in the bow, facing Leston and the shore, watched Wilman and Burton take a couple extra steps into the water, their blue jeans wet up the knees now. Then they stopped, the two of them hands on hips, just watching. Annie'd climbed up into the live oak, almost hidden in the leaves, and watched us, too. Billie Jean, on the wool blanket with Brenda Kay in her lap, hollered out, "Y'all don't worry!" She picked up one of Brenda Kay's hands, waved with it. Brenda Kay's mouth hung open, and even as we headed out onto the lake, my children growing smaller with each stroke Leston made with the paddle, I could see the neat white row of Brenda Kay's bottom teeth.

Then we were alone.

We were silent a few minutes, the only sound the thin wash of water against the canoe as we cut across the lake, Leston choosing to head us south, I could see, away from that old trail, and the possibility of the children following us. I knew what he was after.

By this time—lunch already over, the sun straight up so the only shadows cast onto the lake were those where trees hung out over water—Leston's smoothed-back hair had started to loosen up, strands here and there lifted on the small breeze, his forehead shiny wet with the work of paddling us. He had another cigarette in his mouth, his paddle into the water with the same ease, the same abandon and grace the boys had. The cigarette was burned down near to nothing before he thought to pause in the paddling, take it out, flick it with his thumb and first finger. In the quiet out there, my children already gone from view, I thought I could hear the hiss of the butt as it hit water.

I looked away from him, there on the piece of gray wood that served as a seat, the paddle flat in his lap.

The water was green, a thick green that wouldn't let you see more than a foot or so into it. I looked at the water for a long while, until Leston put the paddle back in, started us on to wherever we were going.

I said, "Mr. Hilburn, how've you been?" I looked up from the water.

"Just fine," he said between strokes.

"Just fine," I said. "That's good." I waited a few moments, said, "But if you care at all to elaborate on that, I'd be glad to give a listen."

"Elaborate," he said.

"Talk more on it."

He stopped paddling, and smiled at me. "I know what elaborate means, Miss Jewel," he said. He ran his hand back through his hair, tried to put it in some kind of order.

"Then go ahead," I said. I let a hand touch the water, watched my fingers go into the green.

"No need," he said, "No need at all." He started paddling again, and I could see we were heading back toward the marsh end of the lake, the bulrushes and sawgrass it was easy to get lost in, to disappear behind.

The first time I laid eyes on Leston I'd been unimpressed.

I'd just started at the school, had attended the East

Columbia Church there only two Sundays, my job as
schoolteacher also to teach the same grades in Sunday
School.

That second Sunday one Mrs. Luvena Hilburn'd
thought it her Christian duty to introduce herself to me,
and told me as we stood outside the bright red door of the
church that she should offer me an empty room in her
house, one that'd been recently vacated by her son, Leston,
who'd headed out to McComb to work in a lumber mill.

Mrs. Hilburn was a heavy woman, but kind all the
same, her eyes a beautiful, clear green, a green I couldn't
know then would be a green I would see the rest of my
days.

Then a tall, thin young man—*a boy*, were the first two
words in my mind that morning—came up behind Mrs.
Hilburn, touched her shoulder, and nodded to me as she
turned around.

"This here's Leston, my boy," she said, "the one whose
room's empty and awaiting you to come and live in. If you
see that as being the Lord's will." She turned back to me,
and Leston put out his hand.

"Ma'am," he said. I hesitated, not certain what it would
mean, a brand-new schoolteacher shaking hands with an
unmarried man, but I shook it all the same, felt the calluses on his fingers, his palm.

There'd been no more thought of him than that: a
green-eyed boy who worked a lumber mill in McComb.
September heat banged down on us all, my throat parched
from talking all week in school, then all Sunday morning
to the same children: the same girl with red pigtails, the
same boy with the black-eye bruise gone to yellow now,
the same fine-blond girl with hands flat on her little white
Bible instead of the desktop.

I looked to Mrs. Hilburn, fanning herself now with a bamboo fan from inside. But unlike the fans of my childhood, the ones I remembered from when I'd sat between my momma and daddy, there were no hymns printed on these, no Psalm 23. Only a gold cross on both sides, lines of gold radiating out, so that, as the cross of Jesus fluttered before me, I wondered how best to find out how much she wanted to rent the room for, and how that amount would seal whether or not it was the Lord's will for me to stay with her.

But I hadn't had to ask. She said, "Two dollars a week is all." I looked up at her. She smiled, said, "Is that the Lord's will?"

"It is," I said, and we laughed.

Her son was already gone. I hadn't even seen him go.

I moved in that afternoon, left the Columbia Hotel, a two-story building with eight rooms and two bathrooms, carrying the new satchel Mrs. Faulk'd given me for graduating Pearl River, in it everything I owned, which wasn't much: one other dress, brown and of the same design as the blue; my underclothes; a few books, including my McGuffey Readers; the fountain pen I'd received from Mrs. Faulk upon graduation from the Mississippi Industrial School for Girls. Tablets of paper. A red pencil. A photograph.

When I got there, her house only a mile or so outside town, I simply knocked at the screen door, called out, "Mrs. Hilburn?" and the door pushed open. This small, round lady with the green eyes and hair done the same as Mrs. Faulk'd always worn hugged me, then pulled back, took in my face, a hand still on my shoulder.

"We're so pleased you saw your way to doing God's will here," she said, laughed again. I laughed, too.

She took the satchel from my hand, set it down next to an overstuffed chair that seemed defeated, its seat flat, the back of it indented where someone'd leaned for years on end. I looked round the front room, saw a fireplace, wood walls painted pale blue, two rockers, the bottoms of the runners just bare wood.

I could live here.

She took my hand, led me back to the kitchen, where sat a table full of people, food heaped and steaming in the middle of it: cheese grits, chicken, red-eye gravy, snap beans and bacon, fried corn and red peppers. All of it hot, filling me up with the wonderful scent of so much home-cooked food. Everybody's plates were empty, all of them about to dig in.

"You timed this just fine, you did," Mrs. Hilburn said, and suddenly I was aware of all five faces at the table turned to me, smiling.

Mrs. Hilburn, my hand still in hers, held her other hand out in a gesture toward the older man who sat at the head. "This here's my husband, Mr. James Baxter Hilburn."

He stood, as did the other two males at the table, the room suddenly cluttered with the sounds of chairs pushed back. "Pleased," Mr. James Baxter Hilburn said, and nodded, smiling. He was tall, taller even than that Leston boy I'd met earlier, and had a thick head of white hair, blue eyes, a white Sunday shirt buttoned up to his neck. He held a hand out to the empty chair and table setting next to him. "Have a seat?" he said.

"I'd be honored, Mr. Hilburn," I said. I let go Mrs. Hilburn's hand, made my way round the table, sidling past the other boy, this one younger than Leston, only a few days into his teens, I figured. Then I was next to Mr. Hilburn, and I sat.

The males all sat, and Mr. Hilburn quick closed his eyes, clasped his hands together in a fierce grip I thought might break bones. He closed his eyes. "Oh Father," he started, all of it so quick my eyes were still on him as he started into blessing the food, the day, the bounty we all of us encountered every minute we walked God's green earth, and giving thanks, too, for this new schoolteacher who'd be living with them from here on out, Amen.

I'd gotten my eyes closed along about halfway through his prayer, opened them only an instant past that last holy word, and saw everyone at the table digging in, shoveling food onto plates like it'd be thrown out in a minute if they didn't.

Then came the introductions: next to me, on my right, was the oldest daughter, Mildred, hair blue-black, eyes the blue of her father's. She turned to me only a moment, smiled and nodded as she pulled a chicken-back onto her plate with two fingers; next to her was the other boy there, Toxie. "The son of my first daughter, Brenda Kay, deceased, may she rest in peace," Mrs. Hilburn said all in a breath, and though I'd felt the need somehow to say I was sorry at that, Toxie'd only leaned forward in his chair so I could see him around his sister, smiled wide, gave a small wave. "Hey," he said.

Next to Mrs. Hilburn, on her right, was Leston, "Who you already met," she said. Leston was eating, his mouth full and chewing away. He nodded, smiled. Next to him was the other black-haired girl, Martha, eyes the same blue as her father's, too, and I started trying to piece things out here: Mrs. Hilburn with a deceased daughter old enough to have had a teenage son; two other daughters with no resemblance whatsoever to the brother, Leston.

Before I could say a thing, not that I would have—I'd

have ended up lying in the dark in my new room here in this house and eventually figuring it all out—Mrs. Hilburn said, "Mr. Hilburn's my second husband. My first was killed in a logging accident years ago. Leston and me took on Mr. Hilburn's name once I married him," she said, "though before that we were Scoggins."

No one at the table got teary, blinked, shrugged. Not even Leston. Nothing. They only ate, and then Mr. Hilburn said, "These here is my daughters, Mildred and Martha. They momma's dead, too. I got two other daughters, they living in Biloxi, married."

"Oh," I said, and looked down at my plate, still empty. "Oh," I said again, and felt a blush coming up on me, as if I'd been the one to pry into these affairs, dug them up like old bones from somewhere.

"Darling, don't you worry none," Mrs. Hilburn said. She smiled, said, "Fill your plate or go hungry, child."

I filled it.

We were near on to the marsh now, and still Leston hadn't elaborated, hadn't given up to anything of what his mind was on, what he was thinking. Even though I knew. But I wanted some of that thinking out in the air here, out on this breeze.

I said, "Leston honey, you remember when we met?"

He was quiet, took one stroke, then another. He said, "I do."

"Tell me of it," I said, and I put a hand up to my eyes, blocked the light from above so I could see his face without squinting.

"You was there," he said, still paddling.

"But I want to hear of it from you. What you remember."

He paused, let the paddle hang in the water a few inches, and I could see the eddy around and behind it, felt the canoe slow up. "What do you want to talk about this for?" he said. He let the paddle sit a moment more, then picked it up, dug into water again.

A few moments later, I said, "Do you remember the watch?"

And just as I'd figured on happening, he gave up with the paddling, his face breaking into the grin I'd hoped would come along with the memories long buried in him.

He shook his head, still smiling, and said, "Now, Jewel, you know I do."

"So tell me," I said. I brought the hand down from my eyes, let it trail in the water, saw the smallest eddies my fingers made of their own.

He lay the paddle across his lap, leaned his forearms on it. "This paddling hurts like hell," he said, and he laughed, the sound he made so foreign, strange and familiar at once after years without it, and I couldn't help but join him.

"You asked," he said, the laugh falling away. "And I can't figure for what." He paused, shook his head. "But the watch," he started, "the watch and sister Mildred and how I gave it to you each night to keep under your pillow and think about me."

"And?" I said. There was no sound now, no water across the bow, no children, no birds close enough to enter the quiet surrounding us.

He said, "I love you, Jewel," and he looked up at me. The words nearly knocked my wind out, words that hadn't come from him in years, not since, as best I could remember, when Brenda Kay was born, the two of us alone in a hospital room. They were words I hadn't heard from him since Before, and all I could say, all I could offer him right there on the water, were my own words, ones I couldn't remember offering up to him myself since then: "I love you, Leston," I said almost in a whisper, and I made sure my eyes were square on his, that I saw as deep into that deepwater green as I could. I wanted him to know I was here, with him, not back on shore and worried with our baby.

Finally that moment was gone, his eyes falling from mine in some embarrassed boy's fall as he spoke: "Once I'd moved back into Daddy Hilburn's house after the mill closed, you and I started to courting. Every night I'd give you my Daddy Scoggins' watch."

He shook his head again, gave a quick snicker. "Kids," he said. "We was just kids," he said. "Silly."

"Not silly, not at all," I said.

He glanced up at me, hands in front of him, forearms on the paddle. "And you took to knocking on my room door each morning early, before you left for school. Before anybody else was up in the house because that's the only place you could work, no quiet in the house with Toxie there." He stopped, shrugged. "Toxie," he said again. "Those early mornings Toxie'd never wake up, even when you came into the room after you'd knocked real quiet, he'd be asleeping. And you'd kiss me awake, and you'd give me back my watch."

He looked up at me again, and he was blushing, the idea of that kiss making my own heart speed up, the trouble and danger and wrath we were asking for, all for me waking him up with a kiss. Because I'd seen in him, even before he'd moved back from the mill, that he was a good man, a good son who loved his mother and step-father both, who took Toxie up with him and fished with him, chopped wood with him, swam at the creek with him. And he loved his sisters, too, though stepsisters they were; gave them while he was working at the mill a piece of his wages in addition to that he gave his momma and stepdaddy, sometimes bought the girls rosewater and ribbons whenever the crew'd made a trip to Pascagoula, brought back to Toxie tiny carved wood animals he'd made the long nights spent at the camp. He was a good man, true-hearted, and as he sat there before me, I saw I'd been right about him: saw the care with which he'd taken showing James how to tie his shoes one winter morning, James on his lap, Leston's arms round him and holding him close and warm, whispering in his firstborn's ear which string to hold where; saw the houses he'd built for us out of wooded land and with those arms that'd seemed so thin when I'd first met him, houses built callus upon callus, thousands of layers of him wearing away with all the trees he'd cut down, all the stumps he'd blasted and hauled; saw the niggers we'd fed and employed for years. Those hands had been through all with him, and now they were almost useless, only good for holding a mug of cold coffee of an evening.

He took in a breath, kept on with what I'd led him into telling. "Then sister Mildred sees you one morning coming out the room, and she comes up behind you, sweeps you out the house and onto the porch outside, and tears into you, tells you you ought to be ashamed of your hussy behavior, sleeping overnight with her step-brother, the two of you not even betrothed."

He stopped again, laughed again, shook his head again. And I laughed, too, because of what was coming, the end of the story.

"And you says to her," Leston said, " 'Why, Sister Mildred, I only stopped in to say good-bye to him for the day. And,' you says, 'we *are* betrothed.' And I'm listening through the wall to all this, you two out on the porch, my heart about to bust out my chest because, I guessed, that was it. Done and done. I didn't ask you to marry me yet, though you knew darn well it was back there in my head somewheres. But that morning it was done and done. No going back."

"No going back," I said, and I scooted forward, rocked the canoe on my way toward one of those hands. I got near to them, took first one, then the other, held them hard.

Leston was looking at me now, the smile gone from his face, just those eyes and his wild hair, the growing-old man who was this growing-old woman's husband, and I leaned to that face, kissed him long and strong and soft, a kiss like none I'd given him in years, not since Before. A kiss like a few whispered words of the lost language we'd once known.

I pulled away. I let go his hands, scooted back to the bow, sat there as before. I smiled, said, "Don't you have some more paddling to do?"

"Yes ma'am," he said, and started toward the bulrushes.

Chapter 16

We made love there in the canoe, the whole of it hidden away in the bulrushes, Leston having maneuvered us in here, weaving along back channels, the bulrushes and sawgrass rising up round us like a curtain grown only for this.

Though I'd feigned ignorance the whole time he was taking us in here, him smiling back without a word, I'd known since he'd come out of our room this morning with hair slicked back, the Old Spice on, that this was where we'd been headed.

Even up to when he jammed the canoe into the thick growth, even until the moment he placed the paddle behind him and started moving up to me, I'd still gone on along with him, let him think he was the one whose idea this all was, who'd forged our opportunity to make love, all this planned because of whatever small relief had come with Brenda Kay taking her first steps, steps a sign something might be headed for the better.

But once I'd gotten him to speak out on the open water, once I'd heard our story in his words, there'd been in me my own desire for this, so that as I lifted my skirts to him, helped him myself with his jeans buttons and gently lifted the suspenders off his shoulders, then felt him inside me for the first time in all that while, there rose in me the low

moans, the sounds I'd heard our first night together in a
hotel in Hattiesburg. There rose up around us the ghosts
of my momma and daddy, the sounds they two made, and
I couldn't help but remember our wedding night, couldn't
help but recall the fear I'd felt, the trembling I'd made at
his touch, the two of us finally alone. He'd been seated on
the edge of the bed, me standing before him, and he
undressed me with careful hands, my dress taking months
to find its way free of buttons and clasps, his big hands
fumbling, trembling of their own. He was young then,
only a boy, me only a girl, our bodies new and unex-
plained, and when finally my dress fell away from around
me, and then my petticoats and slip and underclothes,
he'd leaned back, taking me in with his eyes. And then I
undressed him, and we started in on the long and beautiful task of learning each other.

The love we made on this day, in a canoe on Ashe Lake,
seemed as close to that first time as I could imagine, yet it
was different, changed in that I found comfort in the ghosts
my sounds brought forth, sounds that now, too, Leston
gave out, we two in our forties and making love like the
children we were that first night, the canoe rocking, water
sloshing beneath us. There was comfort in the ghosts of my
parents, some sort of reconciliation, peace in the unformed
words Leston and I made, me understanding suddenly
what it must have been like for my own mother to make
love each Saturday night to a man who'd already left her, a
man she might never get back, and I wondered if my being
here, now, him deep inside me, my arms around his shoulders, my mouth kissing his forehead, I might bring Leston
back from across the deep chasm that'd formed since
Brenda Kay'd been born, from the dark world he lived
nights, sullen with the knowledge he had no work, that his

children were growing up and away, his wife's life filled
with a retarded child, and the cold knowledge the daughter he'd fathered would never be right, never be just a girl,
a beautiful, normal girl named for Leston's beautiful sister.

But then the other purpose took shape in me, twisted
itself into form and being, and I remembered California,
remembered the truth and promise that seemed to shine
from that word. Leston could find work there, I knew;
Billie Jean'd go with no more than the clothes on her back.
Burton and Wilman and Annie were too young yet to dis-
approve. And there was the care out there being offered
for Brenda Kay, just waiting for us, waiting.

I opened my eyes then, saw cut across the blue above
us a single lonely crow, crying out loud and fierce. Just a
single crow across sky, and for a moment I couldn't but
feel myself somehow like Bessy, trading on my body and
what it could do for whatever needs presented themselves, and I remembered her scars, long and cold and
purple, and wondered, too, what sort of scars my plan to
leave this place, to escape Mississippi like it was a nigger
shanty about to collapse, would leave on me, and would
leave on Leston.

Shadows of bulrushes started to fall across us, and I
held Leston even tighter, closed my eyes.

Later, heading back, I said, "Leston, we can do better by
our family." They were the only words came to me for all
the thinking I'd done on how to tell him.

"How so," he said, and pulled the paddle through
another stroke. The sun was still high, a little behind me,
and shone on him, gave even more color to his face. He
was on his third cigarette since we'd finished in the bulrushes. This was the first we'd spoken.

"I have an idea," I said, and stopped. This was it, where all I'd thought over was going to come out.

"I have an idea," I said, "that we ought to think on moving from here."

He was quiet, pulled through another stroke. He said, "From Purvis."

"From Purvis," I said. "From, maybe, Mississippi."

"You want to move to New Orleans," he said, the cigarette at his lips bobbing with his words. It wasn't a question, but what he'd figured the answer to all this. "Or thereabouts," he went on. He stopped paddling a moment, thought better of it, started in again. "Driving in to New Orleans every few weeks to see a doctor don't make it necessary to move there." He drew on the cigarette, the tip going bright.

"Not New Orleans," I said, and swallowed hard. I said, "Not New Orleans. But to a place where Brenda Kay can get what she needs, a place where there's an opportunity for things." I paused. "Things for all of us."

"Things," he said. "Things."

"Like good care. Like something akin to a school. Like maybe a school or something for Brenda Kay." I swallowed again. "Jobs, too. Good jobs."

He brought the paddle from the water entirely, laid it in his lap again. He squinted at me, took the cigarette from his lips, shot out smoke. "Who put these big ideas in your head?" he said. "One guess."

"No one," I said, and then I said, "The *Reader's Digest* is where. There's a place in California where—"

"California," he said, and with that he flicked the cigarette, this one not even halfway done, off into the green water, picked up the paddle, and started in.

"California," I said again, "is where there's a school for

Mongoloids," and I stopped, my last word big and clumsy and strange out here on water, beneath a spring sky, a word that cut off whatever others were lined up in me, stopped them all.

"California," he breathed, the word almost lost in the whisper he gave.

He pulled the paddle out again, set it across his lap. He sat up straight, brought a hand to his forehead to block the sun.

He wasn't looking at me, but behind me and to my right. I scooted around in my seat, tried to see behind me.

We were out fifty yards or so from where we'd put in, afternoon shadows darkening our picnic spot. I couldn't see Annie anywhere, nor Burton or Wilman.

But there lay Billie Jean on her back on the red wool blanket, Brenda Kay straddling her, the two of them lost in whatever game they were up to.

Billie Jean turned her head, saw us. "Hey!" she hollered from where she lay, and waved.

Slowly Brenda Kay's head turned our way, and after a moment that seemed to last longer than all the time Leston and I'd been away, her voice came to me across that green water, traveled as slow and precise as the sun across the sky.

"Momma!" she cried.

1952

Chapter 17

All I could hear was the ringing in my ears, the loud rush of blood through me that choked out everything else, whatever sounds were around me as I ran through the halls of the same hospital my baby Brenda Kay'd been born in, just ahead of me Wilman, his strides long and easy, a man now near on tall as Leston. He was way ahead of me, and had to stop now and again, in his eyes as he turned the fear and pain of what he already knew, what he'd already seen.

Finally, somewhere in the middle of a hall on the second floor, he held out a hand to me, and when I made it to him I took it, held it tight, and we ran together.

He slowed down, pointed to an open door to our left, and I let go his hand, went on into the room without waiting for breath, without waiting for the ringing to stop.

Inside were doctors and nurses, all huddled round the bed. But as I came near they parted, stood aside for me. I didn't even look at them, only at the bed, and at Brenda Kay lying there.

"My momma!" she screamed, "My momma!" and her arms went up to me, arms, I thanked God, that hadn't been burned in the fire, and I saw that her eyebrows, eyebrows that'd been the same fine auburn of her hair, had been scorched off, me still knowing so little of what hap-

pened, only the few words Wilman'd forced out to me on
the ride from the cafeteria here. Only that there'd been a
fire, and that Brenda Kay'd been burned.

"I'm here, honey, I'm here," was all I could say, those
the best words I could offer. "I'm here, my baby, I'm here.
I'm right here."

As I hugged her, held her tight to me, I listened to her
crying, heard her sob in a new way I'd never heard from
her before, a cry too deep, too strong. And I thanked my
God I could be here, and found myself cursing Him in the
very same breath.

I held her.

She feel asleep in my arms, her own arms gone limp as she
gave in to it, but I held her close in her sleep another ten
or fifteen minutes, just to let her know I was there.

Still, she whimpered in her sleep, and when I finally let
her go, the sound of her whimpering was thick in the air,
the soft and quick moans she gave out blasting to pieces,
finally, that ringing in my ears. Even as the doctors started
in on telling me what'd happened, it seemed their words
were only being built around my Brenda Kay's pain. Every
whimper she gave blotted out a phrase or two of what
healing I could hope for, what the chances of her legs
being usable again were, how long before skin might come
back.

Her whimpering even whited out most of what I saw,
so that none of the doctors had faces, voices, just as the
nurses hovering round me and Brenda Kay were only
women in white dresses, all their hair the same color.

Not until one of those nurses took hold of my hand and
as one of the doctors pulled back the sheet that lay across
Brenda Kay did things come alive for me. It was as if I'd

entered the room brand-new and unafraid, my eyes cold
as I looked at my baby daughter's legs, saw what God'd
deemed necessary at this point in her and my life both, a
point three years past when I'd started in on my husband
to move us away from this place.

What I saw:

Her legs had been burned up to midthigh, her right
worse than the left. I took in without blinking, without
swallowing, the image of blackened skin on her right leg
from her ankle on up, skin rumpled and bunched and
blistered where the fire had crept, from midshin to just
above her knee, skin gray and red and mottled, already
oozing.

Then her smell came to me, the smell of burnt flesh,
the sour smoldering and stink of her lying there.

I closed my eyes, closed them, and felt the air in the
room rush past me, as though the roof were lifting off, me
with it, and I disappeared.

Wilman squatted before me. I was in a chair, I knew, in a
hospital hallway, and this was my son, Wilman, his face
close to mine, his forehead wrinkled, mouth pursed, eyes
searching for something.

Me, I saw. He was looking for me, and I blinked a few
times, took in a breath.

"I fainted," I said, and I tried to stand, felt my legs do
nothing, gone to sleep of their own. I pushed on the arms
of the chair, tried to get my legs to work, to move me.

"Momma," he said, and placed his big hands on my
shoulders, held me down. "Momma," he said again, "you
need to have a seat here. You need to sit here for a while.
That's what the doctor said."

I'm right here, I thought, *right here,* and still his eyes were looking for me, searching my face for some sign of recognition, as though it'd been me who'd been burned, my face consumed by flame, and for a long moment, and then for many days and weeks and months and years I wished it'd been me in there on the hospital bed, and I asked myself again, because it seemed there would never be anyone else I could ask this, not even my God Himself, *Is this how He smiles on us?*

Cathedral'd been the one to blame, because blame was what I was after, blame the only thing I had the right to here. My baby'd been burned to where every waking moment she spent for the first two weeks in that hospital were taken up with her crying, holding on to me fierce and hard, leaving bruises on my shoulders I could see in the hospital bathroom mirror when I washed myself at night.

She'd been watching over Brenda Kay like every day I worked at the cafeteria, and the story I'd been handed by Billie Jean and Wilman and even Annie was the same, but it was the story handed them by Cathedral; my children'd all been at school or work themselves: Cathedral was sweeping up in the boys' old bedroom, Wilman the only one living here now.

Burton'd moved out to California five months before to find whatever fortune he thought was there, that idea of California planted by me through all the quiet conversations I'd had with Leston on the subject, me talking at him from across the kitchen table in the middle of the night for the last three years. I'd talked about and showed him and read to him the literature I'd received, brochures shiny and crisp that outlined what the National Association for Retarded Children could do for Brenda Kay out there in

Los Angeles. And Burton'd overheard, and Burton graduated from Purvis High and worked a summer at the ice
cream plant in Columbia and took in enough money to
buy a run-down pickup truck and move. Nothing to it:
Just pure and cold resolve in my son, and as he'd driven
off, waved back at us through the small window of the
cab, I couldn't help but envy him and at the same time feel
glad I'd handed him on something I could lay claim to:
that resolve. He'd gotten a job out there right off, working
at a muffler shop welding mufflers onto cars, all the thousands and thousands of bright and new and perfect cars he
saw out there every day. Now and again he sent a dress to
Billie Jean or Annie or Brenda Kay, and postcards once a
week of piers and seagulls and violet mountains and short
green trees clustered with bright oranges. And I'd gotten a
hat, burgundy with a tiny veil across the front brim. I
hadn't yet had enough nerve to wear it into our church,
where I could just imagine the words that'd pass between
women: *The mother of a retarded child strutting in with a hat
like that! I swan!*

And, too, he'd sent his daddy a lighter, a brass and
stainless steel lighter Leston carried with him everywhere
he went, even in the pocket of his pale green coveralls, his
uniform for work at the ice cream plant. He worked piling
fifty-pound sacks of sugar onto pallets five days a week
now, the job his son had left behind.

Though Leston hadn't approved of Burton's moving,
still deep in my husband the clouded and hopeless dream
of his sons following him into a lumberyard of his own
someday, Leston carried that lighter with him to work
every day, filled it every morning whether it needed it or
not with lighter fluid from the thin blue and yellow can he
kept on the mantel. It was a beautiful lighter, and I won-

dered often enough how much money Burton really made out there in all that sun and in amongst all those cars. But mostly I wondered when my husband was going to roll over and give in to what was so clearly best for my family, so clearly best for Brenda Kay. That lighter, I figured, was a fine start, a piece of California in his coveralls every day, there in his hand with every cigarette he lit.

That same resolve in Burton was what made James a good example of what you could do when you took hold of your life, made it do what you wanted of it: he was in veterinarian school at A&M now, would be out next summer, practicing on his own. And I had a grandchild, too, baby Judy, after Eudine's mother. A baby girl with fiery red hair and green eyes yet again, and who I hadn't yet held. It was a baby they'd planned on having. Eudine'd told me when they'd first called to let us know we'd be grandparents and aunts and uncles, and that notion made me shine inside, the idea one could plan on a child and be smart enough to determine what would happen to your future.

When we'd gotten the phone call near three A.M. one morning ten months ago, James breathless on the other end, the line crackling with interference at some point between here and Texas, I'd said right off to him, "Count 'em up. Count up her fingers and toes, make sure there's ten of each," but right then I'd felt the hollow promise that measure really meant: my Brenda Kay'd had ten of each.

Every time I asked one of my children again how the burn had happened, I could see Cathedral giving out the story, saw her stone still except for the small words she formed, eyes half-opened, her face all straight as she gave to them what she reckoned was God's will in this situation: she'd been sweeping, and heard Brenda Kay scream, dropped the broom right there, ran downstairs to see Brenda Kay in her blue corduroy overalls and white shoes and white blouse, standing in front of the hearth with fire swarming up her legs. Brenda Kay screamed and screamed, then took to running. Cathedral chased her through the front room and on into the kitchen, managed to pull her down from behind and lay on her a moment until the flames'd gone out.

When the story came to this point I always closed my eyes, tried to imagine the scene and what that warmth, that heat was like: Cathedral herself ended up with blistered skin on her right thigh, her thin cotton dress scorched, her heavy leggings keeping her skin from burning any worse.

But I couldn't imagine that heat, couldn't feel that pain. I couldn't feel what it was like for Cathedral, because it was blame I was putting on her—how could she leave Brenda Kay untended at the hearth? How could she?— and I wanted no piece of me feeling sorry for her, feeling there was any way she couldn't be the one to fault here.

Instead, all I could hear were the words Cathedral told my children Brenda Kay was screaming: "My momma! My momma!" even as she lay flat on the floor, Cathedral rising, finally, and going to the sink, filling with water the first thing she could find, a pan I'd cooked that morning's grits in, then rolling Brenda Kay over onto her back, her calling out my name even louder, finding inside her own self that new deeper and stronger sob and scream as Cathedral poured cold January water over my daughter's burned legs.

Then Cathedral laid blankets over Brenda Kay, laid as many as she could find, and ran out to the road, started to waving down any car passing by out there.

At this point, too, I closed my eyes, imagined what it was somebody'd see if they were driving by at that moment: a crazed niggerwoman, arms up in the air and hollering, that Cathedral, the one we all knew spoke in tongues and was given to holy fits for the Lord. That's what they'd think, I knew, and so it was God's blame, too, Him giving her that reputation, and me the first to have seen it come upon her that day out back of Missy Cook's mansion. Now the end result: not one car stopped for a half hour, seven cars passing her by as she screamed and hollered and waved.

It was a nigger, finally, to stop for her, Eleazer Campbell the insurance salesman, one of only three niggers in the county who had a car to drive. He'd been the one to pull over, follow her into the house, lift up Brenda Kay and all the blankets heaped on her. My baby'd passed out by then from the shock and the pain, Eleazer Campbell the one to drive her to this hospital, Cathedral in the back seat with Brenda Kay's head in her lap, stroking her hair, stroking it.

They got to the hospital, and when the nurse at the desk saw what was on, she'd called two nigger orderlies, who took my baby daughter from Eleazer Campbell's arms, him standing just outside the hospital doors, knowing enough not to even try coming inside. And Cathedral behind him, her own burns tended by somebody else later on.

But first she told the nurse who my daughter was, told her Wilman was a junior at Purvis High, that he should be called first, that he could handle it all from then.

She drove with Eleazer Campbell back to the house to clean things up. To get ready, she told my children. And the first thing she saw when she came back in the house was that thin blue and yellow can of lighter fluid, empty,

scorched, the paint bubbled like the skin on my baby's
legs, around it scorched black bricks, the black leading a
trail into the fireplace, the fire now only embers. Brenda
Kay'd reached up to the mantel, and'd pulled the lighter
fluid down, and'd squirted it all over everywhere, and'd
been taken up by flames jumping out the fireplace. It was
a wonder, "A blessing from God above," were the words
Cathedral'd ended the story with each time she'd told it to
my children, that our home didn't burn down to the
ground.

Why didn't she call me? I wondered every time I heard
the story. We had a telephone there in the house, too; why
didn't she call?

But I never asked that out loud, because I knew the
answer: blame had fallen square on her, and she'd known
it.

Cathedral hadn't tended properly to my child, hadn't
kept her out of reach of the lighter fluid. Hadn't called me
away from ladling out dumplings and gravy to children at
Bailey Grammar School while my own retarded child
burned at my home. Blame was hers, hard and pure and
cold.

Chapter 18

Doctors spoke at me, whispered at me, walked the halls with me; nurses smothered me, hugged me, touched me; members of the congregation cried on me, prayed for me, fed me and my family with an endless parade of covered dishes; my children held my hands, brought me flowers, brushed my hair; my husband held the brim of his hat in his hand, and turned it.

I stayed in that hospital room with Brenda Kay for a month, through all the changing of the dressings on her legs, through all the whimpering and crying, through the stench rotten skin gave off. I stayed for a month in the hospital room, doctors saying she'd take pneumonia, that she'd not walk again, that she'd be lucky if gangrene didn't settle in. Dr. Beaudry came in to check on her every other day or so, and each time Brenda Kay let out a scream, her eyes gone open wide, her red mouth a perfect O as she turned her head from him, the memory of his face and the shots still heavy with her, though Dr. Basket'd stopped prescribing them a year and a half before, when it'd come clear to him her bones were as strong as she needed.

Because Brenda Kay had walked everywhere, fearless, it would seem, but not that. She just knew no better: she'd left the house on more than one occasion without any of us knowing, just'd walked. She never got far, always to the

edge of the woods out the back door, or a few yards from
the road out the front before one or another of us would
holler out, take off through the door and turn her back
inside.

But we'd been thankful for the walking, because it meant
no more carrying her, no more toppling of chairs as she tried
to pull herself up, no more climbing of the stairs up to Dr.
Beaudry's office, where we still went once a month for him
to have a look at her. The pall of carrying her everywhere
had become so a part of our lives that when suddenly she'd
took to walking and that gray shroud'd been lifted, I'd
seemed to see more daylight, find better colors in the sunset,
hear rain outside where I'd heard nothing before. Brenda
Kay was growing up, and it seemed there might be some sort
of light at the end of this long tunnel.

One morning late last August, not long before Burton
moved out and long enough after she'd learned to walk—
she was eight now, *eight years old*—she'd simply left the
breakfast table and her plate of eggs and bacon, and gone
to the back door. Everyone was out the house except
Burton and me, Billie Jean already to work at the bank,
Leston in the woods, Annie already done with the morning
chores and now in town with her girlfriends, Wilman to
summer football practice at Purvis. Burton was at the table,
shoveling in his food like always.

Brenda Kay had on denim overalls and a pale blue
blouse with a little lace collar, these as everything else she
wore old clothes from Annie, who'd now started in to
wearing some of Billie Jean's old things, except that she'd
get out the scissors and sewing basket and make her own
changes to those clothes. She'd sheer off a few inches from
an old skirt, fuss up the shoulder seams of a blouse so the
sleeves looked fuller, puffier, all of this without a word to

me. She was learning on her own, me thankful for that, though sorrowed at it, too. Every day I felt there'd been years lost to my children growing up; there were things I'd have loved to teach Annie, even if it was just the trick of cherry Lifesavers and lips I'd shown Billie Jean a Christmas morning too long ago.

Burton had on only a T-shirt and blue jeans, his face puffed and tired and needing a shave. He worked the four to midnight shift over to the ice cream plant, and so I never rousted him out of bed, only let him come on down when he'd finished his sleep. The three of us here in the kitchen was no different than any other morning spent in our house.

The radio was on, too, like every morning, turned to my favorite program, "Sunrise Serenade" out of New Orleans. It was a program I'd listened to for years, had even on occasion danced a little to in the kitchen with Annie when she was smaller, Brenda Kay in her high chair and watching, mouth open for a while before she'd smile at us, wave her arms. Every care of a day fell away when I'd listen to that program and the gospel songs by The Stamps Quartet and Mother Maybell Carter, everything from instrumentals of "Amazing Grace," violins thick and sweet filling the air, on down to "Jesus Loves Me" on a simple, lonesome guitar.

Maybe it was because for a moment or two on that morning it'd seemed somehow that things were on the mend, that the world and this child we'd been given weren't so very heavy a load. Maybe it was the music, or the good knowledge my children—even my Brenda Kay— were healthy, as far as I knew happy, and that I had a grandchild. There was one more life on the face of this earth that I could lay claim to, and I knew I'd never be a grandmother like the only grandmother I ever knew. And maybe, just maybe, the good feeling was because my second son was here at the table, his plans to move to California already laid clear to us all. He was our foot in the door, even though Leston still sat across from me late nights, his face blank while I still tried to persuade him we had to move to California. For the good of us all.

Maybe it was all that together—the music, my children, the prospect of California suddenly shinier than it'd been in a long time—that made me let Brenda Kay walk out the back door. I just watched her from the kitchen window as she made for the woods, her arms loose at her sides, her steps careful and precise in a delicate way, strange steps that involved her lifting one foot, placing it flat on the ground before her, then lifting the next foot and doing the same, steps so gentle I couldn't imagine she'd break eggs walking like that. I let her walk.

"Momma?" Burton said behind me, and I heard his chair scrape against the floor. It was still August, the morning air heavy and thick, edged already with a piece of the heat that would descend on us later in the day. But it didn't matter. What mattered was seeing my baby daughter, Brenda Kay, making for the woods in her awkward orthopedic shoes, shoes that cost twice as much as the shots had, shoes she grew out of every few months.

She was on her own out there. Brenda Kay was outside, surrounded by that green, that sweet smell, that heavy air. Walking on her own.

"Momma?" Burton said again, and stood next to me at the sink, watching. From the corner of my eye I saw him turn to me once, then look back out at his sister.

I said, "You do me a favor, honey, and you go out there and follow her." I smiled, but didn't turn to him, didn't want to take my eyes off what I saw. "You hang back aways," I said, "and you just watch her. See where she goes. Watch out she don't tangle up in any poison ivy." I paused. "I just want to see where she goes, is all."

He didn't move for a moment, and I saw him turn to me again. Then he kissed my cheek, a small little peck, but enough.

He went to the back door, quick put on his workboots without even tying the laces, and he was out the door.

I watched them both now, two of my children, one about to take out to California and a new world out there, the other into a world just as new for her, just as strange and different. Burton did as I said, hung back ten yards or so from her, and as a huge pipe organ played through "Onward Christian Soldiers" on the radio behind me, I smiled. Burton was walking slow, looking down at the ground, hands in his pockets, his steps easy. Brenda Kay was at the edge of the woods on the old trail now, her arms still at her sides, still with her gentle steps. Then she disappeared.

Burton made it to the edge, and stopped. He tapped his toe to the ground, turned to the house. He waved at me. I waved back, and he was gone.

A half hour later here they came, hand in hand. Burton huge and strong, his black hair still tossled with sleep, his face still in need of a shave, but his eyes suddenly brighter than I'd seen them before. And for all the size Burton'd seemed to take on in those thirty minutes, Brenda Kay'd seemed to grow as well, suddenly a little girl and no more the baby I'd had here for eight years. She was smiling the biggest smile I'd seen on her, her top two front teeth missing, most every other tooth showing.

I'd missed that face the last half hour, my morning

routine of care so deep in me that I'd gotten absolutely nothing done in the silence of those last thirty minutes. Because that was what stopped me: silence. The silence an empty house makes, even with a radio going. There was nowhere in my house a single person other than me, and while I'd stood at the kitchen window wringing out a cold dishrag again and again, searching out the trees for signs of my two children returning, I thought I knew something of how Leston could stand here at night, stare out at darkness. I thought maybe there was some comfort he found here in the dark of a house asleep, as close to quiet and empty as he could get. Maybe that silence was what he needed to help him solve what was crushing in on him from out in the dark.

California was what would solve his life, I knew; California was what would change things for Leston. But he'd still have none of it, fresh in my head even two and a half years later the image of his half-smoked cigarette shot out into the water, his whispering "California" with all the disgust he could muster.

Brenda Kay's hand was tight in Burton's as they came toward the house, and I turned from the window and went to the table, picked up as many plates as I could and brought them to the sink.

I went to the back door, stepped out, my hands in fists at my side. "You two," I said, and shook my head, made like I was all bent out of shape over them. "You two."

"Momma!" Brenda Kay said, still smiling, and with her free hand she pointed a thick white finger at her brother. "Burton," she said, "Burton!" His name came out more like Button than anything else, every word she spoke choked off as they were in her throat, each utterance forced and quick. She could say all our names now, could ask for water or milk or more food, could tell me when I needed to take her to the bathroom, tell me if she was cold or too hot: "Momma, cold!" she'd say, or holler out, "Momma, potty!" "Momma, food!" For some reason her mouth couldn't form the sound of an L or an R, and her words came so fast they seemed fallen in on themselves, shrunken up and urgent no matter what, so that the children's names became Nee, Wimn, Button, Bijen, James still no one she knew yet. Sometimes during the day she'd holler out "Miss Wimn" or "Miss Bijen" to let me know she might be feeling lonely, and I'd have to go to her, pick her up, hold her. She hadn't yet attempted Cathedral's name, and only called out "Daddy!" now and again on those few nights he'd pick her up in his arms, walk through the house with her, set her back down, his touch with her always out of duty, I thought: the father's task.

"That's right," I said there on the porch, still shaking my head. "Burton came and got you, now didn't he? I sent him out to get you, and you two take off who knows here. What am I supposed to do with you two?"

Burton squatted, picked her up, settled this suddenly big girl on his hip, and I could see the mud on her white shoes, grass stains at the toe.

"This here's my sister," Burton said, "and she went on an adventure, and I had to save her before she crossed the raging river." Brenda Kay's eyes were on his mouth as he spoke. The words meant nothing to her, I knew, but it was the speaking of them that mattered, just for her to be in his arms and listening. She lifted a hand to his mouth, touched his lips as if they were ice, just tapped them as he spoke, and when he stopped she left her fingers at his lips. Then he snarled a little, his eyes on her, and barked, made like he was gong to bite her fingers.

"Huh! Huh!" she laughed, and hit his nose. "Huh,

Momma!" she said, and turned to me, then to Burton. "Huh! Huh!"

"Now you two," I said.

Inside, Burton set her down on the kitchen floor. She got on her knees, crawled beneath the table, picked up one of the boys' old baseballs I hadn't even known was there. She crawled out, went to the larder door, leaned her back against it. She held the ball with both hands, her fingers so short and thick they hardly seemed big enough to hold it at all.

Burton and I'd watched very move, me at the sink, eyes on her, Burton leaning his back against the counter, his hands on the edge. We hadn't said anything, only watched as she set the ball on the floor, put a hand on top of it, trapped it.

"There's a bit more coffee," I said, and lifted out of the dishwater the first fork, wiped at it with the same rag I'd twisted to death. "Just heat it up a little."

I was waiting for him to talk, waiting for his report. I wanted his words on where she'd gone, but he didn't seem to want to part with them. His eyes hadn't yet met mine since we'd come in here, and the place was silent except for the radio again, "How Great Thou Art" on now, George Beverly Shea's voice deep and warm through the kitchen.

We were watching her again, Burton now leaning against the counter as before, when Brenda Kay started in to her singing. There were no words she sang, only her mouth open and moving, changing the pitch and shape of those sounds so that what came was more a joining of moans up and down, Brenda Kay oblivious of anyone around her. And she sang.

"Tell me," I said, and lifted out my own coffee cup, rinsed it, set it on the drainboard.

"Momma," he said, his head turned to his sister. "Momma," he said again, "it's going to be hard to leave here."

"I know," I said. "But if it's something you have to do, then it's something you have to do." I paused, held the rinsed cup in my hand. "And we'll be seeing you sooner than you think."

He turned to me. There was my second son's face, and no matter how old he would get there'd never disappear from that face the baby he'd once been, the face I'd known at my breast, the face I'd known at his first steps at ten months. There were his dark brown eyes—*my eyes*—his fine chin and jaw. And there was the thin line of a scar back near his left ear where Wilman'd hit him with a piece of wood from thirty feet, back before Burton'd learned the trick of standing just out of Wilman's range so that his little brother would be the one to lose. That was Burton. Here.

He said, "I hope that ain't just a dream of yours, Momma." He paused, his eyes on me. "You coming out to California."

"It's not," I said. "You know it's not." I lifted out a soapy plate, ran a rag across it. "Once you let it turn into a dream," I said, "then it won't ever happen on you. I'm not letting it turn into a dream."

He looked at me a few moments longer while I held the plate in my hand, rinsed it, held it.

Brenda Kay hit a note high up, hit it hard and loud and long, and I quick looked to her, surprised I wasn't yet able to hear the difference between her singing and a wail of pain. She still had the baseball trapped beneath her hand, her eyes hard on it, and let her voice drop down low and soft.

"She didn't look back or side to side or anywhere," he finally said. He was staring out the window. "I just followed her. All the way back to the pasture. She just looked straight ahead and was walking."

He stopped, and I said nothing to urge him on, knew he was building his words to something here. It was in how he looked out the window, how he stared as if there'd be some answer out there.

He said, "When we got to the pasture she just walked right out into the middle of it, on across. Her walking like she does, it's a wonder grass even bent beneath her feet." He gave a small laugh, shook his head. "I was only a few feet behind her. I didn't want her coming up on no snakes, you know."

"Good," I said. I rinsed my hands, done by this time with the dishes except for the skillet.

"Then we were headed into the woods back of the pasture, off towards Casey's place, the back end of his property." He stopped again, swallowed hard. He took in a big breath, held it.

"Burton," I whispered, "what is it?"

"It's nothing," he said, too quick, and let out the breath. "That's it," he said. "She just walked. She was walking right on back into the woods, walking the straightest line I ever saw. She didn't look much at the ground, and when she came up to a bush or old stump or tree or something she just went on around it." He paused. "But then she'd get right back on track," he said. "I finally stopped her when she hit the creek. She was going to walk right into it, shoes and overalls and all. She would've gone right on in if I hadn't come up behind her, took ahold of her hand. That's when she turned to me. She looked up at me, and it took her a minute or so before she recognized me. Before she smiled."

He ran a hand back through his hair, in the move more

of his daddy than he'd ever recognize himself. He turned to me. "And while I was following her back there," he said, looking right into my eyes, "I got this picture in my head of her walking for the rest of her life, right on in a straight line, just walking as long as she lived. And it give me the shivers, Momma. That picture." He blinked, tried to give me a smile, though I knew that wasn't what my boy really wanted to give me. I could see he wanted to cry, to give in to that, but him figuring he was too much a man.

So I took him in my arms, held him close to me, my hands still wet with dishwater, and I held him, and I said, "You just say what you have to say, Burton."

"Momma," he said, and he'd started to cry, my boy about to head out to California and a life none of us could now imagine. "Momma, there's somebody going to be following her the rest of her days, Momma. And I feel like I'm leaving y'all to do that. That's what I feel like."

"You just go on," I said right away, "and you lead your life, and then we're going to come on out there and you'll be serving as our welcoming committee."

I pulled myself away from him, held him by the shoulders. Tears had fallen down his cheeks, and he cleared his throat, wiped at his eyes with the back of his hand.

Already I was thanking God for him, and for every other of my children, even the one singing there on the floor, and thanking God, too, for her voice, the chance and confusing beauty of it. I thanked God for this all, even though I knew it was me would be following her all the way through her time on this earth, unless I took to heart the task before me, the one set up by the same God who'd given her to me: find a way to fix this, not simply watch from behind as she walked straight across the face of her days.

Chapter 19

But whatever I'd been thanking Him for that day seemed now a hundred years ago and lost to the smell of her dead skin, lost to the prospect of Brenda Kay's not walking, lost to the perfect O of her terrible screams. Lost to the point I'd finally turned my face from Him, and took things into my own hands.

The day she went home, Brenda Kay was lifted from her bed and eased into a wheelchair by two nigger orderlies, boys who reminded me too much of Cathedral's own, Sepulcher and Temple, the two who'd carried me only to deliver this child in this wretched hospital, and as Leston and Wilman lifted her into the cab of the truck, settled her there, her whimpering all the way through, I didn't even turn back to look at the place, knew I didn't ever want to see it again.

Leston was even more the stranger now, even older the man: he said nothing to Brenda Kay the entire ride home, knuckles white as they gripped and regripped the steering wheel. It was a Tuesday morning, and he'd taken off from work for this, had on the green coveralls he wore, *Leston* stitched in white thread above his shirt pocket, coveralls a little too big on him so that he seemed that much smaller, that much thinner. He didn't have his hat on, and for some reason I was thankful for that, glad at his not having the damned thing to turn in his hands as he'd stood and done every time he'd come to the hospital.

He was a stricken man, dumbfounded by what'd been tossed at him yet again, but that didn't give him any more reason than the next of us to spend the rest of his days pondering the universe in a coffee cup, not coming to our bed and to his wife. We'd only made love a handful of times since our time on the canoe, and each time I took him into my arms he felt frailer, his skin a touch more toward paper.

But now there was no more time I could spend in persuading him, I saw, as we headed home, him slowing down at each bump, each twist in the road. He had a heart, had love for his daughter, had compassion on us all, but I saw he'd let the grief and bewilderment he carried overwhelm him, blind him to the truth that the world— our world—had to make sea changes in order to get right again, or at least as close to right as we'd ever get.

So that when we finally made it home, and when Wilman and Leston'd finally gotten Brenda Kay into the bed I'd had them move down from her room and set up in the front room, I went to my husband there in the doorway, his hand on the knob and ready to pull it closed behind him as he headed out first to drop Wilman off at school, then back to work himself. I went to him, and I pulled him down to me, and I gave him a kiss, gave it to him hard on the lips, and felt more than anything that it may well have been my kiss good-bye.

Because now we were gone, headed to California, with or without him.

While Brenda Kay napped that afternoon I turned up one of Annie's tablets from her room, and I sat in my rocker next to her, wrote out what I would do.

I figured to start we had to get as much money together as possible, and knew the only way that'd happen would be by selling things off, so I started a list:

> *quilts*
> *radio*
> *furniture*
> *pots and pans*
> *chickens*
> *boys' old clothes*

As I wrote, the old familiarity came back into my hand, the ease with which I'd worked a pencil on paper, the grading of worksheets, and then came the old feeling of chalk in hand, and I stopped, sat back, started in to thinking of when I'd been a teacher and in charge of all those children and with none yet of my own.

But then Brenda Kay whimpered, and I turned to her, saw a dribble of spit at the corner of her mouth, saw her eyes twitching with whatever dream of fire must have been in her, and I resolved right then and there to cut from my mind the luxury of remembering what'd been before for the certain necessity of thinking ahead. I knew it wouldn't be tomorrow, but as soon as Brenda Kay was as better as she would get, which meant I'd stay with her each minute I wasn't working to get us away from here. The sooner she got better, I knew, the sooner we would leave for the next life we had coming to us. It was the future my eye had to be on. No more of the past.

The less we brought with us the better, I thought, and I pictured us pulling into Los Angeles with nothing to our names, simply the money in our pockets and prospects spilling all around us. I saw orange blossoms going strong,

took in the warm sea air and the crystal blue sky; and I saw
a place where Brenda Kay would find friends, teachers, and
saw Leston at work somewhere, doing something, it didn't
matter what. The doing of it was all that mattered.

I hesitated a long while before I put the next word on
the list of things to sell off, but then I wrote it:

home

Such a small word. But one that carried too much of
what kept us here, and so I scribbled through it, and in
place beneath it wrote

house

I was upstairs going through the boxes of the boys'
clothing when I heard it, the knock at the back door. I
went to the attic window, tried to see through the dirty
glass who it would be, though I already knew.

I folded the flannel shirt in my hands, tried to put away
in my head the fact it needed two new buttons before I
could sell it, and I climbed down the ladder, went slowly
along the hall and down the stairs to the kitchen.

I glanced first into the front room, saw Brenda Kay was
coming around, her mouth opening and closing like it
does just before she lets out the first yelp of pain she gave
every time she awoke, the burn a surprise to her, new
every time she came up from sleep.

I had only a few minutes before the tending would start
up in earnest, had only a few minutes to deal with who was
out there, the woman I'd laid blame cold and simple on, the
woman I'd sealed my heart against all those nights on a cot
in a hospital room that reeked of alcohol and dead skin.

I reached for the door, saw Cathedral's outline through the curtains, and the flush of my own pain took me over, and I saw my hand shake at the knob.

I opened the door. There she stood, smiling, smiling and smiling, though in her eyes was some piece of sorrow. She had her hair covered with a worn-out blue handkerchief, had a beat old yellow sweater over her shoulders against the February cool out there, the only button left on it the one at the neck.

I stood looking at her a long moment, felt her too familiar to me. I knew she'd be the one who'd somehow end up laying open to me the fact I was forsaking the heart of my husband to further the good of my retarded daughter, that knowledge coming to me in just that moment, in no time, really, and then I realized that the sweater she wore was one of my old ones, a sweater I'd given her years ago when the times were good, and when we'd fed nigger after nigger at our back door, and when they'd all followed my strong and handsome husband off into the woods to help the United States win the war. That was my sweater she had on.

Still smiling, she shook her head, whispered, "The Lord trying His best to smile down on you, child, but you not letting Him do that."

Before I could think of anything else I could do, any words or gestures or silences, I drew back my hand and brought it full force across this niggerwoman's face, and in that moment all I'd ever fought against exploded in me. I saw Bessy and Cleopatra inside a niggerwoman's shanty stealing her food. I saw Tory's face as I took my beating. I saw myself pulled up by Pastor from the Pearl River, wet and shaking and miserable in the Lord, Missy Cook on the bank and crying tears meant for nothing but effect, and I knew then I was no better than my grandmother, knew no matter how hard you prayed, no matter how shiny the stones in your pocket, no matter how far behind you you thought your old lives were, they were never gone. They were never more than an inch from the surface, battling each moment you breathed, each and every moment of every day fighting to rise up and take you over. And I'd lost, let those old lives win just now.

And at last, in the end of that motion, in the instant of pain in my palm and the pain my palm gave out, I saw Missy Cook's own hand speeding down onto my face. Missy Cook was still a ghost inside me, and I saw you never gave up who you were or where you'd been in your life. I'd refused to let Missy Cook try and reconcile herself to me, just as right now I was refusing Cathedral, and as I felt the pain in my hand, suddenly Missy Cook was only a sad and lonely old woman choking to death on the dry crust of her own history. And now here was my own history, the dry crust of *blame* I wanted forced from me in the form of my hand slapping hard the black flesh of Cathedral's cheek. And then I remembered what I had done after Missy Cook'd hit me, how I'd simply turned my other cheek to her, offered up myself to her, daring her to strike me.

Which was the only thing Cathedral did. Once I'd struck her, she'd closed her eyes, took in a quick breath between clenched teeth. She seemed to fill up her lungs with that breath, held it, then gave her head a quick shake as if to rid herself of the pain I'd given her. Then she opened her eyes, smiled again, and turned her other cheek to me.

She looked at me out the corners of her eyes, and waited. My hands were at my sides, dead, useless, and I took my eyes from her.

"I sorry, Miss Jewel," she whispered. "But you got to think on Job. You got to think on David and him fighting the anointed Saul." She paused. "You got to think on Christ," she said.

That was when I turned from her, stepped inside. Without looking back through the curtains, without looking at anything other than the kitchen floor, I pushed the door closed, then twisted the knob until it locked. I leaned my back against the door, held my hands at my chest. I looked around at all we had in the kitchen: the plain white china and three vases in the glass cupboards above the sink, spoils from those war years; a fine oak table built by Leston; the wall clock that chimed on the half hour, a wedding gift from Leston's mother and stepfather. I looked at everything we could sell and make money from, already trying to gauge in my head how much closer each item might bring us to California.

I heard behind me the slow steps of Cathedral as she moved down the steps, off of our property and toward her own, and though I hadn't known it, I found myself crying, saw the room and its contents shimmer in my eyes.

I pushed myself away from the door, went to the kitchen sink and looked out the window to see Cathedral leaving, heading for the same woods Brenda Kay'd walked through.

I watched Cathedral disappear into the woods, until the last thing I could see was a glimpse here and there of my own yellow sweater deep in the gray and brown of February trees, and then she was gone, and I knew I'd never see her again, knew it just as certain as if I'd lowered her into her grave myself, or just as certain as if she'd lowered me into mine.

Chapter 20

"Jewel," Leston said, "Jewel, wake up."

I opened my eyes to the dark of the bedroom, to the cold and empty side of the bed that had once been Leston's. I ran my hand across the sheets, felt nothing, wondered if I'd only dreamed his voice.

"Jewel," he said again, and I saw his shadow standing next to my side of the bed, at his face the bright ember of a cigarette, the only light here.

He brought the cigarette down, shot out a breath, and I imagined the smoke he let out falling down on me, burying me.

"Get up," he said. He turned, left the room. A moment later I heard his footsteps down the stairs.

I sat up. "Brenda Kay," I whispered, and wondered what was going on. It was May already, and there'd been a couple mornings so far when I'd been able to get her to take a step or two away from the bed, though the pain, it was easy to see, was still there in her legs, dressing still tight on her thighs and on her one calf, us over to Dr. Beaudry's more often than ever now to get those dressings changed. But there'd been no gangrene after all, no pneumonia to kill off my baby, so I didn't know what was wrong. I climbed out of bed, grabbed my robe from the footboard, moved quick to the stairs and down.

Brenda Kay was asleep there in the front room, across her face and body the long shadows cast by the light from the kitchen, her mouth partway open like always as she took in deep and steady breaths. I still hadn't put on my robe, only stood over her, watching her, waiting for whatever my husband'd thought deserved my attention.

"In here," he called, and I turned, saw him sitting at the table, hands around a coffee mug.

I swallowed, looked back at Brenda Kay, then at him. Slowly I shrugged on my robe, left it untied. I backed away from her toward the kitchen, certain there was something about her Leston wanted me to see.

But once I was in the kitchen he wouldn't look at me or toward the front room. Instead, his eyes were fixed high on the wall opposite him. At first I thought he was only staring, lost in whatever thoughts he had, thoughts I'd long given up on trying to understand. I blinked at the light in here, tried hard to focus on him. He had on one of his old white undershirts, his tired green and white striped pajama bottoms. Before him sat his ashtray, heaped with the ends of dead cigarettes. Next to the ashtray lay a new cigarette, already rolled and ready to smoke.

I said, "What is it?" I paused. "She all right?"

He nodded at the wall, and only then did I see what he was onto. I turned, looked, saw the empty space where until yesterday had hung the wall clock.

He said, "My momma and stepdaddy give that to us," his eyes hard. "They're both dead now."

I'd known this moment was heading at me, but'd only put away any thoughts on it, certain I'd be able to piece my way through no matter what. I was certain, too, that with each penny I'd brought in so far, I was bringing us a mile or so closer to California, but at the same time bringing me a minute or so closer to the conversation we were about to have right here, right now.

I'd hoped the words would come to me, in the back of my head somewhere a prayer to God He'd serve me this time, though in everything else I was operating on my own will, on my own cold resolve.

I tied my robe, my eyes on my hands and the impossible task this was, working my fingers to tie a simple knot.

His eyes were on me. He said, "You think I don't see what's going on in my own house, do you?" and he paused. His hands fell away from round the cup, lay flat on the table. A cigarette stub was jammed between two fingers of his left hand, and he brought it to his lips, pulled hard on it.

I said nothing, looked from him to my own hands flat on the table. I opened my mouth, heavy in my head that same prayer for words that would work. And like always, my God either didn't hear them, or chose to let me tread water on my own. I opened my mouth again, closed it again.

"At least tell me," he said, "what you got for it."

I opened my mouth again. I said, "I don't want you to think—"

"Just how much?" he said, his voice low and steeled, his jaws clenched.

I wouldn't take my eyes from the cigarette. I said, "I got twelve dollars."

He laughed, a quick shrug of his shoulders and a shake of his head.

He said, "Let's see. The clock. Four quilts, all the boys' old things. Most all the tomatoes and raspberries and okra and pickles and corn you put up last year. And there's the two vases gone. The two dresses Burton sent Brenda Kay."

He stopped, suddenly sat up, leaned across the table. He looked at me, his eyes open wide now. He whispered, "Anything I missed?"

I pulled back from him, afraid. He wasn't anyone I knew, these the most words in years from him, the laugh, the whisper, the eyes someone else in here with me.

"Or is there more I couldn't come up with?" he whispered, smiling again. "What is it you figure I do down here? You think I sit here, my ass tied tight to a chair? You don't think I walk through my house at night, find my way through the dark to closets and cupboards?" He paused, swallowed air in big gulps, trying to keep up with himself, while all around me the kitchen seemed to grow smaller, hotter. "You figure I can't see what the hell's going on all around me? How you're selling us out piece by piece to some goddamned dream of moving to California?"

His teeth were clenched again, and I could see the faint sheen of sweat on his forehead, veins in his neck straining, sweat coming through his undershirt.

I said, "It's not a dream," though I'd intended no words, hadn't formed or planned on them. They'd only come in a whisper so low I wasn't even certain I'd heard them.

"What?" he said, and leaned even closer, turned an ear toward me.

"I said it's not a dream," and felt my hands begin to shake, my face and neck and back and stomach begin to burn with the effort of only breathing. "It's going to happen, whether you want it to or not." I closed my eyes, felt them begin to smolder.

"So how much you get so far? All sales put together, how much you get for your little jaunt out to sunny California?"

Though I knew the number by heart, kept the tab

running with each item that left our house, I was quiet, the only sound my heart pounding in me, and the silence left by the wall clock, the ticking my husband must have counted on every night, his only company here, now lost.

I said, "Seventy-three dollars and thirty-seven cents."

He was quiet, then said, "More than I figured on. I had it about sixty-five or so."

I looked up at him, saw him lean back again, arms still crossed. He was smiling. "Must be holding out on me," he said. He picked up the single cigarette, held it in the palm of his hand, stared at it.

I said, "I sold the hat Burton gave me. For six dollars."

He laughed again, said, "Seems to me you think you can wrestle the world and win. Ain't so. Simple as that." He let the cigarette roll back and forth in his palm, gave it a small toss, watched it land back in his hand. "Seems if you want to change the world, you might ought to get hold of a few more dollars than that."

He gave the cigarette another quick toss, higher this time, and grabbed it in midair, held it tight in his fist.

"So I want you to see this," he said, "wanted you to come on downstairs here and watch your husband do what he's about to do, so's you'll be able to go at this California whole hog, even with my blessing. My blessing in a big way."

His blessing, he'd said. *His blessing.* I took in a quick breath, my heart and its pounding making me feel my chest might explode with each next beat.

He said, "Way I figure it, the only true way out of here is through raising big dollars, not nickel and diming your way there. Luck you're having, you should arrive in glory land the year 1975." Slowly he brought the cigarette to his lips, creased his eyes closed, anticipating the smoke about to come.

He was staring at me, and I could feel my own forehead perspiring, my stomach and eyes and tongue all burned red. I wanted him to talk more, to say what his blessing was going to be, and I wanted him never to speak again, to leave me alone and let me go on with getting us where I knew we had to be.

Brenda Kay let out a yelp from behind me, and I turned around to her, saw she was only rolling over in her sleep.

"Oh Brenda Kay, oh Brenda Kay," he said, and now he had out the brass lighter Burton'd given him, brought from somewhere when I'd been turned to my baby. He started flicking the lighter lid open and closed, open and closed. He flicked it open one last time, then clicked the flint, shot up the flame, held it on.

He said, "Guess in your head I'm most to blame. Me and my can of lighter fluid's to blame for what's happened, for all the rotting smells in this house and all the tears. Because even though you struck down Cathedral—"

He stopped speaking, shifted his gaze from the flame to me. He wanted to prove he knew things about me I didn't want known.

So I gave it to him. I took my eyes from him, let my head drop. I put my hands together on the table, clasped them hard in an attitude I figured might seem repentant. But all I wanted was for him to be through with this, to get out of his head what'd been festering there for as long as Brenda Kay'd been Brenda Kay.

"Even though you struck down Cathedral," he went on, "I know you still figure it's my fault. The way I see it, if it hadn't been for that can, we wouldn't be here right now having this little talk."

Though I wouldn't tell it to his face, he was wrong. I hadn't put any blame on him, no other blame than the fact he'd pulled out of this family years ago. The truth was we'd been on the road to this night since we'd sat in the cab of the truck on a rainy day almost nine years ago, just down the stairs from Dr. Beaudry's office and that first examination. We'd been on our way to this table since Leston'd flicked on the wipers in a sad attempt to make clear the world we were entering.

But I only nodded my head to his question, wanted him on with this.

"Look at me," he whispered, and I lifted my head, felt my legs set to trembling.

He brought the lighter to the cigarette, the flame twisted to high. He closed his eyes, drew in on the cigarette, let out a small puff of smoke. He brought down the lighter, left on the flame.

"You're selling everything off," he said, his eyes back on the flame, "everything we own. But to my figuring, there's only two things we own you can't sell off. Only two things." He paused, let out another puff of smoke. "Even the truck, I imagine, you could sell out from under us. You probably figure I wouldn't even notice it gone. And all we'd do would be walk everywhere we had to go. Why not? Niggers do it every day, walk to jobs they got, to school, everywhere. Why not us?"

Finally, he let go the flame, snapped the lid closed. He held the lighter with two fingers, turned it back and forth, just looking at it. I looked at it, too, saw how it shone in the light from the lamp above us, saw how cold and shiny and beautiful it was.

"This is one of the two things," he said. "This lighter is one of the two things you can't sell."

He gave it a quick toss, just as he'd done with the cigarette, and caught it, closed his fist tight around it. He looked at me again. "The other's where we are right now," he said, "where our retarded child is sleeping, where our youngest son is sleeping and where our other two daughters is sleeping, and all that's around us all. Right here." He tapped hard the tabletop. "This place," he whispered, "is what you can't sell. And you and I both know that's the only hard dollars you'll ever find. Won't be by selling jar to jar your pickled okra, or a raggedy-ass pair of bib overalls. Not that way."

"Leston," I said, my voice pitched way up high and out of control, tears already coming because what he was saying was right. There was true sorry I was feeling, but a sorry colored with the fact I could see no other way away from here than what I knew he was about to say. "Leston," I said again, and I reached a hand across the table toward him.

"No tears," he said. "This is what you want to have happen, then this is what we'll have happen." He paused, and now it seemed some of the wind'd been knocked from him, that he had to try harder to keep from blinking, to keep his hand steady as he held the cigarette.

He said, "Soon as Brenda Kay's set, soon as you're set, I'll put this place . . ." He paused, his words a whisper so low they'd have been drowned out by the ticking of the clock his momma and stepdaddy'd given us. His eyes finally left me, seemed to wander round the room, finally settling on the empty space on the wall opposite him. "This place I *built* for us," he said, and tapped the tabletop again, "this place and the land we live on, all of it. I'll put it up for sale."

He stopped, held the lighter up to the light again. "But

this," he said, and twisted it in the light. "This is something you're not ever going to get. It'd fetch a good few dollars. And Lord knows there's reason for getting rid of this thing." He paused, still looking at it, and I thought I could see his eyes glistening, ready to give way to tears of his own. "Lord knows that. I been thinking on this lighter. And it occurs to me there's good reason to get the hell rid of it. Because having this thing goes to remind me I couldn't even keep my second son around me, couldn't keep him near to home to give us a hand when we needed it. And of course that leads right on in to my firstborn, and how he wouldn't stay around neither." He swallowed, blinked. "And of course every time I light up I am reminded of how my baby daughter was near burned to death because of this little machine." He paused again, took a drag from the cigarette. He didn't inhale this time, only let the smoke right out. "Reason enough to get rid of the thing," he said.

He sat up straight in his chair, the move so sudden I nearly flinched. He stood, him in his undershirt and pajama bottoms. He held the lighter with two fingers, looked at me, said, "But you're never going to get this. Now you watch. You come with me, and you watch."

"Leston," I said again, but he only turned from the table, started toward the kitchen door.

I got up, followed him to where he stood with the door open now, cool May night air on my face, fresh and welcome in a room that'd seemed to want to suffocate me. Leston stepped onto the porch, and stopped. I stood just inside, saw past him into the dark nothing that surrounded the house every night.

"You know," he said, "all the nights I been walking around inside the house, I never once set foot outside.

Something about how dark it is out here that wouldn't let me." He looked over his shoulder at me. He had the cigarette between his lips, and said, "But tonight. You just watch."

He stepped off the porch, and I went outside, looked out into the darkness. The only light out there was that cast from behind me, the same as on the night Cathedral'd come to warn me about this life I was leading right now, to warn me about the hardship having Brenda Kay would be. True to her word, and true to God's promise, here I was, and here were our lives. And still I couldn't see how this was Him smiling.

Leston turned round at the bottom of the steps, held up the lighter, though I could barely make it out. He said, "You saw me light the last cigarette this lighter will ever light," his voice too huge out here in the dark, and I wondered if Wilman or Billie Jean or Annie'd wake up to all this goings on, and wondered what they would think tomorrow when they came downstairs, how they would see the two of us differently. "You saw me light the last cigarette with this," he said, "but you're not getting it. You won't sell this. It will always be mine, Jewel. Miss Jewel Hilburn, this'll always be mine."

He held the lighter in his hand like a stone, like he was about to skip it across water, and then he cocked back that arm, and with everything this fifty-year-old man had he threw it hard and clean out into the dark, his body swinging around with the momentum he'd made. He threw the lighter farther, I was certain, than anything he'd ever thrown.

And with it went the burning in me, and the weight on me. Even the smells in the house seemed suddenly gone, gone with the strong-arm throw of my husband, and I saw the perfect sense in him, saw the clear-eyed wisdom of his throw, the lighter lost now to the darkness of the woods out there and to everything we'd ever been. Lost, too, to everything ahead of us.

Leston stared out into the dark for a long while, bent over with his hands on his knees, his chest heaving with the effort. Then I saw the cigarette drop to the ground beneath him, thought I could see the small ribbon of smoke snaking up from it.

I went down the steps, took hold of one of his arms, then half-pulled, half-pushed him inside and up the stairs and on into bed, where we slept as though we had died, passed on from this world and into the next.

Chapter 21

The next day, and all the days after that until we moved to California, Leston was a new and different man. Suddenly he was in charge of our moving, him all movement and smiles about the prospect of heading away from the old place, the scene of our lives' miseries for so long. That morning he'd gotten up, shaved, even whistled as he slapped on Old Spice and put on his uniform, then drove Wilman and Annie to school, Billie Jean downtown to the bank. I'd spent the rest of the morning singing along with Brenda Kay, the two of us at the tops of our lungs as "Sunrise Serenade" went on and on, Brenda Kay's words to the songs still all made up. She even took four steps that morning, just after she'd had breakfast in the bed in the front room. "Momma, potty!" she'd hollered out while I was in the kitchen rinsing her dishes, and I'd wiped my hands on a dishtowel, turned, saw her moving all by herself, stiff-legged and slow for the bandages, but moving by herself for the bathroom.

When Leston made it home that night, he was still whistling, ate dinner with a smile on his face. Once we finished, he lit up his after-supper cigarette with a wooden match from a box he had in his front shirt pocket. His eyes wouldn't meet mine as he pulled out the match, struck it on the box, but that was fine with me. Then I looked round the table at my children to see if their faces might betray that they'd heard us up last night. But my children showed nothing: Annie only cleared the dishes like every night, Billie Jean started running water in the sink, Wilman got out the broom and started to sweeping. Brenda Kay sat in her chair next to Leston, watching everything.

"Brenda Kay, oh Brenda Kay," Leston said then, and everyone stopped, turned to him.

He was sitting in his chair, and had a hand up to Brenda Kay's cheek, touched it. Water still ran into the sink, Billie Jean staring at him but with a hand in the stream, waiting for hot; Annie stood between the table and sink, in one hand an empty platter shiny with grease from the fried steak, in the other a half-empty bowl of gravy. Wilman held the broom with both hands, still.

"I think it best we all know right now," Leston said, his eyes on Brenda Kay, who smiled at him, finally, "Daddy!" she shouted, only now fitting that face and the word together. "Daddy!" she shouted again. "Miss Daddy!"

He glanced away from her, gave a smile that seemed awkward and real at once. He cleared his throat, said, "We all ought to know right now that as soon as this here child's ready to go, we're moving to California."

"Daddy!" Annie said, quick placed the dirty plates on the counter, then went to Leston, put her arm round his neck, kissed his cheek. Wilman set the broom in the corner, went to his daddy's chair, put his hand to Leston's back a moment, the closest to a hug or anything else I'd seen him give his daddy since he was three or four. Wilman was smiling, though at the same time I knew there'd be things to worry over for him: starting his last year of school at a new place; leaving not just his friends here but his football—he'd been starting linebacker for two years now on the varsity team. And there was Babs Julien, his girlfriend.

As for Annie, it seemed more than clear there'd be no problems in her coming round to the idea: she'd since taken over Billie Jean's movie magazine pile, knew everyone in Hollywood's birthdate and real hair color by heart, even if it was old information, passed down from ancient *Photoplays*. The skirts shorter than her sister's had been, the jaunty sleeves of her dresses, the makeup and curled red hair and the smiles I'd seen her practicing in the mirror on more than one occasion gave me to know I had nothing to worry over.

But Billie Jean only held her hand at the water. It was her I watched, because she gave nothing out, only turned to the sink, dropped the plug in, swished up the soap with her hand.

I finished with the dishrag and the table, while Annie and Wilman stood over Leston, Brenda Kay right in the middle of it all and slapping her hands together. "Miss Wimn!" she said, then, "Miss Daddy, Miss Nee!" all of it shouted out at the same pitch as always.

I smiled, went to the sink, shook out the crumbs in the garbage can beneath it.

Billie Jean dipped in the first glass, said, "This is fine news, Momma," and smiled.

"You can't fool me, my daughter." I looked at her, dropped the rag into the suds.

"I've got friends, is all," she said. She wouldn't look at me.

"We all do," I said, but there was something in how she tipped her head to my answer, in how she shrugged just then and worked hard to keep her eyes from mine that showed me there were other worries headed for us.

* * *

Most all the days after that seemed to come and go quicker than we could know, as though each week were nothing more than a hail and farewell, the idea of California looming bright and glorious on a horizon closer than ever.

In June we sold off the chickens; in July, the furniture. We took our leads from the progress Brenda Kay made, slow progress, but progress just the same: her walking from the bed to the bathroom in June, in July Leston and Wilman moving the bed back upstairs, her able to move downstairs with the help of one of us.

But even in the face of the fact we were moving, there were still days that seemed like years, and I remember one afternoon in particular when Leston hadn't been able to make it off from the plant, and it'd been Wilman to come with me to Dr. Beaudry's to have the dressings on Brenda Kay's legs changed. Wilman had a job working after school at the soda fountain at Miller's on Main in Purvis, and'd spend most evenings there serving up ice cream to kids from all up and down the county, giving extra heaps to Babs no doubt for nothing. Then he and his friends would drive the county back roads until all hours, and I wouldn't see him until the next morning, dressed for school. "I'm just getting it out of my system, Momma," he'd say whenever it seemed I might be giving him an ugly eye, but truth was I didn't mind, didn't mind at all. He was good about putting his money away, about contributing his time to helping sell off everything, right down to standing by the bushel-barrels of sweet potatoes by the side of the road Saturday mornings, those potatoes selling off for a penny and a half a pound to whoever'd stop. We were heading to California; better, I figured, to get his system cleared here than there.

In late May the heat'd gone up into the nineties, and with the heat had come more and more changes of the dressings, and I remember heading up the stairs to the doctor's door. Once I reached the landing I'd turned to see my son Wilman with Brenda Kay in his arms, his face as stone as he could make it at the stench that rose up off his sister, the smell magnified by the wet heat as he carried her up the stairs.

Inside, Wilman carried Brenda Kay to the examination room, a room as familiar to me as my larder, and set her down on the table. Dr. Beaudry started right in on the same old routine, unwrapping layer by layer of gauze on down to the last lengths drenched in brown and dead and pussy skin, the horror if it near nothing for me, Brenda Kay giving out the same old heart-heavy whimpers, her face squeezed and pinched shut with the pain, while the doctor's low, calm voice guided us along.

That was when I turned to Wilman, saw him leaning back against the white wall, his hands crossed on his chest. His eyes were right on the leg worst burned, the source of the smells, of the giant burden that'd been rolled back on us like a rock we'd thought we'd gotten out from under when she'd started to walking.

Wilman only stared at her legs, and I could see in his eyes tears welling up.

Often enough I thought on my children and what they had to go through, on all the long line of moments I'd lost of my life to Brenda Kay, moments not spent on them.

This was one of those moments. I figured maybe the best thing I could ever do in his entire life would be to go to him right then, to hold him close to me and tell him it was fine to cry, to let go whatever notion he had of a man not crying.

But then Brenda Kay screamed out, and I turned to see Dr. Beaudry give one more small tug with his tweezers at a piece of skin just below her right knee, skin that had to come off before it got infected, and I held tight to Brenda Kay's hand, rubbed her back, rubbed and rubbed, a million gentle circles to get her through this. *Progress*, I thought, and I wondered what that really meant, and saw I'd only figured the idea of *progress* into Brenda Kay's life, and on our *progress* toward her walking, and on our *progress* toward getting to California. I glanced up to Wilman again, saw how the idea of progress with my own children was something I hadn't figured on, how they'd been progressing on their own, how I'd exited their lives for the most part in order to save this one life.

Then Wilman pushed himself off the wall, left the room, and the moment for him and me was gone.

On the first of August we sold the house, got $6,700 for it and the 180 acres around it, more money than we'd seen come through our hands in the last five years. One of the owners of the ice cream plant bought it all, a short fat man who'd never had a farm in his life, and who said he admired the craftsmanship he found in Leston's work. He'd walked through our house touching doorjambs and switchplates, taking off his spectacles now and again and peering into a cabinet, a corner. He'd given us the money within the week, told us we could move out any time that month.

Then, two days before we were to move—there was nothing to pack, nothing for any of us to do but just wait until Leston's and Billie Jean's last days to work—Annie and Brenda Kay and me met Billie Jean at the bank so we could spend her lunch hour shopping for new clothes for us all.

Wilman dropped us off, him having driven his daddy into work that morning. He was headed over to Babs' house for one last dinner with her family before leaving.

All we Hilburn girls walked down Juniper to Main and on into Bancroft's Dress Shop, all of us sopping wet by that time from the heat, and we bought clothes. We bought four outfits that matched from head to toe for Brenda Kay, though I wouldn't permit, would never again permit, anything other than pants for her: enough people ogled my child every time we left the house, whether for Sunday Meeting or Wednesday night supper or just to buy flour and coffee; I didn't need her scarred legs adding to what they saw.

We bought three pairs of cotton slacks, pink and blue and yellow, and a pair of navy blue cotton overalls with a winged dove appliqué at the bib; two white blouses embroidered at the collar and along the front, and two plain-front blouses, one pink, the other pale blue. With each pair of pants I held up to Brenda Kay, Myrtle Bancroft, proprietor, stood back, put her hands on the hips of her green silk dress, and said, "How wonderful, how becoming," the words lost entirely on my daughter. Myrtle acted as though Brenda Kay were trying to win men, which just showed me that, like everyone else, she had no idea what to do with a retarded child, had no idea how to talk or act around her. Finally, after I'd had Brenda Kay try on the third pair of pants, Myrtle'd pulled me aside, whispered in my ear, "Don't she like dresses?" and I'd whispered right back at her, "She doesn't think she has the ankles for it," my small joke lost on her.

Annie bought skirts, though: red and navy and white, even a seersucker blue and white one, cut close to her hips and straight, something I would've never dared dream of wearing or of letting Billie Jean wear. But we were off to California now, where I figured most every girl had skirts like that.

Billie Jean moved slowly through the racks of dresses in the shop, touched things here and there, once in a while pulled something out and held it to her. But it wouldn't be more than a second before she'd shrug and smile, file it back on the rack, take hold of her purse with both hands again.

Then I pulled out a dress for her, a light summer dress with a full skirt and short sleeves, the pattern on the material all kinds of pink orchids. I left Brenda Kay with Annie, went to Billie Jean across the shop from us, and held it up to her. I said, "You try this on."

"But Momma," she said, and she smiled, dipped her head a little again. "This just isn't right."

"What do you mean?" I said. "What's wrong with this dress?" I pulled it away from her, made like I was examining the hem and sleeves for flaws in the stitching.

"There's nothing wrong with the dress," she said, and looked down at it, smiled a smile that let me know she really wanted it, wanted plenty of what she'd looked at so far.

"Then you get this dress," I said, and pushed it at her, "and don't you be worrying over whether or not this is right."

Slowly she lifted a hand from her purse, took the dress. She nodded, said, "yes ma'am," though there was no heart to those two words. She was twenty-two now, a woman with no need for a momma pressing clothes to her body like she was ten, and suddenly the words I'd used on her seemed top heavy and too loud in this small dress shop on the main street of Purvis, and I'd had to swallow, touch a hand to my chest, look around to see who'd heard me.

But there was only Annie and Brenda Kay across the room from us, Annie on tiptoe and pulling down a gray felt hat from the shelf above the dresses, Brenda Kay next to her, hands loose at her sides, white high-top shoes on.

Billie Jean ended up buying only that dress, along with a slip and a plain white blouse with pearl buttons. I'd said nothing more to her on it, finally figured she knew what she was up to.

That night Leston and Wilman and Billie Jean all came home from the last day at their jobs in the Plymouth, a huge and fat and beautiful car pulling up behind the house so that I thought it might have been the man who'd bought the place, out here again to have a look in a kitchen drawer.

By the time I made it out onto the porch, my Leston and Wilman were already climbing out of the car, and it took me a moment or two to see exactly what was going on. Wilman brought me down the steps, and I saw early evening summer clouds reflect up off the hood, saw on the other side of it Leston smiling and smiling, Billie Jean leaning out the back-seat window, smiling just as big, all of them looking at me.

Annie banged past me, placed both hands on the hood, pulled them back at the heat. "A brand-new car!" she hollered out. "I can't believe it! I can't believe it!"

"You best believe it," Leston said, the cigarette in his mouth bobbing with his words. "No way in hell we're heading cross-country in that junkheap truck we had."

"Leston," I said, "watch your mouth," though I was smiling at him, smiling and moving toward the passenger-side door, Wilman standing there and holding it open for me like a chauffeur. Leston'd never said word one about buying a car. Not a word. I'd figured we'd drive from here through to California in the truck, just limping from service station to service station. But a new car.

"Pardon my language, ma'am," he said, and nodded at me. "Nineteen Fifty-two Plymouth," he said, and slapped the hood. "Sixteen hundred dollars cash money."

He grinned. He took out the cigarette, held it away from the car, flicked off the ashes.

I took a big breath, shook my head. "That's a lot of money," I said.

"It's a lot of car," he said. We were all quiet a moment, the only sound the start-up whirr of the cicadas in the trees.

Brenda Kay said, "Huh, huh," her forced laugh as always pitched and twisted in her throat, and suddenly we all laughed right along with her, no matter none of us could know why she'd started.

"How does California sound?" Wilman said.

I went to the car, touched the chrome handle, climbed in. He pushed the door to, clicked it closed. The window was down, and he squatted next to the car, looked in at me.

"Sounds fine," I said. "When do we go?"

"Not soon enough," Leston said from his side, and climbed in next to me. He said, "Everybody in."

We drove and drove the back roads that next-to-last evening in Mississippi, drove and drove, Leston and me in front, Wilman and Annie each at a window, Billie Jean in the middle with Brenda Kay on her lap. Wilman and Annie talked away, Wilman about which roads back here would take us where, Annie about how fine the car would look rolling into Los Angeles, about the clothes she'd bought, about anything else crossed her mind. Leston only smoked and drove, the smell of the new car mixed with that smoke something magnificent. Every now and again I'd feel a touch at my hair, turn to see Brenda Kay's hand up, stubby fingers spread, her eyes on my head, "Momma, haah!" she shouted every time. And there, behind her, sat Billie Jean, turned to a window and smiling, just looking out at the countryside fast growing dark on us.

The next evening we were doing the last straightening up of the house, me scouring the sink, Annie grabbing at whatever cobwebs she could find with the broom, Wilman and Leston outside, the hood of the car up, the two of them peering into the engine like it might speak.

Billie Jean'd been gone all afternoon, picked up at lunchtime by one of her girlfriends at the bank, Ruby Sitwell, who drove a pickup not much different from the one we'd just gotten rid of the day before. They were giving her a farewell party, Billie Jean'd told me as she ran down the front porch steps, her eyes, I'd seen, blinking and blinking at tears coming up. She climbed in the cab, the two of them giggling and crying already. Then Billie Jean'd leaned out the window, blew me a kiss, and the two of them had headed off down the road.

Near sunset I finished scouring the kitchen sink, and turned to see Billie Jean just inside the kitchen from the front room. She stood with her arm looped in the arm of a man we'd only met twice before, one Gower Cross, a plump man whose face seemed too red, maybe even flushed, whenever he talked. He smiled what I figured was entirely too much, but he was a salesman for a tractor-trailer operation out of Jackson, was starting up an office here. All that smiling, I figured, just went right along with the job. He'd been over to dinner a month ago, the first time a month before that, but that was it, and he and Billie Jean'd gone out a few times otherwise. Nothing serious, as far as I could see; she'd had boyfriends on and off, boys I could only recall by how they'd acted around Brenda Kay: some wouldn't come in the house; some smiled too much and patted her head like she was a strange breed of dog; others stood with their hands behind their backs, their eyes never falling on Brenda Kay.

Gower Cross'd been of the smiling variety, just smiling and smiling those times he was over, hesitating with his fork between his plate and mouth a moment or so when Brenda Kay'd smack her lips too loud, or when she'd let fall from her mouth a piece of gristle she wanted rid of, all of it her general manners at the table, no matter how hard I tried to teach her different.

"Gower," I said, and nodded. "Here for dinner? Because all we're having is sandwiches. Tomorrow's—"

"Momma," Billie Jean said, and she pulled him even closer. She had on the orchid dress we'd bought the day before, her eyes and lips and cheeks made up. Then I saw Gower's hair was greased and combed, and he had on a painted tie, his white shirt crisp and starched and clean, nowhere near the rumpled and tired it would've been had he worn it all day. His face was more red than I'd seen it either of the nights he'd been here. Billie Jean glanced up at him, then at me, grinning.

"You two are married," I whispered.

"Oh, Momma," Billie Jean whined out, "you spoiled it," and she let go his arm, came to me, held me and hugged me hard.

I hadn't even the time to react, only stood there with Billie Jean's arms tight round me, my eyes wide open and on this Gower Cross, who stood now with his hands together in front of him, smiling.

Then the force of what'd already happened without any bit of help or hindrance from me took over, and I closed my eyes, held her myself, and I started crying, crying at the shock of it, at the grief of it, at the joy. And I cried, I was surprised to find in myself, at the relief of it. Now I knew what'd been on her mind all this time, even since May when she'd been rinsing dishes and giving what I saw now was a smile she felt obliged to give, right on up to her not buying any clothes, and last night sitting silent in the back seat of the car. Another of my children'd been taken away from me, three down now, the family growing smaller, it seemed, with every day.

I opened my eyes, patted Billie Jean's back, heard her own crying. She pulled away from me, her hands on my shoulders, and we both looked at each other, crying and laughing now, too.

Then she held up her left hand, wiggled her fingers to show me the thin gold band on her finger. She was married.

We turned back to Gower, who was rocking on his heels now. Annie stood back by the kitchen door, her mouth open wide as her eyes. Brenda Kay, oblivious, had gotten hold of an old piece of steel wool from the garbage can, sat on the kitchen floor with it cupped in her hands, looking at it.

"Oh, Brenda Kay," I said, and laughed, went to her.

Gower cleared his throat, said, "I'll take good care of your daughter, y'all can bet."

I squatted next to Brenda Kay, took the steel wool from her, and heard steps up the porch.

Leston pulled back the screen door, stepped in, wiping

his hands on one of the old rags from the shed. He looked at Gower as though he were the only person could be in his kitchen right then. He stopped, Wilman just behind him and with a rag of his own. Leston tucked his rag in his back pocket.

Billie Jean had her arm looped in Gower's again. She'd stopped crying, but gave out a few quick huffs, getting back her breath.

"Won't be any bets about it," Leston said. "I heard from outside. And you will take good care of her."

He put out his hand, his face straight and stone, held it out there in the middle of the room.

Billie Jean gave Gower, who'd suddenly lost his smile, the smallest of shoves. "Oh," he said, "Oh. Yes sir," and the smile came back, and he went to Leston, took his hand, shook it hard.

I waited for something else, some other words or movement, anything. His words, the surprise of his blessing, had startled me, too, and I wondered whether there would come from him any more words, or even a hug for his daughter, my new husband, the one *resolved* to take charge of this family, capable of anything now.

But he only stepped back, nodded again. He reached into his front pocket, pulled from it the roll of bills that was everything we had on this earth, and I watched as he peeled off five twenty-dollar bills, and handed them out to Gower.

"Mr. Hilburn—" he said, and Billie Jean cut in, "Daddy—"

"You take it," he whispered, "and you do with it what y'all see fit. No more arguing over it."

"Take it," I said, my eyes on Billie Jean's, hers brimming again. She looked at me, tried to smile, and I nodded. This was the way, I saw, my husband believed he could best bless his children, his loss of work, his selling bundles of kindling for so long a humiliation only overridden by money, and what it could promise.

Gower went to Leston, slowly brought up his hand. He took the bills without looking at them, put them in his pocket. He shook Leston's hand again, pumped it hard and hard, his face so red I thought it might burst.

Wilman stood next to Leston, held out his hand to Gower, who quick dropped Leston's, started in on Wilman's. My second son only nodded at Gower, Wilman's deep brown eyes never blinking, no smile coming across his face. He could have been Leston thirty years ago, I thought, his face so straight and serious, the perfect mirror of his father's right then.

Finally Gower let go his hand, and Billie Jean stepped in, hugged her daddy, who hesitated a moment before he brought his own arms up, wrapped them round his daughter, and smiled. He smiled, his eyes closed, and I could see inside him some same sense of relief I'd felt: here was another one gone.

Then Billie Jean hugged Wilman, then Annie, whose mouth still hung open, and then she squatted, hugged Brenda Kay, still on the floor, legs spread.

Billie Jean pulled away a moment later, turned and pointed to Gower, still smiling and with his hands in front of him. She said, "Brenda Kay, this is your brother-in-law, Gower."

Brenda Kay turned to the garbage can again, reached in, but Billie Jean caught her hand, pulled it out. "Gower's part of our family now," she said, looking into Brenda Kay's eyes.

"Bijen," she shouted, and smiled. Then she lost the

smile, reached up and touched at Billie Jean's eyes as though they'd been wounded, as though maybe, I thought, she'd been burned too: her eyebrows knotted up, and she made an O with her mouth.

"I'm okay, darling," Billie Jean said, and sniffed. "I'm fine. I just want you to say hello to your new brother, Gower." She turned from Brenda Kay, looked at her husband.

Brenda Kay followed her gaze, finally settled her eyes on Gower. "Gow?" she shouted.

"Yes," Gower said, and rocked on his heels again. "Yes, hello, Miss Brenda Kay." He brought up a hand, gave a short wave, almost a salute.

"Gow," Brenda Kay shouted, "you fat!"

And the news and shock and surprise of it all was over, none of us able to hold back. The laughing started right up, though I'd said "Brenda Kay" as stern as I could, and though Gower Cross lost his own smile a few moments, a hand going right to his stomach and touching it like he was trying to hide. Even Billie Jean was laughing, a hand covering her mouth as her shoulders shook. Then Gower took it up once he'd seen there was no fighting it, and he laughed, laughed and laughed too loud and long, but he laughed.

Above it I could hear Brenda Kay's "Huh huh huh!" again and again, tuneless and disconnected, but laughter all the same.

A few minutes later they drove off in Gower's truck, a black company-issue Ford, Billie Jean's hand waving the hankie out her window. We were all on the front porch, and once they were gone we were silent. Annie and Wilman and Brenda Kay turned back to the house, went on inside, leaving my husband and me out there in the growing dark.

"Well," I said. "Another one down." I turned to Leston, saw him staring off after the truck, though it'd already disappeared. His hands were in his back pockets.

He turned to me. I could see only half his face in the light from inside. He was smiling. He shrugged, then leaned over, kissed me on the lips. He hadn't even taken his hands out of his pockets.

He said, "Not much time to worry over them. We got our own lives to go." He paused. "We're going to California tomorrow."

I only looked up at him, surprised at his kiss, his smile, at his saying in words we had a life to worry over.

He turned, went to the screen door, held it open. "Miss Jewel," he said, "after you."

That night we slept on mattresses on the floor, and near morning a storm rolled in, filled the house with low thunder and the soft call of summer rain, chilling down the air round us all. At five we got up, washed our faces, ate cold biscuits and sausage I'd cooked the night before, and we left.

The children'd barely woken up, were already on their way back asleep as we backed away from the house, the front of it suddenly lit up brighter than any day I'd ever known by the headlights of our new car. The house seemed almost to call out to me, to want me back in it, back in the comfort of knowing what the life we were leaving was all about: no money, Brenda Kay and healing her up and taking her to the bathroom and washing her and wiping up after her, Wilman and Annie to school, Leston and his uniform and cigarettes. Then came Cathedral and all the children I'd served at the cafeteria, then all our days before, the

niggers out in the dark eating food I'd cooked. Leston and
JE and Toxie and Garland and the tips of their cigarettes
waving round in the dark mornings, the smell of pine tar
and engine oil thick in the air all day long.

I looked to Leston, his arm across the top of the seat,
his head turned as he backed out.

I looked again to the house, watched it go dark as we
turned, the headlights poking out at first the heavy green
forest, then the road before us, and I could feel my heart
picking up, the fear in it and the clear hope, and I looked
at Leston again.

He stopped, shifted gears. Before he gave it the gas, he
turned to me, smiled, though I could barely make out his
face in the dark, could see beneath the brim of his hat only
the hint of his mouth, the corners up.

He said, "Miss Jewel Hilburn."

I smiled, said, "Yes?"

He said, "Miss Jewel Hilburn, we're taking care."

"Yes," I said, and swallowed, my heart still going away.
"I guess we are," I said.

He nodded, gave the pedal a push, and we were off,
headed for California in our brand new '52 Plymouth,
new clothes in old suitcases in the trunk, my retarded
daughter settled between my last two children in the back
seat. I turned, saw all of them with their heads back,
mouths open in sleep.

And I saw beyond them, out the rear window and fast
disappearing in the distance we were putting behind us,
the house. No dust whirled up behind us for the quiet rain
we'd gotten, and I kept my eye on our old home until I
lost it for the trees and bushes and all else green there in
Mississippi.

BOOK TWO

BOOK TWO

1952

Chapter 22

This was a heat I'd never known. The sun wasn't even up yet, and already the small of my back was wet, my hair and eyes and hands hot.

But it was a dry heat, and as I watched the sun come up above the jagged mountains to the east, mountains we'd cut through late yesterday afternoon, mountains that let out into the miles and miles of sand hills we'd passed through before finally hitting this town, Indio, I took in that heat, decided I would want it with me the rest of my days.

I stood in the motel parking lot, the rising sun turning mountains that'd been gray in the twilight before sunrise suddenly black as it rose above them. I started in on my first day in California, and wondered if that sun could possibly be the same one that'd seen over every day of my life so far.

The sun was different, yes, and the air, and the light, and the shadows cast once it'd gone down last night. The mountain to the west—what the waitress at the diner last night had called Mount San Jacinto, spelled with a *J* instead of a *Y*, like it sounded, her mouth working a piece of gum all the while, her too-black hair whipped high up atop her head, her makeup so thick I couldn't be certain how old she might've been—that mountain swallowed up the sun early, yet still the sunset oranges and purples and reds all around lit up the desert so that it stayed light and hot and dry long into the night, and made this an even stranger and more beautiful place than I could have imagined. This was California, and last night had been our first night here.

"Momma," Wilman said from behind me, and I turned, saw him loading one of the suitcases into the trunk of our brand-new car. Here we were, in California, in summer heat and desert, Mount San Jacinto purple in the light from the new sun.

"Momma, get Annie out here to give me a hand, hey?" Wilman said, and lifted the suitcase in, a beat old cardboard thing tied with ropes, and I was glad it'd be hidden away in the trunk when we finally arrived in Los Angeles today. The car was what I wanted seen of us, our brand-new car.

We'd spent the first night in Natchitoches, the second just outside Ft. Worth, Leston letting Wilman take over the wheel for a half hour every hundred miles or so, so he could nap. The next night we spent in Big Spring, where we met up with James and Eudine and Judy, who'd driven down from Plainfield where James'd set up a practice taking care of livestock.

I'd called them from Ft. Worth the night before, asked where we could meet them, as Eudine had family down there to Big Spring. We ended up having to meet at the parking lot of the grocery store in the middle of town, then following them to Eudine's Aunt Charity's trailer just west of there.

I'd figured on the reunion in the parking lot being just as loud as any meeting with Eudine could be, but when she stepped from their car, her blonde hair stringy and wet, her face sweating at the heat, and'd stood up to show she was wearing a maternity smock, her belly poking out near to finished, I cried out even louder than she did, went to her, held her.

Then baby Judy came out from the back seat, her eyes heavy with sleep, perfect bangs cut across her forehead and plastered there with sweat, her red pigtails dark and wet. I leaned down, picked her up, though she made to push me away for a moment or two before settling herself on my hip, this feel of a baby in my arms as much a part of me as how I made biscuits, as lacing my shoes.

"She's a sweet three-and-a-half-year-old," Eudine said, holding her hand as Judy yawned. Eudine looked from Judy to me to Annie, half-whispered in the way she had so that everyone in attendance could hear, "They say the worst is terrible twos, but I think this age ought to be called throttle-'em threes," and she laughed, showed she was chewing on a big piece of pink gum. She hugged Annie, started in on how grown-up she looked.

Meantime, James and Leston and Wilman were all shaking hands, eyes meeting only a moment or so before darting out to the flat desert prairie at the far end of town, to the horizon that might as well have been a million miles away.

"Where's Billie Jean?" I heard James ask, even though Eudine'd already started in about the sheer hell of diapers, and how she and James weren't willingly walking into having this next baby, if we knew what she meant.

Leston smiled, shook his head at James' question. He took off his hat, swiped at his brow with the sleeve of his shirt. "Damndest thing," I heard him say. He looked at the oiled dirt of the parking lot, rubbed a toe of his boot in it. "Got married day before we took out. Man named Gower Cross." He looked up at James, who still had his hands on

his hips. Hot wind picked at all their hair, lifted it and settled it again and again.

"You don't mean it," James said.

"Don't mean what?" Eudine cut in. "What y'all keeping
to yourselves over there, huh?"

But she wasn't really interested, I could see; she reached
into the back seat of our car, took hold of Brenda Kay's
hand. "Come on out here, baby-doll," she said, and slowly
Brenda Kay moved toward her, a smile starting to come.

"How's them legs of yours?" Eudine said, and knelt as
best she could, hugged Brenda Kay still sitting on the seat,
her legs dangling out the door. "How you doing, baby?"
she said.

"You fat!" she hollered, and Eudine laughed that loud
laugh of hers.

"You're telling me, sweetheart!" Eudine laughed, then
climbed into the car next to Brenda Kay, pulling Annie on
in with her, the three of them taking up the back seat of
the Plymouth. "And y'all got yourselves a brand-new car
to boot," she said, ran her hand along the top of the seat
in front of her.

I kept an eye on Brenda Kay to see how she'd be around
Eudine. But instead her eyes were on me, and on the child
in my arms, and I realized it was Judy and me she was
most interested in, my attention and love suddenly given,
she must've thought, to someone else. Not to her.

"Daddy!" Judy cried out, and started to fidgeting in my
arms, and I let her go, watched as she ran to her daddy,
my son James, who picked her up and swung her round
like a sack of flour, set her on top of his shoulders.

I turned back to the car, saw Brenda Kay looking at me.
She eased back in the seat, comforted, I was certain, by
Judy being gone, and started watching Eudine talk on and

on at her about how much food was going to be over to
her Aunt Charity's, how she was barbequing up Texas
steaks and roast corn and cutting up fresh cantaloupe
from down by the Pecos. Brenda Kay just kept blinking,
not certain who this was, why she was here.

Finally, the men came to the car, and James said, "Now
y'all just follow me. Wilman and Judy'll go with me, and
then we can visit for real." Judy, still on his shoulders, had
hold a hank of his hair, pulled at it like it was a set of reins
in her hands.

Leston nodded, and James pulled Judy from her perch
up there, set her on the ground. Then he put out his hand,
held it for his father to take.

Leston took it, and the two shook, but it was what happened after that that made me swell and smile, made the
dirt and travel and sweat so far worthwhile: they finished
shaking hands, but for a moment or two they only stood
there, looking at each other, holding hands firm and hard,
but holding hands.

A heavy gust of prairie wind barreled through the parking lot, shook the car, the sound of grit against the side of
the car the only sound around us, even Eudine quiet for a
second.

But then she broke it, yelled, "Now let's get on out of
here. There's steaks the size of this car to be eaten," and we
were gone, headed for a trailer somewhere in the town of
Big Spring, Texas.

We ate too much, then spent the night in Aunt Charity's
trailer, all nine of us covering every bit of floor space she
had and using up every blanket and sheet and towel
before we were out of there. Our leaving the next morning was filled with kisses and crying and fussing over

when we might see each other again; filled, too, with the deep and shiny ache I carried in my heart when I'd had to surrender baby Judy back to her own momma. There was a certain wonder in the fact of a normal child, I came to see with the weight of one back in my arms, a wonder in all they could prove out to be, the world set before each and every one of them like a fine table set for a feast. And here was baby Judy, ready and raring to go out into the world as she squirmed to get free from her momma's arms once we were in our car and backing away from the trailer. Eudine finally let my first grandchild down, and no sooner than Judy's feet touched dirt did she tear off around the side of the trailer, and disappear.

Eudine shrugged and made a face at me, and I smiled, waved again, that ache grown even bigger in just that moment, when I'd not been able to wave good-bye to Judy.

Leston put the car in gear, and we were gone.

Before we were out of Big Spring and back on the desert, I made Leston stop at a hardware store, had Wilman go in and buy a galvanized bucket, then fill it with ice cubes at the service station we gassed up at. I sat with the bucket on the floorboard between my legs, passing out cubes to whoever wanted one and soaking down one of Wilman's T-shirts—the last clean one he had—and passing that around, too, each of us given five minutes with it wrapped round our necks until I had to soak it down again, pass it on to the next person.

The next night we'd stayed in El Paso, Wilman pestering us to head over to Juarez for a bullfight, but James having warned us off that for fear we'd end up knifed and robbed; the next night we'd spent in Demming, New Mexico. We hadn't got near as far as we'd intended for the car over

heating once we were up into the mountains and off the
flat of Texas. But we'd managed to limp into Demming,
Leston knowing even before the Plymouth dealer in town
did it was the thermostat needed replacing. We bought
cowboy boots for Leston and Wilman and even Annie while
we waited, then found a motel and spent the night, got up
early the next morning and started across Arizona, made it
to Phoenix by dark. By that time the hot, dry air had been
with us for a few days, and I could feel my lips going
chapped, kept us all salved up with a tube of Chapstick I'd
bought back in El Paso.

Then had come the next to last leg, us crossing over the
green Colorado at midday, stopped at the California side
for a fruit inspection, then sent on to Blythe where we
filled up the tank and the bucket both. Then a hundred
miles of nothing, only desert, then those mountains, the
sand hills, and the Desert Moon Inn.

Wilman settled the suitcase into the trunk, pushed it back
aways to make room for the other four, all the worldly
goods we had left, but there was joy I took in traveling this
light, everything shucked for now.

Wilman went back inside, the Plymouth parked right in
front of our room of the low, flat motel. The sign for the
place—script letters way up high spelling out *Desert Moon
Inn* in flashing blue neon, a lit white bulb the size of a basketball dotting the I—was what brought us in from
Highway 10 yesterday evening, hot and tired and so
worked up about finally being in California we didn't
notice how close the place was to the train tracks. After a
supper that cost us twice what the same in Mississippi
would have, we drove back and forth on the main street, a
four-lane road lined with huge date palm trees that swayed

in the late evening breeze beneath a sky that seemed impossibly huge and littered with brand-new stars, then pulled around to the back of a Texaco station so that Wilman could throw up the date milkshake he'd finished off his meal with—Indio was the date capital of the world, our waitress had told us. Then we spent the night listening to freight trains, the whole room trembling with the slow weight of the cars as they edged through town, the whole room lit on and off with blue neon coming in through the thin curtains. None of us slept, except for Brenda Kay, no bandages on her legs now, no wraps. Only the red and scarred skin that would always be red and scarred. She was the only one to sleep, the four of us—Leston, me, Wilman and Annie—only turning and turning.

Inside the room Leston was shaving at the sink. Annie, in the seersucker skirt, leaned at the mirror above the dresser, penciling at her eyebrows, her hair still in the rag-curls she'd put in last night, her cheeks rouged up, her eyelids a pale blue. Brenda Kay was still asleep on the bed, wrapped in the sheet and curled up tight.

"Annie, don't you think you're overdoing this a bit?" I said, and stood behind her, looked in the mirror at her.

She stopped with the pencil, glared up at me.

She said, "I guess you don't realize what we're doing today, do you?" She looked at me a moment longer, started up with the pencil again.

"I know," I said, "that you're my daughter, always will be, and I know that fact won't ever give you the right to talk to me that way, young girl." I tried to force my eyes to go hard on her, tried to grit my teeth in a way she might fear and respect. But that didn't happen: I couldn't do anything other than smile at her, here in a cheap motel in Indio, California, date capital of the world, my daughter getting dolled up in the hopes some Hollywood director would spot her as we rolled into town.

"Yes, Momma," she sighed out, then put down her pencil, started taking out the rags. "I'm sorry, Momma," she said in her teenage way, the words only enough to get me off her back. She wouldn't look at me, only at the mirror, and suddenly she stopped, leaned even closer to the glass. "Look at the bags under my eyes!" she yelled.

Leston said, "The last two suitcases are for you to put in the car, Anne," and tapped his razor.

We ate breakfast at the same diner we'd eaten at the night before, served by a waitress might as well have been the same one we'd had last night except for her too-blonde hair, then we gassed up at the Texaco station Wilman'd thrown up at last night. Before we headed out, Leston asked the attendant if we could borrow the hose lying next to the restroom doors at the side of the place, and the man'd shrugged, said okay. Wilman got out, showered the car with water to wash off as much road dirt as possible. Brenda Kay clapped in the back seat as Wilman sprayed the rear window, while Annie, her chin in hand, sat shaking her head at all us white crackers. By eight-fifteen we were out on Highway 10, headed for Los Angeles in our clean and brand-new car.

Mountains surrounded us for a long while, rocky mountains that jutted up on either side of the flat desert floor, nothing but brush and rock leading away from the road and toward those peaks. We drove past a sign that said Palm Springs, and Annie near-pitched a fit in the back seat, screaming on and on about how that town was Hollywood's desert playground, where everybody came to sit in the sun after working hard on their movies. We passed through a couple of towns, Beaumont and Banning, the reasons they even existed there in the desert I couldn't see; after a while we started coming into farm country, on either side of the road green rows of lettuce and tomatoes and summer squash skimming past like spokes on a wheel as we drove.

Finally the mountains beside us seemed to part, those on our left peeling back and south, those to the right retreating aways, and we came to a rise in the road.

Leston slowed down on the highway, pulled to the shoulder, and we stopped.

I leaned forward, a hand to the dashboard, and looked out the windshield.

It was a flat valley we were heading into, huge and wide, but green as far as you could see, a flat green with few trees. This was California, as much like glory land as anything I'd ever hope to see. California.

Leston had a hand on the steering wheel, with the other took the cigarette from his lips, hung it out the window.

"She's pretty," he said, his eyes squinted at the light, at all the light the sun above us gave off. Though it was still in the nineties, and though the bucket of ice on the floor-board was half-melted, sloshed back and forth with each bump in the road, somehow the heat didn't matter, and the struggle it was to keep my eyes from squinting closed at the light didn't matter. Nothing mattered, because here we were.

Cars shot past us, and I looked to the back seat, saw the faces of my three children staring at the view, even Brenda Kay looking, taking it in and making of it whatever her mind made of things brand-new and foreign to her, her having no way to know she was gazing down on a place where she'd be helped beyond measure, where we'd come closer, God willing or not, to fixing this life.

Leston leaned his head out the window, looked behind him. He gave it the gas, and we were back on the black-top, rolling down to our salvation, and I got out the brochures I'd gotten from the National Association for Retarded Children, unfolded them, careful not to rip them, pieces of worn and soft paper three years old, and I read them out loud again for the fiftieth time this trip.

An hour later we were still in farm country, only now there were more cars, more intersections, more stoplights and stores and service stations and homes coming in closer to the road. Now and again, too, we'd pass a dairy farm, the smell on this August afternoon swallowing us up. Then we'd be back in the middle of cabbage fields or more toma-toes, the smell as welcome and comfortable as any Mississippi afternoon, only better, the air still dry and hot.

We passed through towns with strange names, all the while making certain to stay right on Highway 10, just as Burton'd instructed. We passed through a town called Redlands, then Bloomington, passed signs pointing to places called Fontana and Rialto, Ontario and Montclair, all of it farmland and farmland.

Then the road was bordered on both sides by rows of low, thick green trees, branches heavy with pale green fruit.

"They look like limes," Wilman said from the back seat, and I said, "They're too big."

"Oranges," Leston said.

"That's oranges?" Annie said from behind me. She sat up, her face out the window. "That's oranges?"

"Looks like," Leston said. "This is California, you know."

"Oranges," she said.

"Ohnge," I heard from Brenda Kay, and I turned, saw her peering out the window right alongside her sister.

"Y'all sit back," I said, "just sit back and hold tight. We'll be there soon enough."

"Look at that," Leston said, and I turned to see us pass a green sign, ENTERING LOS ANGELES COUNTY in white letters across it, and I heard Annie and Wilman holler and clap in the back seat, Brenda Kay starting in with her Huh huhs, and I could do nothing but shake my head, call out a time or two more for them to settle down, Leston grinning all the while.

The farmland started giving out, fewer and fewer strawberry fields and broccoli and lettuce, all of it turned over to houses, stores, streetlights and more streetlights. We were passing through more towns, too: Covina, West Covina, Baldwin Park, low buildings coming up now, cars swarming up round us when we came to intersections. Yet there wasn't anywheres on the map Burton'd sent us any indication we were getting very close to where he would meet us, Bundy Mufflers at the corner of Olympic Boulevard and Bundy Avenue. Now and again, too, we were getting honked at, cars pulling right up behind us and near tapping the bumper back there, and suddenly I'd seen that our car wasn't much to shout about in the middle of all these cars; we were just another of a thousand brand-new '52 Plymouths on the road, only we had Mississippi plates on. There was nothing special about our car.

But I started over on that thought, tried to set in my mind the truth of where we were: California, not some back road in Lamar County, Mississippi. Everyone here drove new cars. That was the plain and simple truth of where we were.

Leston pulled into a Shell station. As best as I could tell, we were in a town the map called El Monte, still a ways from the area Burton'd circled on the map for us to head to. I could see on the map, too, there was the Freeway coming up, Burton warning us in his last letter about how all the cars went fast on it and how there were no stop signs or lights anywheres, only Exits on certain streets. He'd warned us of it, but'd told us, too, there wasn't much to fear if you just stayed the speed everyone else was going, and stayed on it until it ended on Garvey; once we reached there we wouldn't be far at all from Bundy Mufflers.

I glanced up from the map at Leston, who had both hands on the wheel, holding it tight. His jaw was set, and only then did I see he'd gone through some middle place already, had lost something of all the light we'd been feeling coming in, and I knew right away it had to do with the cars, and the streets and the buildings and the driving. All of it.

The attendant came out. Leston told him to fill it up, then climbed out, quick walked away from the pumps and across the lot to a beat-up flatbed truck heaped with empty bushel baskets.

"Momma, what's wrong?" Wilman said.

I put down the map, pulled my leg up over the bucket, climbed out. "You just stay here," I said to them, and went to my husband.

He was rolling a cigarette from the pouch he carried in his front shirt pocket. His hands shook with the effort, his eyebrows knotted with the task at hand.

He finished, rolled the cigarette in his one hand while he stuffed the pouch back in his pocket. He licked it, put it to his lips, pulled from the shirt pocket the matchbox. His hands'd stopped shaking, but I'd seen it, and he knew I had.

He lit the cigarette, took a long pull at it, then looked

up to the sky. The air was filled with the sound of cars, somebody honking here and there, cars speeding up and slowing down, speeding up and slowing down.

"Getting tired," he said to the air, let out the smoke. He took off his hat, waved it in front of him like he was cooling off. "Driving in this heat's tough."

"Yes," I said, and I crossed my arms, pretended to see in the sky whatever it was he was looking at.

I said, "Wilman can drive."

Leston nodded, took another pull. He still hadn't looked at me, though he and I both knew that same fear, the fear I'd thought beaten with the toss of a lighter into woods, had just reared up in him in some small way. We were in new territory, new ground. This was the new world, I thought, and it was no wonder that fear could show up this quick.

So I played along with his bluff of a fresh cigarette, eyes to the sky. The traffic and sound and light and noise and sun were all things he somehow couldn't take this day, the day he arrived in a place I knew he'd promised himself a million times he'd never come to. Now we were here, and I figured he had every right to bluff, every right to want me to talk him into letting his youngest son—and not himself—end up being the one to drive us on into Los Angeles.

"Leston," I said, and I reached up to him, touched his collar. "Think how proud it'd make him. You letting him drive in to his older brother's shop. Think of that."

He was quiet, took two more pulls, let out the smoke. He looked at me, said, "That'd be nice for him, wouldn't it."

I said, "Give you a rest, too." I touched the collar of his shirt again, then touched his cheek. "You can't help but be tired," I said.

He nodded, dropped the cigarette to the asphalt, rubbed it out with his toe. He put a hand to my waist, then bent to me and gave me a small peck at the cheek, and turned, went for the car. The hood was up, the attendant holding the dipstick, looking at it.

Leston came up to him, said, "Looks fine," and handed him a couple dollar bills for the gas.

The Freeway was just as fast and loud and frightening as Burton'd told us, but Wilman took it all like he'd done all this before: he had both hands on the steering wheel, his eyes on the car in front of him, yet he was sitting back in the seat, an elbow hanging out the window, and kept shouting at us to look at this building, look at that. It was near three-thirty, and we were headed due west, the sun about to slip down beneath the visor in front of him. The Freeway was built up high off the ground so that it was like we were floating above everything, cars all cutting in one on another, brake lights rearing up red and then moving right along. Wilman was keeping up with it all, but stayed in the right lane, and for that I was thankful. I was in the back seat and behind him, next to me Brenda Kay asleep, at the other window Annie calling out street Exits while I read the map in my lap. Leston was up where I'd sat most of the trip, his hat in his lap, a hand on each knee.

Then the Freeway ended, and we drove to the bottom of a ramp and back down onto streets, around us now more buildings and more cars and more stores and what-have-you than I'd seen my whole life. New Orleans was only a stick in the mud compared to this.

Everywhere were huge signs trying to sell Camel cigarettes and Beeman's gum, Nehi and Firestone Tires,

Chevrolets and Buicks, the buildings all made out of concrete and stucco and circled with parking lots.

We stopped at the light at the bottom of the ramp, and Wilman said, "Where to now?"

"We're on Garvey?" I said, trying to read both the map and Burton's letter at once.

Out the corner of my eye I could see Leston's head bob a little, looking for a street sign. "Garvey," he said. "Looks like."

"Then we go to the right, and we start looking for Olympic Boulevard," I said, figuring from what all I had in front of me that was the best way we'd ever find this Bundy Mufflers. Already I held some kind of awe for Burton's moving out here and finding a job in the middle of all this noise and confusion. *My son*, I thought, and reread the directions yet again.

Wilman drove, and drove, and drove, dodging between cars while we all read any street sign we could find, looking for Olympic Boulevard. But somehow we weren't coming up on it, and so Wilman drove, still around us all the billboards and grocery stores and big intersections.

Near four o'clock we came up to the tallest of all the buildings we'd seen so far, a white one poking up what looked a couple hundred feet in the air. Annie called out from her side that it was the Los Angeles City Hall we were passing, and then Wilman tooted the horn, put a hand out his window and waved, hollered, "Hello, Los Angeles City Hall!"

"Wilman," Annie whined, stretched his name all out in how embarrassed she was, and shrank back away from the window. Still Brenda Kay slept, and still Leston sat stiff in the front seat.

Finally I told Wilman to turn around, head back the

way we came, and once we did, it seemed only a minute or so before he hollered "Olympic Boulevard!" and stopped at the light. He turned to me, said, "Now which way?"

I turned the map round and round, then set it in my lap what I thought might be the right way.

"Turn right?" I said.

He shrugged, said, "Lucky we're in the right lane," and turned to the front.

I had no clear idea where we were any of the next ten minutes, everything here looking so much like everything else, street signs missing or twisted or hiding behind more street signs and telephone poles so that I was just about to give up, drop the map out the window, when Wilman said, "Well, will you looky here." He clicked on the blinker, turned left at the intersection, then made a quick right into the parking lot of Bundy Mufflers at the corner of Bundy and Olympic.

It was a long, low building painted a light yellow not much different from the color the sky had turned the last few minutes, a big yellow billboard up on the roof with *Bundy Mufflers* spelled out in black script letters. Across the front of the building were five or six garage doors standing open, in each a car high up on a lift; at the far right of the building was a glass door into what I figured must be the office.

Wilman pulled the car up to the first bay, shut off the engine. The man working beneath the car in front of us stopped only a second, flipped up the visor he wore against the shine of his welding torch. His face was black with grease and dirt, and he was squinting. He had no front teeth, and said nothing, only gave a quick nod of his head, and the visor snapped into place. He popped the torch to high, started back in on the car.

I opened my door, climbed out, leaving Brenda Kay still asleep on the seat. There she lay, mouth open and hair matted down with sweat, the front of her pale blue blouse sweat through.

My baby daughter had arrived, sweaty and hot and asleep, in the promised land.

Leston and Annie and Wilman were already out, each of us just standing next to our own door. We were all looking around, just looking, waiting for whatever was supposed to happen next. Heat shimmered up off the asphalt of the lot, and I took a step, felt the ground give with my weight, smelled the black and sharp odor of it.

Then from the third bay down came Burton, walking at us and working off his leather gloves, a smile on his face, that face just as dirty as the man with no teeth. He had on gray coveralls, *Burt* stitched in green thread just below the words *Bundy Mufflers* above his chest pocket, and though I felt like running to him, hugging him, the energy wasn't in me. We all just stood next to our own door, and smiled back at him as he came to us.

He went to me first, and I held him, pulled him close and patted his back, rocked a little with him in my arms.

"Momma," he said, and pulled back, looked at me. He was sweating even more than us, of course, and wiped the back of his hand at his chin. "You made it," he said, "you made it."

"We made it," I said, and looked into his eyes for some clue as to how his life had been this last year. I said, "I told you this wasn't going to be any dream."

He looked puzzled a moment, a moment long enough for me to feel exactly how tired I really was from the trip, from the heat, from the noise and light. Cars still honked, still slowed down and sped up, and suddenly I could feel the weight of it all on me, on my legs and arms and eyes, all of me just standing out here in the soft tar of the Bundy Mufflers parking lot.

Then he realized what I meant, smiled and shook his head at the memory, I figured, of our talk after Brenda Kay'd walked off into the woods. He said, "Yep, I guess you're right," and he let go of me, moved back a little. "And I'm your foot in the door."

He stood looking at me, at the car, at all of us, no one else having yet said a word to him, all of us just as tired as me, and what I saw, buried beneath the grime and sweat and the Bundy Mufflers uniform, was a man. He was older by only a year since I'd seen him drive away in his pickup, but he was a man. It was in how he stood, how he was sizing up us all; and it was in his eyes and what I thought I'd seen there: hard word and hard work, a big sun high up in the sky every day shining down on him and his hard work, his own life. He was already burrowed into the real world, already dug in for the long fight he had the rest of his life to try and win.

Wilman stood with one arm resting on top of his open door, the other at his hip. He said, "Drove us in here myself."

"Indeed I am impressed, little brother," he said, and put out a hand. They shook hands like men do, no hint anywheres that it might mean something, though when Burton let go and came around the back of the car to where Annie stood, bent down and kissed her on the cheek, I could see Wilman grinning a boy's grin, proud at himself and at his big brother both, the two of them, I could already see in his smile, in cahoots here in sunny California.

Annie said, "Billie Jean's married, got married the night before we left."

Burton straightened up, put a hand to his neck. He looked from her to me, said, "No."

"Yep," Annie said, and I nodded. She said, "To Gower Cross of Jackson. You should have seen them when they came in. She was all—"

"Gower Cross?" Burton said, and looked to Wilman, to Annie. Then he looked to Leston, who was leaning against the car, his arms crossed. He said, "Gower Cross, Daddy?"

Leston nodded, pushed himself off. "Why?"

"I know him," Burton said. He rubbed at his neck, looked at the car. "Know of him. Used to sell pallets over to the ice cream plant." He shrugged, looked up at me again, then to his daddy. "Don't matter though," he said, and now he held his hand out to his daddy, smiled. "What matters is y'all made it."

Leston took his hand, shook it, let it go. He turned to the car, slapped the roof. "Brand-new," he said. "Sixteen hundred dollars cash money."

Burton whistled, touched the top of the trunk with a hand, then took it away. "Don't want to dirty it up," he said.

"We hosed her off in Indio," Wilman said.

"Hilburn!" someone shouted from inside one of the bays, a huge and deep voice that made Burton's eyes dart toward the building.

He started moving away from us. He was putting on the gloves, walking backwards and toward the bay he'd come from. "I get off in an hour or so," he said. "Y'all just do what you want until then." He got on the gloves, started to wave, then stopped. He said, "Where's Brenda Kay?"

"Asleep," I hollered, and I moved aside from my open door, pointed in to where she lay.

He smiled, shook his head. "Asleep," he said. "Asleep upon her arrival to California." He laughed, then turned, ran back toward the bay just as "Hilburn!" thundered out again.

I turned, saw the rest of my family was still looking to where he'd disappeared. Then Leston leaned against the car again. He brought out the pouch, rolled another cigarette, lit it up.

He said, "Burt." He'd said it to no one, just himself, but we all heard it, and we looked at him.

Finally, Wilman said, "Daddy, what do you want to do?"

I looked from him to Leston, watched him shoot out smoke.

He was quiet a while, long enough for Annie to look at me, plead with her eyes for us to get out of here and back on those streets and back to driving around Los Angeles, California.

He said, "Why don't we just wait here until Burt gets off." He paused. "Looks like they got a soda pop machine inside this office here," he said, and nodded toward the glass door. "Think I see one inside."

Then that door opened, and a man leaned out. He was short and balding but had thick, hairy arms. He had on a white short-sleeve shirt and thin black tie, black pants.

"Can I help you with something?" he said.

"Nope," Leston said. He crossed his arms, left the cigarette in his mouth. "Just waiting on Burt to get off work."

"Oh," the man said. He paused a moment there in the door, then gave a half-smile. "Burt?" he said.

"One of your mechanics," Leston said, and gave a nod back toward the bays.

"Oh," the man said again, still with that smile. He let go the door, disappeared inside.

We were quiet, the four of us. We stood there at our doors for a while, and then Wilman said again, "Daddy?"

Finally Leston said, "How about those soda pops while we wait for Burt?" and turned to me, looked at me across the roof of the car, across the glare of the sun on cream-colored paint, and I could see his face shivering in the heat waves up off the metal.

We'd made it into the new world, made it here on my own sheer resolve. I'd been handed the dream, my dream of California.

But something in my husband, in his shivering face across from me and how he looked at me just then—eyes squinted at the light, lips tight around the cigarette—made me remember being handed by God the answers to my prayers for my own daddy, that he never come back.

Now we'd arrived, myself the one to have answered my own prayers, me the agent to get us here, and for an instant as I took in that shivering face, took in this heat, and the cars all around us, and this yellow sky, I wondered what sort of curse and blessing I'd given myself with this newly answered prayer. Wondered, too, if God had abandoned me now I was in a new world, or if at some point He might bring me back into His fold, forgive me for whatever was about to happen.

I looked at Leston, looked at him for a moment that seemed longer than the entire trip out here. I looked at him, and felt a drop of sweat roll down my temple and cheek, felt it hold on at my jaw. I touched it, rubbed it away.

I said, "Let me see if I got some change in my purse," and I turned, sat down in the car next to Brenda Kay, still asleep. I touched her forehead, felt her cheek. Then I got my purse from the floorboard, started digging for any change I could find in there.

Chapter 23

"It's not that you don't have the money for the down payment," the man behind the desk said, him there in his brown pinstripe suit and vest, clothes that made it ever so easy for him to say that to us.

Leston and I sat in two hard-backed chairs, me on the edge of mine. Leston, in his white shirt and navy blue tie—the only one he owned—sat leaning forward, his elbows on his knees, in his hands that hat, always that hat. His eyes were on the man telling us our money was no good.

"Not even with that new Plymouth out there as collateral," Leston said.

"I'm afraid not," the banker said, his face straight, mouth all a thin line.

"So what do you propose?" Leston near whispered. "You propose we just sit in a motel for the rest of our lives, until such time as we have years of gainful employment behind us?"

"Leston," I said, and did my wife's best to smile at the banker, apologize with my eyes, at the same time reaching to touch Leston's back.

His eyes fell from the man to the hat, and suddenly what went through my head was the whole idea of Leston's life falling in on itself again, of those nights when he'd stared too long out the kitchen window. Already, there in the motel, we were in separate rooms, Brenda Kay and me huddled on the one single bed, Annie on the other, Leston and Wilman with their own beds apiece. We weren't together, and I wasn't there to hold onto him through the nights, give to him whatever magic holding him gave, let him live his days with his chin a little higher, him standing a little taller.

The problem was that I only bussed tables. Two weeks after we moved into the motel on Pico, I'd gotten a job working at Hughes Cafeteria over to the airport, bussing tables four hours a day, my days of being a server at Bailey Grammar finally bearing fruit, I sometimes laughed to Leston, though there'd been no reaction to that, only his stone silence.

Leston hadn't even found anything yet, though it was the truth to say he hadn't yet started to look. He just drove around each day, I knew, smoking cigarettes, taking Annie and Brenda Kay—Wilman over to Bundy with his brother—up and down the boulevards, just looking at Los Angeles, and the sheer size of the place and the number of people and all those cars pushing him into a corner, even if he was in the process of making that corner himself. And now here was the corner: the bank, of course, not only wanted the two of us working, but wanted us to have had those jobs for at least a year.

We wanted to put a down payment on a house with the money we'd brought with us, it dying away each week we were parked there in the motel, us renting two rooms, one for Leston and Wilman, the other for we girls. In each room were two single beds, a hot plate on a nightstand between them, on the walls paintings of big green ocean waves breaking on black rocks, which was nothing of the beaches we'd seen so far: there was only sand here, sand too hot to walk on, sand and sand and sand on out to the blue-green sea almost invisible from the road. After a month of living in the motel, the car parked out front, school about to start for both Wilman and Annie, we'd finally decided to commit to buying a house.

The house we wanted was in an area of the town of Venice called Mar Vista, though calling anything out here a town seemed ridiculous. It was all of it just one big city. The house was a block off Bollona Creek, and we'd heard stories from the real estate agent who'd shown us the place, a man not twenty-five years old and already losing his hair, dressed in a sharp black suit and driving a Plymouth even newer than our own. He told us of the great days of Venice in America, and how a Mr. Kinney'd designed the whole thing to be a place where people'd feel like they were in Italy and just naturally soak up the culture such an atmosphere'd give off. But the water we'd seen wasn't much more than a dumping ground for the oil wells around.

The house itself was a three-room thing set on a parcel of ground so little I heard food cooking in the kitchen next door when I stood in the bathroom, the tiny window above the tub open. It had stucco walls outside and in, a front yard no bigger than our front porch back in Mississippi, chain link fence round the back yard. One thing was for certain: we wouldn't have to worry about Brenda Kay wandering off into any woods anymore. And though what the agent was asking for the place seemed a huge amount, he'd shown us how, if we got the right loan, we could afford the $12,000 he wanted.

I glanced away from the banker, who eased himself back in his overstuffed chair. Outside in the lobby people were bustling back and forth, people with money to deposit in a bank, people who owned houses and held jobs that didn't depend on the courtesy of customers eating in a cafeteria to give you tips. I looked to Leston's hands, and saw the black grease beneath his nails, there no matter how hard he worked to get it out, there every day I'd ever known him, there when he was working the lumber mill the first day I met him after church, there when he was out blasting up the woods for the Government, there when he was scratching at those same woods and selling lightered knots to niggers. This was his life, I thought in that moment: grease beneath his nails, always there, never leaving.

The banker said, "You could rent a house, at least until you've both been working solid jobs long enough. There is certainly a great deal of economic growth going on right now in the Los Angeles area, thereby making solid jobs relatively easy to find." He paused, glanced at Leston to see, I figured, if he'd get any response out of him for that remark.

But Leston didn't move, only looked at the hat, and the man went on. "Or you could just sit on this down payment for a year or so, and resubmit an application for a mortgage." He tilted his head to one side, reached with one hand to the desktop, straightened the thin pile of papers there. "Or you might go the easy route, deed this house you want with a second party, have someone cosign this loan for you." He put a fist to his mouth, cleared his throat. He looked up from the papers, smiled, his eyes giving away nothing. He said, "Do you know anyone who might do that for you? Someone, of course, who has been working a job for a while."

Leston gave a quick laugh, shook his head. He, too, was smiling, in his smile the same nothing as the banker's. This was all mere pleasantry here, business hiding, I saw, in how we were all of us supposed to act as human beings: courteous, smiling, as though owning a home were not at stake at all, maybe all of this only over buying a steer, a used sewing machine.

Leston said, "I sure do know that someone," and he stood, his eyes right on the banker, who was suddenly standing, too. Leston trying his best to hold onto things, surprise us by standing, putting out his hand to the banker.

The banker put out his hand, said, "Well, then, good. Good." He let go Leston's hand, placed his fingers on the desktop. He said, "That's good."

Leston nodded, turned. "We'll be back here. You just hold on to them papers." He hadn't looked at me yet, was already pulling open the glass doors, was heading out into the lobby.

I quick turned to the banker, nodded at him, my purse tight in my hands. I smiled, and he nodded back. I pulled the door to behind me, had to walk quick as I could to catch up with Leston, already pulling open the green glass front door.

When I made it to him he stood facing the street, hands in his pockets. We were on Main Street, cars flying past, midday traffic here in downtown Los Angeles, people moving past us as we stood there on the sidewalk. To the right, poking out above the buildings and above these cars and above these people passing, was City Hall, that monstrous white building too white, too tall, looking down on us and everyone else.

Leston looked one way up the street, then the other, as if he were waiting for some sign to give him direction.

I stood next to him, looked up at him. Still he wouldn't look at me, only squinted up the street, then down. The air was hot, dry, the sun too bright; I'd heard on the radio coming over here something called the Santa Ana Winds were picking up, hot wind off the desert that, the announcer'd said, always meant brushfires in the hills.

I said, "Who do you know?"

He looked down at me, finally. His body was still turned to the street, so that he was almost looking over his shoulder at me. For a moment or two the brim of his hat blocked out the sun.

He said, "You don't know?"

"No," I said.

"Well," he said, and shook his head. His face took on a dead smile. He turned, looked up the street again, and the sun fell into my eyes, burned into me for an instant before I closed them, turned from him.

He said, "Why, it's the famous Burt of Bundy Mufflers we'll get to deed the house with us." He paused, and I looked at him again, a hand up to block that sun.

He was looking at the ground now. He gave a small, dead laugh, as dead as the smile he'd given a moment ago. He took in a deep breath, straightened his shoulders, looked to the street again.

"We'll get our son to deed the house with us. He's been here long enough." He paused. "Burton Hilburn," he said. "Our son'll have to cosign for us so's we can own a house."

He stopped, shook his head, and I could see that same smile still on him. "Burt," he said, just that one word, but I could hear on it, even above all this commotion and noise out here on the street, the certain dead sound of that old word he'd uttered on the canoe back on Ashe Lake, the word he'd said just before he'd flicked away a brand-new cigarette: *California*.

I swallowed, looked down at the sidewalk. I blinked a

couple times, in my eyes still burnt-out purple circles of
the sun. But then they slowly started to disappear, and I
saw there on the sidewalk our shadows, short, thick midday shadows of the two of us standing here on Main
Street.

Leston's shadow turned from mine, disappeared so that
it was only my shadow on the sidewalk now, and I turned,
saw him moving down the sidewalk toward the huge
parking lot next to the bank, his hat on tight in this wind,
hands in his pockets.

Chapter 24

But the world didn't crack around us because of that deed; our son only walked through the tinted glass doors of a bank with us, sat down with his daddy and momma in front of the loan officer and anyone who wanted to take a look through that office's glass walls at a young man with a bright blue suit on, lapels wide as his shoulders, a tie round his neck painted with a picture of a palm tree and a sunset too gloriously bright for the real thing. That was all, really, that happened: Burton Hilburn got dressed up, took a morning off from the muffler shop, and we picked him up from the apartment he shared with three other boys two blocks from work. Annie stayed home from school—they were in their second week already—to take care of Brenda Kay while we were gone, and we three went to the bank, where Burton signed his own good name over.

No, the world didn't stop because of that humiliation I knew Leston was savoring up, letting fester in him, and no matter how close Leston was to the brink of whatever abyss he seemed to totter on, I wouldn't let him fall in. I had a hard hold of him those first days we were here, sometimes felt like I had him by an ear and were leading him around that way: once we'd signed on to the house, once we'd shaken hands all around with the banker, once we were out of that ugly glass and brick building and out on the street and in the Plymouth headed to Mar Vista and the house we were about to own, I said from the back seat, "Leston, let's stop over to the furniture place back by the motel. That place, remember?"

"Pico Furniture," Burton said, and glanced back at me from where he sat in the passenger seat, him still smiling, face all light, fresh from the victory I knew it was for him at the bank. He'd grinned and grinned when he'd held that pen in his hand, grinned and signed and grinned more. "That where you're talking about, Momma?"

"Yes," I said. I leaned forward, touched Leston's shoulder. "You know where I mean?" I said.

"You want to buy furniture already, and we haven't yet bought the house." He wouldn't look back at me, wouldn't even glance at me in the rearview mirror, only held tight to the steering wheel.

But I was bound and determined right then to touch what he'd started to let sour in him, wanted to let him know that now we were here, now we were going to own a house in California, now that his children were in schools out here and his second oldest son in fact co-owned our house, there was nothing he could do to drag us down with him. I wasn't going to sit in an empty bed for years waiting for him to come up from the kitchen anymore.

I leaned back in the seat, looked out my window, and gave up a smile, one that built in me some small beginning of relief, because our family, no matter how broken it seemed now, no matter how scattershot and tentative and cracker Mississippi we seemed, was coming to order. I could see it taking shape now, saw it in the palm trees out there that lined the street on this particular stretch of Washington Boulevard and how tall they stood, how smooth the line they made from the sidewalk to the tops of the fronds up there. I could see the way our life was taking shape, too, in how Burton sat up next to his daddy, a boy who'd had enough *resolve* in him to make his way out here, set up his life, sign that paper as a result of it.

Our family was taking shape before my eyes, taking on order, though that order would never fall full into line, not until I'd finished the last thing I had to do, the one thing that scared everything in me near to pieces when I thought on it. But once the papers would be signed on the house, once we'd buy furniture and have it delivered, once I'd be cooking on a stove in a kitchen in a stucco house—I'd fry up thick steaks, I decided at that moment, steaks with home fries and corn on the cob for our first dinner in our new house—there would be only that last lone task before all would be straight.

I'd take Brenda Kay to the Exceptional Children's Foundation, a place on Adams Avenue, off Western.

So far, those two street names meant nothing to me. I'd been too scared to look at a map, too scared even to ask Leston or Burton, because what I'd found—and I'd told no one yet, hadn't told Wilman or Burton or Annie, and there'd be no way I would tell Leston this—was that the National Association for Retarded Children, those people I'd dreamed on saving our lives for the past three years, was only an office in a building somewhere in downtown Los Angeles, and that there wasn't much they could do for me, other than point me to this other organization, the Exceptional Children's Foundation.

I'd called them from a pay phone at a gas station near the motel one afternoon the second week we were there, Leston gone job hunting, Wilman over to Bundy Mufflers, where he sat sipping on a Nehi Orange most afternoons and watched his brother work. The boss there didn't seem to mind, and I couldn't figure any better thing for him to do while Leston was out with the car.

I left Annie with Brenda Kay in the room, Brenda Kay asleep on the far bed. Annie'd sighed and pouted and carried on about having to babysit like every time I had an errand to run or work to go to, but then I stood at the motel room door, and pulled from my purse the brochures I'd carried with me these years, the ones on the National Association for Retarded Children and all they could do for us.

"This is why we're here," I whispered hard to her, and held them up, the paper limp and tired in my hand. "These are the people who're going to help us, help your sister. And you will watch over her, and you will do as I say."

Annie crossed her arms, still held the pout. She turned, went to the bed, fell back on it. She had on jeans and Wilman's white dress shirt, the sleeves rolled up, her red hair spilled back behind her on the motel's ugly yellow bedspread.

"Yes ma'am," she said to the ceiling, and I tried and tried to see in her the little girl who'd given up her nye-nye so many long years ago to that sleeping sister in the next bed, but could not.

I left her, pulled the door shut behind me. I still held the brochures in my hand, crossed the motel parking lot to the Shell station right there on the corner, and went to the phone booth.

I closed the glass door. It was hot inside, afternoon sun in through the glass, and I thought I smelled somebody's vomit. I looked down at my feet, pulled back the hem of my dress to see if I was standing in it. I couldn't see it any-wheres, but I knew that's what it was. Somebody's thrown up in here.

But I still kept the door closed. This was the phone call,

the only one that'd matter for the rest of our lives. I didn't want the street sounds out there cutting in on this moment, didn't want car horns and brakes screaming out to destroy this.

I put in my nickel, dialed the operator, asked for information. I told the woman at the other end the address for the National Association for Retarded Children, felt my eyes going hot as she gave me the number.

Then I called.

"N-A-R-C," a woman answered, and I'd been only silent, not certain what I needed to say, though I'd rehearsed it in my head enough times: *Hello, I have a daughter who's . . .*

"Hello?" the woman said again, and I finally managed to open my mouth, said, "Hello?"

"Yes?" she said. "Can I help you?"

"I hope so," I'd said, and then, half-crying, half-laughing, I'd sputtered out all it was I had to say, about how we'd moved here for them, how we'd planned to get Brenda Kay there as soon as we could, how I'd read in the *Reader's Digest* all about these medications and about—

"But Miss," the woman cut in, and suddenly I heard how long I'd been running, how many words I'd let spill. "I'm sorry," I said. "I'm so sorry I just—"

"The service we provide," she started in, me still with more words lined up in me, three years' worth of words ready to go, "is as an umbrella group of sorts. We publish a newsletter bimonthly, work to keep abreast of new research in the field of mental retardation, and otherwise refer specific cases to specific groups. We're not equipped here to—"

I couldn't hear her words then, for a moment the notion in me that the telephone connection'd gone bad, or that maybe I'd called the wrong place altogether. But just as quick it came to me: this was the rush of blood through me, the sound three years of hope made leaving me: *Research. Umbrella Group. Not Equipped.*

"Hello?" the woman was saying, and I opened my eyes, though I hadn't known they were closed.

I looked around, saw the cars on Pico, saw the Shell station with its rows of bright cans of oil in the window, stacked so perfect it seemed they might be the only thing in the world that meant anything, a perfect row of cans, labels all facing out and straight.

"Hello?" the woman said again.

"I'm here," I said into the receiver, though I'd figured she'd see through my words, see that, in fact, I was not here, was nowhere.

"I suggest you visit the people out at the Exceptional Children's Foundation, located at two-one-five-one Adams Boulevard, just before you hit Western," the woman went on. "Mr. Nathan White is his name," she said, "and after some preliminary testing, they might very well enroll your child there."

I swallowed hard, closed my eyes again. I tried hard to concentrate on her words, on what she'd offered up to me, and only then did I take in her word: *Enroll.*

"I said, "Enroll?"

"Yes," she said.

I said, "Mr. White?"

"Nathan White," she said.

So I let myself smile as we drove away from the bank and all the papers we'd had to sign, though my smile was just a small one. I said to my husband, "You know where I'm talking about. Pico Furniture."

I turned a moment from the window to see what his reaction might be, and caught him looking at me in the rearview mirror. His eyes jumped away as soon as he saw me looking.

I picked out two single beds for the girls' room, a fold-out sofa bed Wilman'd sleep on in the living room, a double bed for our bedroom; picked out, too, a big over-stuffed chair for the living room, a dinette set for the kitchen.

And then, once we were up and ordering our furniture, putting money down on it, money perfectly fine with these people, perfectly acceptable, the man at the counter tilted his head one way, looked at Leston, and said, "You wouldn't be new to Los Angeles, would you?"

Burton'd been leaning back in an easy chair a few feet away, and I heard him say, "They've been here only a little more than a month so far."

Leston, next to me, had his wallet out, in his hand the dollars that would fill our house. He blinked, his head bowed to the wallet.

Then Burton was next to him, put his arm round his daddy's shoulder. The man at the counter said to Leston, "Would you be in need of a job?"

He stopped, folded the wallet, held it in his hands. Slowly he raised his head, looked the man square on. Burton'd let his arm drop, had lost the smile he'd had, too. We both knew what was going on here, Burton and me, and he gave a glance over at me. He took a small step away from his daddy, who was putting the wallet back into his pants pocket.

This was a moment could go either way, I knew. Either Leston'd want to leave California because of this moment, this humiliation unfolding with no help from us at all, or we would stay in California because of this job unfolding with no help from us at all. This moment.

And in that moment I thought of those streets, Western and Adams, thought of that row of oil cans, and of my son Burton and his tie and jacket, and found in all those pictures in my head that it was me, too, making a decision right here, right now. I decided that, no matter how much more humiliation my husband would feel, if he turned down this job, I'd step in front of him, and tell that man behind the counter Yes, indeed, he would take the job. I'd make a fool out of my husband and me both; I was bussing tables, making my piddly money each day while he drove our new car back and forth through Los Angeles. He'd take this job, whether he wanted it or not.

Leston looked at him, took in a breath. He said, "Depends," and I felt my hands clutching tight my purse, felt my heart go faster.

"Driving is what we need. A driver, a man who can handle big trucks. Some lifting, too. But it's a driver we need." The man crossed his arms, and smiled at Leston. "There's just too much happening here these days, too much the boom. We need people."

"I know trucks," he said, and smiled, still without looking at me or his son.

I took a deep breath, felt how hot my neck and face had gone, thankful I didn't need to do what I'd resolved. Thankful, too, for whatever slow coming around my husband seemed to make here in the showroom of Pico Furniture.

Chapter 25

Frank was the name on his khaki shirt, him locking the door of our house in California behind him, then turning to Brenda Kay and me. I'd dressed Brenda Kay up in one of the outfits I'd bought back in Purvis, and we'd gone out to the Plymouth parked there in the short driveway—the tail end of the car actually hung out over the sidewalk, the drive was so short—and waited for Leston to come out.

It'd taken me this long—almost two months—to get up the nerve to finally take this step, to finally find in me the stone piece of resolve I'd thought was so full in me all these years of persuading my husband we needed to move here.

But for two months I'd found things to do, things to do, settling us all in until there was no more settling to do, no more reason or time to put off what it was we'd moved here to do. Now here was the time, the day. Leston was going to drive us to Pico Furniture, then I was going to take the Plymouth to Adams and Western and the Exceptional Children's Foundation, a place I'd never been to, a place I'd never called, too afraid of what they might say.

And there he was in his Pico Furniture uniform, somebody else's name stitched in red thread above the front shirt pocket. But it was a clean shirt, pressed last night

with the new iron I'd bought over to the Sears Roebuck
the week before, along with the ironing board and the pots
and pans and glasses and dishes and all else went into cre-
ating a new life in a new world. We'd started with the
$6,700, then'd bought the car for $1,600, given $100 to
Gower and Billie Jean, spent $120 on the trip out, paid
$1,200 down on the house, spent $230 on food and the
motel for that month and on gas and what have you while
we were trying to buy the house, then'd handed over
another $1,000 for the furniture and everything that went
into filling up an empty house, then around $600 for a
refrigerator and stove and washer and dryer, the washer
and dryer hooked up on the porch out back, Wilman and
Leston building a two-by-four and plywood roof to cover
them both.

   That'd left us with a little under $2,000 to begin, but
each week saw bits of that money flaking away, what with
food for us all and books for Wilman and Annie, more
clothes for Annie, who, it'd turned out, decided she'd
bought all the wrong things back in Purvis, where that
Myrtle Bancroft in the dress shop, in Annie's words,
"wouldn't know fashion if it ran over her on Sunset
Boulevard." And that word *enroll* kept coming back to me,
its weight and value solid and good in my heart, but the
idea of the cost that word carried right along with it something I hadn't counted on.

   A million things were going on then, our children's
lives swirling up and into movement: the first piece of
mail we got at the new house had been a letter from Billie
Jean telling of how she'd already settled herself into married life in Purvis, though Gower was on the road most
days of the week. They were planning on having kids right
away, which made my heart fall and rise at the same time:

who knew if they were ready, but, once those kids were there, wouldn't that *make* them ready? We'd talked on the telephone to James and Eudine, got word Eudine was farther along than they'd expected, that the next baby was due any day rather than two weeks from now, like the doctor'd first said. Burton was dating five or six girls at once, had managed even to hook up with one Julie Hesmer, daughter of the owner of Bundy Mufflers.

Wilman'd walked on to the field for football practice at Venice High School the first day of school, and'd ended up being a starter at fullback; Annie'd already ingratiated herself with a clutch of giggling girls at the junior high, though I hadn't met any of them yet, only'd answered the phone an endless number of times to have some little chatty girl at the other end say, "Umm, is Annie they-err?" and then laugh, doing the best to imitate the drawl Annie'd brought with her and, it seemed, was maybe even more pronounced now we were here. Maybe that was how she'd got in good with whoever these girls were, her posing as a Southern Belle at school. Who knew?

And there'd been the beach as often as possible for Burton and Wilman, and a section of Venice Beach up almost to Ocean Park everybody called Muscle Beach, where one Saturday Brenda Kay and Leston and I'd gone down to see exactly what all the fuss was, why Burton and Wilman insisted on spending every free minute they had there.

We parked right smack at the end of Venice Boulevard, lucky enough, I figured, to get a spot in one of the slots in front of the row of shops there, the sand starting only a block of storefronts down. The sidewalk was jammed with young people and older folks and all in between, all of them hurrying to whatever it was one did at a beach. We

walked past a Woolworth's; next a little shop that sold
only bathing suits, mannequins in the window wearing
next to nothing, two-piece suits that showed your midriff
out there for anybody to take a look at, and I wondered
how soon it'd be before Annie was asking for one of those.
Next to that was a fish and tackle shop, and a lawyer's
office, and then a store that sold liquor right off the
shelves, right here at the beach. California, I thought,
California and California and California. Two-piece swimsuits and liquor and lawyers.

Then the shops ended, and we came to a strip of concrete like a narrow road that ran parallel to the ocean, still
what looked a good quarter mile away across the sand. A
short brick wall stood across the strip, separating the sand
and the street, these houses behind us, the shops and cars
and all of Venice and Los Angeles and the rest of the
world. This was where land stopped, where the beach
started.

I looked to the left, wondered when we might find this
Muscle Beach Wilman'd given us the loosest directions to:
"Just on down to the end of Venice, Momma," he'd said
that morning, pushing the front screen door open with
one hand, his towel in the other. Burton honked his horn
again, him out there in the ten- or twelve-year-old green
pickup he'd bought for fifty dollars from somebody at the
shop. "You'll see us," he'd said, and left. He hadn't even
had any breakfast.

I looked down the beach to the right, squinted, saw
what looked like steel pipes set up like a swing set way
down there, people all standing around, all of them
Wilman's age, it looked like: girls with those two-piece
suits on, boys in black swimming trunks. Beyond them I
could see a pier out into the ocean, on it a roller coaster

and buildings and flags and the like: Ocean Park, the place Wilman and Burton went, I'd heard enough times from Annie, every time they left at night.

"Down there," I'd said, and swallowed, closed my eyes a moment at the idea of walking through all these people with Brenda Kay in tow. It wasn't shame, I knew, that made me feel this way; it was the looks we all got, the looks we'd gotten all our lives, and how people didn't even know how to look at us. I held Brenda Kay's hand tighter in mine, started off on that thin road, Leston right beside us.

Of course we got the looks from everyone, everything from the shocked, mouth-drop-open look at Brenda Kay most of the kids gave as we moved along, to the look that was no look, eyes darting away from Brenda Kay. And, too, there were the smilers, people who purposefully met our eyes and smiled a smile full of pity, eyebrows knotted in the smallest way, lips never parting. All looks we'd lived with every time we ever left the house, and it occurred to me for the first time since we'd been in California that, in fact, these people weren't so different, weren't so strange and new. We'd gotten the same looks in Purvis. Always.

We came to the knots of people I'd seen, only to find there were two or three wooden platforms set up on this side of the steel bar structure, platforms covered with canvas, dumbbells and bars and round heavy weights laid out on them. Boys and men I hadn't been able to see from back where we'd started from were standing in the sun and lifting the bars, holding them up above their heads. Girls all ages and some boys, too, stood round and watched, sometimes clapping when the bar had a bigger number of round weights on them. They were all tan and grimacing, tough boys, I thought, waiting for the girls to see them. On another platform a few feet up the beach was a man and woman. They were holding hands, and then the man picked up the girl, and the girl arched her body up there in the air while the man lifted her above his head, him grimacing and tan, too, the girl with a smile that looked painted on, pretend. She had on one of those two-piece bathing suits, her midriff all tan, tan as her legs and arms and face. He held her up in the air a few seconds, and then he gave her a toss straight up, and she twisted, turned, and fell back into his waiting arms, her own arm out into the air all poised and graceful, her still with that smile. Then he lifted her again, and this time she put her hands on his shoulders, and pushed herself off his stomach, swung herself up somehow until she was doing a handstand on his shoulders, and the grimacing tan man put his hands on his hips, stared out into the crowd. Everyone clapped at this, too.

California, I thought.

The bars I'd seen were at the far end of all this goings on, and we stopped ourselves at the edge of the sand, the pipes about twenty yards out.

There, each swinging from two metal rings they held tight in their hands, rings that hung on chains attached to the steel crossbar, swinging like monkeys there up above us all, only a handful of boys and girls standing and watching them, were Wilman and Burton, my sons' muscles taut across their chests and stomachs, their skin already a deep and shining tan, so that at first I didn't recognize them as we came up, and I thought for a moment these were just two strangers putting on a show like everybody else. They just weren't drawing the crowds.

Burton pulled himself up until his hands in those rings were at his hips, and he held himself there, Wilman next to him, just hanging. They both had on black swim trunks, their chests just sprinkled with the beginnings of dark hair. Burton's face jittered with the strain of holding himself above the sand, his eyes closed. Wilman was smiling, arms above him as he hung there, in his face some strain, but nothing like in his brother's.

Someone in the crowd hollered out, "You do it, Bill! Don't be a weenie!" and everybody laughed, started up chanting *Wee-nee, wee-nee!*

Wilman smiled even more, started laughing himself, and it was only then I figured out: this was his new name, just as Burton'd been cut down to Burt. *Bill,* I thought. *Bill.*

I turned to Leston, Brenda Kay between the two of us, her just watching, taking in all that lay before us: the sand, beyond it the green smudge of sea, her brothers here and hanging on the rings.

But it was Leston I wanted to see, his reaction I wanted.

I'd thought he'd turn, want us to leave at this newest attack on him and who he was, yet another of his children rechristened in the land of plenty.

He was only watching them, in his eyes almost the same blank look as Brenda Kay. Then he glanced at me, and smiled.

"Them boys," he said, and shook his head. He had a cigarette at his lips, took it out, let go the smoke, the wind out here making it disappear as soon as he gave it up. "Burt and Bill," he said, and he nodded at them. "Already charming the girls."

I only looked at him, the surprise of his words like cool water, or like the warm breeze that blew in off the ocean at us right then, right there, a breeze sharp with the salt of it, strange and wonderful. Welcome.

I turned, saw Wilman—*Bill*—was pulling himself up,

the cries of *Wee-nee, wee-nee!* rising round him, the words, it seemed, lifting him up, making him move. Then his hands, too, were even with his hips, his face as shaking as Burton's had. He was up, and most everybody—*their friends,* I saw, *their friends*—gave out a big groan. Some girls clapped and hollered out for him, and Wilman just smiled and smiled, at the same time his face filled with the hurt of holding himself there. Burton—"Burt," I whispered to myself—still held his hands tight on those rings, pressing down to hold himself up.

"Let's go," Leston said, and I felt his hand at my elbow, turned and saw him with Brenda Kay holding his other hand, the two of them already headed for where we'd parked.

He smiled, the cigarette at his lips burned down near to nothing. He said, "They don't need us here," and he winked. "Burt and Bill," he said. He took hold my hand, and we started back.

Now, today, the day I was to finally call to order our lives with simply showing up to a place on Adams off Western, here came my husband, the front door to our home in California closed behind him, his furniture store uniform on, somebody else's name on his chest, and I was filled with dread and fear and joy at once. This was the day.

He came to the car, opened his door, and I said, "Morning, Frank," to which he'd only stared at me a moment. I reached over, touched a finger to the name on his shirt pocket, said, "Don't you know anything? In California, Burton turns to Burt, Wilman to Bill, Leston to Frank." I smiled again, and hoped he hadn't seen how my finger'd shaken as I'd pointed.

"Fank?" Brenda Kay shouted in the back seat, and leaned forward, both hands on top of the seat between us.

"You're nervous," he said to me. He smiled, started the engine, put a hand on the top of the seat, backed us out. He said to Brenda Kay, "Miss Jewel Hilburn's moved us all the way out here to Los Angeles to meet with them folks at the Association of Retarded People, and now she's afraid of why she did it."

"You are just too perceptive," I said, and felt my hands holding too tight to my purse once again. "Just too, Mr. Leston Hilburn." I paused. "And it's the National Association for Retarded Children." I still hadn't told him of the Umbrella Group; hadn't told him I was headed somewhere else this morning, a place I knew nothing of.

He smiled again, fished in his shirt pocket for a cigarette he'd already rolled, his fingers digging under *Frank*. He pulled one out, put it to his lips. He looked at me, his eyes all squinted up as if it were already lit. He said, "You don't think I know the name of this outfit?"

We were out on the street now, and he put the car into gear, but didn't give it any gas. We sat in the middle of the street a moment, and I said, "Shouldn't we get a move on?"

"Just don't you worry now," he said. "You don't. About today."

"Remember who you're talking to," I said, and tried to give him a smile might convince him just to drive us to Pico Furniture. I just wanted to get him out the car, leave me to find out what we'd come here for.

Chapter 26

I had no problems finding the place; just as the office girl at N.A.R.C. had told me, it was off Western, which I'd taken down from Pico and just followed light to light to light until I hit Adams, then turned right.

They were nice homes set back farther on the lots than most houses I'd seen since we'd moved here, houses with green lawns and flowerbeds and bushes, honeysuckle and climbing roses and palm trees. The houses were older, you could tell by the gingerbread and touches they had, and'd seen a better time than right now: some were clapboard with a little chip here and there where the paint was bubbling up; some had that white stucco, but with the faintest tinge of green to it where moss'd started in; and some were brick, now and again the mortar loose and crumbling. But most all of them were in fine shape, positively better than the house we lived in. I wondered as I crawled the car along, looking for 2151, how pleasant it'd be to live here.

Then I spotted it, a gray house with white trim, a big porch out front almost like what you might find back in one of the finer homes in Purvis. The second story had dormers poking out, and in the front yard stood a magnolia.

A magnolia.

The first space I could find to park was four or five houses down, where, I saw, I'd have to parallel park this monster of a car, and I could just imagine what any passerby might think when he saw what was going on: a woman with Mississippi tags on her car, a retarded girl in the front seat, the woman trying to maneuver this car too big for her into that tiny spot. But it was the only spot I could see for the next block or so, the street jammed with cars all sparkling and clean and new.

I pulled up even with the car in front of my spot, then turned in the seat, put my arm on top of it like I'd seen Leston do a million times before, and I started backing up.

A little nigger boy stood on the sidewalk back there. He was looking at me, and waved a hand at me, motioned me to back up.

I smiled at him through the rear window, started back as he waved and waved. Then he put up his hand to stop me, made a whirling move with his hand, what I took to mean *Cut the wheel the other way*, which I did.

We went like this a minute or two, him motioning, me following, until I'd finally got the car nestled into place, snug between two cars.

I climbed out, came round to give him my proper thank you, but he was already gone, moving up the sidewalk. Though his back was to me, I could see for the first time how well he was dressed: navy blue pants with a sharp crease, a white short-sleeve dress shirt, shiny black shoes. Hung from his shoulder was a leather strap cinched round a pile of books that bounced on his back as he walked away.

I called out, "Thank you!"

He turned, walked backwards a moment. He had on a thin, black tie, and he gave the smallest of nods, his chin jutting up in the air only a moment. He turned back, headed off.

I didn't know what to think: though he'd been the one to help me, done me that favor, nigger children in Mississippi never just jutted their chin when you spoke to them, but always gave answer. And they didn't— couldn't—dress like that, except on Sunday mornings. But, as with everything I'd discovered so far, this was a new world, one I had no way to figure how it worked.

I turned back to the car, opened the door for Brenda Kay. She stared out the windshield a moment longer, as though she, too, were watching the boy.

I said, "Let's come on now, Brenda Kay. There's people to meet." I reached down, touched her hair. I had it back in pretty red barrettes today, had her dressed in pink slacks and a pink and white striped blouse, her shoes all shined up pretty and white. I reached to her lap, took her hand. "Come on now, Brenda Kay," I said, and then, for no other reason than that I'd never heard the words from me before, I said, "There's a new world here and waiting for us."

There'd been no one to hear them, only my daughter. But they were the best words I knew I could speak right then, could pass on to my daughter. This was why we were here: Brenda Kay, and that gray house with the white trim and big porch.

I held her hand tight, felt my palms begin to go wet, and I pulled her up. Brenda Kay turned in the seat and placed her white shoes out onto the curb, and stood.

"There," I said. "There," and I looked at her. She still had no look in her eyes, her mouth clamped shut for whatever reason. I said, "Now give us a smile here," and reached to her hair again, tucked a single thin strand of it back behind her ear.

"Let's see a smile," someone said from behind me, and

I quick turned, startled at the sound of a different voice out here.

A niggerwoman stood there on the sidewalk, in front of her a baby carriage. She was looking at Brenda Kay, smiling, and I could feel my own smile trying to come up on me, trying to make its way onto my face.

I said, "Good morning," and thought I'd said it maybe too quick.

She nodded, our eyes meeting and holding a moment. She was a high yellow, but it was her hair I saw and took in first: straight, bobbed under at her shoulders, parted at the top in the middle. Then I saw what she had on: a pale lavender dress, pearl buttons up the front, a lavender belt at her waist, the skirt of the dress all flounced out and full. And she had on lavender high heel shoes.

She said, "You of course are with the Foundation," and, still smiling, nodded toward Brenda Kay. "We're happy you folks are here."

But her words weren't meaning much to me just then; I only watched her lips moving, saw she wore deep red lipstick, saw, too, she had on rouge, and that her eyebrows'd been penciled in.

"Yes, we are," I struggled out, the words feeble and useless, I knew. "At least we're about to be, that is," I said. "With the Foundation."

"Mississippi," she said, and leaned back a little, nodded to the rear of the car. "I saw your plates," she said, and looked back at me. "My grandfather was from Mississippi. Up around Oxford, I think."

"Oh," I said, then said, "We're from Purvis, down near to Hattiesburg," and found my breath was slow and shallow, me here on the street and talking to a niggerwoman I'd never seen before, just passing the time of day. And her wearing clothes I'd never imagined I might wear. *Lavender shoes.*

"Momma!" Brenda Kay said, and I felt like her word was some sort of salvation, her demanding of me my attention, and I'd forced my smile again. "We've got to be getting to the Foundation," I said, however hollow I sounded. They were only words.

"Nice to see you," she said, and nodded. She pushed the carriage along again, a carriage shiny and new, the wheels as they turned making no sound at all, and suddenly I saw a picture of Cathedral barefoot on the road out front the old house in Mississippi, one or another of her boys when they were babies bundled up in an old quilt and tied off on her back, a papoose there as she walked.

From across the street another woman's voice shouted, "Dorinda, how's little Leon?"

I looked, saw on the porch of a red brick house another niggerwoman, this one in a bathrobe printed with all kinds of flowers. She had her arms crossed against her chest, her hair cut short and curled. Her skin was a little darker than the one with the carriage, and I could see her smiling, her white teeth.

The one pushing the carriage, this Dorinda, called out, "He's doing just fine. A little of the croup, but nothing this fresh air won't help."

"You call me, girl," the other woman hollered, and I watched as she went to the edge of the porch, stepped down to the concrete walk that went up the middle of the lawn, and bent over, picked up the newspaper lying there.

"In a while," Dorinda called out, still pushing the carriage, and the woman with the robe waved, went back up on the porch, and disappeared inside.

They lived here.

I took Brenda Kay's hand, my eyes looking everything over, wondering what could go on in this neighborhood, what caused niggers to live this way. There were four houses we had to pass, and I found as we walked along the sidewalk that the concrete suddenly seemed cracked and cracked, narrow strips of grass growing up between those cracks to make it look a little more shabby than when we'd driven up. And the green in the stucco of these homes seemed a shade heavier, the loose mortar even looser, though I knew it was all in my head, all me and my making up reasons why these niggers couldn't live in such fine houses, when we ourselves lived in a house with a driveway not big enough to hold our car.

Each step I took seemed filled with a new and uneasy feeling, as though the world were breaking up beneath us as we moved. My life was being swallowed up more and more each day by this strange place, California: liquor stores and lawyers, two-piece swimsuits and luxurious niggertowns, at the center of it all my Brenda Kay and me, struggling with each step we took just to stand in the middle of this brand-new place.

Then we came to 2151, and I stopped, looked to left and right. This was it, the place where whatever'd start next in our lives was going to start.

I took Brenda Kay's hand, held it tight, and we started up the walk, moved up the three steps and onto the porch. The door was a big oak affair, stained and beautiful, with a leaded glass window I couldn't see through. Next to the door was a brass plaque, not much different than the one Leston and I'd walked up to and read at Dr. Basket's office in New Orleans all those years back. But now we were at 2151 Adams, and this plaque was shiny and looked new, and held out to me a whole barrel full of promise, not like

the somber fear Dr. Basket's old and tarnished plaque had
given me. This plaque read:

The Exceptional Children's Foundation
Nathan White, Director

Though there was a small black button on a switch-
plate next to the plaque, I didn't want for whatever reason
to push it, didn't want to hear a doorbell sound through
the glass before us. We were small, I suddenly saw, me
only a cracker from Mississippi showing up here to the
door with my retarded child, my Brenda Kay, and so I
reached up a hand to the leaded glass, hesitated a moment
longer—just one more moment of this life, because who
knew what would come next? Who knew, other than God
up in heaven, what would come next?

I knocked. I looked at Brenda Kay, saw that single
strand of hair fallen back out of place. How could I have
missed it when I'd pulled back her hair this morning? I
wondered, and I reached up, tucked it back behind her
ear again, her eyes straight ahead, mouth still tight closed.

My hand still there at Brenda Kay's hair, the front door
opened up wide, and there stood yet another niggerwoman, this one young and beautiful, high cheeks and a
fine straight nose. Her hair was pulled back tight into a
bun, and she had on makeup, too, and was smiling at us.

I took my hand down from Brenda Kay's ear like I'd
been caught red-handed at something. I swallowed. I tried
to smile, tried and tried, and finally tore my eyes from her,
glanced aside at that shiny plaque. I said, "We'd like to see
Mr. White, if we could."

She stepped back from the door, opened it even
wider, and made a sweeping gesture with her free hand

to lead us in. "Please," was all she'd said, and it sounded like a word from a movie the way she said it, her mouth all in a smile, her eyes smiling, too, really meaning it. This from a niggerwoman dressed in a white blouse with a high collar and a black skirt, and though I was glad she wasn't all gussied up in lavender like the one on the street, already I was wondering if, were I to end up enrolling Brenda Kay here, she'd be in a class full of retarded nigger children.

She closed the door behind us, Brenda Kay's hand in mine now, and said, "Do you have an appointment?"

I turned, faced her, said, "No, actually. We do not." I glanced at the floor: sparkling hardwood, buffed and polished and gleaming; a shaft of morning light fell in through a window to my right and lit up the wood, and I could see in the air dust motes sailing and sailing, just hanging there in the air.

"Well then," she said, "we'll see if we can't get you in to see him." She paused, and I looked up, saw she was looking at Brenda Kay. "My name's May," she said to her, and Brenda Kay looked to me a moment, just like she always did, then back to the woman.

"This here is Brenda Kay Hilburn," I said, and reached out, touched my daughter's arm. "I'm her momma," I said, "Mrs. Jewel Hilburn. We just moved here not a long time ago, a couple months. The people over to the National Association for Retarded Children said we'd do best to come see y'all."

"Hey!" Brenda Kay said, and smiled. Then she looked at me, said, "Thedral, Momma!" and turned back to May.

"No," I said to her, "not Cathedral," and I was surprised at how she'd remember her from three years past. There hadn't been talk of her even allowed in our house.

I turned to the woman, saw she had a puzzled look behind the smile she held. I smiled, said, "She's talking about Cathedral, a niggerwoman who took care of her when she was little. Back in Mississippi."

She lost the smile as soon as that word *niggerwoman* crossed my lips, and I knew right then it was the wrong word, though I'd never in my life felt any kind of embarrassment at uttering it. But I knew it was the wrong word, here in the foyer of a fine home in Los Angeles in a nigger neighborhood, a foyer suddenly too much like Missy Cook's old place in Purvis: a few feet away a staircase ran up to a landing at a window that looked, I imagined, out onto the back yard, and I thought a moment on seeing my and my momma's clothes burned in the pecan orchard back of Missy Cook's house, and on my momma's rocker going up in flames, too. To my left was what looked like it'd been a dining room, big windows looking out on the front yard, chairs spread against the walls; to my right was a smaller room with a big oak desk, on it stacks of paper, a blotter, a telephone, a lamp; next to it, on a smaller table, was a typewriter.

And as I took all this in, I realized what I was really doing: avoiding the eyes of this woman, May.

"Okay," May said. She turned from us, headed into the room with the desk. Once behind it she smiled again, pointed to the room behind us, where the chairs sat. "You can have a seat, and we'll see what we can do."

I nodded, smiled, turned to Brenda Kay. We two moved into the dining room, where in one corner, next to the window, stood a potted tree, something I hadn't seen from the foyer. Brenda Kay walked right over to it, took one of its small leaves in her hand, rubbed it between her fingers. I sat on the smallest, hardest chair I could find, some sort of punishment I couldn't figure out why I was giving myself.

From where I sat I had clear view into the parlor across the foyer, and to May, who was half-turned from us, the telephone to her ear. She was talking low into it, and then she stopped, listened a moment, nodded. She had a pen in her hand, was writing something on a piece of paper on the desktop. Then she smiled, her eyes on the piece of paper in her hand, and said one more word, hung up the phone.

"Mr. White will see you now," she said, and stood. "He's only got a few minutes while the children finish up with morning exercise. Then he'll have to be back in the classroom."

I stood, went to Brenda Kay, still at the tree, and took hold her hand. Then we were in May's office, her leading us to a door to my left.

She opened the door for us, and our eyes met, the two of us smiling, and for one last moment I wondered whether this Mr. White himself was a nigger, the irony of his name right there in my face, Mr. White, and I wondered if that wasn't what she'd been smiling at all along.

I led Brenda Kay into a room with potted plants all around, in the windows and against the walls, and there in the center of the room sat a desk bigger than May's, Mr. Nathan White perched on the corner of it.

He was white. Too white, in fact: he was pale and thin, his forehead high and pasty. He had the thinnest moustache, too, and wore a white dress shirt and red tie, tan vest and pants, and I couldn't help but feel as we walked into the room for the very first time that here was a white boy, out to impress us with his maturity and poise, what with the way he sat there on the desk.

"Be seated," he said, and pointed to two chairs in front of the desk.

I led Brenda Kay to the chairs, and we did as we were told, sat down, me on the edge, my back as straight and proper as I could make it, knees together, hands on my purse in my lap, Brenda Kay leaning forward in her seat, her hands clasped. She was already slowly rocking forward and back, and I said, "This is Brenda Kay Hilburn. She's eight years old, nine in October." I paused. He looked at her, but wasn't smiling. Instead, he had a finger to his chin, started tapping it.

I said, "I'm Jewel Hilburn," and I smiled even harder, hoping he might take it up, me not certain what Brenda Kay was up to, her with that rocking. She was watching him, waiting. Just as I was.

"We moved here two months ago from near Purvis, Mississippi." I paused.

He smiled, nodded sharply. "Briefly," he said, and cut his eyes over to me, "let me tell you what we're about. We will test your child, let you know what level we perceive her learning abilities might reach. We test our children each year, determine areas in which they might excel. And we teach them. There are two classes here, one for the younger children, like your Brenda Kay, a class taught by Mrs. Becky Hamby, in whom I have all faith; the second class consists of older children, teenagers. I teach them. We are both authoritative and gentle in our approach. Firm and careful." His voice was big for him, as if maybe he'd taken voice lessons somewhere in his life, and felt it necessary to use what he'd learned. It wasn't unpleasant, wasn't intimidating in any way I could see: Brenda Kay was still rocking just a little, but now her eyes were gone wandering, looking at the plants in the pots around the room.

"You go ahead and have a look around," he said. "Go on, Brenda Kay. You can touch them if you want."

Her eyes shot to his when he'd said her name, and now she was looking at me.

I nodded, and she stood right off, walked around his desk and went to a plant with pale purple leaves hanging in a basket from the ceiling. She was in the sunlight now, Mr. White's back to her, and she touched leaves here and there, just fingered them.

"If I may," he said, "I would encourage you to enroll her as soon as possible, Mrs. Hilburn. That will allow us to begin that lifelong process of learning as much as she possibly can, as much as her level of retardation will allow."

"But—" I began, and'd meant to ask him the question all these plants, all this shiny hardwood and oak furniture and the fine rugs on the floor had screamed for me to ask: how much would enrollment cost?

"In reality, this endeavor might seem hopeless," he said, and now he was off the edge of the desk, swooping toward me, his eyes on mine as he came near. "But hope isn't what we find at stake here. It's educability: helping the child find his or her own level of learning, and proceeding from there. Finding at what point the child's learning abilities taper off. Finding where we can begin working with what they already know, what they need to know, what, in fact, they *can* know."

Now he was pacing, his arms still across his chest, that finger still tapping out his chin. He hadn't raised his voice at all, hadn't ranted. He was only speaking, giving out to me what was going on here at the Exceptional Children's Foundation. I felt my neck go hot, my breath so short with all these words, with his movement and seriousness and authority. And I listened.

"We cover such topics as the alphabet, simple addition, money value, et cetera, as well as storytelling, exercise—that's where they are right now—" He pointed behind him, and for a moment I glanced that way, as if I might see something. But we were only in a room, his office.

He stopped, stood by the edge of the desk, leaned against it. "I suppose you'll want to know who I am," he said, and he gave a smile, however rehearsed or insincere it may have been. Still, I thought, it was a smile. "I am a philanthropist, I make no bones about saying that. There's no pride in my revealing this fact, no boast. I come from upstate New York, studied business management in school. But I found that the sort of business I was most interested in involved helping retarded—what I call Exceptional, of course, hence the name of the Foundation—children." He paused. "I had a retarded brother. A younger brother, and I can remember his being brought home from the hospital, and my parents staying up and weeping all night long for weeks."

He said all of this matter-of-fact, even that word *weep*, a word I wasn't certain if I'd ever heard spoken before except in the sanctuary at church, and then it'd been Jesus who wept. *Jesus wept*, I thought: the shortest verse in the Bible.

I glanced over at Brenda Kay, wondered if I could just go ahead and tell him all about her, about how long in labor I'd been, about Cathedral's boys Sepulcher and Temple carrying me downstairs, eyes locked on each other, and about the drive to New Orleans the first time, and about the burns on her legs, and how we'd finally moved here. I wondered if I could tell him all of that, any of that, but he gave no room for me to speak.

"They finally placed him in an institution, my younger

brother only a month old. That was the beginning of the journey, the journey that has ended here. You see," he said, and now he uncrossed his arms and put his hands on the edge of the desk. He was still looking at me, eyebrows knotted up, eyes all concern and care, though, like that smile, I still couldn't tell how much heart was behind it. "You see, I saw my brother grow up," he said. "I saw him being raised in an institution, saw him go from a month-old infant to a child to an adolescent to a teenager to a young man. I saw all of it, because we as a family made it a point to visit him once a month. It was a fine institution, fiscally sound and with a caring staff. And we loved him, gave him cookies and candy when we came, spoke carefully and lovingly to him, touched him and hugged him and smiled at him. Still, it was an institution in which he lived every day, and over the years I began to see in my brother's eyes a certain spark, a certain unspeakable something deep inside him I believe went untapped, and when he died at age twenty-one, I grieved. I grieved not for my mother or my father or my older sister or myself. I didn't grieve for any of us."

He paused, and he was off the desk now, and sat in the empty chair next to me, leaned close to me. I saw he was older than I'd first thought, saw flecks of gray in that black hair, saw his skin wasn't as soft as I'd thought before, but was aging, aging like all the rest of us.

"What I grieved for was that spark, that undeniable spark behind his eyes, *in* his eyes, that had gone untapped. I didn't know what that spark meant, didn't know what it might have meant. But it was gone."

He finished, and I brought my eyes from his, settled them on my hands holding my purse, at my old hands here in front of me. Then I looked at Brenda Kay. She stood at the window, had both hands up to the glass. She was looking out at something in the side yard of the place, then turned to me, the sun falling in on her to light up her face.

She pointed a finger to the glass, said, "Momma, look! Matoes, Momma!"

She smiled, and I thought I, too, could see a spark of some kind in her eyes, her green eyes illuminated by the sun so that the color'd become gemlike, green and light.

"Tomatoes, that's right, Brenda Kay," Mr. White said, and stood, went to her at the glass. "That's another of our projects here. In addition to class time and exercise, we also work on our garden out there. Cherry tomatoes, for some reason, seems to be the vegetable of choice for these youngsters."

He put an arm on Brenda Kay's shoulder. She didn't flinch, didn't even move, as though already she'd known who this man was and why he was here.

"That's what we used to grow back at home. In Mississippi. Tomatoes, and all else you can name," I said, and suddenly I felt stupid. Words about vegetables. I didn't want him to think me the cracker I was, wanted him to know I, too, was a teacher, had gone to college.

But he only looked at his watch, turned from her and picked up the tan suit coat from the back of his desk chair, started shrugging it on.

He said, "I know you are thinking at this moment that here is a man who wears his heart on his sleeve, exhibiting his family's failures and his retarded brother's plight as well as his own grand designs on the world for all to see. But the truth of the matter is that that is how matters we pretend do not exist change. Living in closets, hiding away the exceptional and pretending they do not exist, pretending

that God is in His heaven and that all is right with the
world, none of these antiquated notions serve the exceptional child. They only bury these young people, only turn
our eyes from finding that spark in every one of them. And
I am convinced that there is a spark in each child. That
may be a simplistic view of the world, may even be ridiculous; some retarded children never learn to wipe their
noses, never learn to chew food. Perhaps for those the
institution is needed. But not for the children to whom we
address ourselves here at the Foundation."

He paused, the coat on now, and ran a hand down the
tie, placed his hands in his pockets. He tilted his head to
one side, said, "Now, what do you think?"

I took in a breath, not ready for him to turn this around
to me. I'd been listening, hearing his words, words that
made sense to me, but words so forward, his handing
them all out to me so abrupt and straight that the only
words ready in my head left me just as quick: "You are a
pompous man," I said. "But right."

He laughed, laughed out loud and long, leaned his
head back and laughed and laughed, and shook his head.
Brenda Kay turned quick to him, and then she started to
laughing, too, her "Huh huh huh!" filling up whatever
room for laughter was left in here, and I felt myself begin
to smile.

He said, "Thank you, Mrs. Hilburn. Thank you," and
he came around the desk, held out his hand for me to
shake. "And I'll expect you and your daughter here tomorrow morning at eight for her first set of tests, and for
enrollment."

I finally stood, glad to be out of the chair, swearing to
myself already I'd never sit there again, never let him boil
over me like that, though I knew what I'd said was true:

he was right. And I knew, too, we'd be here tomorrow morning, would arrive out on that street at seven-thirty just to make sure we weren't late.

I took his hand, a hand that seemed too frail in mine, and we shook. "Enrollment," I said, and felt my smile leave. Now was the time: "Enrollment," I said again. "How much will that cost?"

He stopped shaking my hand, but still held it. He said, "What you can afford, you pay." He paused. "Remember? I am a philanthropist. Pay only what you can afford."

He let go my hand, touched his tie again. He said, "I admire your candor, and look forward to more of it. I need the occasional kick in the pants. Refreshing, certainly." He turned from me, started toward the door.

"Brenda Kay," I said, "come on, honey, let's go."

I held my hand out to her, the same hand I'd shaken with Mr. Nathan White, Philanthropist, just held it out to her.

She was facing the window, both hands to the glass again. For a moment or two she stared out to where those tomatoes must have been, then dropped her hands to her side, turned and came around the desk to me. Then we were standing before the closed door, Mr. White with his hand at the knob, ready to pull it open.

He smiled at me. "One last item," he said. "The word *nigger*. It's an outmoded word, to say the least."

"Oh," I said and felt my face blush, "oh, I—"

"Don't worry," he said. "There's simply the word *colored* or the word *negro*. By no regards new words, certainly. But ones which we employ here. I hope you understand."

"Yes," I said, "yes," and then I felt something settle over me, a calm I took and wrapped myself in, Brenda Kay's warm hand in mine.

He smiled again, and pulled the door open, followed us out to where May the *colored* girl sat. She was on the telephone, but smiled up at us anyway. Mr. White leaned over the desk, took a pencil and piece of paper from the desktop, scribbled something on it. She read it, nodded at him even though she was in the middle of a sentence.

Mr. White turned to us, quick glanced at his watch again. "May here will fill you in on what we'll expect tomorrow, how long the testing will take, et cetera." He looked behind us and up, and I could hear scuffling from above, sounds I knew well: the scrape and scratch of desks across a wooden floor.

He said, "If you wish, you may take a look in either of the classrooms for a moment, just to give you a concrete glimpse into what happens here." He looked at me only an instant, and turned, went into the foyer and started up the stairs. "If you like," he called. "Otherwise, we'll see you tomorrow."

He was already on his way up, two steps at a time.

"Now, Mrs. Hilburn," May said from behind me, and I turned to her, saw her smiling, nowhere in her face any show of that word I'd used, the one I'd been raised on, the one that'd never meant anything wrong in my life. But a word, I knew starting then, I'd try my best to keep from speaking.

She said, "Let me have your address and home phone number, to start with."

Brenda Kay and I made it to the landing on the stairs, and we both looked out the window onto a long green lawn, fenced off on all three sides, honeysuckle and climbing roses and oleander growing up against those fences.

"Brenda Kay," I whispered, "how'd you like to play out there?"

She nodded hard, smiled.

"Let's go see where you might go to school," I whispered next, and put my arm round her, held her close as we went up the rest of the stairs.

Then the word sank into her, and she stopped, turned her face to me.

"Schoo?" she said, her mouth open, eyebrows up.

"School," I said. "Like Wilman and Annie. Like your momma used to teach long before you ever came around. School."

"Wimn?" she said, then, "Nee?"

"No, not here," I said, and started us on up to the second floor.

We made it to the top, and I saw across from us a door partway open, saw just the shoulder of Mr. White's tan suit, him up at a blackboard—*a blackboard*—and talking away.

He moved a little to the side, and now I could see his face. He caught sight of us out here in the hall, and pointed his thumb over his shoulder, meaning, I figured, Brenda Kay's class was the next door down. He hadn't even stopped talking, only motioned us on.

We moved along the hall, a window at the far end so that the place was filled with light, something I was more glad for than I would've ever imagined I could be: sunlight in a hallway.

The next door was closed, and so I let go Brenda Kay, leaned my ear close to the door, and heard a woman's voice, no other sound than that.

I smiled, looked at Brenda Kay. She smiled at me, and I reached a hand to the door, quietly knocked.

"Come in," came the voice, and I reached down, turned the knob, slowly opened the door.

There were things about that moment I will always remember: Mrs. Becky Hamby, her blond-white hair parted on the side, curled under just where it reached her shoulders, her standing in front of a blackboard just as Mr. White had; the big storybook she held in her hands, the pages facing her audience, the picture there a drawing of three policemen at a busy intersection with their hands up, holding back traffic so a line of ducklings could make it across the street. And there was the smile she gave to us, the nod, and the way she started right back into the story she'd **been reading**, her voice a song there in the room: "When they came to the corner of Beacon Street there was the police car with four policemen that Clancy had sent from headquarters—"

But of course it was the children and the slow turn of all their heads to the two of us standing in the doorway that I would carry with me from then on, kids with black hair and blond, red and brown; kids with freckles and teeth and no teeth and glasses and no glasses, new clothes and old clothes, even a couple of colored children, and I can remember making myself think that word: *colored*. And all of the children, I figured, here for the same reason: parents who loved them, parents who held out hope.

Mrs. Hamby stopped reading when she saw she'd lost them, every one of them looking back at us, what seemed a sea of retarded children, though there were only a dozen or so, some with small eyes and wide faces like my Brenda Kay's, some with just open mouths and sullen eyes, but all of them looking at us.

"We have visitors," Mrs. Hamby said, still with the book open. She was a good teacher, I could tell already: she wasn't going to lose sight of reading time, wasn't going to put away the book simply because we'd shown up; and too, she wasn't going to shut down the natural interest they all showed in our being here. She would make of this what she could.

"I'm Mrs. Hamby," she said. "And you are . . ."

"Mrs. Hilburn," I said, and nodded to her, to all the children.

Their eyes weren't on me.

"And this is Brenda Kay," I said. "Brenda Kay Hilburn," and I turned to her, smiled. "My daughter," I said.

Brenda Kay only stood there, looking at all the children, and I tried to imagine for a moment what she might think, might feel at suddenly seeing all these children so like her, so in need of all we could give them. But I would come up with nothing, could think of no one but myself, and the joy of this moment, this fine start.

1960

Chapter 27

Brenda Kay stood at the foul line, hands holding the basketball between her legs, knees bent, eyes on the net. Behind her were the rest of the children.

"Let's go, Brenda!" the woman, this Mrs. Klausman, hollered, and it was all I could do not to shout from where I stood with the other mothers, *Brenda Kay, it's Brenda Kay!* But I said nothing, only held my arms tighter across my chest.

Mrs. Klausman blew her whistle, a short bleat of a sound, but loud enough to make it echo off the brick walls of the gymnasium, and scare the living daylights out of most every child. Dennis, the boy behind Brenda Kay, had been standing quiet and still behind her, but now quick brought his arms up to his chest, started to twitching his whole head like he does, his thick glasses near falling off with each move. The little girl behind him, Candy was her name, started to twisting back and forth even faster than she'd been doing before. Another boy, Randy, him short as Brenda Kay, his hair near the same color, let out a low deep growl, started lifting one foot and then the other, one foot and the other. The two children who'd already shot, Marcella and Jimmy, sat on the floor behind this Mrs. Klausman, knees tucked up under their chins. Jimmy was already shivering, Marcella swaying back and forth.

Brenda Kay was breathing faster now, her eyes still set on the net, her so small there on the floor, that net so far away.

This was the first day to the high school, the children's first gymnasium day. There'd been talk from Mr. White about this eventuality for the last six years, since I'd started in helping at the center and being paid for it. Six years of talk about getting the children across town to West High School to use the gym during the off period, 11:45 to 12:30, so they could get hold of better exercise, better facilities, have more fun.

Until today, exercise time'd been at the old Presbyterian church off Torrance Boulevard. Behind the church was a parking lot painted with stripes for a volleyball court, and we'd all of us march the two blocks up the hill from the Health Center where Mr. White and I held class, the children and the two or three other mothers that showed up each day all holding hands. We'd walk on the sidewalk, beside us the cars on the street, some of them honking at us now and again, teenagers the same age as Brenda Kay hollering out things these children didn't need to hear, but which most likely meant nothing to them: *Morons, Retards.* But we'd sing songs or just talk, and then we'd be at the church parking lot, and I'd pull from the duffel bag I carried over my shoulder the ball, and we'd play there on the broken asphalt a game something akin to volleyball.

I myself had only seen it played on the beach whenever Leston used to feel like going to see Wilman and Burton at it, back before they'd gotten married. Now whenever they got to the beach it was with kids in tow, my grandchildren: Burton's girls, Susan, Jeannie and Jill; Wilman's boys, Brad, Robert and Timmy. But there'd been a time not too far back, before they'd had to carry playpens and diapers and umbrellas, when the two of them were out on the beach every afternoon, all day Saturday and Sunday, back at Venice Beach and showing off to any girl that'd put eyes on them.

The version we played at the church, though, had no net, no poles, just that painted square on the parking lot. We'd give the ball to one or another of the children, show them again and again how you held the ball in the palm of one hand, then brought the other up under it, hit it hard so it flew up and into play.

But that didn't happen too often, of course; most of the time the child missed the ball, or only held it in her hand like you showed her, and stared at it or you or the ground. Marcella was the worst about that, her black hair in a ponytail so tight you'd swear she had to work to close her eyes. She'd simply stare at the ball no matter how softly you talked, no matter how calm your hand on her back, no matter how many times you took her hand in yours and swung it up under that ball just to show her. Other children—Dennis in particular—knocked the stuffing out of it, sent the ball flying high and, usually, behind him, to where it'd bounce off the hood of a churchworker's car. One time the pastor himself had been in his old DeSoto, inching out of his slot at the back door to the sanctuary, only to have a ball Dennis'd slammed too high and far bounce off his roof. Pastor'd jammed on the brakes and looked everywhere, startled and scared, his old man's red face bleached white with the *whump!* that ball had sounded. All he'd seen, too, was a parking lot full of retarded children and three mothers bent over laughing, hands covering our mouths in some small attempt at hiding. We joked for months after that, about how Mr. McKnight must've thought God was gearing up to speak to him there in his DeSoto, pounding his car roof to get his attention.

The children had fun, even when the ball went too high, or never left a child's hand. We women spoke to them as if they were children, kids out for fun, and that seemed the trick to it all: just to treat them like they were kids themselves, though they ran in age anywhere from fifteen, which was Candy's age, to twenty-four, Dennis' age.

Brenda Kay was one of the younger ones at seventeen. She could get the ball up into the air on occasion, where sometimes it'd make it a couple of times back and forth, one child to the next keeping it in the air. Sometimes it only fell off her hand, rolled a few feet away. But they were playing outside in the open air and moving themselves, their arms and legs.

Then West High School finally caved in to Mr. White, and of course all we mothers, not to mention Mr. White himself, nearly jumped for joy at the news, at the idea of our children in a real school, if for only an hour or so a day. Mr. White'd had to guarantee in writing the school would have no liabilities for the whole thing, and guarantee the children at the high school would hardly see our children. Even the gym door would be kept locked from the inside, so as not to disturb any of the normal children.

Mrs. Klausman also came with the deal. She was the girls' PE coach, and'd been assigned this duty, her job supposedly to help out the children with organized play time, but, I figured, also to see they didn't destroy the place, didn't each of them go into mad rages and start to tearing the mats off the walls at either end of the court, didn't throw up and bleed and bash in the wooden bleachers. I'd dealt with people who had no idea what retarded children were about long enough to be able to

spot them a mile away. She was one of them; I could see
the fear in her by the way she'd tried to smile while telling
us at the start of the period what she perceived her role as
being: "Coach and friend, friend and coach." Her eyes
never landed on the children around her, but always
keeping on us, as though we might throw her some life-
line, reel her in from whatever hell she thought she was
drowning in.

I wasn't certain how long she'd last: blowing that
whistle, hollering out to the children to throw. Marcella'd
started swaying so hard she looked near to falling over
there on the hardwood floor; when it'd been her turn,
she'd merely done what Marcella always did: stared at
the ball in her hands for a while. But then maybe because
this was a new place, a big building with brick walls and
championship flags hanging from the rafters, Marcella'd
finally held the basketball just like we'd shown her to
hold a volleyball, and for the first time ever she put her
other hand beneath the ball, swung it up hard and quick,
and gave it a good solid slap. The basketball popped up
only a few feet, but it was the action that'd counted to we
three mothers over here seated on the bleachers. We'd
clapped and cheered, Crystal Holloway—Jimmy's
momma—and Terri LaCoste—Dennis' momma—and
myself all standing up in our seats.

But Mrs. Klausman had only blown her whistle, shaken
her head, and walked to pick up the ball. She held it at her
hip, the whistle in her other hand, and stood next to
Marcella, bounced the ball a couple of times. Then she
shot, making that ball go in a perfect arc so that it fell right
through the net without even touching the metal hoop.

"That's how you do it," she said, and she'd turned,
smiling, to where Marcella'd been.

Marcella was already over on the floor, curled up with her knees under her chin like she was right now.

Jimmy'd held the ball with two hands like it was a huge rock, his knees buckling a little under him, and he'd pushed it toward the basket, made it bounce twice before it rolled away to the right, where Mrs. Klausman stopped it with her foot. Then she'd done the same thing: stood next to him, shot, turned to him. He'd only looked up at her, his big ears poking out at either side of his head, his hair in that crew cut his momma said made him look at least a little more attentive than he would otherwise. Then he'd turned, gone and sat next to Marcella.

And now it was Brenda Kay's turn. Still she stared at the net, still she held the ball between her knees. She opened and closed her mouth with each breath she took, her eyes, it looked from here, already going red at that whistle.

Mrs. Klausman popped the whistle again, just a short moment's worth of sound, but shrill nonetheless. Randy, at the end of the line, gave a small yelp just as Brenda Kay swung her arms up, let go the ball.

It sailed straight up above her in a perfect line. Brenda Kay looked up at it, watched it a moment before she ducked, turned to get out of the way, bumping hard against Dennis, his hands still at his chest.

The ball came down, bounced on the wood floor, and everyone, even Mrs. Klausman, only watched, let it bounce until it finally stopped, sat right there at the foul line.

Dennis started laughing, his laughter even louder than Brenda Kay's, the sound way up high and cackling like some wild animal's. I wasn't sure what he was laughing at, whether it was Brenda Kay's shot or the ball settling right square back on the line or Brenda Kay ducking and banging into him. But he was laughing.

Brenda Kay turned to him, stared at him a moment, then let out "Huh! Huh! Huh!" almost as loud, and suddenly each of the children was laughing, the gymnasium echoing with laughter so hard and unafraid it was more a haunting sound than anything else, like laughing ghosts in a movie. None of them knew enough to be restrained in how they laughed, that matter of *manners* and *politeness* a notion that only operated in their heads when Momma or Daddy was with them.

Mrs. Klausman hadn't yet picked up the ball, only stood staring at them, the whistle in one hand and close up to her mouth, like she'd been ready to blow it, but couldn't quite get her hand there. Then she shifted her eyes to us, we mothers there on the bleachers.

None of us did anything to help. We only watched, and from the corner of my eyes I could see in each of us a piece of satisfaction with what was going on, in how the children had set her on edge, let her know they weren't little zombies she could point in the right direction and expect to have operate just fine. We each of us sat there perfectly still, backs straight, chins up high.

We'd gotten this far alone, was what I was thinking on the way home from the high school. Mrs. Klausman'd finally given up after she'd been unable to stop the children from laughing. Even Jimmy quit his shivering once he'd started in, his laughter more a silent snickering.

That was when we mothers rounded them up, then went out to the station wagon, herded them in—Dennis and Brenda Kay in the front seat with me, Marcella and Candy and Jimmy in the back seat, Randy all the way in the far back in the fold-up seat. Crystal and Terri climbed into Crystal's car, a '57 Chevy she hadn't yet decided to give up to her seventeen-year-old son, Mark, Jimmy's younger brother. And then I set off for the drive back to the Health Center, Crystal to take Terri home.

I pulled the station wagon into the Health Center parking lot, yet another of these squared-off stucco buildings I'd finally grown used to here. By this time Randy in the far back had started in to his growling and yelping, and no matter how hard I tired to cut that sound out of my head, it was no use. The first gymnasium day was fast on its way from bad to worse: I'd already gotten a headache, and here it was only a little after noon.

There'd be Mr. White to answer to, report on how it'd gone with Mrs. Klausman and basketball. Then Arts and Crafts this afternoon, all that clay I had to water down and knead up before the children could start with it. We'd roll out the clay into long strings, coil it up on itself into little vases we'd let set in the windows, then paint up, take home sometime next week. It was something we'd done before, but nearly every art project we did we'd done before.

I pulled the keys out of the ignition, turned and opened my door, hollered out to the children to line up on my side of the car, hold hands for the walk back to the classroom, and I wondered exactly how many coil vases and ashtrays and paperweights and doorstops and unidentifiable other clay whatnots we'd made these years. A hundred at least, I thought, all variations on the same old idea: get them working with their hands, make something they could hold and think *I made it! I made it!* and have it be the truth. For that, I figured as I looked back at them already lined up—Candy and Marcella and Dennis and Brenda Kay and Randy and Jimmy, him shivering again there at the end of the line—maybe all those red coils of clay were worth it. Dirt well spent.

"Everybody holding hands?" I called out, and turned to the building.

"Ohhhn!" Marcella gave out, and I turned to her, her eyes wide open with the ponytail. Her head was tilted to one side, her mouth open, jaw jutted out. "Ohhn!" she said. "Dennis! Dennis!" she said, and she held up the hand she was supposed to be holding with Dennis, just put it up in the air, empty.

Then Randy gave his yelp, put his hand up the same as Marcella'd done. His hand, too, was empty, that hand supposed to be holding on to Brenda Kay's.

I looked at Dennis, at Brenda Kay. They were holding hands, both of them with their heads down, staring at the pavement, mouths closed. Dennis' glasses had slipped down his nose, just barely hanging on at his ears.

I looked at their hands, saw how they were holding on: their fingers were laced together, as soft and gentle as could be, the two of them holding hands like they were courting.

I said, "Now stop that," and a feeling I'd known would come but which I'd refused for so long finally broke in me. It rose in my throat black and hard, and I took two steps to them, reached my hands to theirs, and pulled them apart. I said, "You, Dennis," and took hold of his elbow, pulled him away out of line, "you just stand yourself right on down here next to Randy. You just stand right there," I said, and directed him to the back of the line.

He moved slowly, lifted his free hand and pushed his glasses up. They were heavy horn-rimmed glasses, black, and made his face turn owlish. They made him somehow look intelligent, the thickness of the glass distorting the shape of his eyes so they didn't look so Mongoloid, so tapered at the outside edges. When he was at the end of the line, I looked into those eyes, looked into them maybe a moment too long, but a moment I figured needed to be spent this way.

I said, "Now you know we don't hold hands that way. You know that, Dennis," and I tried to hold my eyes firm on him, tried to make myself *authoritative*, a word Mr. White'd stressed for so long, since the first day I'd ever met him.

But he smiled at me, then looked at his hands, stared at them with that smile on his face. He moved his right hand down to Randy's, his eyes on his hand the whole time, and took hold of Randy's hand, held it tight.

He moved his eyes back to the other hand, slowly moved it toward me, and took hold of my hand. Carefully he laced his fingers in mine, held my hand the same as he'd held Brenda Kay's.

He looked up at me. His glasses'd slipped again; my hand in his, he reached up, with his middle finger pushed them back into place. He was still smiling, and looked at me.

"Okay lunch okay?" he said, and nodded.

I paused, looked at him in that authoritative way I thought I had, eyes boring in on him even through the thick glasses he had on. I hoped he might hear what I was saying, really: *Don't touch my daughter the way you might want to some day.* Then I pulled our hands apart, took hold of his the way I wanted him to: palm to palm, fingers together and holding on.

Still he smiled, and I saw it was lost on him, what I was doing lost on them all; they only started to fidgeting there in line against the station wagon.

I looked away from him and his smile, looked up the line to Brenda Kay. She leaned toward Marcella, said something, a single word. Marcella's eyes were open wide, staring off. Then she got the smallest glint of a smile, her eyes changed somehow, the corners of her mouth just turning up.

Brenda Kay turned, looked at me, said, "Lunch now, Momma!"

"All right," I said, Dennis' hand in mine. I thought to grip it hard, but decided against it. We'd be inside in a minute, and now I didn't know if I'd even have to report this incident to Mr. White, this little holding of hands that might not have been just holding of hands.

"All right," I said again, like I might've been trying to convince myself eating lunch was the only thing needed doing in these children's lives. "Let's go to lunch," I said, and I started toward the building.

Chapter 28

Our eight years in California:

Brenda Kay tested in that first year at a four-year-old's level of intelligence;

Leston worked driving truck for Pico Furniture and lifting and carrying more than his boss had ever let on he'd be doing, but it was work, money coming at us, even though Leston was fifty-two years old by then, a man too old for standing and lifting and carrying furniture. Every night I'd had to rub his back down with Ben Gay, his flesh never building up the way it might have were he a younger man, what with all that exercise and work, and I'd had to rub and rub and rub until he fell asleep under my hands;

Brenda Kay brought home a pencil holder she'd made out of an old Campbell's Soup can and swatch of wallpaper;

Wilman graduated Venice High, got on at Pico Furniture, Leston and him working together and moving furniture anywheres from up to the Hollywood Hills on down to Long Beach;

Burton married one Sarah Kaminski, a Jewish girl he'd met on a blind date set up by Wilman and his girlfriend of the time; a girl Wilman'd known when he was at Venice High and who, Wilman'd confided in me once she and Burton'd announced their engagement, had had what he called a "nose job" since their days in school; a girl who wore her hair cut way short above her shoulders and who seemed not to like me at all though she wanted me to think she adored me; a Jewish girl, the two of them married by a judge in Santa Monica so's there'd be no conflicts about any kind of ceremony whether Jewish or Baptist, though we'd lost the practice of attending church or Sunday School, since we'd moved here;

Brenda Kay's teacher, Mrs. Hamby, asked me to step in for her one afternoon for Arts and Crafts when she had to tend to a dentist's appointment, and I'd had them all gluing popsicle sticks together into whatever shapes their hearts desired;

Annie had a string of boyfriends a mile long through high school, all of them pretty boys with handsome, hard jaws and crew cuts and plaid shirts and khaki trousers, and it'd seemed like we saw each one no more than three times apiece. Then she'd run in from that third date all crying, falling apart,and it'd be my role to go into her room, pat her on the back, console her and agree with her about the stupidity of Men, though I hadn't yet seen a man around the house looking for her. Just pretty boys;

Mr. Nathan White hired me on as assistant to the smaller children, and I quit working the Hughes Cafeteria, took to bringing in the clay and papier-mâché and colored macaroni;

Leston and Wilman both lost their jobs when Pico Furniture closed up and declared bankruptcy, and Leston got a job as a maintenance man over to El Camino College in Gardena for thirty-seven dollars a week. Wilman went down to the unemployment office in the hopes of only collecting money so he could lay out on the beach; instead, they'd made him go over to Watts to the Royal Crown Cola

Company and apply for some job called Truck Sales, a job involved driving store to store and selling soda pop—Nehi, Royal Crown, Par-T-Pak—off the truck and filling store shelves with it, a job he promptly got, started at fifty-two dollars a week, him still living at home;

Brenda Kay at age twelve tested in at age five;

James and Eudine had their third baby, David, company to the other two, Judy and Mark;

Billie Jean had first Elaine, then Matthew back in Jackson. Gower transferred up there when the Purvis dealership closed down;

Brenda Kay and the rest of her class made handprint ashtrays, hers kept filled by Leston so that I had to empty it each morning before Brenda Kay and I headed up to the Foundation in the second car we had, an old '49 Chevrolet Burton rounded up at Bundy;

Wilman met a girl named Barbara Holmes while he and his cronies from high school were out one Saturday night to the ballroom at the end of Santa Monica pier to see Spade Cooley. Wilman and Barbara'd danced, then gone over to The Clock Drive-In, where, he told me the next morning, she wouldn't let him kiss her, this Barbara Holmes a Baptist girl from East Texas and whose daddy was an actor himself and who'd been in a few movies, even with John Wayne one time. Her momma'd been a singer with Kay Kaiser and his Kollege of Musical Knowledge in the 40s, and Barbara herself was a Job's Daughter. All of this was reason enough for Leston and me to give approval to them marrying eight months later at a church wedding in Culver City, to which Wilman'd been late because of his route taking too long that day. The two of them honeymooned up to Las Vegas just over the weekend, Wilman back at work Monday morning, Barbara back to work at the telephone company, where she was an operator;

Mr. Nathan White talked the Health Department down in Redondo Beach into giving up its old storeroom to him, there being now thirty-two children holed up each day in the Foundation's house on Adams. I was in charge of organizing the carpool down there in the South Bay, each of us mothers trading off driving, though I was there each day one way or the other;

Burton and Sarah had Susan; Wilman and Barbara had Brad, and those two traded having children for the next few years, baby girls to Burton, baby boys to Wilman: Jeannie, then Robert, then Jill, then Timmy;

Brenda Kay at age fourteen tested in at age six;

Leston was made supervisor of the heating and cooling plant at El Camino, and I talked him into selling off the house in Mar Vista for something farther down the coast, our lives now moving south from Los Angeles, what with Leston in Gardena, me and Brenda Kay in Redondo Beach. We made three thousand dollars off the house in Mar Vista, bought a two-bedroom bungalo off Sixth Street and Ingleside in Manhattan Beach, not three blocks from the ocean;

Mr. Nathan White put me in charge of yet another of his big ideas, the families of all the exceptional children in the Redondo Beach class saving up Blue Chip Stamps in order to buy a station wagon. A year and a half later, in December 1959, we had enough for the station wagon, and I had another aspect of my job: driving that station wagon each morning and picking up the children, driving them home each afternoon;

Leston was promoted to Head of Maintenance at El Camino College;

James gave up being a veterinarian for teaching high school Ag. in Leveland, just outside Lubbock;

Wilman was made the first Pre-Salesman for Royal Crown, quit driving truck and was given a company car, a black 1960 Rambler, and started driving from store to store and selling from sheets of paper instead of off the truck, the truck showing up the next day with whatever the store ordered;

Burton quit Bundy, took a job at Royal Crown, and for a few months followed Wilman's Rambler with his Royal Crown delivery truck, until he, too, started as a Pre-Salesman;

Annie graduated Lawndale High School still followed by that string of boys, but ended up getting engaged two years later to a California Highway Patrolman ten years her senior, him having stopped her on the new Harbor Freeway for speeding, then writing her up, then asking her out;

Billie Jean wrote and said she'd be out with the babies for the wedding in December;

James called and said they'd all be out for the wedding;

Brenda Kay at age sixteen tested in at age six;

Brenda Kay at age seventeen tested in at age six;

Today she'd held hands with Dennis.

Chapter 29

"The temptation is," Mr. White started up, and rose from his seat behind the desk, "to make more of certain things than is necessary." He came round the desk and sat on the corner like always: arms crossed, chin down, eyes on the floor.

For a moment I thought he was talking about Brenda Kay and Dennis, though I hadn't said a word to him yet, had just come into his office from passing out the lunchboxes to the children, each box masking-taped shut by their mothers, a practice we'd all gotten into what with the number of times they dropped the boxes walking to and from the station wagon, or moving into the classroom. One little girl no longer with us—her parents moved to Sacramento last year, freeing up room for Candy—even pushed her lunchbox out the station wagon window one morning; all I'd seen of it was a sort of small explosion in the rearview mirror: a sandwich and chips and apple all flying up into the grill of the car behind me. Now the windows were kept rolled up, all except mine.

I'd gotten the lunchboxes passed out, had the tape open for each of them, when Mrs. Walker, one of the secretaries for the Health Center, came into the classroom, told me Mr. White needed to see me right away, that she'd watch over them for me.

I'd turned to the children, saw all of them eating away, Brenda Kay slowly unwrapping her sandwich as if it might've been gold. She picked up one half of it with both hands, leaned over the table until her chin almost touched the tabletop, and bit into it. Fried egg sandwich. Her favorite, what I made for her most every day, either that or pimento and cheese.

I'd looked round the classroom, certain I was doing it, surveying it all, just to put off meeting with Mr. White. I knew, too, he wouldn't come down hard on me for what went on; I just knew I'd have to tell him the truth of the matter: our first day at the high school had been, in fact, a disaster.

Not that anything bad had happened, actually; they were just themselves today. On the batteries of tests the Foundation gave, not one of them had ever placed higher than a ten-year-old's capabilities; as far as the public school system out here was concerned, these children could make coil ashtrays and miss baskets for the rest of their lives and still get no better at it, still break down into laughter at whatever they thought was funny.

But that wasn't what I was in this for, the simple ritual of just killing time in these children's lives. I'd signed on for the long haul, certainly; I'd be with my Brenda Kay until the end of my days, but not just so I could keep treading water. There was a way to fix this thing, I knew, and it had something to do with getting these kids over to West High School even if for only an hour or two a day. Only an hour out in the world, but one they might not otherwise get, some head start at the end point I figured all we mothers and fathers and brothers and sisters of these children were aiming at: solving these lives. I could just picture Mrs. Klausman doing her part to end it all before it'd even started, her marching into the principal's office and laying in on him how horrid these children'd been, how worth nothing they were. They couldn't even dribble a ball.

I'd given one last look at the classroom, a room that'd been a big storage room for years before we ever came around. Now there was a blackboard on one wall, two big tables set up in the middle, the children all in their appointed chairs and eating, a heavy and huge braided rug under it all. On the walls were pictures of Lincoln and Washington and Eisenhower, circling the top of the walls cards with alphabet in printed letters. It could have been any classroom, could have been, I saw, the classroom where I'd started teaching back in Columbia, these kids roughly the same mental equivalent as all those ornery children I'd had to deal with so many years ago.

Then Jimmy glanced up at me, him with his crew cut, those ears, and he shivered hard, nearly dropped the banana in his hand for it. He'd seen me looking at him, and turned his back to me, took a bite off the banana, and I knew where I was: in an ex-storeroom, a room with no windows.

But better than no room at all.

"Got the call from Mr. Mooney, the principal at West," Mr. White went on. He shook his head, brought a hand from his chest to his chin, and rubbed it: his same old moves. "Doesn't look good."

"Of course," I started up, "Mr. Mooney's got all his information from the girls' PE coach, Mrs. Klausman. That's his first mistake."

I stood behind the chair he always kept positioned in front of the desk; he still swooped off that desk edge and stood up, came close to you and started his pacing, all of it, I knew, designed to intimidate, to force into you who was in charge. But he wasn't a man who wanted to be in charge for the thin reason of just having power. No, he wanted in charge because he knew how to get things changed.

"Gym day," he said, pacing again, the same man as the first day I met him, "is our foot in the door, our way of making ourselves known to the school board, to the public education system at large. Imagine the burdens lifted from parents, imagine the opportunities afforded our children. Public education for the retarded."

He stopped then, arms crossed, and said, "But you've heard this before," and smiled.

I tried to smile, tried hard. I'd heard it all before, knew there was hope for that new way of teaching in California, knew we'd come worlds from where we'd started, knew that there might come some day—some day soon, if any of my prayers were answered by the same old God up in Heaven—new ways to change her, bring up her learning level.

But there were things to deal with now, today.

I said, "Maybe there's nothing to this, but . . . ," and I paused, waited a moment before I could line up the words I wanted to give.

"There's always something in everything," he said, and circled back to his desk. His office was the opposite of that sun-filled room back up on Adams: the desk was strictly school district issue, gunmetal gray with a slate top, his chair the same color gray with a hard green leather back and seat. May, the receptionist, was still up at the old house, down here was Mrs. Walker, a white woman with hair swirled up high and sprayed into place, lips fire engine red. Who knew what the children thought when they saw her?

"Maybe, maybe not," I said, and half-smiled, looked up at him. His own lunch was spread out on the desktop: an apple, two Oreos, a half-eaten sandwich on dark bread. He sat down, leaned over the desktop, picked up the sandwich, bit into it.

"Seems I may've caught a couple of the children up to something." I paused. "Holding hands, namely."

He looked at me over the tops of his glasses, stopped chewing. He held that look a moment or two, then slowly started to chewing, leaned back.

He swallowed, said, "Well. It's about time."

"What?" I said, and for the first time in years I wanted to sit in that chair, wanted to plant myself there, lean my head over into my hands.

"It's about time," he said again, and now he was dusting off his hands, smiling. "I've had to deal with this on more than one occasion, believe you me," he said. "You wouldn't believe the sorts of liaisons that begin to happen once this sort of discovery takes place, especially with this age group. Why I've seen—"

"It's my Brenda Kay," I said, quick put my hand to my forehead, let it cover my eyes.

He stopped, and I heard him stand right up, come around the desk. Then I felt his hand on my shoulder. "I didn't mean to make it seem . . ." he began, but stopped. "I mean," he said, "it's happened."

"There's always something in everything," I said, and brought down my hand, tried again to smile at him, still held on with the other hand to the back of the chair.

He said, "It's bound to happen. And it does. It has. It will. But the only way I've found to deal with it is simply to let them know they're not to behave that way. Now," he said, and let go my shoulder. He went to the edge of the desk, stood looking at his food. He turned his head to me, nodded at the empty chair. He said, "Would you sit down?"

"Only if you promise not to go on the attack like you do," I said.

"Promise," he said, and looked back at his food.

I sat down, glad for the weight off my feet, glad my legs could ease up, let me relax. Brenda Kay and Dennis.

"Maybe you won't want to hear this," he said, "but holding hands is not the worst thing that could happen. Not at all. But, first, do not give them opportunity. Don't let them have the chance to hold hands." He paused, turned to me. "Who's the boy?"

"Dennis," I said. I looked down at the gray linoleum floor, a far cry from that gleaming hardwood, from when I'd only had to worry on enrolling my daughter, on getting red clay wet enough to work.

"Dennis," he said. "He's responsive. He hears. He'll listen." He paused. "But if they carry on, keep holding hands even if we instruct them not to, there's not much else we can do. Much worse can happen here. Maybe holding hands will be outlet enough."

I looked up. "Outlet for what?" I said, but I'd already figured it out, already knew.

He still looked at the desktop. "Growing up," he said, matter-of-fact.

He stopped, looked at me once again. He reached up, took off his glasses, crossed his arms. Then he sat on the corner of the desk, the same old perch, and here came my old life, this same series of days that lined themselves up in front of me and told me the same thing again and again and again: take hold of it by the throat, make it work.

Puberty fell on them, that word so filthy gone unspoken, but what I already knew was upon my baby girl. She was already seventeen, her body going through its own motions like there were things it had to do, wild things my daughter's brain never dreamed of: every night when I gave her her bath, there were new signs: her breasts growing larger, more thin wisps of hair between her legs, all of it a mockery, I knew, sheer spite from God once again. Now here she was holding hands with a boy, their bodies like blind animals making their way along, searching, not knowing what it was they were looking for.

And one morning some five months ago Leston and I'd both woke up to Brenda Kay hollering out from her bedroom. I'd rolled right out of bed, rushed to her room, alive in my head the memory of her burned legs, the pain of them even as she rolled over of a morning, memories so fresh we might as well have been still back in Mississippi, the house filled with the stink of old and soaked bandages.

I opened her bedroom door, saw her standing next to her bed, a finger pointed at the mattress. "Momma!" she hollered. "Momma!"

"What's wrong?" I'd said, but by that time I already saw what she was pointing at: a bloodstain there on the middle of the sheet, and I'd had to swallow hard, keep myself from crying as I turned to her, looked at the seat of her nightgown, saw more blood there. She'd started her monthlies.

"Jewel?" Leston'd called from the bedroom. "What's going on?"

"Nothing," I'd said, then went to the bathroom, headed for the box of napkins I'd kept under the sink for the last three or four years, me never certain when this morning might come.

"Morning accident," I called out to Leston, and let him think she'd just wet the bed again.

Take hold of it, grab it by the throat, make it work.

Mr. White was right, of course: they'd have to be separated, separated as much as I could make certain. And there'd be much worse could happen, too. But I wasn't going to let that happen, not at all. I'd been in charge of her all this time, I wasn't about to surrender to letting that foot in the door. No.

I stood, didn't need the chair anymore. There were ways to fix this world, and us in it. There were simple ways: keep the two separate.

"You're right," I said. I started for the door. "It's an outlet," I said, and steeled myself for whatever I had in front of me to do.

"Good," he said from behind me, and I knew he'd sat back down, had started in on his lunch again. "And gym day does not cease as of today. Gym day will be on our regular agenda, every Monday, Wednesday and Friday from now on."

I had my hand on the door, turned the knob.

He was chewing, spoke with food in his mouth. "We're on our way to having our children in the public schools," he said.

"Fine by me," I said. I pulled the door open, stepped out, pulled it to behind me.

"I'll be down there in a couple of minutes," he called after me, but I already had the door closed.

Eight years in California. Good enough for a lifetime, I thought as I headed down the corridor toward the old storeroom, and knew something'd changed inside Mr. White's office just now. I knew somehow things were different, and suddenly it had to do with him and the fact he'd never had any children of his own, never seen them grow up and away like I'd seen all five of mine. And no matter how much the philanthropist he was, no matter how hard he'd grieved at that spark lost in his brother's eye, he had no retarded child of his own. No matter how many cases he'd known, they were all still theory, all of them—all of *us*, I thought—just ideas played off his own ideas. Holding hands wasn't the worst could happen, he'd said. But I knew it was the door standing wide open for the next thing to come.

Mrs. Walker stood at the desk when I got back, the children quiet, still, slowly chewing, eyes of some lifting up from their food to take me in, others' heads bowed to the task at hand: lunch.

She quick turned to me, flew a hand up to her chest. Her fingernails were long, the same red as her lips. "You scared me to death!" she said, and smiled, then made her way past me. "They've been just like this," she said at the doorway. "Angels," she said.

She was gone, and I turned, looked back at them.

Brenda Kay was in her place, her sandwich finished. She held one of the chocolate chip cookies I'd baked last night, held it in her hand and looked at it.

"Dennis!" she shouted, looked over to him seated across from her at the far left corner of the table. "You want?"

Dennis' shoulders went up at his name, and he cocked back his head, looked at her through those thick lenses, the glasses far down on his nose. He clutched half a sandwich with both hands, held it there at his chin.

He looked at her a moment, then nodded his head hard.

But by this time I was already away from the desk, had my hand out and took hold of the cookie as Brenda Kay was standing, leaning over to him. I took it, said, "Now I baked these for you, Brenda Kay," and placed a hand on her shoulder, gently pushed her down into her seat.

She looked at me, her mouth open. She had a few last bites of the fried egg sandwich there in her mouth: yellow and white and brown.

"Now if you don't want this, I'll go ahead and have it myself," I said, and I brought it to my mouth, nibbled it. "Thank you, Brenda Kay," I said, and tried to swallow, tried hard, but couldn't. I just chewed on that small piece of cookie in my mouth.

I glanced over to Dennis. He looked at me, then at Brenda Kay, then let his head fall, took the sandwich in his hands.

Chapter 30

That night Annie stood on a stool in the living room in her wedding gown. Mrs. Zafaris, the seamstress from the wedding shop over on Crenshaw and who lived one block over, tucked here, tucked there, her mouth full of pins. Annie the whole time was lifting a fold of white and lifting, looking at herself and turning, looking and turning, Mrs. Zafaris hollering at her the best she could with those pins in her mouth to hold still.

We were in the kitchen, Leston and Brenda Kay at the table, eating the pork chops and gravy and collards I'd made, me busy at cleaning everything up. We'd gotten the call from Billie Jean last night, her in Phoenix, that she'd be in near seven as best she could figure. It was quarter till now.

I hadn't seen her in eight years, and knew it to be a crime, knew it way deep down. We'd been so filled with our lives out here, so carried along with just making do, I knew we were the ones heavy at fault. We hadn't seen our oldest daughter in eight years, hadn't even seen our two grandchildren, what I still called our babies, though Elaine was six now, Matthew four. No longer babies, but children, and as I hurried to wash up the skillet and pans I pictured James and Billie Jean at the same age as Elaine and Matthew, Burton brand-new and still nursing back then. I knew I'd missed worlds of my grandchildren's lives, knew that at that age they were already gone, James already the independent boy he'd find himself later on, insisting he not work with his father, insisting on joining to fight the war, all of it without his parents' approval not out of spite, but simply because he knew he could do it on his own. Once, when James was six, Elaine's age, he'd come home from a fistfight with one of the Skokum kids at school, the Skokums a family more cracker than we'd ever hope to be. He'd had a black eye and a scrape across his cheek like somebody'd taken heavy sandpaper to his face. When Leston'd gotten home from the woods and we were all to the table for dinner, Billie Jean barely able to see up over the edge to the food on her plate, Burton suckling away, Leston said, "'You going to tell us what happened?" then acted like it was no matter to him what the answer he got was. He only reached across the table for a biscuit from the basket of them, heaped hominy onto his plate. I'd made a big fuss over it, of course, when he'd walked in the door from school, painted the scrape up with iodine, pressed cold washrags to his face, hoped that black eye'd disappear before Sunday church.

James'd shrugged, said, "Alton Skokum."

"Alton Skokum what?" Leston said, and buttered his biscuit.

He was quiet, shrugged again. "Called you a nigger-lover." He reached for a biscuit himself, started forking it open.

Leston finally looked at him, knife in one hand, biscuit in the other. "So you fought him? You think I need defending?"

James said nothing, only went at the biscuit. "I don't know what that means, Daddy," he said. "Nigger-lover. But

I knew it wasn't good, the way Alton said it. That's why I had a fight with him."

He had the biscuit open then, steam up off it, and he looked at me. "Momma," he'd said, "you pass me the honey?"

It'd taken a moment or so for me to nod, smile, pass it to him. That was that. End of story, the beginning of James' life and the revealing even that far back as to who he'd end up being: teaching high-school Ag. in Levelland, Texas, because, Eudine'd written us enough times, that was what he wanted to do.

And there at the sink in our house in Manhattan Beach, where I could smell the sea through the open windows at night, and where the bedsheets were heavy with the damp air, I thought of whoever my grandchild this Elaine was, Billie Jean and Gower's six-year-old, wondered at what'd happened in her life so far that would already set her and who she was in motion, and I was sorry, too, that there hadn't been a part of me in there, a hand in raising her and Matthew. And then there were James and Eudine's children as well, three of them, Judy and Mark and David, all these lives on the face of the earth and me able to touch on them so little, all of them well on their way to not knowing who their grandma was already. We lived in California.

But there were the other grandchildren, the ones I took what comfort I could in when I wasn't tending to Brenda Kay. All the attention she took every day and the job of driving and assisting Mr. White exhausted me, so that when, on most Saturday mornings, Burton and Sarah showed up with Susan and Jeannie and Jill, and when Wilman and Barbara showed up with Brad and Robert and Timmy, it was all I could do to make a few batches of biscuits and slice up some bacon for their breakfasts while Wilman and Burton worked on the yard, mowed it up nice for Leston, and did whatever else was needed, whether weeding the flowerbeds or painting the shutters or fixing a shingle. That was all my grand-kids would remember me by, I figured: biscuits and bacon, their daddies at work on our yard.

The grandchildren were a hardship for Leston: he didn't know what to do with them, usually ended up getting mad at them for whatever reason—Jeannie and Susan pulling each other's hair, Robert digging a hole in the yard, Jeannie and Brad just running through the house, getting energy out they otherwise would have spent at the beach. Eventually he'd holler at all of them to be quiet, then'd look to me to provide entertainment of some kind. Sometimes he'd take a child up into his lap, then do the trick of rolling a cigarette with one hand, the child's mouth open and watching this strange magic take place right before their eyes. Then he'd let that child down, light up the cigarette and hold the smoke in his lungs as long as he could, all the grandchildren down around his knees and counting out loud how long he could hold it, him smiling all the while, winking at them. But that sequence of events'd only last long enough for Burton to get the ole-anders over to the side yard trimmed up a bit, only long enough for Wilman to pull a couple screens off the win-dows before the children'd lose interest, wander off. Most times they ended up playing with Brenda Kay, scribbling right alone with her at the kitchen table with the boxes of crayons I always had for her, the tablets of colored paper I kept. That's how Saturdays went.

But, finally, Leston got what he wanted out of this life, so far as I could tell. In these eight years he'd come

around from the man moving furniture to the Head of
Maintenance at El Camino College, seventeen men
under him now; he'd come around from the man with
his hands jammed into his pockets to the man who
could call up either or both sons, tell them he wanted
them over of a Saturday morning to change the oil on
the Plymouth, to help wallpaper the bathroom, to dig up
the little strip of ground along the back fence where
Leston grew okra and snap beans and tomatoes. And
they came, which, I knew, pleased my husband no end.
They came, usually brought their children along, sometimes the wives, neither of whom much liked the way
things went: Saturdays, if Leston so wanted it, were his
and his alone, and whatever plans the wives made,
whether a trip to the beach or mowing their own lawns
or weeding their own flowerbeds, were lost. Burton and
Wilman were the sons following Leston off into the
woods, it was easy to see: Hilburn and Sons Lumber
Company, the company that never happened, but happened in its own way nonetheless.

A little over a year ago he'd come home from work and
stood in the kitchen in his gray maintenance uniform and
held me tight in his arms, lifted me off the floor and
laughed. I'd thought at first maybe he'd lost another job,
him gone crazy over so much loss of himself through his
days. But no. It was because he'd been told by the president of the school to buy white shirts and dark pants and
a slew of new ties, that he'd be wearing that sort of outfit
from now on. Starting immediately he was Head of
Maintenance. No more pressing uniforms, either: he'd be
taking all his clothing to the dry cleaners—he had a
cleaning allowance now—and that was when I'd laughed,

too, Brenda Kay laughing right along with us, there at the kitchen table.

That night we'd made love for the first time in over a year, and in his hands I'd felt some return of reason to him, of the power he held over his world. Here was my husband, as good as returned from the dead, that old language of our bodies resurrected. Here was my husband of the years Before once more, though my breasts had long gone the slack of age, my legs up around him merely the flesh and bones of a woman fifty-six years old. It was a slow and pleasant making love, not like when we were children ourselves and on our honeymoon in Hattiesburg, and suddenly I'd remembered the two of us taking a bath together there in the hotel room, naked as jaybirds and quick to make love as many times as we could before we'd have to go back to Purvis.

And as we made our slow love that night, I couldn't help but think on those days, the days Before, Before and Before and Before, when what Leston and I'd had, I finally saw, was love. Love was what he had, and Leston, finally brought to the point of being ready to move inside me, seemed suddenly filled with the kind of love we'd had then: not the passion of the body, but of the heart. We wanted one another, wanted to feel each other as close as we could, and I marveled at what went on in the world, at how many times this world'd had to spin before the language we knew of each other surfaced in our lives, spoke again.

We made love that night, and we were happy in it. We were happy, and when, finally, he was inside me—my husband now sixty years old, even more of his hair gone, the flesh on his back soft and loose in my hands—I saw the same twenty-four-year-old I married, the same man I met at Sunday church in East Columbia, Mississippi, the same man with callused hands and dirty fingernails and an easy smile. This was the same man whose sounds mixed with mine our first night together to remind me of my own parents in our bedroom in Manhattan Beach, the two of us grandparents eleven times over and living in what might as well have been a foreign country, even after those many years we'd lived in California. Not the life I'd ever thought would happen when we'd made love our first time so long ago, but sounds we'd made that night now old friends come to visit us here, my husband a man who'd wear a tie to work from then on.

And this Saturday was Annie's wedding, the day after tomorrow, Gene O'Reilly her suitor, the man who'd been nicknamed Frog by his fellow Highway Patrolmen. He was a motorcycle patrolman, and was short, thick, friendly. His was a true and friendly smile, eyes big, mouth wide so that, yes, you could see he'd be called Frog by men who weren't afraid of him.

So far Annie hadn't called him that but once, that time on an outing to The Rock, a place Burton'd brought us to our first months here, and which we'd made our own beach since then. It was way up north of Mar Vista, all the way up near Port Hueneme, black rocks and waves crashing and a stretch of sand as well. We'd go there Sundays and picnic, and Leston would fish in the ocean—what Burton informed us was called surfcasting—and Brenda Kay would set her feet into the cool water. Usually there was nobody about, nobody for us to worry over seeing her legs, seeing our daughter. Just us.

Gene'd come along that time as a sort of baptism: all the grandchildren screaming and carrying on down to the edge of the water, burying each other in the sand; the

wives yapping on about all the food; Leston out at the
water with his pole; Burton and Wilman throwing a football back and forth up and down the beach. All of this,
and Brenda Kay, too.

But he took to her right off for some reason, a reason I
couldn't figure out: while Annie was helping me and Sarah
and Barbara lay out the food, Gene had knelt next to Brenda
Kay there at the end of the blanket we always used at the
beach, one of those ugly green moving blankets Leston'd
brought home one time and'd promised he'd return, baby
Timmy and baby Jill crawling round on it, droopy diapers
and all. Gene knelt next to her, touched her back, talked to
her in a quiet way, then pulled from the pocket of his
Bermuda shorts a small, thin square box, black. He touched
a finger to it, fiddled here and there, and then I could hear
a radio station, the call letters KTLA, then some music,
Hank Williams' voice small and tinny, but there.

We women stopped, food wrapped in wax paper in our
hands, and watched as Gene handed the thing to her.

"It's one of those transistor radios," Barbara said.

"My," Sarah said. She was quiet, then said, "Think it's a
bribe?"

"If it is," Annie said, "then I hope he bribes me, too."

Barbara laughed at that, and I smiled, watched my
daughter while they went on unwrapping the food.

Brenda Kay looked up at him. She had on slacks, like
always, and a blouse, her feet bare, her last toes jammed
together like they would always be, a jumble of toes.

Gene held out the radio to her. She glanced from it to
him and back. Then she looked to me, saw I was watching.

I nodded, and she reached her hand to the radio, took
it, held it to her ear.

"You want to hold it that close," I could hear Gene say

quietly, "then you want to turn the volume down." He hadn't taken his eyes off her, not even when she'd looked at me. Gently he took the radio from her hand, touched the side of it. Hank Williams' voice went even smaller, and he gave it back to her, placed it back in her hand, lifted her hand to her ear. "There," he said.

"Hey, Frog!" Annie called out then, and Gene turned to her, got that smile. "Time to eat!"

Gene looked at the ground, slowly shook his head, poked a finger in the sand. Brenda Kay sat with the radio up to her ear, was already rocking away to the music. Then she let out the first moan, her singing. Gene glanced at her only a moment, looked back at the sand, drew something there with his finger. He was still grinning.

He said, "Annie, I wish you wouldn't've said that."

"Frog!" Burton called from down the beach, his arms up to catch the football Wilman'd just thrown. "I heard that, Frog!" He caught the ball, and already he and Wilman were running up toward the blanket and the food, both of them hollering "Frog Man! The Frog Man!"

Of course Annie was all smiles, and went around the blanket, knelt next to Gene, Brenda Kay still rocking. She said, "But you still love me."

"Maybe," he said, and Barbara and Sarah and I all laughed at that, the grandkids swarming up now, all of them calling out "Frog! Frog! Frog!"

"Let's go ahead and eat," I said, "before sand gets all in everything," and Gene stood, went to the ice chest, pulled from inside it a can opener and started in on cans of soda pop for the kids: Nehi grape and orange and lemon-lime; next, he opened cans of beer for the men, Sarah and Annie taking one right along with them, Barbara making a tsk-tsk sound and grabbing up a Nehi orange for herself.

I went a few feet toward the rocks, where Leston was casting, cupped my hands around my mouth, hollered out, "Come on in, Leston!"

He was reeling in his line, and turned to me. "First quiet I've had today!" he called, his voice nearly swallowed by the wash of the waves. He was smiling.

"Suit yourself," I said, though only to myself, and I turned back to the family, everybody eating now, Gene with his head back and Annie feeding him potato chips one at a time like they were grapes. Jeannie and Susan were giggling, mocking them: Jeannie's head was back the same as Gene's, and Susan held a chip just above her mouth. "'Oh, Frog!" she said, and they both fell down, laughing. Burton said, "Now y'all cut that out," and Sarah, next to him, a piece of fried chicken in her hands and almost to her mouth, stopped, said, " 'Y'all.' You're never going to lose that."

"Damn right," Wilman said, and Barbara laughed, slapped at his leg. "Bill," she said. "Watch your mouth."

Bill.

Brenda Kay gave out a moan seemed even louder than normal for her, and I went to the grocery bag the paper plates and napkins were in, pulled out one of each. I said, "'Now we'll get you some food, Brenda Kay," the words just me talking to myself.

But before I even had a spoonful of potato salad on the plate, there was Gene handing Brenda Kay a can of Nehi grape. She stopped her rocking, smiled up at him, took it.

"There you go," he'd said to her.

I had every dish cleaned and put away now, the table cleared and wiped clean. Brenda Kay was still at the table, the transistor up to her ear, Leston in the front room with

Annie and Mrs. Zafaris. It was seven-twenty already, and I
had pictures in my head of Billie Jean having rolled her car
somewhere between Blythe and Indio, that wasteland she'd
die in thinking this was all California was: desert and rocks.

Then the doorbell rang, and I went into the front room
just as the door pushed open, Brad and Robert rushing in
and grabbing me round the knees, the two of them calling,
"Gramma! Gramma!"

Next came Barbara, Timmy in her arms, asleep. "Sorry
about the doorbell," she said, "but Robert wanted to do it.
No way to stop." She smiled, and I patted the boys' heads,
said, "Nothing wrong with hearing your doorbell ring.
Kind of nice, I think."

Leston stood as Wilman came in. Wilman said, "She's
not here yet?" and Leston shrugged, said, "You know Billie
Jean."

They shook hands, and Barbara turned, headed back
toward our bedroom. "I'm going to lay Timmy down," she
said, but Wilman was already talking to his daddy, the two
of them speaking low on how Wilman's sales route was
proving out, how the additions at El Camino were progressing.

Brad and Robert had let go of me, were over now at
Annie, her still up on the stool. The two boys put out
their hands, just touched the white material, and Annie
glowered down at me, whispered, "Momma."

"Come on now, boys," I said, "Brenda Kay and I baked
some cookies the other day, and there's still some left."

They turned right then, took off for the kitchen.

By eight-thirty, Burton and Sarah and their children were
here, and still there was no sign of Billie Jean. Mrs. Zafaris
finished with the dress and was gone, clearing out at least

that much room for the grandchildren to tussle and fuss
in, Timmy still fast asleep in the bedroom, Jill on her
hands and knees and laughing and drooling, trying to
keep up. Wilman and Burton and Leston sat in the front
room talking mostly of Royal Crown and all the goings on,
the same talk as always. My two sons threw out the names
of their bosses and shook their heads, Leston all the time
nodding away like he knew these men they talked of,
when I knew all along it was just pride in his sons: they
were doing fine, Wilman and Barbara getting ready to buy
a house all the way down in Buena Park, out in Orange
County, Burton with an eye on a house closer in, just over
to Torrance.

Annie was in the kitchen with us, huddled against the
wall phone, face to the corner of the room, whispering
and laughing to Gene. She turned around now and again
to wave off a laughing grandchild or two tugging at her.
Brenda Kay was eating a cookie, scribbling on a pad of
paper with one of those old red pencils left over from
when Annie used to use them, just scribbling away and
moaning to the music from the radio at her ear. It was near
on to her bedtime already, and she still had to have her
bath. Already, too, she'd started in to whining about all the
ruckus the grandchildren were making, her leaning her
head to one side like she does, then letting out with a loud
"Momma, *please!*" testy-like, almost crying. She was used
to the quiet of a house this time of night, not to all these
people, all this noise.

Then, above it all, I heard a car pull up and stop out on
the street, me already standing, ready for it to be her.

Everything else carried right on, no one hearing a
thing, and I went into the front room, cut through the
middle of the men talking, weaved my way round chil-

dren, and made it to the door, opened it. "Momma, please!" I heard Brenda Kay call out behind me, then heard Barbara say, "Boys, quiet down."

A car was parked on the street, the engine already ticking down. It was dark out there, the only light that from a lamppost four or five houses down, so I couldn't tell who was inside until the driver door opened up.

Then Billie Jean stepped out, cried, "Oh, Momma!" and came to me across the lawn. She had her arms up, a purse hanging from the crook of her elbow, and when she made it to me she almost knocked me down, so much force in her hug. She hugged me and hugged me, eight years' worth of a hug, and I turned with her in my arms, the two of us making a slow circle there in the yard.

I pulled away from her, saw in the dark a woman's face now, thinner, longer, her eyes harder, deeper somehow, her hair poofed up and sad high on her head, a week away from whatever fashionable Mississippi hairdo she'd gotten before she left. I saw all this in the dark of a lamppost so that she looked gray, her skin and eyes and hair all different shades of gray. Billie Jean.

"Now where's my grandchildren?" I said, and I turned toward the car, my arm round her waist, hers around mine.

We started to the car, and I thought I could see in the back seat the shadow outlines of two children. "Elaine?" I said. "Matthew?" and squinted at the darkness inside, us almost to the sidewalk.

Billie Jean let go, went to the rear door, opened it. She stood there a moment or two like a chauffeur, her standing tall, then she leaned in, said, "You two come on out now."

She stood up again, and I saw first two shiny black

shoes, then two legs in black pants, then a white shirt and black bow tie, then a boy, a little boy standing at the curb, hands at his side, just standing there, looking at the ground.

Billie Jean let go the door handle, squatted next to him and fiddled with the tie, though it seemed perfectly straight to me.

"Matthew," she said, "I want you to go over and give your Grandma Hilburn a big hug. You do that."

He didn't look up from the ground, but started toward me, and I went to him, scared as he must have been at meeting me on a dark street like this, an old woman he'd never met, him tired as he was after five days on the road.

I took him in my arms, hugged him, Billie Jean's baby, him already four, *four,* his hair greased and combed and parted in the middle. I said, "I'm so glad to meet you, Matthew. I'm your Grandma Hilburn, and I want you to know I love you."

I tried to get him to look at me, for his eyes to meet mine so he could see exactly what I meant, that in fact I loved him, though I didn't know him, knew him only through the parade of letters and photographs she'd sent over the years, letters filled with the daily news all our lives were filled with. Only in this way could I know how he'd busted open his chin after falling down the front porch steps not a week after he was walking, and that it'd taken seventeen stitches to put him back together. Nor could I know his first tooth had come out only two weeks ago but through his momma's words to me on paper, and that the tooth fairy'd left him a nickel under his pillow, which he swallowed the next morning in the belief the money was needed to grow the next tooth back into place. And only through letters could I know the other

child, the one still inside the car, my granddaughter
Elaine, and how she refused to let Billie Jean pick out her
clothes for her, coming out of her room each morning
neat and clean and dressed better than Billie Jean herself
could do. Little Miss Independent, Billie Jean called her
in her letters.

Still, I looked at Matthew's eyes, trying to get him to
look at me. I said, "Show me that place where your tooth
used to be," and I smiled, touched his cheek. But he
wouldn't look at me.

Billie Jean was whispering hard into the back seat now,
and I thought I heard a small slap, thought maybe it was
just her spanking the car seat to get her child moving, but
then I heard Elaine start in to crying, and I wondered what
it was to set her off.

"Billie Jean?" I said, and stood. "You okay?"

She was pulling Elaine out, her crying loud and long
now, and then I could see her: frilly dress gray out here, her
hair pulled back in a tight ponytail, her face screwed up
into a cry, Billie Jean holding her by the wrist and sliding
her out onto the curb next to her brother.

"This is a fine how do you do you're making for
Grandma Hilburn," Billie Jean said, and still the child
cried, put her free hand to her face, rubbed back tears I
couldn't see.

"There, there," I said. "It's been a long trip, I know."

"We'd of been here earlier if it weren't for the traffic,"
she said above her daughter's crying.

"And if we didn't have to stop, put on Sunday clothes,"
Matthew half-whispered, his head still down.

I laughed at that, trying hard to calm down the air out
here, but it didn't work. His comment only served, it
seemed, to set Billie Jean off.

"Now don't you start up with me, Matthew," she said, and I could tell her teeth were clenched. "Just you don't."

"I won't," he said.

"He can if he wants," Elaine said, all that crying suddenly gone. She wasn't even breathing hard. "He can pitch a fit if he wants. We can do whatever we want. Papa told us so."

"Don't," Billie Jean whispered. "You don't."

"They're divorced," Elaine said right then, her eyes on her momma.

"What?" I said, and swallowed hard, took a breath.

Elaine's mouth was straight, no smile or frown or anything there. Only this child's gray face, a gray dress, beside her her gray brother and her gray momma. She was watching her momma, watching her, I saw, to see what she'd do.

"Oh, Momma!" Billie Jean cried out even louder then, let go Elaine's hand. She made fists of her hands, put them to her eyes, my oldest daughter like a child all over again, crying.

"What?" I said again. I let go Matthew, felt dazed, though my body automatically did what a momma needed to do right then: I went to Billie Jean, held her tight, rocked her. And then I cried, too. I opened my eyes a moment or so, saw the two of them, these displaced children, surprised and puzzled at all of this as any children would be, their momma suddenly made small enough to be a child, the child of this old woman they'd never laid eyes on.

"Two years," Billie Jean cried, "two years," and she sobbed.

A moment later I felt new hands on me, and I opened my eyes, saw Barbara and Annie and Sarah crowded round us, smiles on their faces, and I realized they hadn't heard Elaine's words, them believing these tears we were giving out were tears of joy, tears being spent on a long overdue welcome to Billie Jean and her children.

The knot of us turned, headed toward the door, where more people spilled out, Burton and Wilman, then the grandkids, all of them clustering round us as we finally made it to the door, where Leston stood, hands on hips, smiling.

"Daddy," she said, and she tried her best, I could see, to sniff back her tears, catch hold her breath, smile up at him. But it was no use: she looked at him a moment longer, then burst out again, her face in the light from inside all red now, no longer that dead gray out at the curb. Her face was red with crying, and I leaned hard into her, held her tight. *Take hold of it,* I thought. *Make it work.*

My breath was hollow, short, my fingers tingling with the sharp edge of the news she'd brought, real news, not that she'd passed off in what now seemed useless letters. *Gower Cross,* I thought, and suddenly saw Burton flinching at that name the day we'd driven into Los Angeles and'd told him his sister'd married him. All I knew of this Gower Cross was that he worked long hours and traveled a lot. That was all I knew of him, and then, just as suddenly, I saw how little I knew of my own Billie Jean, her able to hide so well her life from us, only to have the darkest and biggest secret she could carry coughed up by her own daughter.

I held her even tighter, whispered into her ear just loud enough for only her to hear in the midst of all this commotion: "You just hug your daddy. We'll talk about this later. Just don't you worry none." And still I didn't know what I'd say to her, how I could keep her from worrying, and now the tingling moved from my fingers into my hands, started creeping into my arms. I knew nothing of what to do next.

She nodded through her crying, and left my arms for her daddy's only a couple feet away.

I turned from everyone, looked back for Matthew and Elaine.

The other grandkids stood round them out at the car, Matthew and Elaine dressed up and shiny, the others messy and beat from a day at hard play. They all stood off from Billie Jean's children, a loose circle, none of the children saying a word, only sizing each other up.

I crossed the lawn and neared them, said to the regulars, "Now y'all scoot, let these children get some air," and slowly they scattered, Brad and Robert and Susan and Jill backing away a few steps before jumping into the old routine of running and screaming, this night an extra treat, I knew, what with staying up late and being out on the street in the dark. "On in the house," I shouted after them. "Go introduce yourselves to Aunt Billie Jean," I said. They stopped the circles they were making in the yard, arms out, Robert and Jeannie already staggering a little though they'd just started twirling. "Now get on," I said.

They turned, headed back inside, where they started laughing again. "Momma, *please!*" I heard Brenda Kay cry, even out here in the street. "Bath, Momma!" she yelled.

But I stooped down there in the yard, looked Elaine and Matthew straight in the eye, and I said, "Now I don't want to start out things in the wrong way. I want you to know right out that I love you both. I'm your grandma." I paused, said, "You understand that?"

They looked at the ground then, at the grass, slowly nodded. "Yes'm," Matthew said, and Elaine whispered, "Yes, ma'am."

"Fine manners," I said, and smiled, though they still wouldn't look at me. "I don't know what you all been through, but I'm certain of one thing only: it's not been pleasant."

At this Matthew started to sniffing, reached up and rubbed his nose.

"But you're at my house now, my and your granddaddy's house, and we're here to take care of you, because we love you." I paused again, said, "Do you understand that, too?"

They both nodded.

"Then what I want you to do for now is just to keep quiet about the problem. You know, about the—"

"The divorce," Elaine whispered. She looked up at me, and put two fingers to her lips, made the old move like she was twisting a key. "My lips are sealed. Matthew?" She nudged him with an elbow.

His head still down, him still sniffing, he quick brought two fingers to his mouth, twisted them like a key just as his sister had.

"It'll come out, and everybody'll know," I said, and smiled, though suddenly the huge size of all this slammed into me.

"It'll come," I said again, "and we'll all of us know, but you got my guarantee there's nobody going to love you any less for it. Nobody. I love you. Your granddaddy loves you. Your ants and uncles and all those cousins love you. They do." They were words just coming out of me now, loose and free, but taking on their own meaning in spite of that. It was the truth: we loved them, we did. Maybe I even loved them more now than I would have because of whatever it was they'd gone through.

Divorce. Divorce was what they'd been through, and I saw how little I knew, too, of that whole ugly territory. All

I knew of it was a man walking toward my house when I was a little girl, a man who smelled of pomade and who patted my head. I never even knew if my parents were divorced or not, though they might as well have been. And that was when I reached a hand to both of them, touched the cheeks of both my grandchildren, because what I did know was the pain I'd carried with me, the pain buried deep in me, planted by the sorrow in my own mother, the touch of my father's hand on my head. These two children had their own pain, no pain I could ever know because it belonged to them. But I had my own, and hoped that by my touch they might see I knew a piece of what they held in their own hearts. Just a piece of that pain.

"Now let's come on in," I whispered, and stood, brought my hands from their faces, held them out for them to take.

Matthew was the first, though he still hadn't looked up. He took my hand, and then Elaine took the other, and I turned with them, headed toward the front door.

I looked up from the two of them, and saw the silhouettes in the window of four children, just standing there. They saw me looking, and disappeared in a swirl of laughter.

Billie Jean sat next to Brenda Kay at the table, an arm around her. Brenda Kay'd taken the radio from her ear, was grinning and grinning.

"Bijen!" she shouted out to me as I came in, and I nodded, said, "Your long lost sister." I smiled, smiled at all the faces of my children, all of them here except for James, who'd arrive sometime tomorrow with his own group in tow. They were all here at the table, Sarah and Barbara leaning against the counter and smiling, too. Everyone

smiling, from Leston there at the head of the table right on
down to Brenda Kay. I'd dropped Matthew and Elaine off
in the front room with the grandkids, figured it best to let
them settle in that way before being forced to face all these
adults, and Brenda Kay.

But though Billie Jean was smiling, of course there was
the huge and awful secret I knew of her. I could see right
off that sorrow hidden in her face, in her smile, in the way
she reached up just then to Brenda Kay and tucked a lock
of hair behind her ear. There was behind her smile, her
moves, her eyes the knowledge of something I'd never
faced before, never knew, never would.

It was my mother's face I was seeing. That was what I
recognized in her: the look of defeat, of love lost or squan-
dered or never found at all. My mother was seated at our
table, and I felt my heart squeeze down on itself, felt my
throat knot up, felt my eyes ready to brim over.

Divorce was there in her fingers as she brought that
hand down and laced it together with the fingers of her
other hand on the table and held them tight together, too
tight, and I wondered how anybody couldn't see there was
something wrong, so wrong in my daughter.

Burton and Wilman blabbered on and on with their
questions about how things were back home, asking after
old girlfriends and high school football teams.

There sat Leston, too, him smiling all the while and
nodding, a cigarette smoldering in his hand. He didn't
look at me, his eyes on his daughter and on his sons, them
surrounding him in just the manner I knew he dreamed
of. He drew in on the cigarette, held the smoke, and I
wondered at what had held our own marriage together all
these long years. Love was in us, certainly, but even when
I'd decided to move our family to California without

Leston's blessing, I'd still pictured him going with us, even if I'd had to tie him to the roof.

We'd been through it, I knew, too, and for a moment I marveled at the fact we'd *not* gotten divorced after all. Then Leston finally let out the smoke, chuckled at something Wilman said, and in that smile, in that smoke, I thought that it was precisely because of all we'd gone through that we were still together. Him without me wouldn't have worked, just as me without him would have failed. I drew power from him, he from me. And now he was a new man, a confident and successful man allowed to laugh and smoke and call his boys over to work for him. Head of Maintenance. Leston Hilburn.

I looked back at Billie Jean, and wondered from where she drew the power to smile as she did, to keep up the hiding she seemed to be doing so well. I wondered how long it would last.

She answered the boys' questions as best she could, gave out numbers and names and shrugged, too, when she didn't know, then asked questions herself after this Gene her baby sister was about to marry: how tall he was, how they met, her all the while smiling.

And again the magnitude and depth of what she'd been through pierced me, and I saw how all these words were working for however short a time to cover her, to keep her from the real topic that'd come out sooner or later. Again I wondered what it was I'd do to make good on that promise to her we'd talk about it, and the promise, too, I'd made to her children, that everybody'd know, that the truth would come out, that things would be fine.

I had no idea where any of that would start.

I called out, "Brenda Kay, bath time," and went to

her, took hold of her hand, tried my best not to let my
eyes meet on Billie Jean's for fear of what she might see
in me: Fear. Cowardice. Seeking refuge in my retarded
daughter and what routine I could use to put off whatever a momma was supposed to do here and now, a
divorced daughter and two new grandchildren on her
hands.

Brenda Kay stood right off, the transistor radio in her
hand.

"That radio's from Gene," Annie said to Billie Jean. "It's
so cute. She won't go anywheres without it. Momma even
lets her bring it in and listen to it while she's taking her
bath."

Gene, I remembered. And Annie getting married day
after tomorrow, and suddenly it was like Mrs. Zafaris and
Annie in that dress had all been years before, not on this
night. Not tonight at all.

"Night, all!" Brenda Kay called out as she walked along
behind me into the front room, and I said, "We'll be back
for hugs good-night in a few minutes."

"I love you, Brenda Kay!" Billie Jean said.

"Love you," Brenda Kay said.

The grandchildren were sitting in a circle on the floor,
Matthew and Elaine right there and part of them. They'd
gotten a deck of cards from the end table drawer. It was a
Crazy Eights deck, on the cards pictures of clowns instead
of diamonds and spades and clubs and hearts, and as we
walked through the middle of the circle, Brad said,
"Susan, do you have a six?"

"Go fish," Susan said.

"Liar," Jeannie said, and I spoke up, said, "We'll not talk
like that here."

I glanced down, saw Matthew and Elaine both with their

mouths open, staring at Brenda Kay, their hands fallen down in their laps to reveal every card they held.

I stopped, said, "This is your Aunt Brenda Kay," and smiled.

They said nothing, said Brenda Kay said, "Momma, bath!"

"Say hello, Brenda Kay," I said.

"Hello," she said. She wouldn't look at them.

Brad said, "You guys, hold your cards up so we can't see them."

But Matthew and Elaine didn't move, only stared, and I saw in their faces how much there was to do, how much. These other grandchildren, the regulars, knew how to act around Brenda Kay—just talk to her, smile, hug her when they came over. That's all. And when she got cranky like this, just ignore her. It was my job to take care of her, get her bathed, lay out her clothes for the next day, get her to bed, keep her happy. My job.

Robert said, "Matthew, do you have a nine?" and Brad reached over to him, pushed his little brother's shoulder, said, "It's not your turn, dodo."

"Y'all behave now," I said, and we moved on toward Brenda Kay's bedroom, and the refuge giving her her bath would give me. Matthew and Elaine'd be here tomorrow morning. They'd be here, and so would Billie Jean. Tomorrow.

I turned on the light in Brenda Kay's room, and there on the bed lay Jill and Timmy, curled up and pink and asleep, oblivious to everything, just babies not yet walking, asleep here in a house not their own, in a bedroom not their own. My grandchildren.

"Babies, Momma," Brenda Kay whispered, and for a moment it was as if someone else had spoken, as though there might be some fine and lovely ghost haunting the room, the words easing themselves into my ear like warm light.

She'd whispered, a sound she'd never made before, her words all these years so tight and forced and hollow in her throat. Brenda Kay whispered, and I turned quick to her, saw her with a finger to her lips, saw her mouth pucker up and watched her blow air out, what I knew was her imitation of somebody saying Shhh.

Her seventeen, and still learning. Seventeen, and this new move in her, and I felt myself smile, felt my hands moving of their own up to her and hugging her, holding her hard, harder, maybe, than I'd held Billie Jean out there on the lawn. I held her tight, until finally I let go, pulled back, saw her smiling at me.

I said, "Now where'd you learn that?"

She shrugged, still smiling. "Babies," she whispered, again that new sound out in the air, here in the universe, a new sound that signaled me there was always hope, even in the face of whatever ugly surprises the same old God could dish up.

I gave her one more quick hug, then took her by the elbow and guided her back out into the hall, cut off the light behind me, led her into the bathroom, closed the door behind us.

I sat on the toilet seat, said, "We can just undress in here tonight," and reached down, untied her white shoes. "Lift, " I said, and she lifted her right foot, then her left as I took off the shoes. She lifted the right foot again, let me slide her sock off, did the same for the left.

Next I reached up, started unbuttoning her blouse for her like I did every night.

She was still smiling, still had a hand up to her lips,

still blew out, so very pleased at my reaction, at what attention she'd gotten out of it. I finished with the last button, started to slip the blouse off, and said, "Now you tell me who taught you that, little girl. Mr. White?"

"Whisper, Momma," she whispered, and brought her hand down just long enough for me to take off the blouse. Still she smiled.

"Now turn around," I whispered, and she smiled even bigger, her teeth showing now. Our moves were rote in us both, us here at our nightly task, and she turned her back to me so I could unfasten the little white cotton brassiere she started wearing two years ago. But it was the whispering that was different, and I wondered how long this game might go on in our lives, how many days or weeks or years. I smiled.

I undid the brassiere, dropped it next to the blouse, whispered, "Let's turn around," even as she was turning. I whispered, "Was it Mr. White?"

She shook her head, her finger still to her lips.

I reached up, put my hands to the elastic waist of her slacks, started easing them down over her hips. Once I'd gotten them down to her knees, revealing like every other night the series of scars across her legs like red maps of some strange and made-up countries, scars that made my stomach twist the same every time I saw them, I closed my eyes, whispered, "So who was it taught you to whisper? Was it Annie?"

The slacks were down at her ankles now, and she lifted her feet again, slowly kicked them off. I opened my eyes. She stood before me in just her cotton underdrawers, her finger still up, the transistor radio tight in her other hand. There were her breasts, small and insignificant, the nipples the palest pink imaginable.

I leaned over to the tub, twisted on the water, let it run on my hand. I looked up at her, said, "Was it little Susan?"

"Whisper, Momma," and I could barely hear her for the water into the tub. It was warm now, and I took the white plug from the edge of the tub, settled it into the drain, and felt the bathroom warming up. The tiny room was suddenly a fine and beautiful place, green tiles up the walls around the tub, wallpaper Burton and Wilman'd put up earlier this year on the rest of the walls: great sailboats out at sea, sails all rigged up and full. Two gold-painted plaster angelfish hung on the wall behind Brenda Kay; a magazine rack filed with old *Reader's Digests* sat next to me between the wall and the toilet; a soft and pale green rug lay on the floor in front of the sink beside Brenda Kay. Steam lifted into the room now, and I breathed it in, filled my lungs.

I sat up from the water, kept on with the game. I whispered, "Was it little Susan?"

She shook her head.

I reached to her waist, started peeling down her underdrawers. The little window up above the bathtub was open, let the warmth from the water fog up the room more than otherwise, and now the room was cozy, the refuge I was looking for, what I wanted while I thought things out, put off *taking hold* and *making it work* for however long I could, even if just until we were through with this bath. Just that much.

"Then who was it taught you?" I whispered.

I got Brenda Kay's underdrawers down to her ankles, let her lift her feet up yet again, and saw it.

The steam in the room made me have to hold the underdrawers up closer to my face, and I held them in my hands, held them and stared.

There at the crotch was a bloodstain the size and shape of an egg.

Nothing new, yet still a surprise, a simple and sad gift from God.

I looked up at her, saw her through the thin steam smiling at me, whispering something, her finger at her lips and the rush of water into the tub keeping whatever word she uttered from reaching me.

Yet even through the rise of tears in my throat, through the rise of the knowledge of what exactly this in my hands meant, even through that I managed to whisper, "Who taught you to whisper?" one final time.

She leaned closer to me, didn't even see the blood-stained underdrawers in my hands, or if she did, didn't think it had anything to do with her, which, I saw, was the truth: her bleeding every month'd never mean anything other than dirty underdrawers, than her momma having to check the seat of her pants four and five times a day just to make certain she wasn't soaking through. What I held in my hands would never mean anything.

Her smiling face wasn't six inches away when she stopped leaning toward me. She took her finger from her lips.

"Dennis," she whispered, and put her finger to her lips again, blew air out.

I let my head drop, closed my eyes. I said, "Get in the tub."

"Whisper, Momma," she whispered, but I only leaned over to the faucet, turned off the water, said full-voiced, "Get in the tub," and heard how the sound of my voice banged off the tiles in here, how it ricocheted and rounded in this tiny room, at the same time shattered any sense of *refuge* might've been in here to start. It was gone, and suddenly I knew it'd never existed. Refuge from my life wasn't possible, of course, not even here, in a bathroom in a house in Manhattan Beach, the house filled with children and grandchildren.

And then, as if God's slap had been lost on me, as though I hadn't just seen in the bloodstain in my daughter's underdrawers, in her whispered word that you could never take refuge from your life, never get away from what you had to do before you, somebody knocked on the bathroom door.

No surprise at all. Enter trouble. No news here.

"Momma," Burton said. "Momma, you better come on out here," he said. "Billie Jean, she's crying out here. She's crying, and so are Matthew and Elaine." He paused. "Momma," he said, "all hell's breaking loose out here."

"Just a minute," I said. I was still there on the toilet, still had my eyes closed. "Just wait," I said.

I heard Brenda Kay climb in the tub, settle herself, then heard the transistor radio come on, some silly rock and roll song, a girl asking again and again for somebody named Kooky to lend her his comb.

"Momma?" Burton said, and I opened my eyes.

I said, "I'll be out in a minute or so," I said, "Crying's good for you," and I swallowed hard, stood from the toilet, then got down on my knees before the tub, took the washrag from where it hung on the faucet. With my other hand I reached for the bar of soap nestled in the corner where the walls and tub met. I put my hands with the soap and rag into the warm water, started lathering it up.

"In a minute," I said, and started in on Brenda Kay.

1962

Chapter 31

What more can I say except that I understood Leston when he came home from work one evening in April, him in his white dress shirt and thin black tie, his black pants and shined wing tip shoes, standing there in our kitchen. Brenda Kay sat at the table, the transistor to her ear, in her other hand a thick green crayon held tight, her hand squirreling out with the greatest of efforts the rows of letters she'd been making for three months now, the huge and joyful triumph of them:

$$\text{ЗI B ВЧВ ЯЭ В Я}$$

What is there for me to say, except that I understood him when he smiled down at Brenda Kay, touched her hair with one hand, with his other loosened the tie at his throat, then looked at me. A cigarette hung there at his lips like always, across his face a smile that creased his eyes nearly closed, this man Head of Maintenance at El Camino College, my husband.

He tapped ash into the handprint ashtray Brenda Kay'd made so long ago, and said, "We're moving back."

What is there for me to say, except I understood him? Because I did.

Though I hadn't known it was coming, I could have seen it if I'd dared to pay that kind of attention to him. There were clues, his life moving along with no help from me, as I could tell. Just moving, while I'd always been all eyes on Brenda Kay.

The first clue had come years ago, when I'd stopped pressing the gray uniform he'd worn for so long, traded in for the dry-cleaning allowance and the shirt and tie. And there had been the way he'd made love that night, the power that'd returned to him and his hands, how he'd held me.

And lately there'd been the clue of his new interest in what Brenda Kay was interested in. There was a new program on the television, "American Bandstand," a man named Dick Clark running the thing, on the program all kinds of musical bands every Saturday morning. We'd gotten the television as a gift from Burton and Wilman not long after Annie and Gene got married, my little Annie and her husband with a baby of their own now, Laura, and with another one on the way. Brenda Kay watched the program every time it was on, and now she could *see* the boys and girls who sang the songs she listened to on the old transistor Gene'd given her, her eyes wide when those groups sang, even wider when the children in the audience were shown dancing. On Saturday mornings when Burton or Wilman or, now, Gene weren't over and helping out, Leston'd sit right there alongside her and watch with her, point out to Brenda Kay teenagers dancing who seemed funny, the two of them laughing in the front room while I went about my Saturday chores of cleaning the kitchen, vacuuming, all else I had to ignore during the week when I was at Brenda Kay's school.

Leston'd been there through Dennis, too, had assumed a sort of position in things by volunteering himself to go over to his house, square off with his parents, even Dennis himself. I'd just smiled at his ideas, at how he still thought children and their problems could be solved with muscle and weight, as though Brenda Kay and Dennis were nothing more than kids whose parents didn't want them to date each other. For two years now the battle'd been on: I'd forbidden the two of them to ride together, sit with each other, share food or pencils or anything else. All of it in vain, of course: still Brenda Kay would come home and whisper to me, laugh at the mention of his name, or she'd see a boy and girl on "American Bandstand" dancing away, point at the two of them, holler out, "Dennis! Brenda Kay!"

But nothing more than that came of the two, no wavering in the way things between them fell. I didn't know if it was because of me and what I'd resolved to do that night two years ago when she'd first whispered his name to me, or if it had to do with Dennis' mom, Terri LaCoste, her full aware of what was up and as resolved to keep the two apart as I was. Nor did I know if it weren't just the two of them themselves, this seeing each other in the faces of teenagers on the television all they could know of love.

And there had been the giant clue Leston'd given as to the future of our days here in California. It was a clue I hadn't seen at all, one that came the day she gave to him the first row of letters she'd ever made, those B's labored and forced and hard, but B's all the same. Mr. White'd been stone resolved not to start her in on letters and such, her not testing in at a sufficient level for him. But I'd seen him working with the children for years on their letters, and I took to filling in the afternoons until Leston pulled

in, with working on her name one letter at a time: first
through the curves in the letter B, then the straight lines,
until she was making one and two and three of them of an
afternoon. We never told Leston what we were up to.

Then three months ago I'd pulled the surprise on him,
had Brenda Kay make an entire row in one afternoon.
When Leston walked in the door, there stood Brenda Kay,
all smiles, a hand behind her back. I stood in the doorway
between the kitchen and front room, a dishtowel in my
hands, behind me the kitchen filled with the smells of
fried ham and mashed potatoes and biscuits, and I said,
"Go ahead, Brenda Kay. Show your daddy what you did."

She quick brought the hand from behind her back,
held out the sheet of lined paper straight out of a tablet
just like the ones I'd filled my whole childhood. There was
a look on my Brenda Kay's face, one I'd never seen before,
a sort of startled surprise and pride, her eyebrows as high
up as they'd go, her mouth in a big open smile. And there
was a look much the same on my husband, who took the
paper from her hand, looked at the row of gnarled letter
B's there, then bent over and kissed her cheek.

It was then he uttered the words it'd be months before
I'd realize meant more than they did: "We did it!" he
hollered out, and hugged his baby daughter tight, an
eighteen-year-old girl just completed her first line of letters, all of them capital B's.

We did it. I thought nothing of those words, only went
to him and kissed his cheek, then kissed Brenda Kay, her
already laughing. "B, Daddy!" she shouted, and Leston'd
said, "B, Brenda Kay," and laughed more.

But suddenly, this evening in April, Leston's tie already
loosened, supper almost ready, I felt all these clues fall

suddenly into a big and intricate shape I couldn't quite recognize. Still, I knew what he meant when he said, "We're moving back."

"Moving where?" I said to him, though no name had to be uttered.

He put the cigarette to his lips again, took one last drag, then stubbed it out in the tray. "Home," he said, his eyes on the wisps of smoke up from the dead cigarette.

I was at the counter, slicing up a green tomato I'd picked from the small strip of vines that grew along the back of the house. Leston liked the green ones sliced up and fried, then spread with mayonnaise and sprinkled with pepper, and I looked from him to the tomato on the cutting board, the knife in my hand. I closed my eyes a moment, opened them, sliced right down and through the tomato, and again.

I said, "So we can run our lives right back into the ground. Run right back to that cracker life we had before." I paused, though I kept cutting away. I said, "And this isn't home?"

I nodded at Brenda Kay. I said, "'You see what she's doing there? You think we'd be able to get this far back where you call home?"

"We got this far," he said.

I wouldn't let my eyes meet his, instead stared hard at Brenda Kay wrestling those letters in her head to the paper, fighting hard for them, the crayon nearly snapped in two for how hard she gripped it. But still I saw him out the corner of my eye, saw him looking at me as he pulled the tie on through his collar, slowly folded it up in his hands.

"We got this far," he said again.

* * *

That night we lay in bed, me on my side and facing him, but as far away from him as I could get. Leston, I could make out in the dark, lay on his back, eyes open, his hands behind his head on the pillow.

I whispered, "But she's writing. She's got the first letter of her name down so well she don't have to look at the letter *B* anymore to write it." I paused. "I heard they'll all be starting up to Lawndale High School soon. Part of the day. It's in the works." I paused, whispered, "We can't leave."

He whispered, "You taught her what she knows. You taught her to write that first letter to her name. Just like you taught who knows who all back home how to read and write. You're a teacher. That's you."

I was quiet, then whispered, "Your job."

"My job," he said, and in the light from the small shard of moon through the window I thought I could see the shine of his eyes, wide open and unblinking, him staring at the dark ceiling above us.

Then I saw him smile. He whispered, "The reason I got my job is because it's nigger work. That's all." He paused. "I got the position I do because it's a nigger job, and I was the only white boy willing to do it. I never told you that."

He rolled onto his side, faced me, and I lost his eyes, saw only his silhouette, the shape of his head and shoulders, then the folds and lines where the blanket and sheet took over. There was that word, right here in our bedroom, the two-syllable one that brought on the specter of our old lives, that shadow never far from us at any given moment, only one word away. I'd always just said the word *colored* to him each time he used the word *nigger,* nothing more. But enough from me to let him know I didn't approve of its usage around our home. This time, though, I was silent in a darkness that suddenly seemed thick and full.

He said, "The man I replaced was a nigger, and he never got to wear a tie and wing tips the whole time he was with the college. Gray uniforms every day. *Moses* on his shirt. Every day." He stopped again, and now I felt myself slowly move over toward him, felt my body go from the comfort of sheets I'd already warmed up to a new place in our bed, new terrain, the sheets cold but forgiving, warming up quick enough to where the cold couldn't seep into me, chill me to the bone like the fog did early mornings. Then Leston's hand was on my shoulder, just resting there.

He whispered, "But it don't matter, because I did it. I did the job." He took a breath, held my shoulder a little tighter, then eased up. "I won," he said, "and you won. We beat this place. Brenda Kay's near on to writing her name, I wear a shirt and tie to work. We're sitting in a house worth enough money to buy a palace back home."

I closed my eyes, had seen enough, even though the room was dark.

I whispered, "What will we do there?"

"Live," he said straightaway. "Eat. Sleep." He paused. "Fish," he said, and I could see him smile, even through my closed eyes, even through the dark. He whispered, "I been in touch with Toxie. He tells me there's a place'd be perfect for us, down near to—"

"Toxie," I cut in, "you been talking to Toxie."

That was when I sat up in bed, started in on the hard fight I was ready for. Toxie. Mississippi. Fishing and smoking cigarettes. I said out loud, loud enough, I wanted to make sure, for Brenda Kay to wake up, "You sure got the nerve to go on ahead and start making big plans for this family. You sure got the nerve."

He still lay on his side, the room silent a few moments,

moments dark and full and empty at once. I hadn't lived here ten years just to see all hell break loose. I said, "Just who you think you are? Just who you think took care of Brenda Kay every day of her life? Just who you think took care, too, of your daughter, of Billie Jean and Matthew and Elaine while they got set up here? Who you think's got a job to do at a school for retarded children? You think you're going to lead me by the nose down the primrose path you think moving back to Mississippi is going to be?"

I stopped, breathed hard in and out, felt my face hot and flushed in the dark, my hands in fists, palms sweating. I listened for the struggle of sheets that would be Brenda Kay waking up in the next room, waited for her to cry out in the dark for me to come save her. But nothing happened. She slept.

"Talk to me of nerve," Leston said then, his words heavy and sharp and black in the room, some huge ax through the darkness. "Talk to me of making big plans for a family, about going right ahead and doing what you want for your family." His voice was as solid as I'd ever heard it, and I knew then it wasn't only me with *resolve* in this family, wasn't only in my children, too. It was here in bed next to me. I knew what was going on in his head, knew how he was leading me.

"Talk to me of nerve, Miss Jewel Hilburn," he said, "and selling off a house bit by bit, sending to magazines for brochures. Selling a clock off a wall with nobody's blessing but your own." He paused, and the words still hung in the air around me, shiny, black words just hanging there. He'd brought me and what I'd done back to fight me, slapped me cold with my own history, with the tight ball of nerves and flesh that made me me and nobody else.

Leston rolled onto his back again, put his hands behind

his head again, looked at the ceiling again. He whispered just loud enough for only me to hear, his voice total control: "I been here ten years for you. You railroaded me into this place, and I stayed. I stayed, and now we beat this place." He stopped, and still I was breathing hard in and out, because I could see the future already, saw in the dark hollow where his eyes ought to be a place two thousand miles east of here, where the air was thick and wet and hot, where things moved slowly and carefully right on to their deaths.

He whispered, "It took you three years to get me out here. Now I been here ten," his words even more quiet now, each of them almost a ghost of its own in this room, a room not a half mile from the Pacific, where waves beat against the shore every day, this world spinning round to reveal what that day could bring: things as strange and full as rows and rows of the letter B, as strange and empty as the idea of Mississippi.

"And," he whispered again, his voice now down to nothing, only a dream of real words, "you are my wife."

The only sound then was me, breathing in and in and in. Only me, and then I swallowed, took one last huge and hard, deep breath, because I understood him.

Chapter 32

I never knew my husband to be happier.

We sold the house nine days after we listed it, made more money than it seemed we would know to do with. Three days later Leston went right out, bought another new car, and when he came home driving a beige four-door with wide whitewall tires, I wondered if he weren't just and always the child, joyful at things he could drive, a life he could control the way he'd controlled his voice in the dark of our bedroom, and the way he'd controlled the lives of his children these long years, James the only one to escape early enough on; and the way he controlled the colored men who worked for him at El Camino, and the niggers back in Mississippi, all of them controlled by him.

Except Brenda Kay, of course, me part and parcel of her. Now we were moving to where he called home, and now, I'd seen as he pulled into our driveway that night with the new car, this would be his return in triumph, and his last stand at controlling me. *You are my wife.* Hilburn and Wife Lumber Company, trooping off into the dark, deep woods of Mississippi.

He cut the engine, leaned his head out the open window. "Well," he said, then opened the door, climbed out. He slammed the door closed, slapped the roof, smiled at me. "What do you think? Studebaker Lark Regal."

Behind him the early evening fog'd begun to bank up, the sky to the east a brutal, deep blue, the gray out over the ocean suddenly soft and obliging.

I said nothing, only turned, went back into the house. He knew what I thought. No need for words.

"Momma," Anne said, little Laura in her lap, a pacifier plugged into her mouth—now there were twelve grand-children, an even dozen, and my Annie already expecting another one, too. "Momma, there's just no sense in this," she said.

We were in the kitchen, Annie, Billie Jean, me and Brenda Kay, her at the table with her paper and crayons and making swirls and lines and jagged circles. Annie sat across from her in Leston's chair. Laura held a saltine in one hand, banged on the tabletop with the other, her eyes moving from me to Brenda Kay to her momma and back again.

Billie Jean had on her white uniform, the nurse's hat she wore all day long now off her head and on the counter, her hair down. Most afternoons she dropped by on her way home from the hospital, Annie coming by two or three afternoons a week, too, and stayed for a cup of coffee. Matthew and Elaine were taken care of by a lady with two children of her own two doors down from Billie Jean's apartment, Annie always on her way running an errand or three, and so it always seemed a rush of time, that cup of coffee. But at least my daughters came to see me and Brenda Kay, and for that I was thankful.

But today the rush was gone, and when the two of them'd shown up to the door at precisely the same moment, the looks on their faces the same somber look, eyebrows knotted up, mouths closed tight, I knew right away they were here on business.

"Can't Daddy see what this'll lead to?" Billie Jean said, and pushed herself off the counter, set her cup down. "It's not a place people want to move to, but from. Annie's right, there's no sense in this at all."

"So you tell me," I said, and finished rinsing the beans in the sink, wiped my hands with the dishtowel hung from the refrigerator handle. "You two tell me what makes sense here. Your daddy knows what I feel about this. There's been words passed. It's not that I'm stumbling through this with no regard for my Brenda Kay or me." I took a breath, put my hands together, as though that might turn my words into sensible ones themselves, not just ones telling of my surrender. I said, "He is my husband, and he has let me know in no uncertain terms that we're going back." I paused, took another breath. "I am his wife."

"Dammit," Billie Jean said, and crossed her arms.

"Watch your mouth," I said, and glanced at Brenda Kay, transistor to her ear, her crayon still at work. She hadn't heard a thing, had no idea how her world would soon tumble back what felt like a hundred years, a thousand. Mississippi.

I looked at Billie Jean, saw the anger play across her face like I'd seen it play too many times before. She'd lived with us for three months when she moved back, months too filled with the bickering of her and her kids, too filled with Brenda Kay whining out Momma *please!* all afternoon and night long.

I knew the look on her face, knew it told of the blame and anger and sorrow she put on that whole idea of *marriage,* of *love.*

Before she could say anything—if she'd even thought to—I said, "You just drop that thought. You best understand even entertaining the idea of the word *Divorce* in this kitchen will get you booted right out into the street. Understand that."

She shot her eyes at me, as did Anne. Laura still slapped at the table, quiet music still came from Brenda Kay's radio.

"Momma," Billie Jean started, "it's just that—"

"Don't," I cut in. "There's more that's passed between your daddy and me than you'll ever know. And there's more to just *me* than you'll ever know, too. There isn't any escaping this, that—"

"Divorce don't always mean escape, Momma," she said, and her hands were on her hips, her teeth clenched. "Don't you put that on me, Momma."

I was quiet. We'd had this fight enough times, the two of us scraping our way around the house some days, me with the notion she was trying to hide from the whole idea of marriage, that commitment, her with the knowledge of what she'd left, so that she was always right, the one to win. I always had to remember the real truth: she was the only one could know whether she'd done the right thing by getting divorced, just as I was always the only one could know my own history, know why I wasn't one to give up.

But here I was, my willingness to move as good a sign as any I was giving up.

"I'm sorry," I said, and I looked in her eyes, tried to smile. I said, "I just know from the life I've lived that what God hands down to me has to be found before I can lay any plans. Before I can see what I can do." I paused, still tried to smile. "I don't know what's going to happen out there. You both know I don't want to go back there. You know that," and I moved my eyes from Billie Jean's to Anne's, saw hers were brimmed up, tears ready to fall.

"Annie," I said, and I went past Billie Jean to her, touched her shoulder. Laura reached up, touched the front of my blouse. "Don't cry," I said, though it seemed this was the only thing left for any of us to do.

"Momma," she said, her eyes never leaving mine, and now a single tear slipped down her cheek. "I don't want you to go."

Then I felt Billie Jean's hand on my shoulder. She said, "I don't want you to go, either, Momma." She paused. "That's all there is to say. We don't want you to go."

"Then don't say another word," I whispered, felt tears on my own cheeks now.

I leaned to Annie, kissed her cheek, then turned to Billie Jean, and held her. My two daughters, still and always my children.

Yet still my children came by each night, spoke to me in the kitchen in low voices of how we ought not to move, while Leston sat in the living room reading over contracts on the house, the owner's manual for the car, and studying hard the three photographs of the place Toxie'd lined up for us. It was a rental house on a bayou near McHenry, a gray wooden house six feet off the ground with a porch across the front, two windows like empty eyes. Behind the house was the bayou, sawgrass and water. In the third picture was Toxie himself, standing at the top of the steps up to the porch, one hand resting on a support post for the porch roof, the other hand—the hand with only two fingers—there on his hip. He had on overalls and a short-sleeve shirt. He was smiling.

The pictures came the day after Leston'd informed me we were moving, and I never got a straight answer out of him as to when he and Toxie'd worked all this out. What

I wanted to know didn't matter to him, I could tell; all he needed were those photographs, the ones he brought with him to work each day, that he'd shown to every one of his underlings there, that he'd shown to every one of his grandchildren, right on down to baby Laura, him laughing and smiling all the while with the joke of that— "Start 'em thinking about heaven when they're young," he'd laughed to Gene—though all I could see in those pictures was heat, and sawgrass, and no single thing for my Brenda Kay—nor me—to do there.

On the last few Saturdays and Sundays before we moved, the children were at the house with us, packing up what we had into boxes. The grandkids had no idea, so far as I could tell, of what was going on, simply danced around the cardboard boxes and laughed, ran out in the yard or were at the beach with Barbara and Sarah and Gene, and I envied them that. I wanted to know again what it felt like to be a child, the life you planned for yourself lined up and ready to be played out in whatever way you wanted, perfect joy in the belief your life was in your own hands.

But mine'd been taken from me now, wrestled free of my grasp with simple words: *You are my wife,* my husband banking, and banking correctly, on a promise to love, honor and obey I'd made him thirty-six years ago. Now none of what was happening—not the packing, not the money, not the true happiness in my husband—none of it felt real.

Nothing was real, not even when Leston brought home the newspaper the week before we moved, there on page twenty-six of the *Gardena Chronicle* a photograph of him smiling in his white shirt and black tie, his face at a three-quarter angle to the camera.

"Read that," he said, and put his hands on his hips, smiled, tilted his head.

I looked at him, me puzzled, surprised, somehow afraid; he'd given no word to me that this was coming: an article about him, the headline reading "ECC Head of Maintenance to Retire."

"Out loud," he said.

I looked at him again, tried a smile, and read the article.

Leston Hilburn, Head of Maintenance at El Camino College, will be seeking early retirement, announced ECC president Lawrence Baldwin yesterday.

"Mr. Hilburn has been of great value to the College for the last eight years," Baldwin was quoted as saying in a press release from ECC. "In that time he has not only decreased turnaround time for both major and minor repairs to various College facilities and machinery, but he has also increased morale among our maintenance crew and served as a model of efficiency."

Hilburn, who will be 61 this year, has chosen to retire early "so that I can head back home to Mississippi," he said in a telephone interview with the *Chronicle*. "We've been here in Los Angeles for ten years," he continued, "and now my wife and I figure it's time we went back to where we're from."

There was more, but that was where I stopped. I looked up at him, said, "I figured no such thing."

"What would you have me say?" he said, the smile gone, his chin up and head straight. "I make the paper, and you figure I'll just say out there to God and the world my wife don't want to go."

"I don't," I said, and I quick folded the paper up, handed it back to him.

But what I wouldn't tell him, and what didn't seem

real at all, was that for a moment I thought the picture in the paper was of my own Jacob Chetauga. The smile and head and white shirt and black tie seemed the same man as in my old photograph, buried somewhere in this mess of boxes we were readying for the move. That feeling'd lasted only a moment, an instant, but I'd felt it, and then I couldn't help but wonder if in these last ten years Leston hadn't lived through his own death and won out over it, just like my grandfather had. The broken rope had been proof of God's hand on all our lives, no matter how hard we tried to will our lives in our own direction. Maybe this was God's will, I thought; maybe I'd already seen my husband live out his death, and now he was coming up grinning and walking away, just like my granddaddy'd walked away from a crowd ready to kill.

But then, for the first time in my life, for the first time ever, I wondered if maybe, just maybe, it'd been only a broken rope, no more than that. An accident, and suddenly I saw this forced turn our lives were taking might only be my husband's sad belief he knew what he was doing.

It'd been my momma, dying before my eyes, who'd prayed my granddaddy would have died the day he was hanged, my daddy on an aunt's shoulders, watching it all. It'd been my momma who'd wished my daddy would have seen his own daddy die, because she thought he'd be a better man for it, one who knew the difference between God's will and his own, the difference between right and wrong. And for an instant—an instant no longer than I'd thought the picture of Leston was of my granddaddy Jacob Chetauga—I let the same sort of prayer pass through me as before, me full aware of what prayer could do. It'd been me, of course, who prayed my daddy'd never make it back to our house from that thick woods he disappeared into each Sunday afternoon, and me, too, who pulled back the gray wool blanket, revealed him dead to me and my momma and the entire world. And me, finally, to pray for ten fingers and ten toes on my Brenda Kay. That was the power of prayer.

So I prayed, Leston already unfolding the paper and reading out loud the rest of the article, about his boys Bill and Burt working for Royal Crown Cola in Watts, a third son in Texas, James, teaching high school, and about his son-in-law Gene O'Reilly being a California Highway patrolman. I heard the article talk about a house in McHenry already rented out, while I let a minuscule prayer course its way through me: *Whatever death it is he's known these ten years,* I offered up to my God, that distant and puzzling and convincing God I thought I sometimes knew, *let him have died enough to see what's best for us.*

I paused in the hallway, out of his line of sight— Brenda Kay was in her room, waiting for me to usher her to the bathroom, bathe her—and I listened to him read the rest of the article, listened for word of his wife and her job, listened for word of Gene's wife, Annie, or for word on his eldest daughter, Billie Jean, who'd taken a few night courses over the last two years, then gotten a job as nurse over to Buena Park Community Hospital in Orange County. And I listened, most important, for word of his retarded daughter, Brenda Kay, and the rows of letter *B*'s she filled her days with.

But there were no words of that sort, only a few more about the brief and happy history of my husband's rise at El Camino College, and so I let my prayer move through me again, eyes closed, face to the floor: *Let him have died enough.*

In my head, though, was the picture of Billie Jean in my kitchen, arms crossed, hair undone and down to her shoulders, teeth clenched. Whose will was being done here? I wondered. Was this God's will? Could I escape the will of God?

Did God have any hand in this at all?

Billie Jean's image was in my head, the frustration she felt magnified in me. *Let him have died enough.* I prayed again, but this time with a few more words added for good measure: *to see there's a wife and daughter here with him.* Here was the brink of the old world, one I didn't want to enter, satisfied, finally, with the new one I had, yet my husband bound by pride and an old dead dream of a place called Mississippi to bring us away from here.

I prayed.

We left for Mississippi anyway, left on a Saturday morning in the midst of thick, cold fog and untold tears: from Billie Jean, who promised she'd visit soon as she'd worked up enough vacation time; from Barbara and Sarah both, though the two of them, I knew, must have been glad their husbands'd be returned to them for weekends; from baby Laura crying away at her two new teeth working in, and from Elaine and Matthew, the two of them dressed up nearly the same as the night they'd been brought here, Billie Jean with some strange notion our taking leave needed Sunday clothes. The rest of the grandchildren were crying, too, all of them lined up in the front room of the empty house, our furniture—what we couldn't jam into the U-Haul trailer we were toting with us to McHenry—divvied up among the children.

Wilman and Burton, of course, weren't crying at all, but grinned and fidgeted, afraid, I knew, they might let go what they felt about their daddy taking off without them. Wilman had on his Royal Crown shirt and pants and tie, was planning to take Brad and Robert to merchandise a bit of his route down in Long Beach; Burton'd set his eyes on painting their kitchen. "I've been waiting three years for this," Sarah'd whispered to Barbara in the kitchen earlier as we were taking the last kitchen things—the coffeepot, the skillet I'd cooked our last morning's breakfast in—out to the Studebaker, Sarah certain, I figured, I couldn't hear. Or maybe certain I *could*.

Annie cried the most. She cried and cried, and I knew it was because I'd never had the moment I'd had with the rest of my children with her, never'd been told by her she was leaving for her own, though she'd been married for near two years now. There'd never been a moment like the one I'd had with James at supper back in Mississippi, nor a night like the one when Billie Jean'd brought Gower home to us, told us they were already married, then'd driven off into the dark, waving behind her. Burton'd followed Brenda Kay back into the woods behind our old house, the talk we'd had of dreams and making them happen what I always considered my true good-bye to him; and for whatever reason I always thought of my boy Wilman's driving us in to Los Angeles, the ease with which he'd worked the wheel, the way he'd chewed his gum and waved out to City Hall and'd delivered us right to the doorstep of Bundy Muffler—that was his good-bye, I believed, him suddenly grown after that, as good as gone.

There'd never been any good-bye from Annie: Gene hadn't so much taken her from us as he'd become a Hilburn himself, ever since the day on the beach and the way he'd handed Brenda Kay her can of soda pop, showed her how to twist the dial on the transistor radio. Anne'd never said good-bye.

And she never would, I saw this morning, the fog outside the windows pushing in on us, pushing so hard on the glass I thought perhaps it'd pop, burst on us here in an empty house.

She'd never say good-bye to us, because now it was us who were leaving, her momma and daddy and baby sister taking out on her. We were the ones to leave her, not the other way around. I hugged her, felt her heavy tears through my blouse as she cried into me, felt snug against me the small swell of her next baby, my next grandchild, and I thought of her when she was a baby girl herself in a house in Mississippi. I thought of a ragged, worn blanket she held out to me, a gift worth more than any Brenda Kay would ever receive: her nye-nye, a small bit of cloth surrendered to Brenda Kay. Surrendered, given out of a child's love for a sister we didn't even know yet was retarded. But Annie'd known, even then. The blanket'd been a gift to a sleepy sister, the sorrow and work of Brenda Kay's life already begun back then, Annie already seeing it.

So I let her cry into me. Gene put a hand to her shoulder, whispered, "Anne, it's okay," and gave me a small smile, a shrug. I nodded at him, smiled. I closed my eyes, held her even tighter, because I knew this was the closest I'd ever come to letting her go, slip through my hands, me leaving her to Los Angeles and whatever might happen without me here. She was in good hands, certainly: Gene's, and Burton's and Wilman's and Billie Jean's. But not mine.

Finally, Leston cleared his throat, said, "We got to get moving. Want to make Phoenix at least."

She pulled away, her eye makeup all streaming down her face—leave it to my Annie to have made herself up before coming over to see her family off, even though it was only eight in the morning—her mouth a crumpled smile, her hair the most beautiful red I knew.

"These are for Brenda Kay on the road," Barbara said from behind me, and I turned, touched my own eyes with the back of my hand. She handed me a paper T.G.&Y. bag, and I opened it, saw inside a 64 box of Crayola crayons, a couple coloring books, three candy bars.

I looked up at her, smiled, said, "Thank you," though my tears were going full now, too. Then Barbara cried more, and Sarah, and before we three hugged one last time, I caught a glimpse through my tears of Leston and Wilman and Burton, all with their arms crossed, all three shaking their heads, all three grinning. My boys, the only one not here my James, who we'd be seeing once we made it to Texas, probably on Tuesday.

We let go each other, and I wiped my eyes with a Kleenex Barbara handed me from her purse, we three wiping and smiling and nearly laughing at all these tears.

Then I looked around the living room, said, "Where's Brenda Kay?"

"Already in the car, ready and waiting," Gene called out, his head just inside the door. The room was empty save for we three women; everybody'd gone outside.

We went out the door onto the front walk, the fog still just as thick, just as cold, but it didn't matter: I'd grown used to the fog, even found I liked the way it hid the day ahead, the way it started things out cool and damp no matter how bright and hot the day'd reveal itself later on.

I was the last one out the house, closed the door behind me, turned the knob to make sure it'd locked. Then I turned, saw all the grandchildren huddled together on the lawn, all of them except James and Eudine's. Though the children weren't in any special order, were just a peck of kids out on a foggy Saturday morning lawn in Manhattan Beach, I laid them out in order in my mind, somehow there being comfort in that act, in being able to know just who all these children belonged to: first Billie Jean's Elaine and Matthew; then Burton and Sarah's Susan, Jeannie and Jill; next Wilman and Barbara's Brad, Robert and Timmy; last, Anne and Gene's baby Laura, her standing all wobbly, there in a little tutu-like skirt and white baby shoes, a white blouse with embroidery round the sleeves and neck. Her hand was tight in Susan's, a little baby girl looking up at me.

There they stood, all these children strangely silent on the lawn, none of them more than seven years old, all of them just watching me. Behind them was the soft gray background of fog, so that I couldn't even see the house across the street clearly, and then I moved toward them out onto the grass, knelt before them all and gave each a kiss and hug, said good-bye. I felt on my back gentle pats like fragile wings just touching me, touching me: my grandchildren's hands.

I stood, turned from them to the car and trailer parked on the street. Burton leaned against the front fender, Wilman against the trunk. Billie Jean stood at the open rear door, and I could see Brenda Kay already inside, the transistor to her ear. She started to swaying, then let out a moan, her own song, and though it bore no resemblance I could make to the song she was hearing, I knew it was the new Ray Charles song playing everywhere these days, "I Can't Stop Loving You."

She started to singing, her voice wandering up and down like it wanted to settle somewhere, find home, and then came the refrain. Brenda Kay let out even louder, slow and long, "Ah ahh stop, love you!" She leaned her head to one side, and her auburn hair fell off her shoulder, the transistor tight to her ear.

"Sing it, Brenda Kay!" Wilman said, and I turned to him at the back of the car, saw him with his arms still across his chest, still grinning. Barbara, now next to him, reached to his shoulder, slapped him. "Now you cut that out," she said, but she was smiling, too, and I looked around, saw everyone was smiling, from Laura on the lawn along with all the grandchildren right on up to Annie. They were all smiling, all looking at me.

I stood next to Billie Jean at the rear door now, looked in at Brenda Kay, said, "You sing it for us, Brenda Kay. All the way to Phoenix."

But she was turned to her window, lost in the tune, her voice off wandering again.

Billie Jean took hold of me then, held me, and I said, "No more tears, now," and I felt her nod, her chin on my shoulder. "Yes, Momma," she whispered.

Then came the last hugs from my children, and all the good-byes from the grandchildren, who suddenly broke up, exploded into running on the lawn, circles and circles and circles, Laura in the middle, hands up, looking for someone to take a hold.

"Let's get a move on," Leston said as he shook hands with first Wilman, then Burton, then Gene. He climbed in the driver seat, pulled his door closed, started up the engine.

"Lark Regal," Gene called out above the engine, took a step back from the curb onto the lawn. "She'll get you there easy."

I was already settled in my seat, saw Leston nod at him, smile. He gave a small wave to his sons and son-in-law.

Annie leaned in my window, held me one last, long moment, then stood, took a step back from the car. She had on a red and green plaid smock top, green stretch-pants with stirrups and these huarache sandals everybody wore out here, and when she put her hands on her hips, I reached out the window, patted her tummy, said, "You take care, my Annie."

She smiled, quick nodded, her forehead and eyes wrinkled up, ready for tears again.

Before she could give in to it, Leston put the car in gear, and slowly we pulled away from the house, our headlights making sad stabs at lighting up the gray street. It was fog, clean and simple. Nothing for it but to drive slow as you could, watch for other headlights coming at you.

I turned in my seat, saw out the rear window Annie and Gene, him with his arm around her shoulder, her with her arms crossed; and I saw Wilman and Burton turn from the curb, head up the lawn, where Barbara stood holding hard to Brad's arm, heavy words down at him for whatever offense he'd made, while the rest of the grandchildren swirled round the two of them; and where Sarah leaned against her and Burton's Rambler parked in the driveway of our old house, purse already on her arm. I saw all of them back there, all of them disappearing into the fog behind us.

I looked at Brenda Kay. She brought the transistor from

her ear, held it with both hands in her lap, stared at it a moment or two, then with one finger touched the side, gently twisted the dial to change the station.

She turned it, turned it, then stopped, and here came that Ray Charles song again, this time on a different station. She looked up at me, eyes open wide, mouth open in the closest thing to amazement I figured she could know.

"Momma!" she said, and held the transistor at arm's length, nearly touched my face with it. "Ray Cha!" she said.

I said, "Sing it, Brenda Kay," and she smiled, all those teeth again, then held the radio to her ear, let out her song.

I turned to the front, saw the lighter in the dashboard pop. Leston had a cigarette out, reached over and pulled out the lighter, touched it to the cigarette.

Here was cigarette smoke in a new car again, a smell I'd thought ten tears ago a magnificent smell, a mix of the new and familiar with me inside a car that, in 1952, had been heading west toward a new world.

But now here it was inside a '62 Studebaker headed back to the old, and I shuddered at that moment, shuddered from the base of my spine right on up to my neck. It was a reflex, I figured, that showed the amazement I felt myself, the open-mouth awe that had hold on me because of how quick a life could change, how, like lightning, some unforeseen force could bust in, burn your world right out of your hands, leave you dazed. I was just along for the ride back to Mississippi, a place I'd called home once. A month ago I never thought this'd be happening. Now it'd already come to pass.

So I left my window rolled down, let cold fog fill as much of this new car as it could, crowd out both the cigarette smell and the new car smell. I wanted the fog to fill us up, swallow us whole before we headed out onto the deesrt, where the rocks and mountains and greasy brush'd play itself out in backwards motion, our lives going the same way: backwards, backwards.

We pulled to the stop sign at Highland and Sixth. Leston honked the horn for any cars he couldn't see coming at us, then eased right onto Highland.

We were only a few yards past the intersection when I said, "Turn left on Manhattan Beach Boulevard."

"Left?" he said, and glanced at me. "You mean right. We got to head out Manhattan Beach and hit—"

"I mean turn left," I said, surprised at the ease of my own words, how simply they'd come. I hadn't gritted my teeth, hadn't the need to swallow hard. I'd only said words, soft and clean.

I knew where it was I wanted to go right then, and knew how to get there. It seemed like the most simple thing I'd ever known in my life: just turn left at Manhattan Beach Boulevard instead of right, head west to the end of the street, and to the pier. It was the ocean I wanted right then, what I wanted to draw into me, hold onto. When we hit the desert later today, and, even later, when we moved into a house on the bayou in Mississippi, I wanted the ocean with me, my last look at it, even if it'd be shrouded in fog. I wanted that look, and Brenda Kay's voice behind me, singing away to what'd suddenly turned into the saddest song I knew I'd ever hear.

"Ah ahh stop, love you!" she sang out, and I said to Leston, "Turn left at Manhattan Beach Boulevard, and head on down to the pier."

"It's nothing but fog—"

"I am your wife," I whispered, my eyes never turning to him, only staring out into the fog.

He said nothing, and when a few moments later the gray gave way to a hazy pinpoint of bright and red ahead, both of us well aware that that was the stoplight at the intersection of Highland and Manhattan Beach Boulevard, he let out a deep breath to signal how much of a discomfort my last request was to him.

Because that's what it felt like, my last request: get us to the Pacific, that west as far west as you could get.

There was nothing to see at the end of the street. Leston pulled into a slot in the small parking lot where the city pier went out, and we sat in the car, before us the broad, dull gray of fog. All I could see was a few feet of sand, the first few pylons of the pier like the black ribs of some huge and long dead animal jammed down into the beach, the rest of it all fading into the gray. Now and again a fisherman walked past us out of the fog, started on to the pier, pole over his shoulder, tackle box or bucket of bait in hand. I thought to say to Leston, *Look, fish here. Fish here, instead of a bayou in McHenry,* but I knew it was no use, and so I kept the words to myself. And in the minute or so we sat there two boys in swimming trunks walked past, hair blond as could be, shirts off, chests bare to the west air. Each carried, too, one of these Surfboards that'd become all the rage, and just then I heard Brenda Kay sit up behind me, saw shoot between Leston and me in the front seat her arm, her small, pudgy fingers forming a fist, then pointing with the first finger at the boys as they disappeared out onto the sand.

"Look!" she said. "Momma, look!"

I said nothing. Her fist and pointing finger hung there

in the air for a minute or so, the arm stiff, fingers so tight I thought they'd turn blue.

She pulled her arm back, and I heard her lean back in the seat, heard her skim through ten or twelve radio stations before settling on one, Elvis Presley singing "Good Luck Charm."

"That boy's from Mississippi," Leston said. "That Elvis boy."

"This isn't Mississippi," I said.

I turned in my seat, reached over into Brenda Kay's lap and took the radio from her, clicked it off.

I tried to smile at her, said, "Let's leave this off for a few minutes, honey," handed it back to her.

She smiled at me, whispered, "Quiet, y'all," and for the first time in two years I found relief in that sound, in her whisper. Quiet was right, and I reached a hand to her lap, gave a small squeeze to her hand.

I faced front. The car was silent, and only then did I pick up what I realized was the real reason I'd come here: through the fog, fog so thick you'd have thought nothing could make its way through, even through that fog, I heard it:

Waves broke out there, somewhere inside the fog that'd eaten us up, somewhere out past the sand before us. I heard waves beating down out there in the gray, beating away, pulverizing the earth with every crash, wearing away the world with each rise and fall of water.

That was what I'd come here to find: the sound of the world being eaten away, the good knowledge that no matter what any of us intended the world still kept giving way.

That would be me, I thought. Me. I'd keep pounding, even with this next life in front of me, a life that wasn't new at all, just a return to the old.

But I would crash. I would crash and crash and crash,

crash until all I knew turned into sand, moved the way I wanted it.

"Let's go," I said, the sound of pounding waves heavy in my ears, a sound that suddenly melted into the roar of my own blood through me. "Let's head to where you think we ought to live," I said to my husband, and let my words start crashing away.

Chapter 33

We got to McHenry near sundown Friday night, pulled up in front of the house on the bayou, lights on inside the windows and coming out through the screen door. Though the light was warm, a soft and smooth yellow, those windows were still empty eyes, the front door only an open mouth.

In front of the house was an old green pickup, no tailgate, the back window cracked and shattered like a spiderweb across one half of it. We parked next to it, and Leston shut off the engine.

I didn't move. The car was silent save for the thin hiss of static from Brenda Kay's transistor behind me. We'd already replaced the batteries twice since we left.

Leston said, "Well, here we are."

I turned in the seat, looked back at Brenda Kay the same way I had near a week ago. But now she was sweating, single hairs of her bangs plastered to her forehead, the neck of her blouse sweat through, her eyes rimmed with sweat. She had the radio in her lap, her eyes looking all around out her window.

I faced forward, opened my door. I was the first one to step foot on this foreign soil, a place I hated without even giving it a chance. But that was my right, I figured: if I gave it a chance, I'd lose. And I wasn't going to lose.

I reached for Brenda Kay's door handle as Leston climbed out, and here came the front screen door pounding open, Toxie moving fast across the porch, the light from inside silhouetting him for a moment.

"Jewel," he cried out like I'd been ever so close to him all my life, when what little I could recall of him involved that first Sunday afternoon supper at Leston's mother and stepfather's, the little teenage kid, Leston's nephew, who'd leaned forward, said "Hey!" to me, then gone on and eaten while I served up food for myself. Just that moment, and the lost three fingers to a quick fuse, and the picture of him following Leston and all the niggers— they were niggers once again, I knew now, always only niggers here in Mississippi—to work, me always at the sink inside the house and looking out at them, the children round me and howling out for good. That was all I knew of Toxie.

Now here we were again, right back where we'd started. Toxie gave me a hard hug, his hair at my cheek thick with some sort of hair oil—not even pomade—and wet on my skin, the two-finger hand on my back patting like some wounded bird trying to take flight.

He pulled away, looked at me in the growing dark. I smiled at him, said, "Toxie, how you doing?" though I willed myself not to recognize him, not to see in the shape of his mouth and in his eyes any resemblance whatsoever to my husband. It worked: he was a stranger, and I was only exchanging pleasantries with him after a long, hot trip.

He said, "Fine, we fine," and I turned from him, opened Brenda Kay's door.

I said, "Come on out, Brenda Kay, and say hey to Uncle Toxie."

Toxie put his hand in his pockets. He glanced up and over the roof, nodded at Leston, then ducked down to see inside the car.

Brenda Kay scooted across the seat, let her legs touch ground out here, her white shoes all the whiter for the closing dark.

"Some shoes you got there," Toxie said.

I wouldn't look at him, only reached a hand in to Brenda Kay, helped her out.

Leston came around the front of the car, and Toxie, I could tell, was torn as to what to do: should he hug his uncle, an uncle not but a few years older than himself, and welcome him Back Home where he ought never to have left, or should he stay here, make introductions with his mother's namesake, this retarded girl?

Leston gave a quick nod at him, then looked at Brenda Kay, who stood now, arms loose at her sides, in one hand the transistor, static hiss still filling the air.

"Let's us turn that thing off now," I said, and reached to take the radio from her.

"No!" Brenda Kay shouted, and shook my hand away from hers, brought the radio to her chest. She looked at me, then at Toxie, then me again.

"Suit yourself," I said, and I turned, smiled at Toxie. I said, "Brenda Kay, this here's Uncle Toxie. Toxie, Brenda Kay. A little cranky after this trip."

"I know you, Brenda Kay," Toxie said. "I come to see you when you was in the hospital over to Purvis." He rocked on his heels now, hands still in his pockets, and I couldn't remember his ever coming to see her after she'd burned her legs, not that I'd necessarily remember. But it didn't matter to me, because I was willing myself not to know this man. I was out here and living in Mississippi and this bayou shanty for one reason and one reason only: to break my husband, get us back to California and to the progress our lives'd made, get us back in that line toward fixing our lives.

Brenda Kay smiled, clicked off the radio. She brought her eyes from his, and I could tell she was looking down the length of his arms, stopped when her eyes landed on his pockets, where his hands were hiding.

"Two finger!" she shouted, then laughed: "Huh huh huh!"

"You remember!" Toxie laughed. He brought out the maimed hand, reached to beneath her chin, tickled her.

She laughed harder, squeezed up her shoulders with his tickling. "Two finger!" she shouted out.

"Now that's enough," I said, and I smiled, though the dark'd probably made it difficult for anyone to tell I was. Toxie stopped right away, put his hand back in his pocket.

"He was only tickling the girl," came Leston's voice in the dark, his words quiet, meant to carry extra weight with how soft he'd spoken.

But I wasn't here to lose, and if I put Toxie down this early on, all the better. It was Leston I was aiming at; if I cut out Toxie, there'd be that much less work to do on him.

I said, "It's been a long and tiring trip for all of us. She doesn't need any more winding up." I paused, looked up at Leston. I wouldn't let my eyes meet Toxie's, not now.

Leston stood with his hands in his pockets, too. In the dark I could make out his mouth, a tight thin line, his eyes only shadows.

I said, "Let's just go on in and see where we're going to live now, hey?"

Toxie shrugged right away, glanced up at Leston, then

to me. "Sounds fine with me. Let's do it," and he turned, took a step for the porch.

Then he stopped, looked to the car like he'd not seen it parked there next to his derelict truck. He took a hand from a pocket—the five-fingered hand—and slowly ran it across the hood. I could see the windows of the house reflected in the metal, saw his hand interrupt the shine there as he let his fingers trace the line of the fender.

"What the hell kind of car is this?" he said.

"Your language, please," I shot right out, and slammed closed Brenda Kay's door, took her hand.

"Beg pardon, ma'am," Toxie said, and took his hand from the hood.

"Studebaker Lark Regal. Brand-new," Leston said, though he wasn't looking at Toxie. He was looking at me, and as I started for the porch I said to Leston, "Excuse me," moved toward him so that he had to stand aside, lean into the car to make room for us.

"Studebaker," Toxie whispered. He gave out a low, soft whistle in the dark, and I wondered at how little he could see of what was going on here between Leston and me; marveled, too, at how easy he'd been to put away.

Inside, Toxie skittered round the place, going from room to room, eager to impress upon us just how lavish our accommodations were: the house, owned by an older gentleman in Gulfport, a plumbing contractor Toxie worked for, was partially furnished—a sofa in that front room, a bed in both the bedrooms, a kitchen table with five chairs—had electricity, a dock out back, a gas stove and stocked refrigerator, even a washing machine. But what impressed Toxie most, and hence what he spent the most time showing off to us, was the plumbing itself. "No lead pipe in this here little palace," Toxie said in the kitchen, him rocking on his heels again while Leston crouched, peered beneath the kitchen sink. When he pulled his head out, he looked right away to me, and I said, "A palace," a word I thought'd been Leston's a month ago when he'd described what we could afford. Leston only smiled at me.

Toxie made certain, too, I turned the water on and off in the bathroom and kitchen, saw how shiny the stainless steel fixtures were, touched the showerhead above the tub. He even talked me into turning the shower on so I could see how smooth was the flow of water.

When finally he'd shown us every visible inch of pipe in the house, had flipped on and off the light switches in the bedrooms, had even turned on the washing machine for a moment, then flicked it off, we three moved into the front room, where Brenda Kay sat on the blue corduroy sofa, the radio still in her lap, still turned off.

That was when the treefrogs started in. All the windows in the house were open, and the sound whirled right in on us, a dull, thick hum that swelled in an instant to the same deep and sharp-edged drone I'd lived through the first forty-eight years of my life. It wasn't a welcome sound, certainly, nor was it a surprise, but I knew if I gave myself a second's chance I'd find that sound ushering in old thoughts on other times, times when we lived back here, times when the children were growing up in the old house and the boys or Annie'd complain at the sound ghosting its way into their rooms.

But I wouldn't let myself remember that, only went to the sofa, said to Brenda Kay louder than I needed, "Don't you get worked up about those treefrogs," though there was nowhere on her face any evidence she'd even heard them. She'd remembered Toxie's two fingers from a trip he made to her hospital room ten years before; why couldn't she remember the sound—the comfort, in fact, if I'd let myself feel it—of those nights years ago, when she was a child?

Leston and Toxie'd gone into the kitchen, though, hadn't even taken note of the signal I'd tried to send them about the annoyance of treefrogs. Then, just as suddenly as they'd started, the treefrogs stopped, the quick loss of sound now making this house seem all the more empty. The room was entirely empty, the room and this house and the whole bayou out there, the woods and everything in this state completely and utterly empty. Just as empty, I knew, as the shadow of our lives here, the future a huge and empty room we'd never fill.

Now came the sound of the refrigerator door opening and closing, and I heard first one and then another small spray of sound, two cans of beer being opened. Next came low whispering, two men together who hadn't seen each other in years, well aware their words weren't meant for any woman, whether normal or retarded, to hear.

I turned from Brenda Kay, who'd clicked the radio back on to more static, and faced the doorway across the room that led into the kitchen. I couldn't see either one of them in there, saw only the shining stainless steel faucet, two shining stainless steel knobs for hot and cold running water. Still, I watched, certain something was about to happen.

And it did: Leston leaned back from where he stood in the kitchen into my line of sight, lifted the can of beer in a sort of toast to me, then took a sip.

I figured it was nothing Toxie'd see meant anything: just a little gesture made by his uncle to me, Leston's recognition, maybe, of our triumphant return to

Mississippi. We'd driven in in a Studebaker Lark Regal, after all.

But I took the gesture for what it meant, for what I'd seen in his eyes as he held up the can, at the way he hadn't blinked taking that sip of beer: nothing I'd done so far to make this as difficult as I could had been lost on him. His little toast meant he knew all about what was going on inside me, thirty-six years of marriage to me giving him enough indications as to how I worked. And I was working now.

But before he could lean back into the whispered conversation, the plans for fishing and coon hunting and beer drinking that Toxie, I was certain, had already laid out for him, I gave him a gesture of my own, one I knew he'd recognize: I smiled at him, my lips never parting, just turning up at the corners, and I nodded once, stared hard right back at him. *This battle has begun,* I signaled him.

He disappeared, and I heard the whispering again, a low cold laugh from the both of them.

The treefrogs started up again, drowned out the sound of their laughter, and I turned to Brenda Kay, saw a mosquito right there on her left cheek, already parked and working away.

I quick reached up, flicked at it with my finger. Brenda Kay flinched a little with my move, and I smiled at her, met her eyes with mine.

I took my hand away then, saw where my finger'd left a small swipe of blood on her cheek; saw, too, the smashed mosquito on my fingertip.

This battle has begun, I thought.

Toxie didn't stay too much later, and then Leston and I dug in the dark through the trailer to find the box marked *linens* so we'd have sheets for the beds, towels and washrags for in the morning; next we pulled out the box marked *pots and pans* so I'd have something to cook breakfast on. All this time no words passed between us, the two of us knowing already what was in store.

Toxie showed up at seven the next morning with three colored men, men I knew would never believe other coloreds could live in houses as fine as those in the neighborhood where the Exceptional Children's Foundation had been. I saw it in how they slowly rolled out of the bed of Toxie's pickup when he pulled in, three men in ragged overalls and undershirts; saw it in how they wouldn't even mount those steps up as Toxie came to the door, him there in a green cotton shirt and blue jeans, me stopped at the sofa and tying Brenda Kay's shoes, watching all this through the screen door. The door and all the windows were already open for the heat of the morning, and for that wet air, air that seemed thicker and wetter than any foggy morning I'd known in the last ten years.

He knocked on the doorframe, and I stood, called out, "Leston, Toxie's here," to which Toxie, startled—he hadn't seen me through the screen—cleared his throat, cupped his hands to the screen and peered in. He smiled, said, "Got the road crew here this morning to help y'all." He motioned behind him with his good hand, then stepped away from the door. "Boys from down to the shop."

He put his hands in his pockets again, waited for me to open the door. He looked back at the coloreds, then to the screen, squinted, looking for me.

"Leston out fishing already?" he said. I made it to the door, paused a second before I pushed it open an inch or so, let him finish opening it himself.

"Nope," I said without looking at him. "Shaving," I

said, and turned, headed back to Brenda Kay and her other shoe.

"Unc Tox!" she shouted out, and Toxie laughed, pulled that hand from his pocket, made like he was coming at her with it.

She laughed "Huh huh huh" there on the couch, squirmed as he came closer, her foot pulling out of my hand with the movement.

"Gonna tickle the bejabbers out of you, honey!" he said, and I'd had to reach for her foot, take hold hard to it.

"Brenda Kay," I said, low and strong, and she stopped, looked at me. "Tox, Momma!" she said, her forehead screwed up, eyebrows high in a way I knew meant I should leave her alone.

"Yes, Toxie's here," I said, and slipped on the shoe. "He's going to be working hard today, unloading all our things so we can move in proper to this palace."

"Palace, that's right," he said. "Miss Brenda Kay, you're living in a regular palace." He stopped, put his hands in his pockets as I finished off tying the shoe, then half-pushed, half-pulled myself to standing: one hand on the arm of the sofa, the other on my knee, I slowly made it up.

Toxie still smiled, his hands still in his pockets. Then he sniffed, looked around, sniffed again. "I don't smell it," he said. He turned, sniffing, and headed toward the kitchen.

"What's that?" I said, and gave a hand to Brenda Kay, helped her up from the sofa.

"Breakfast," he said. "Your biscuits, grits." He disappeared into the kitchen, and I followed him in.

He stood at the stove, looked over it like it was some dead animal. "Like the old days," he said, and looked at me, smiled. "Your breakfast for the crew."

"The old days," I said. I put my hands on my hips. "What gave you the idea I was here to make breakfast for y'all?" I said, and paused. "Just like the old days," I said. This was a war.

"Leston," he said, still smiling.

"That's right," Leston said from behind me, and moved past me into the kitchen. He was barefoot, had on an undershirt and gray workpants, something left over from the old days at El Camino. Above the neck of the undershirt was a spray of gray hairs, and he had a towel round his neck, rubbed at his chin and cheek with one corner of it. His hair was slicked back, still wet from his shower. He looked at me, his mouth straight.

"Told him last night we'd have breakfast over here before we started in on the trailer," he said. He finished wiping his face, took the towel from round his neck. "Guess I forgot to inform you," he said.

"I imagine you'll be wanting the whole works, of course. Biscuits and bacon and grits and eggs."

"It's a whole trailer out there we got to unload." He balled the towel up in his hands, said, "Then we got to get down to Gulfport to the U-Haul, turn it in."

"That's a good day's work," Toxie put in, and I cut my eyes at him, saw him shrug, smile.

"And the coloreds outside, I suppose I'll be feeding them, too."

Leston nodded, said, "Suppose so," the towel tight in his hands.

"Coloreds?" Toxie said then, and it was as if my looking at him sharp as I had didn't mean a thing. "Coloreds?" he said again, and gave a chuckle, the same low and cold one he'd given with Leston last night. "That's a California word if ever I heard one," he said, still smiling. He said,

"Them's nothing but niggers out there. No better or worse than that."

I looked at him. I said, "You call them what you want, Toxie, and I'll call them what I want. You understand that?"

He looked down, nodded. "Yes ma'am," he said, and he looked again like nothing more than the teenage kid at the supper table, ill-mannered and ready to eat.

"If I'm feeding this whole brood," I said, and I paused, weighed out a few seconds while I gathered up my words, not certain how they'd play out here: I was thinking right then on May the secretary and how I'd had to learn that word *colored* all on my own, and I was thinking on those two or three retarded colored children that first morning ten years ago in the classroom at the Foundation, and I was thinking hard, too, on that colored boy who'd helped me park our old Plymouth, and the woman in the lavender dress, her baby Leon with the croup.

And though it brought shame to me even as we stood there, whatever hell was about to break loose here, I was thinking on what ammunition I could bring to things, get him to see the truth of Los Angeles, the promise we'd already wrung from it: a row of letter B's, basketball, a classroom with the pictures of our Presidents on the walls.

Then I said it, said the unimaginable, half because a piece of me believed it somehow the right thing to do, but another half, the half I was already ashamed of, because I wanted to use those colored men out there to my advantage.

I took a breath. "If I'm feeding this whole brood," I said again, "then I think the coloreds ought to come on inside, eat in here."

They were stupid words, I knew as quick as I'd said

them; stupid for the way they showed my own hand instead of forcing his; stupid for how they revealed me and all the plans I had in my head.

"God damn," Toxie whispered. I blinked once, twice at Leston's granite face, then looked to Toxie.

"Your language, please," I managed to say, though I knew the tight pitch of my voice'd already betrayed me, shown me to be nothing more than an old woman working to get her way.

"God damn, Leston," Toxie whispered again, and he looked up first at me, then to his uncle. "Y'all didn't go out to California and come back goddamn nigger-lovers, now did you?"

Toxie was smiling, but it was a different smile now, no longer the child, but the man, the same man who'd driven here in that old pickup out front, the same one who'd loaded up three *niggers* to spend a Saturday helping his uncle and wife and retarded cousin move Back Home. The same man who, just by the color of his skin, dictated to those three men exactly how far back of him they had to walk.

Now he was a man, I saw, ready to say what he wanted, and I saw that in fact nothing'd been lost on him. He knew all about what was going on between Leston and myself; knew, too, by how he lifted his jaw, took a breath, that he'd thrown in with my husband. I hadn't put him away last night at all.

But Leston spoke at just the right moment, said to his nephew, "You watch your language in this house, Toxie," and I looked to him, saw him in profile, his face turned to Toxie.

Toxie nodded, lost the smile. "Beg pardon," he said.

"And no, we are not nigger-lovers," Leston said, and

slowly turned to me. "What's fair is fair," he said. "Them boys out there—niggers, coloreds, whatever you want to call them—they're going to work today, so we'll feed them." He paused, brought the towel up to his face, swiped at a dab of soap below his ear. He said. "They'll eat outside, too. Just like they used to."

"Fine," I said, and brought my eyes from his, right away set about banging open and shut the cupboards in search of a skillet, a pot to boil water in. I wouldn't look at either Leston or Toxie, embarrassed at having my own bluff called in this way, mad I'd lost this first round.

And, I realized, I wouldn't look at them, especially Leston, because I was savoring the small piece of victory I'd found: Leston'd looked first to Toxie, told him to watch his mouth. Told him, in fact, this was our house, no one else's. That was a victory.

I found a skillet and pan in the cabinet next to the sink, precisely where I'd placed them the night before, though I couldn't recall putting them there. I set them on the stove, Toxie moving out of my way, hands still in his pockets. Then I opened the refrigerator, took out the slab of bacon in there.

"Get out the kitchen," I said, still without looking at them. "I've got food to cook." I went to the sink, filled the pan with smooth-flowing water from a shiny stainless steel faucet. I fixed my eye for a moment out the window above the sink, out there the bayou, sawgrass and water, waves of heat already shimmering up off it all.

Chapter 34

I lay awake every night the first month, wondering how it'd come about, and come about so quick. The open windows above the headboard seemed only a prank there in the dark, the air inside no cooler, no less stagnant than that out on the water and in the woods. The only thing close to movement was the soar and tear of night sounds out there, sounds louder and more rambunctious than any late-night siren or honking horn I'd heard in Venice or Manhattan Beach.

Leston lay next to me, sleeping away; he spent much of each day, as he'd said he would, fishing or crabbing, or just tooling around in the Studebaker, a regular country gentleman now, him with no need for a job and with all the money we had from selling off the house. The wad of it was settled into a bank down in Gulfport, waiting for us to find a house we wanted to buy, or a parcel of land we'd want to build on, all of it part of his big plan for the end of our lives.

Sometimes we went with him on his rides, the three of us stopping at a hamburger stand in Gulfport and getting oyster po'boys, then sitting on the picnic tables set up out front, eating away while that Gulf sun beat down on us.

Once, too, we went right down to the water, trudged through a beach wider than any California beach I'd ever seen, the sand here like sugar, white and fine. When we finally made it to the water, I rolled up Brenda Kay's pantlegs, held the bottom edge of my skirt in one hand, took hold of Brenda Kay's hand with the other. Then we walked out what felt a half-mile before the water even got up to our knees.

Brenda Kay and I kept a few paces behind Leston, him leading the way, his pantlegs rolled up, too, to reveal the pale white skin of his legs: an old man's legs, I saw that afternoon out on the water. Then I looked down at my own legs, saw the blue veins crisscrossing just beneath skin that seemed transparent as new ice, and I saw that I was only an old woman. Most days of my life'd already passed through me, and not once in the last ten years of those days had the picture of me walking out in the Gulf of Mexico with my husband and baby daughter wheedled its way into my head. Then I pictured California, and the waves there, remembered the power of them I'd drawn into me the morning we'd left for this place.

I said, "There's no waves out here, Leston," and I stopped, let go the hem of my skirt a moment, held a hand up to my eyes and looked out to sea.

Leston stopped. He put his hands on his hips, looked out to sea, too. I glanced at him, saw the round, wide patch of sweat on the back of his shirt.

He said, "Kind of nice, no waves."

"If you don't like waves," I said. He turned, a puzzled look on his face, and I was glad he couldn't know what I meant, glad for the secret of the sound of those California waves breaking in my head.

He turned from us, said, "Let's keep going," and started off.

I gathered up my skirt, looked at Brenda Kay, smiled and said, "Just a little farther and we'll head back in."

She smiled up at me, started walking, and for a moment I let play across me the notion we were actually having a good time, Brenda Kay liberated in some way, barefoot in the Gulf of Mexico. Her steps through the water were slow and gentle and exaggerated: with each step she lifted her foot clear of the water, brought it forward, set it back in the water, did the same with the other foot.

I watched her move this way, watched her smile, then heard Leston say, "Take a look at this."

I turned from Brenda Kay, saw Leston point at a boat way out in the water, when Brenda Kay's hand jumped in mine, her screaming out at the same moment.

I turned to her, felt her hand hold tight to mine, nearly crush my bones. She was staggering, her feet moving quick beneath her. "Momma! Momma!" she screamed, though her eyes were on the water, her head darting, looking, looking.

Then she looked up at me, crying now, and said, "Momma, foot! Momma, foot!"

"What, honey?" I said, and took both her hands. "What happened?"

"Maybe stepped on a ray," Leston said, and now he was all movement next to me, reached down and lifted her like a baby into his arms, up out of the water. "Take a look at her feet, see if there's any marks."

"Marks?" I said. "What kind of marks?" But I was already poring over her feet with my eyes, touching all over, searching for welts, cuts, bites, anything.

She'd gone to silent tears, her breath in short, quick spurts as she took air in, cried it out.

I found nothing on her feet, nor up her legs to the knees. Only her scars, the same old evidence of an accident years before.

"Probably stepped on a flounder is all," Leston said, his voice gone calm, and I saw a chance, another avenue for ammunition, and I said, "You knew there were rays out here?"

He looked at me, eyes squinted for the sun. Brenda Kay had hold of his shirt collar with one hand, the other clutched at the neck of her own blouse. She was still crying.

"She didn't get stung," he said. "She maybe stepped on a flounder."

"There's rays out here, and you knew it, and you let us out here." I stopped, peeled Brenda Kay's hand away from her blouse, took it in mine. "There," I said to her soft as I could. "We're heading back in now. We're going home now."

I looked up at him again, knew I'd done the best I could with what I had at hand: we wouldn't be back here, wouldn't step back in the Gulf of Mexico.

I lay awake at nights wondering on how quick we could get back out. There wasn't any doubt in me; we'd be back there, and I'd be back to the Foundation, back to driving the station wagon, back in the classroom and doing what was necessary for Brenda Kay's life. That, I saw, was what I was doing late nights lying awake: already fixing this, mending the bone-break our moving here was.

Instead of remembering my life back in California, I found I was imagining what would be once we returned, emerging once again from this jungle called Mississippi into Los Angeles, but this time without having to break all new ground, without having to live in a motel or bus tables or work for a moving company.

The treefrogs starting up, the night owls and cicadas and various other animals outside our open bedroom

window making their nightly racket, I pictured Leston
heading off to work at ECC each morning in his shirt and
tie, saw him at the table of an evening, rubbing black
shoe polish into the toe of a wing tip with an old rag,
then buffing it, shining it up, brushing it with the brush
from the shoeshine box there on the floor in front of
him. I saw him spending Saturday mornings with the
boys mowing the lawn, saw him with older—and
more—grandchildren circled round him as he rolled cigarettes with one hand at the same kitchen table. And I
saw him smiling while surfcasting at The Rock, maybe
Brad or Matthew or Susan next to him, him showing
them a thing or two about fishing.

I saw, too, a party for Brenda Kay when she came back;
not the party Mr. White had thrown for us leaving, a party
that'd involved me having to clear from the walls of the
old classroom all Brenda Kay's drawings, sheets of con-
struction paper I'd labeled "Easter Sunday" or "Our
Garden" or "Three Rainbows," though Brenda Kay'd never
given any of them names. There'd been a whole file folder
full of them I'd had to take down while Mrs. Walker
passed out cupcakes she'd made, and Mr. White'd poured
Kool-Aid into Dixie cups for us all.

No, the party I saw was one that welcomed her back to
the classroom, a classroom where, after more cupcakes and
more Kool-Aid, she'd settle in, be quick to finish learning
the rest of the letters of her name, so that the next crop of
pictures she'd have stapled to the walls would have her sig-
nature at the bottom, no matter how shaky the letters.

And I even saw in my plans, plans like the kind of
dream I'd told Burton of years ago, the kind of dream you
had to make happen, or it wasn't worth dreaming at all—
in my plans I even saw Dennis, saw in the time I'd had to

devote to keeping the two of them apart some piece of joy: I had that job to do, had my baby daughter to keep from him. A job.

The day after Leston came home with the Studebaker, I told Mr. White that we were moving back to Mississippi, some sort of true proof in my husband's purchase of a new car that we'd really be going. Mr. White'd only smiled, put out his hand for me to shake.

We were in the gymnasium at West High, the children out on the court in four teams for two games of badminton. Long ago we'd gotten rid of Mrs. Klausman, now had two Long Beach State PE majors paid by the Foundation to lead the children in their daily activity time. There were two station wagons then, too; another woman, Mrs. Cox, and I traded routes in the mornings and afternoons so we wouldn't get too bored at making the same rounds every day.

Word had it—Word always had it at the Foundation, Word about new and fantastic events coming at us, those Words floating through us like the rumors they usually were, but sometimes taking hold, proving out to be true— that not too far off was some sort of short day program at Lawndale High. Mr. White's plans to get the children onto the campus of a public high school for at least a small amount of class time each day were supposedly coming close to actually happening after all these years of fussing and tussling with school board after school board. All the way back to the old Foundation office on Adams he'd been talking about this happening, our children showing up to public schools. And just before we'd moved, the Word had started its rounds: soon they'd be in real schools, not jammed into an old storeroom.

But that day in the gymnasium, he'd only shaken my hand, put his other hand to my shoulder, and smiled. A whistle blew, and one of the college boys, Neil, a big bear of a boy, black hair in a crew cut, shoulders broader than either Wilman's or Burton's ever were, called out to the children, "Okay, people, let's swing the racket up. Everybody!"

I glanced to the children, saw them swing their rackets up as close as they'd ever get to together, then looked back at Mr. White.

He let go my hand, took the other from my shoulder, buried both hands deep in his pockets. He said, "If we were in my office, I'd make you sit in that chair in front of my desk, and I'd put you through my lecture on how valuable you've been to the Foundation." He paused, looked down at the parquet floor, said, "But I think you may already know that." He smiled, said, "And I don't think you'd sit in that chair, either."

"Certainly not," I said, and smiled. "You know me better than that."

"Of course," he said. "I, being the pompous and arrogant man I am, am right." He laughed, and I did, too, though I found it hard to. This was the end of things.

I looked out to the children, saw the other college boy—Stan was his name, a boy as blond as one of those surfing boys we'd see disappear into the fog the morning we would leave for Mississippi—standing behind Marcella, his arm on hers, gently lifting the racket in a fine arc from her knee to just above her shoulder.

Mr. White cleared his throat, said, "But what I'm not certain I understand is why you're leaving. And why," he said, his voice gone low, almost to a whisper, "to Mississippi. Perhaps you're returning to your family—"

"I have no family out there," I cut in. I swallowed, said, "I was orphaned at age eleven."

"Oh," he said. "Oh," and I saw only then how thin this relationship had actually been all these years: he knew nothing of me, knew only I'd been a teacher once, two or three lives before this one. He knew nothing of a logging shack, or of pomade or bamboo fans printed with Bible verses, or of leather belts or blasting stumps for the Government. The fact was that I'd known more of him after our first meeting in an oak-paneled office on Adams than he knew of me right now, after eight years of helping him.

But what I found most strange was that I took comfort in that, because it only proved I'd been successful in my mission so far: this relationship was bound up in Brenda Kay, and how I'd been able to lend my hand to helping fix her life, and the lives of these other children. That was where I'd wanted the focus of my life to stay, and, judging by how little he knew of me, I'd made that happen.

"I'm sorry to hear that," he said, his face all serious, and I'd had to make myself laugh for him, ease the obvious strain I'd put between us. He didn't know what to do with what I'd just told him.

"Thanks for feeling sorry," I said, "but it happened quite a while ago." I smiled.

He looked down. He said, "Yet I'm still surprised you'd choose to move back. What with the unrest there, the racial tension going on."

"Racial tension," I said.

He looked up at me. "Why, yes," he said. "I'm speaking of the freedom marches, the bus rides. Dr. Martin Luther King."

"Oh," I said, and I glanced again out to the court. Stan and Neil stood together now on the far side of the gym, arms crossed. They both had on the same outfit they wore every day: gray sweatpants, gray sweatshirts, whistles round their necks. Stan was saying something to Neil, both of them looking at the children swinging away. Then Neil busted out laughing, shook his head. "Carrie," Stan called out, "hold tight to the racket," and left Neil to his laughter.

"I've been hearing about that for quite a while," I said. "But it won't have anything to do with us." I looked to him, smiled. "We're just poor crackers moving to a bayou."

He looked at me, shrugged. He said, "Well then, why are you moving? From all this—" he brought a hand from his pocket, gestured at the crowd of children. "And from what's coming up soon."

"You mean Lawndale High School," I said.

He smiled, said, "That must be common knowledge now." He paused. "So why are you moving?"

I swallowed again, took in his words, because now he was asking for the truth, not stumbling on it, like he'd stumbled on the small pebble of my history I'd just revealed to him: me an orphan at eleven. He was asking straight out for the one true reason we were moving, and I had to swallow again, struggle out the words.

I forced a smile, said, "My husband, my Leston, wants us to."

I said nothing else, felt myself bite my lower lip, felt a drop of sweat cut a small swath down the middle of my back.

"Oh," he said. He took his hands out of his pockets, crossed his arms. He had a navy suit coat—suits being his own uniform of sorts, and I remember looking at him as he half-turned from me, looked away from me and out onto the court.

He said, "I've certainly no experience in that department, as well you know. Marriage, I mean." He paused, nodded at the children. "I'm quite pleased with the performance of these young men."

I turned to them, too, saw that Stan and Neil were lining the children up in order of height, little Carrie first, followed by Marcella, Brenda Kay two children back from her, Dennis, I was thankful, five children back from Brenda Kay. They each still had a racket in one hand, and stood a few feet back of one net. Then Stan ran around to the opposite side of the net, a birdie in one hand, racket in the other. "Ready?" he called out, and Neil, next to Carrie, him so big and brawny next to that tiny child, took hold her wrist as Stan'd done with Marcella. "Ready!" Neil said, and Stan batted the birdie high up and over the net, Neil swinging up Carrie's racket so that she batted it right back.

Stan made a big stunt out of backing up and backing up, trying to center himself under the birdie coming back down to him, his arms flailing about as he backed up even more, then finally fell down on the floor, only to have the birdie drop dead center on his chest.

Neil cheered and clapped at Carrie's making contact with the birdie, her so pleased with herself she dropped the racket, clasped her hands together at her chest and started stomping the floor, a smile wide across her face.

Then the clapping and cheering was picked up by the rest of the children, healthy sounds of young people happy at what success they could find.

Mr. White turned to me, smiling, "You see what I mean? This program is certainly a triumph. A far cry from a church parking lot. And a far cry from that dismal start with Miss what's-her-name."

"Klausman," I said, and he nodded, looked back to the children, Marcella stepping up for her chance now.

But I was looking at his navy suit coat, at how, with his arms crossed, the cuffs of his white shirt poked out the sleeves, the cuff links he had on with some insignia on them, and I remember thinking how this was his own uniform, his identification, the clothes he wore saying simply *philanthropist*. And suddenly I saw Leston's white short-sleeve shirt and wing tips and black ties, his uniform: *Head of Maintenance*, it spoke, and there came to me the picture of my two sons wearing their Royal Crown uniforms: *Salesman;* and I wondered, too, if James, standing before his high-school Ag. class, didn't wear a white laboratory coat like my old science teachers at Pearl River Junior College wore, those coats saying *Teacher.* And I thought of Billie Jean, her white outfit and paper hat tacked high up on her head: *Nurse.*

I looked out at the children there, Stan doing the same act again with Marcella's birdie, the birdie arcing high, then falling, falling, and I looked at Brenda Kay, at what she had on: blue cotton short-sleeve blouse, blue slacks to hide her scars, white orthopedic shoes: *Retarded daughter.*

And finally, I looked down at my own clothes, at the gray and blue plaid dress, buttons down the front, thin little collar, black shoes with a low heel.

Wife.

Mr. White turned to me again, uncrossed his arms, jammed his hands back into his pockets. Those cuff links'd gone, just disappeared. "Your husband, I imagine, has family there? In Mississippi."

"Oh, yes," I said, nodded, thought of that photograph of Toxie, his two fingers there at his hip. "Spread around the state. We'll be seeing them."

"I want you to know how truly sorry I am to hear this from you, hear of your husband's choosing to leave," he said, and here came his hand to my shoulder again, him on stage as always, his touching me meant to convey how genuine was his emotion.

He said, "I've never been married, so I can only imagine how difficult it must be to have to form your own will to someone else's. It must be tremendously difficult, and for that I admire you. Giving up one's own will for the judgment of another," he said, "even at the risk of sacrificing Brenda Kay's education." He stopped, slowly shook his head, then said, "I can only imagine."

And though I nodded, knew in his words was a kernel of truth—this was not the best thing for Brenda Kay— another part of me seethed, wanted his hand off my shoulder, his words out of my head. I nodded, while inside I shook my head as hard as I could: *You can not imagine,* I screamed. *You can not.*

He smiled, gave my shoulder a gentle shake. He said, "We'll have a party for you and Brenda Kay before you go."

I lay awake each night, and each night my mind and the pictures I came up with worked right through the same cycle: first, what new occurrences I could use as ammunition against my husband, crash away at him and his own wrongheaded *resolve* to make us stay here, even if Brenda Kay'd been so scared by that fish beneath her feet she wouldn't even dangle her feet off the dock now, wouldn't even climb into the jonboat Leston'd bought off a friend of Toxie's. Each night I hoped for more occurrences such as that one in the waters of the Gulf of Mexico, even if they'd be at the expense of my baby daughter.

Next came pictures of the life ahead, those pictures

prophecies, I knew, the image of Brenda Kay's name scrawled across the bottom of a picture I might name "Waves at the Beach" as great a glory as I could figure on seeing in my life, a glory I knew would some day be mine.

And lastly there came to me each night that blue and gray plaid dress, my eyes looking down at it, the word *Wife* and the uniform I knew I'd wear the rest of my days no matter what clothes I had on come to haunt me, me still lying there awake in bed, still here in Mississippi, still trying to find some way back.

I never knew when or how I fell asleep, only knew that when I awoke each morning I sat straight up in bed, my nightgown soaked with sweat, and shot my eyes round the room in an effort to remember where I was, and who this man in bed next to me was, and why that word *Wife* still circled me, swirled round me like a fearless ghost in the pale, wet light of dawn on a bayou, outside the open window behind me the lonesome, measured drone of a woodpecker high up in a cypress, this next day in Mississippi already begun.

Chapter 35

But it was Leston to call down God's answer to my prayers, my husband to make happen our moving back to California, though he'd no way to know that was what he was doing. On just one day my husband put into motion our lives in a way that led to our leaving this place, and put us back on the narrow path.

One morning in July he woke up before me, and when I sat up in bed he was already at the dresser, pants on, cigarette at his lips. He tucked in the old shirt he had on, then started to buckle the belt, all with his back to me. Sunlight came in from behind me, through that open window, so that his clothes seemed to shine, white in the light as I blinked my eyes, rubbed back the little sleep I'd gotten.

He said, "Taking Brenda Kay fishing. If that's fine with you."

He cinched the belt, reached to the dresser for his pocketknife and change. He half-turned to me, smoke snaking up from the cigarette. He blinked at the light shining in on him as he looked at him. "No need to worry," he said, and smiled. "You get her dressed, and I'll entertain her awhile. Give you some time to yourself." He paused. "Thought maybe, too, we'd take a drive after lunch."

In his smile was that same confident and powerful man,

the one who, the evening he came home and told us he wouldn't be wearing a gray uniform anymore, had lifted me off my feet, nearly swung me round the kitchen, and for a few minutes while I got myself dressed, then made my way to Brenda Kay's room, roused her from sleep and led her to the bathroom, there seemed some jagged edge of remorse in me for giving him all the grief I knew I did each day. There'd been the business I'd given him about his knowing there were rays out in the Gulf, for example, or the ten or twelve new mosquito bites Brenda Kay woke up with each morning, me leading her into the kitchen where Leston sipped his coffee and rolled his cigarettes. Then I'd stand his baby daughter in front of him, lift the bottom edge of her nightgown, point out the small red welts. Each morning I said, "Take a look at these, Leston," the red welts on her scarred skin an even deeper red than those about her ankles or arms. Then I always turned Brenda Kay around, led her right back out the kitchen and to her room before Leston was able to say a word.

Yet still here was my husband, up and out of bed and, I could hear through the bathroom floor, already down in the storeroom under the house, fiddling with his tackle box, making ready, I knew, the old bamboo pole he'd found down there when we'd moved in, fixing right then a bobber to the line, a hook and weight, so that his daughter could fish with him, this same daughter sitting on the toilet and yawning.

Remorse is what I felt, even through the humidity and heat of the day rising up around me. I reached down, reeled off the right number of sheets of toilet paper for Brenda Kay—she'd already jammed the toilet four times for using too much of it, the water pressure here nowhere near what it used to be in Manhattan Beach—and I smiled at the fact it didn't matter how fine the plumbing in a house was: if a pipe got plugged, it got plugged.

She finished, and I heard Leston stomp up the porch steps, the screen door bang closed.

"Ready yet?" he called out from the front room, and Brenda Kay stood, pulled her underdrawers up, flushed the toilet. She watched it like she does, watched it until the water swirled down and disappeared. She looked at me, smiled, proud.

"Daddy's taking you fishing today," I said, and that remorse I was feeling made me smile all the harder, guilt working its way through me. I said, "You're going to have a fine time with him. You two catch some fish and I'll fry it up for supper, all right?"

"Fish?" she said, and slowly lifted a hand to her head, scratched.

"That's right." I turned on the water at the sink, said, "Now let's wash up first, then we'll get dressed and you can head out the dock."

She bent to the sink, put her hands under the water like every morning, but then turned her head, looked up at me. "Fish?" she said. Her hands were still beneath the water, her eyes steady on me.

He'd never asked her to go before, never showed her a thing about surfcasting, nor crabbing. Nothing. This was a fact I knew, but only now did I see what was different about all this: it was Brenda Kay who'd realized it, too, her eyes on me a question, asking, *Is it true?*

It hadn't taken me long to find out how little I could teach Brenda Kay on my own: for all the hours I spent each day working on the alphabet at the kitchen table with her, showing her her name printed out carefully in big block letters on tablet paper, Brenda Kay never once made an effort to write out the letter R. Instead, she dissolved into tears after the first twenty minutes of my urging, my holding her hand and tracking the letters, so that still all she churned out the first two months we were here were rows and rows of letter B's, and scribble drawings, and collage pictures we made with white glue and pages clipped from the *Reader's Digest*.

But that spark she had, the spark I was determined not to let die, was still here: this early morning in July she'd perceived a change in her daddy's behavior herself, one more piece of evidence that there was hope for her. There was a spark in her eyes, the same spark I believed must have been in the eyes of Mr. White's baby brother himself, and I thought of how that spark'd been lost, burned out. This was my baby daughter, and I knew that if she were only in the right place and surrounded by the right people, the right activities, she could grow, could find a way to write her name, to figure the number of sheets of toilet paper she needed. She needed those other children around her, needed the teachers, needed the time swinging badminton rackets in order for her to learn.

I called to Leston, "Out in a minute," took the bar of soap in my hands, lathered it up hard and fast.

I had sausage already going on the stove, and stood now at the sink filling the coffee pot. I could see the two of them on the dock, the sun above them now so I didn't have to squint so hard. Leston's plan was that I'd make a little breakfast, bring it out to them when it was ready, then the three of us could relax awhile outside, watch whatever he or Brenda Kay pulled in.

I finished with the pot, brought it to the stove. It sounded like a fine enough plan to me, but when I went

back to the cupboard by the sink for flour for the biscuits—the house wasn't that much of a palace, after all,
what with no pantry, food stocked just into shelves, the
washing machine planted right here in one corner of the
kitchen—I glanced out the window to see Brenda Kay, her
already given in to swatting at mosquitoes.

Leston said something to her, took hold of her pole and
lifted it so that it pointed up, the bobber some ten feet or so
out away from the dock. He stood next to her holding his
own pole in one hand; he hadn't yet cast out. He towered
over her, and spoke at her. His words, though I couldn't
make them out, were loud, as thought she might be hard of
hearing. With his free hand he pointed at the water, then
made a few quick circles in the air with his fingers.

Brenda Kay said nothing, didn't nod or otherwise suggest she'd heard any of it. Instead, she stood with her
mouth open, her eyes on the water. Then, slowly, she let
the tip of her pole start moving down to the water again,
and Leston reached to it, quick brought it back up again.

Brenda Kay swatted at her cheek.

Leston spoke to her again, made the same circles in the
air, then bent down close to her, smiled hard at her. Still
she wouldn't look at him.

He looked at her a moment longer, then took a few
steps down the dock, bent over a tobacco tin, laced a
worm through the end of his hook. He checked the line,
cast off from the end of the dock. The worm and hook and
bobber dropped to make smooth, clean circles on the
morning water out there.

I smiled, reached for the flour tin and the baking powder both, brought them down. Biscuits and sausage it
would be for breakfast; nothing heavy. So far it'd been a
prosperous day, that look of puzzlement in Brenda Kay's

face enough to keep me going at least the rest of it. Remorse was gone: I had more evidence now that we needed home, and soon. All I needed was a way to introduce it to my husband, make him see in the surprise on her face a call for us to head back to the Foundation, to his children and grandchildren.

I poured out the flour, pinched in a little baking powder, mixed it up with a fork, made a hole down the center of the flour to the bottom of the bowl. I tipped a little buttermilk into the center, worked it around with my fingertips, then picked up the ball of it, rolled it between my palms, laid it on the baking pan on the stove.

I had eight or ten of them made when I heard Leston's voice again, thought maybe he or, if this day was shaping out the way it'd started to so far, maybe Brenda Kay herself'd caught something, and I went to the window, fingers heavy with biscuit dough.

Brenda Kay's pole was dipped down into the water now, and she was swinging it back and forth, cutting up the water. Then Leston was beside her, and grabbed the pole out of Brenda Kay's hands. He was talking at her again, this time no smile. She swatted at her cheek once, then at her neck, then her chin, three swats right in a row.

Leston swatted at the back of his neck, waved a hand in front of his face, shooing away mosquitoes. He was still talking to her, two poles in his hands now.

He set his pole down on the dock, pulled her line in, lifted it to show the hook was bare. He stepped over to the tobacco tin, brought up another worm.

Brenda Kay turned to him, swatted at the back of her neck, and I could see already a small circle of sweat at the base of her back.

Leston held high the worm, quick twisted it onto Brenda

Kay's hook, and I saw her shiver with his movement, with the way the worm simply slipped through the hook.

Leston moved to the edge of the dock, dropped the line into the water. He was trying hard to smile, I could see, and he made again the circles in the air, talked at Brenda Kay again, and handed her the pole.

She wouldn't take it this time, only stared at where the bobber sat in the water.

Leston smiled harder, most all his teeth showing now, and held out the pole to her. She still wouldn't take it. Then he pushed it at her, his move nothing giant, nothing hard, just a gentle push, the pole touching her arm.

She moved quick away from the touch, her eyes on the water.

That was when I turned on the faucet, started rinsing off my hands. I'd seen enough in just these few moments. I'd seen enough, and there flashed through my head the image of Billie Jean what seemed centuries ago, her bent over at the waist, Leston with his belt pulled out and ready to bring down on her, we three out behind the barn at the old place. I saw in my head the lipstick on Billie Jean's face, saw her eyes looking up at me, and heard Leston's whispered words at me: *Go on inside,* he'd said, and because all those years ago it'd been his job as the daddy to administer the punishment, I'd turned and headed back to the house.

I knew he wouldn't try that on Brenda Kay, figured maybe the most he might do out there would be to let his voice go even harder, push the pole a little stronger at her. But I trusted a part of me right then, the part that signaled something might happen if I weren't out there quick enough.

My eyes on Leston as I worked the dough off my hands, I realized I couldn't remember him ever spending any time alone with her, spending any piece of his life with just her and her alone. It was a fact, a huge and awesome truth that hit me like a revelation: her life and how it'd been spent had always been in my hands, and always would. Certainly he loved her, had never been one to be ashamed of her, as far as I knew. But there came to me no pictures of the two of them alone, just me and every day of my life since she'd been born taken up with taking care of her.

So how, I wondered, could I ever let Brenda Kay's life get out of my hands this way, so far out of my hands I'd thought she could go out fishing with her daddy? He was a man who had no idea, I was certain, how to take care of his baby daughter, how to talk to her the way I did, take her to the bathroom, bathe her, read to her, hold her hand and trace the letters of her name even while she cried through it all. He had no idea at all.

And suddenly I saw Mississippi for what it was: enemy territory, deep and troubled and ugly, even here was my husband to protect me, care for me as he thought fit. This place would never be the same place he'd thought it would be by our simply moving back, taking up residence in the place he'd seen his glory, come and go. This was not the same place.

Nor was I the same woman. Just as there'd been lives I'd passed through on the way to this detoured one, maybe there'd been different *mes* on that same road, different Jewels. Right now I wasn't the same Jewel Leston'd had to tell to take care of herself that morning lifetimes ago, the first morning I'd known Brenda Kay was in me, him perched on the edge of our bed and smiling at the promise a next new child had held out back then. I'd been a different Jewel that morning, a morning even before Cathedral'd come and stood outside our kitchen to call down the curse of God on me, reveal to me the truth of the hardship of this life, a life that'd started in Mississippi and that, if my husband had his way, would end here.

But I wasn't going to let that happen. I took hold the hand towel hanging from the oven door handle, started drying my hands, and looked out the window one last time before I went out.

There stood Brenda Kay, still out on the dock, but facing the kitchen window now, eyes trained right on me as though she'd known I'd seen it all. Her mouth was open, her bangs already a little wet with heat. Behind her stood Leston, still trying to pass off the rod to her. He'd lost the smile, his words heavy and hard at her, though I still couldn't make them out for what they were. Maybe they were words of encouragement, maybe he was swearing at her not paying attention. I didn't know. All I knew was that she was looking at me, waiting for me, and that I was already on my way.

I went out the kitchen door and down the stairs, nearly ran through the yard back of the house and out onto the dock.

"Here she comes," Leston said, his jaw clenched. He dropped the pole, let it hit the dock with the wooden clatter he knew it'd have. He turned from her, from me, and headed out the end of the dock, cast out his line. "Saving the day," he said almost in a whisper, but one loud enough for me to hear.

I said nothing. I only made it to Brenda Kay, put an arm round her shoulder, led her off the dock and through the yard, up the stairs and into the kitchen.

A little before two Leston came in with the mail and milk and bread. Since we'd moved here he was always eager to find reason to go to town, ride up onto the blacktop road in his Lark Regal. Then he'd park in one of the slots in front

of the only grocery store in town, a little place Wilman
would call a "Mom and Pops" for how small it was. Getting
milk and bread was no chore, nor was picking up the mail
from the cluster of eight or nine boxes a mile up the road.

I was at the washing machine, pulling out sheets and
making ready to put them on the line. I still wasn't
speaking to him.

He set the brown paper sack on the counter, and held
up two pieces of mail.

"Looky here," he said, and held them until I looked up,
saw what he had in his hand: an envelope and a postcard.
I saw, too, he still had the same smile when I'd awoken
this morning, the same impervious smile, the one that
seemed to shout at me we'd never leave this place, that
this was the end of the rainbow.

He dropped them on the table, where Brenda Kay sat
coloring in one of the books Barbara'd bought her, the transistor radio next to her and turned to low. Country was the
only music she could find down here; no more rock and
roll. Right now it was Jim Reeves singing out low and sad.

"Well," Leston said, and gave a thin whistle. "Bugs
Bunny with blue fur." He was looking at the coloring book,
then grinned, said, "From Eudine and Annie." He tapped
the mail without looking up at me. He squatted next to
Brenda Kay, said, "That's a pretty picture, Brenda Kay."

"Thank, Daddy," she said, a sky-blue crayon in her
hand, her still scribbling away.

I lifted the basket of wet sheets, set it on top of the
washer, and went to the counter, put away the milk, then
picked up the mail from the table.

I looked at the envelope first, saw it was from Eudine,
her big and looping letters a dead giveaway. The postcard,
then, would be from Annie, and I hit it away in my apron

pocket, saved it. I loved Eudine, certainly, but I wanted to go slow with word from my daughter, savor it and any word of life out there in Los Angeles.

I crossed the kitchen to the counter, leaned against it as I opened the envelope. Inside was just a two-sentence note on a piece of scratch paper—"Sorry this took so long to get developed. Will write soon as I can breathe!"—and signed only with a big *E*.

Inside, too, was a photograph, a color one of all of us standing outside her house in Leveland when we'd stopped in on the way here.

Leston, the tallest, stood at the left, awkward and stiff next to Eudine. He had an arm on her shoulder, her holding onto his hand. She was smiling, her lips that same bright red as always, though she'd started wearing her hair up and close to her head, and there were the tiniest wrinkles beside her eyes. Next to her stood Brenda Kay, both hands at her sides, her looking off to the right at something none of us'd ever know. Next to Brenda Kay was me—*that's me,* I thought as I looked at the picture, me a black-haired and smiling old woman who seemed even shorter than I thought, my arms thin and aged round the baby I held in my arms, baby Jane, grandchild number four from James and Eudine. In front of me stood the two boys, Mark and David, both tan and barefoot and wearing only shorts, both with crew cuts, both with their faces screwed up into monkey grins at the camera. Next to me stood Judy, my first grandchild, her already thirteen and smiling, her head leaned over and resting on my shoulder. Those pigtails she'd had in the grocery store parking lot in Big Spring, Texas, ten years ago had given way to long tresses of strawberry blonde hair she wore curled and loose. She had on jeans and a shirt of her daddy's, the front tails of it knotted just above her waist so you couldn't tell it by the photograph, I knew she'd already gotten a young woman's curves, Eudine's mouth running all through dinner about the number and size of the boys who'd already started to coming round.

There we were, all of us in the photograph. Except for James.

I held it in my hand, touched at the images of my grandchildren with my fingertip, all the while a piece of me sorry it hadn't been me to take the picture instead of him. I wanted his image there in front of me right now instead of this old and tired woman smiling out at me. Then I found myself looking at the images of his children and his wife and his retarded sister and his momma and daddy, just trying to muster an image of James in my head, trying to see in all of us something of him. And now I knew I was growing old, because all I could get together was a gray outline, like a picture out of focus: him at the dinner table, him in a uniform, him shaking his daddy's hand ten years ago. Only that.

"What she send?" Leston said. He stood next to me, reached for the picture.

I handed it to him, said nothing. But, like all day long, that silence didn't seem to matter to him.

"That's a fine picture," he said. "Those boys of his," he said, and gave a short laugh. "Two goobers," he said.

I turned from him, moved to the table, pulled out a chair across from Brenda Kay. I sat down, brought out the postcard.

It wasn't a picture postcard, but one of those preprinted ones, "This Side of Card Is For Address" and a three-cent Liberty stamp printed in purple on the one side, her message on the other. But I looked first at our address written out in Anne's fine, solid handwriting: "Mrs. Jewel Hilburn, McHenry, Mississippi" and I wondered what she'd thought of when she wrote that out, wondered what she'd remember of this place from her childhood.

I turned the card over, slowly read it.

July 13, 1962

Dear Momma,

Just a short note while I have a minute this morning. We are all moved, but are still putting away boxes & such. We bought a beautiful Coldspot refrigerator from Sears. It is really a dream & has a large freezer section. Barbara had a Tupperware party & I stocked up on all kinds of goodies that will come in handy. Laura seems to like her new room just fine, although she has to call me every now & then just to make sure I'm still here. It seems like there are a million bratty kids around here, but at least there are children for her to play with. She is now quite proficient at feeding herself; you should see her. In fact she gets real mad if you try & help her. Guess that's about all the room I've got.

Love,
Annie

That was it. Just the note she said it would be, nothing more. There were things I could take from her words, I knew: the image of Laura, alone in a room and happy until she saw she was alone, then calling out; a Tupperware party at Barbara's. Barbara like always bubbling over and happy at everything; a shiny new refrigerator. But that was it. I couldn't even picture the new house they'd bought, only knew it was in Torrance, sat at the peak of a hill in a new tract of homes.

Leston said, "Soon's you have the sheets up, we can take our drive."

I looked at him. "So long as it's not Gulfport," and broke my day-long silence.

He laughed, reached a hand up to his hair, smoothed it back. He said, "Not to Gulfport."

"Dive?" Brenda Kay said, and we both turned to her.

"Yep," Leston said. "Surprise destination."

She looked at me, puzzled. "Supise?"

I nodded. I still had the postcard in my hand, hoped that maybe by just holding onto it something else'd come to me: a picture of that house, the sound of Laura's voice. Maybe even the sound of waves crashing that foggy morning, a sound that seemed suddenly fading in me this day, a day I felt I was fast losing hold of. I couldn't even picture my oldest son.

I said, "Your daddy's got some surprise up his sleeve for us," and I smiled at her, turned to the washing machine, took up the basket. I went to the back door, turned and pushed open the screen door with my back.

I said, "You want to come out back, help Momma put up the sheets?"

"No," Brenda Kay said right out, no hesitation. She was still coloring away, her eyes never leaving the paper.

Leston looked at me. He shrugged.

He said, "I'll be out front," and turned, headed out to the front room. A moment later I heard the front screen door open, close, next his slow footsteps on the porch.

*   *   *

Outside I put up the sheets, clipped and clipped and clipped, my arms aching with the work of it. The slow afternoon breeze was almost as wet as the sheets, and I hoped it wasn't too late in the day to be putting them out.

But what I hoped most for, and what I never heard, was Brenda Kay's voice come down to me from that kitchen window, her calling out to me like baby Laura, making certain she wasn't alone.

Chapter 36

I wasn't long in figuring out where we were headed. I kept my mouth closed about it, figured I'd let my husband believe in his ability to surprise me for as long as I could, so when we turned left, headed on 13 up toward Carnes, there was nothing left for me but to sit back, see how he planned to play this out.

We drove on through the woods, trees reaching over the highway. Once, a little while north of Lumberton on 11, when the trees seemed to stretch out over us for as far ahead as you could see, Brenda Kay hollered out behind us, "Tree tunnel, Momma!" and both Leston and I laughed, him shaking his head, grinning.

I said, "That's right," and nodded.

A mile or so farther on Leston said, "No doubt you know where we're headed."

"You tell me," I said, and it was as if our having laughed together a few moments before might have happened a year ago, or ten. I said, "This is your surprise," and looked out my window at a green so thick you could see only a few feet back in, and I thought of my daddy, of him disappearing into the same thick green of a Sunday afternoon in a place not far from here, not far at all. Because that was where we were headed: back to the old places.

"My surprise," he said, and the dashboard lighter

popped. I didn't hear him pull it out, a moment later glanced from my window to the dashboard to see it still there.

Then I looked at him, at his profile sharp against all this green shooting past him. His hair jumped with the wind in through his open window, the unlit cigarette jammed between the first and second fingers of his right hand holding the wheel, his left arm hanging down out the window.

This was my husband. This was Leston, and I swallowed hard, because I knew what I was doing, knew for every second I breathed what I was doing: fighting him, trying my best to beat him.

I took in a deep breath, held it, looked out the windshield. Afternoon light fell in places through the trees to the road, dappled it with light, my window open, too, my hair jumping just as much as Leston's. The air moving round us seemed fresher, the shattered bits of light out there on the blacktop making the drive feel that much cooler. But I knew better, knew this wind through the car was only a brief fix-up of the heat we had to live in, sleep through.

I hung my arm out the window, too, held it palm forward so I could feel like I could catch the air, hold on to it, keep it cool in me.

Leston popped in the lighter again, said, "Dealer's choice," and drove on.

We were just this side of Purvis when he finally slowed down, hit the blinker, turned left onto an old dirt road, not even oiled, and I knew where our first stop would be.

The trees seemed even thicker than I remembered back in here, that green giving way now and again to fields already thick with rows of more green: watermelon, sweet potatoes, corn. Then just as quick the fields would disappear, and here came the green again: honeysuckle, kudzu, wild grapevine. Now and again, too, a shanty'd poke out from the woods: porch, tin roof, a dog or two.

He slowed the car to a crawl, eased it to the right, and stopped. He let the engine run a second or two before he cut it, then all I could hear was the sound of crickets.

"There," he said, and lifted his arm, pointed to my right, his hand in front of me. "Right there," he said.

I looked. Shrouded in magnolia and longleaf pine and vines of all sorts was our first house, the cabin Leston'd built. Our first home, here on Rosehill Road.

That same dappled light shone on the house, on the rusted tin roof scattered over with pine straw, on the black and rusted-out pickup off to the left and up on bricks, no wheels.

I could see the rough wood sides of the house, exposed logs, gray mortar between each. The windows weren't busted out, what I took to be a good sign for the place, and the chimney seemed in order, only a brick or two missing off the top. Otherwise, it looked just about the same, except that when we'd had it Leston kept the front and back and side yards cleared.

Brenda Kay said, "Davey Cockett," and we two laughed again, though we didn't look at each other. I was only looking out the window, taking in this place that seemed so long ago my memory of it might as well have been a dream, a chapter out of a book I'd read when I was a little girl.

I said, "It's a log cabin, all right, Brenda Kay." I paused. "This is the place where your brother James and your sister Billie Jean were born. Right here."

"Bijen?" she said. "James?"

"They're not here," I said, and I knew without even looking behind me she had her face out the window, scouring the place with her eyes for her brother, her sister. "But this is where they were born," I said.

I wasn't thinking about those children, though. I was thinking about how this was the house Leston and I'd come back to from Hattiesburg, a house that'd seemed in its own day a palace those many years ago, a palace to a girl who'd been thrown from a mansion in Purvis on to the Mississippi Industrial School for Girls, from there to a bedroom in a house in East Columbia, tossed and tossed, one life to the next. I looked at the place, me sitting in the powerful silence of no engine running and the whir of crickets round us. This was where I'd landed those many years and lifetimes ago, me with a handsome husband with deepwater green eyes, dreams of his own lumber company and a family large enough to carry it on into the future.

"Something's missing," Leston said, and I touched my lips with the tips of two fingers, felt the bottom lip tremble, and tried hard to get my mind off what I knew would lead me right on down the road to tears. He said, "You remember what's missing?"

I turned, looked at him. He was smiling, cut his eyes to mine a second, then brought them back to the house. He nodded at the place, and I turned back to it, looked hard at it.

"Shutters," I said a minute or so later, and felt myself smile, remembered the shutters he'd put up for me after James'd been born: his gift, those white shutters with the pinetree silhouettes in the center.

"Kills the place, those shutters gone," Leston said, and I blinked at his voice, nodded, my eyes on the bare log walls. "But looks like it's holding up good enough."

The front door opened then, and a colored girl with a sleeping baby in her arms came out. The girl had on an undershirt and a pair of faded green pants, the pantlegs cut off just above her knees. She nodded at us, and I smiled, nodded back. I judged she was maybe ten years old, if that.

Leston opened his door, and I turned to him, saw he was already standing, leaning against the doorframe, his arms on the roof. All I could see of him were those gray pants, his yellow shirt, his belt.

"Momma," Brenda Kay said, "Nancy."

"No," I said, "that's not her," and I shook my head. Nancy was one of the retarded colored children from our days up on Adams at the old Foundation house, a girl we hadn't seen or heard of in years, and I wondered at what all Brenda Kay had stored up, what memories of her life were jammed in her head, looking for escape if only the right object or face or word passed before her. And I wondered, too, what all of this living in Mississippi she'd recall, at what point in her life she might shoot out the name *Toxie*, the word *fish*.

Leston called out, "How y'all?"

She stood right there in the open doorway, and now another child came out, stood just behind her, this one a little shirtless boy.

"Fine, sir," she said, and nodded.

"Your momma and daddy home?" Leston said.

"No, sir," she said. "They working."

He was quiet a moment, and I looked back at him, at his middle. I said, "Leston."

"I built this here house," he said to her.

"Yes, sir," the girl said, and now the baby in her arms woke up. It lifted its head off her chest, looked around, stopped when it saw the car.

"Leston," I said again.

"Shh," Brenda Kay whispered behind me. "Baby."

Leston was quiet a moment, then said. "Well." He tapped the roof of the car twice, said, "Well now, you take care," and then he was sliding back into the seat, pulled the door closed.

"Yes, sir," the girl said, nodded.

I said, "Bye-bye," out my window, and waved.

Leston started up the engine, and the boy took a step back at the sound. The girl waved at me, and the boy, given bravery, I guess, by his sister's wave at me, stepped back up to her, then moved in front of her. He waved, too, and Leston eased out onto the road, started off.

I turned from the children to Leston, saw he was smiling. He glanced up at the rearview mirror, said, "Brenda Kay, where to next?"

"Home," she said, and for some reason, again one we'd never know, she started singing: "Ahh ah stop, love you!"

"Home it is," he said, gave it the gas so that behind us, I knew without looking back, there trailed a cloud of dirt.

The next road we turned off on was an oiled one, a step up on the quality of the lives of those living round here. When we'd lived here, though, it'd been just dirt. Now there'd be no dust cloud to follow us, trail us like a hound trying to find some animal on its way back to its nest.

The road, too, was a little wider, and by the time we made it to the other house, the one where Burton and Wilman and Anne'd been born, the sun was starting on its way down, the shadows cast on the road nowhere near as clean and sharp as those on our way here.

Leston slowed down, pulled even with the house, cut the engine.

"Home," he said.

"Home," Brenda Kay said.

I said nothing.

Leston turned in his seat, said to Brenda Kay, "You remember this place? You remember when we lived back here?"

"Home," she said again, no question on her voice. Just that word.

"Well," Leston said. He turned to me. "Here we are. Scene of the crime."

"What crime?" I said, my eyes still on the house.

He was quiet a moment, then said, "Figure of speech." He popped open his door, climbed out. He crossed in front of the car, was already in the yard and headed for the house before I called out, "What are you doing?"

He took easy strides across the yard, the grass thick in places, other places worn down to dirt as though whoever lived here used the front yard for a parking lot. He didn't look back at me, didn't turn and smile or say a word. He only lifted one hand, gave a short wave back at us, and kept going for the door.

That was when I opened my door, stepped out onto the thin grass next to the road. I stood, turned to Brenda Kay.

I said, "Honey, you wait here for a minute or so. Momma and Daddy's going to have a look."

She quick nodded, her mouth open and eyes looking over the house, and I thought for a moment maybe she did remember the place. Why not? I thought, and then I opened her door, reached in for her hand. I said, "You just come along, Brenda Kay. We'll have us a look around here."

"Home?" she said, and looked up at me. Finally it'd become a question for her, and I smiled, said, "Once."

Leston knocked at the door, three quick raps that cut through the thick air, made our stopping in here more an intrusion than it already was, though there didn't seem to be anyone around: no cars, the spots in the yard where grass'd been rubbed bare speckled with oil stains.

He knocked again, this time harder, slower, but still no one answered. He stepped off the stoop, went to the window to his right, the front-room window, and peered in.

"Definitely not niggers living here," he said, his hands cupped to the window, his face to the glass.

"Leston," I said.

"Coloreds, what have you," he said. "Whatever, they're not living here."

I still held Brenda Kay's hand, took a step toward him. He stepped away from the house.

"How can you tell?" I said, and thought of a lavender dress, of a colored boy helping an old white woman park a '52 Plymouth.

He looked at me over his shoulder. "You serious?"

I shrugged, went to the window he'd stood at. Now I was curious, wanted to peek in at what someone'd done to the house that'd been our home. I knew the rising danger in that curiosity, in giving over to what was Before instead of eyeing what could come. Still, I let go Brenda Kay's hand, went to the window.

Inside was furniture: an old divan and a chair, the stuffed back of it worn at the center. In one corner, there beneath where the stairs came down, stood an old radio, big and boxy, just like we'd had. And to my right was the fireplace, the hearth, on it a stack of what looked like magazines.

Scene of the crime, I thought; these were the stairs I'd been carried down by two colored boys after too many hours of trying to give birth to the eighteen-year-old girl behind me; and this was the fireplace, where there'd been a can of lighter fluid left out.

My life in a single room.

I turned from the window, saw Leston standing away form the house, looking up at the place, Brenda Kay just behind him, hands at her sides, her looking up at the house, too. Just my husband and my daughter.

It was a frightening image, the two of them there in the yard, our Lark Regal behind them on the oiled road, all shined and bright—Leston and Toxie washed it every four days or so, Leston letting his nephew tinker under the hood most every evening he came by. But it wasn't just the car out there that scared me, or my daughter still looking at the second story, or my husband, his neck craned to take in the house.

What frightened me was the way the sun suddenly worked on it all: Leston stood in the shadow of the house now, his face no longer squinted against anything, only examining the other house he'd built for his family. Brenda Kay, though, stood just past the line of shadow, out there in July sun, heat beating down on her, shining hard on her head, on the auburn hair she'd gotten not from me, but from her daddy. And the sun shone on her fair skin, her eyes squinted near-closed, her brain never having been granted the privilege of common sense: she could just lift a hand to her forehead, help block out that sun, or just take a step forward, past that shadow line, and be in shade. And the sun was working just then on that shiny car, symbol of what Leston thought we'd achieved in ten years, success measured by the width of a whitewall, the hum of an engine.

"Look up there," Leston said, and I moved toward him,

then past him to Brenda Kay, took her hand and pulled her into the shadow of the house. Then I looked to where Leston pointed, an upstairs window on the right side of the house.

"Look at that," he said. "You see that screen?"

I nodded, not certain what he was after. The window itself was up, inside it thin curtains, still in what had become a breezeless afternoon.

He said, "Look at the screen, will you?"

"I am," I said. I was looking, and I wasn't seeing what he wanted.

"There's a rust stain down near to the bottom, in the center. It's a rust stain, a circle." He paused, brought the hand down.

I saw the stain, saw the faintest trace where an already rusty and old screen was even rustier, then looked at him.

He was smiling at me, slowly shook his head. He said, "You don't remember."

"It's the boys' old room," I said. "That what you're after?"

He gave a small laugh. His eyes went to the window again, and he nodded at it, said, "That's the boys' room, right. But that stain. That stain's where Burton and Wilman used to pee when they was too tired or scared or cold to head out to the privy." He paused, still smiling. "That is, before we had the indoor plumbing." He looked at me again. "You remember?"

"Yes," I said, and nodded, at the same moment felt myself suddenly falling into the chasm he'd led me to, felt myself smiling all the way down into a darkness he wanted us to hole up in the rest of our days, that abyss called Memory. He wanted me to spend the rest of my life like he and Toxie did every evening he was over, the two of them out on the porch as the sun set behind cypress and oak, them both talking on what they'd done with their days.

I was falling because I could hear two boys' whispers like silver in the night, steps to a window, that window sliding up slowly, as though we wouldn't hear the long quiet pull of wood on wood as the window went up. I closed my eyes a moment out there in the heat, and heard those sounds again, even above the crickets, of two boys peeing out a second-story window, their whispers, silent laughter, all of it right here in my ears.

I opened my eyes, looked at the house, took it in in the way Leston was doing: the clapboards were still the same white, though the paint'd blistered up; what little lawn there was out here was trimmed up, short: whoever lived here at least wanted that much to look nice.

But it was our house, I saw, the same one that'd been illuminated by the headlights of the old Plymouth ten years ago as Leston'd pulled out and away from our old lives. Wilman and Anne and Brenda Kay all asleep in the back seat, and I fell even deeper, faster toward the point Leston was aiming me for.

I smiled, and Leston nodded again at the screen, said, "Those two boys were goobers, too." He looked at me, smiled, and started round the side of the house.

Brenda Kay and I followed, the lawn in the side yard just as neat and trim as that in front, and I reached out, touched the side of the house like it was some big and hairy beast. I just touched it, afraid it might move, might jump at me, memories cascading down on me so hard.

To my right was the barn, behind it the repair shed, neither of them any more broken-down now than when Toxie and Sepulcher disappeared in there each morning to fiddle with the engines on the machinery we'd owned. I caught glimpses, too, of the field back behind the shed where we'd kept the cattle before selling it off, and where, later, we'd grown sweet potatoes to sell for medicine for Brenda Kay.

Calcium glucanate, I remembered. Some sort of drug these backwoods doctors figured on curing mental retardation, and I smiled, shook my head.

We were behind the house now, spread out in front of us the woods into which I'd let Brenda Kay walk just to see where she went, a teenage boy named Burton following behind her, and I remembered him stopping at the edge, kicking the dirt with his toe, him the undercover man, and I shook my head at this, too, me smiling.

"What's so funny?" Leston said. I turned from the woods to him, there with a hand up to his forehead, us no longer hidden from the sun by the house.

I said, "I'm smiling at just exactly what you want me to, I know it," and finally let go Brenda Kay's hand. This was safe haven here, a place more familiar than the faces of my grandchildren, more comfortable than a down bed in a mansion in Purvis proper. Here we were.

I smiled, came toward him. A piece of me was ready to surrender to it all, to this point he was trying so very hard to make by visiting these old places: we had come a long way in our lives, had beaten more than most people were handed out. That house six feet above ground on the bayou was, in some ways, a palace. Our boys and girls were men and women now.

And as I came nearer him, I remembered those mornings with the children even sharper, even clearer, remembered the tussling and fighting between Burton and Wilman and Annie, her tagging along, and I remembered Billie Jean when she was only a girl, before she'd lost the piece of herself she'd given to Gower Cross, and before she'd found, I could only imagine, the heavy and ugly knowledge only going through a divorce could bring.

I moved closer to Leston. In spite of all the waves I wanted crashing in my head and the feel of cold, thick fog round me, even in spite of all we had to do in California to save our baby daughter, those waves and that gray started to melting away with each minute we stood out here in the sun beside our old house. This was our home, I was beginning to see. And I was headed straight for what, I figured deep down in a place I was about to stop listening to, would certainly be our deaths: Leston's, mine, Brenda Kay's.

Still, I touched his chest with one hand, smiled up at him, the sun lighting his face. Here was the man I'd sworn allegiance to, the man I'd married, the one who came even before all the Before this house brought with it. Before, though it seemed there'd never existed such a time, even Brenda Kay. This was the man. *I am your wife,* I heard rise up in me, and smiled at the man who'd built this home for us.

I let my hand go to his face, placed my palm at his cheek, gently rubbed there with my thumb, this touch just the smallest utterance of the dying language of love our bodies'd once spoken. This was Leston.

I said, "You know I love you."

He reached up, took my hand, and I could feel the strength in him, in his calluses and rough skin and bones and muscles.

He said, "I love you too, Jewel."

I said, "Scene of the crime," still smiling.

"Scene of the crime," he said. He grinned, let go my hand.

He put his hands in his back pockets then, looked past

me back toward the barn: just my husband after all, this
moment of closeness maybe a bit too much, or maybe just
enough: he shrugged, still grinning. Without letting his
eyes light on mine, he said, "Think I'll have a go look to
the shed. See what shape she's in."

He glanced down at me, shrugged again, and started
away. "Brenda Kay," he called out, "you want to come see
the old barn and shed I built?"

"Momma?" Brenda Kay said. She was waiting for me,
eyebrows up, mouth open, those white teeth.

"Brenda Kay?" Leston said. He was next to her now. He
was still smiling, but I could see it was something he had
to think about. He knew what was going on: his own
daughter stood next to him, but waited for me to nod, to
signal what she should do.

Leston put out a hand to her, him turned to the barn,
Brenda Kay turned to me. He reached down, took hold
her hand, gave it a small shake. "Come on now," he said
without looking at me. "Let's go."

Brenda Kay's hand was dead in his, her eyes still trained
on me. I said, "Now you do what your daddy says," and I
nodded, smiled.

She turned, went right away with Leston, and I
watched the two of them march off hand in hand along a
path clouded over with green.

I turned back to the house. Scene of the crime, I thought,
and I went to the steps up to the kitchen door, steps I'd
mounted too many times to count, after calling my children
in from the woods, or hauling up the breakfast plates the
coloreds stacked on the ground next to the bottom step, or
carrying up the wind-dried sheets and towels and clothing,
and I thought of the sheets I'd hung earlier this afternoon,
wondered if they'd be dry by the time we got home.

I stood at the bottom of the steps, put one hand on the rail, and suddenly all those times I'd mounted them didn't seem such a burden, such a chore, and I saw I was about to hit the bottom of that abyss Leston'd led me to, the one I'd tottered over and into all by myself. It was my *resolve* I was about to lose, I saw.

I lifted a foot, set it on the first step up. This was comfortable, the wood strong and sturdy, exactly what I needed to feel beneath me while I carried up a load of laundry or a child with a skinned knee or an apron full of summer squash or corn, and so I took another step, and another, let my hand on the rail guide me up and up, closer and closer to the kitchen door window.

Finally I made it to the top of the steps, stood on the little porch there. I cupped my hands to the window, looked in at my own kitchen, and knew it was me, *me,* I wanted to glimpse walking across the floor in there, a skillet of bacon and eggs in my hand, my apron for a potholder; and hoped, too, I'd see Burton and Wilman come tearing into the room, Annie right behind them, trailing nye-nye and crying for them to wait for her. It was all of that I wanted to see, and knew I would if I let myself, let the ghosts of past lives, ones I'd thought for years were behind me, breathe all over in me, illuminate this old kitchen.

And suddenly there was movement inside, a swirl of color and shape before my eyes so that I had only time enough to swallow, feel my heart lurch and heave with what I saw. I staggered back a step, saw before me a girl in a flowered dress as she swung open the door, a hand to a hip, her head to one side.

She said, "What y'all want?" and I saw her dirty blond hair fall off one shoulder, saw smeared red across her lips, her bare feet.

She was just a girl, a girl no older than—and I'd had to think a moment on who she seemed no older than, and the only girl who came to mind was my own baby daughter, my Brenda Kay, tromping round in a broken-down barn just then.

"Well?" the girl said. She quick tilted her head the other way, a hand still at her hip, the other on the doorknob.

"I—" I started, but didn't know how I might lead her to see what I'd hoped I might find inside my old kitchen.

"We," I said, and now she'd taken to tapping a toe on the floor, the floor painted a dark red, and not the old stained wood we'd had it. "We just were looking at the place," I said.

"We saw you," she said right out, but then her face lost its edge, retreated to reveal she was in fact only a girl, no woman in charge of this place. She blinked, said, "I saw you," and brought her head up straight, let go the doorknob, put that hand to her hip. She gritted her teeth, tried to regain whatever power she'd had over me, but she'd lost it.

"Somebody in there with you?" I said, and crossed my arms.

She gave the quickest glance to her left, tried to see behind her without looking all the way. Then she drew in a breath, seemed to kick her elbows out at her sides even broader, hold her shoulders even higher, and I knew I was wrong about how old she was, knew only then she was at most fifteen.

It'd been in the hair, the color and snarl of it, that I'd misjudged her age, and in that lipstick, the dress. It was a Saturday-night dress: puffed short sleeves, the skirt just above the knees, the flowers in the material a shade too bright, the neckline cut just a breath too low.

The dress buttoned up the front, starting at the waist, and as she brought up her shoulders I could see where she'd missed a couple buttons, the two below the top one. It was a dress a little too tight for her, a girl with breasts, I could see, that'd send her at her age out to find lipstick, to color her hair this shade, to buy a cheap dress a size too small, and I wondered who her momma was, and where she might be, and who the boy inside the house with her was.

Because as she stood taller in some child's attempt at intimidating an old woman who'd seen all I'd seen about the way this world works, from the quick and simple death of a father to the slow and hateful one of her mother, from the birth of a retarded child to the arc of a basketball in a high school gym, I saw between the open front of her dress the two curves of flesh where her breasts met, small turns of pale-milk skin men lived their lives to find, where only minutes before, I knew, some boy most likely no older than herself had found strange comfort, a feeling I figured must be foreign and familiar at once, some memory of a mother's breast buried deep inside him, at the same time a dream of the future, of the moment when he might enter her and the world would be his, so that memory and the future were locked in the same moment, the same touch of tongue on flesh, the body able to accomplish with no more than mere human touch what it was I wanted in my life: to remember what'd gone before me, but to push out to what might be.

Only then did I see I hadn't yet fallen into the abyss, but still tottered there, still stood with my toes on the edge, about to fall toward the end of a life that'd be spent here, in Mississippi, among the bones of my old dead lives, ghosts or no ghosts.

I said, "You're showing, honey," and nodded at her chest.

She looked down at herself, saw the buttons, started doing them up, when from behind her came the boy's voice: "Tell 'em to head out."

She still fumbled with the buttons, glanced at me, said, "You heard that."

I said, "My husband built this house," and I turned, not because of the boy's words, but because there seemed nothing more to say. I took each step down from the porch one at a time, savored them for what they were: past history.

But when I reached bottom I turned, looked up at her, and it seemed there was something else I wanted to say, on my own tongue words I figured might help her, and might help me.

She stood with a hand back on the doorknob, the other at her side.

I said, "Don't let a man speak your mind." I paused, said, "You want us out, you tell us."

She took a breath, glanced behind her again. She stood straight again, said, "You head on out now."

"Fine," I said, and I nodded at her, smiled.

She closed the door, but stood at the window a moment. She turned her head away from the glass, and I could see through the window her shake her head, that dirty blonde hair moving back and forth in long locks. Then she faced me again.

I put up a hand, gave a small wave, hoped whatever it was happened here wouldn't be lost on her, or on me.

Her face was blank, no look to it at all. Just her eyes on me, that hair down the sides of her face, her smeared lips.

Then she raised a hand, gave the smallest of waves, just a shake of her fingertips, but enough to make me wonder what my life would've been like if my last child, the daughter named after my husband's dead sister, were born a normal child; and I wondered if that child inside the window might well have been named Brenda Kay, her momma out to work somewheres—Bailey Grammar, serving up lunches right now to summer school kids—her daughter shut up in an empty house right now while a boy had at her, the two of them finding the surprise and sorrow of love.

And I felt then, too, some of the burden and joy, perhaps, that Cathedral might've felt by passing on words I could use, giving to me fair warning of the life to come while she stood here at the bottom of these steps on a cold March night, me there at the top of them while from behind me spilled warm kitchen light, light that fell out onto the cold hard-packed ground out here, light that seemed to illuminate Cathedral herself.

The girl turned her head from me, nodded to the boy I couldn't see, the boy I was glad I'd never lay eyes on. Then she quick turned back to me, her mouth and eyebrows and eyes filled with nothing, and she disappeared.

Leston opened Brenda Kay's door, and she climbed in. I was already in the front seat, windows all down, my forehead and neck and chest and back all drenched in sweat. I hadn't wanted to stand outside the car while I waited for my daughter and husband to come back. I just wanted in the car, wanted gone from there. Leston closed Brenda Kay's door, came around to his side, climbed in.

He put the key to the ignition, started up the car, and I looked at him.

He seemed scared somehow, his face flushed even more than it would for the heat. He smiled too hard at me, wouldn't let his eyes meet mine for more than an instant.

He faced forward, both hands on the wheel, and I wondered if he hadn't been out scouring the woods behind the place, looking for a brass lighter.

I said, "What happened?"

"Nothing," he said, shrugged. He put a hand to his shirt pocket for another cigarette, came up empty. "Maybe the heat. I don't know."

I looked out the windshield, said, "Where to next?"

"Well," he said, and looked straight ahead. He blinked a couple times, said, "Figured I named the first place, Brenda Kay told us to come here. Figure it's your turn. You tell us where."

I was quiet a moment, the only sound the low hum of the engine. I said, "Cathedral's."

I turned to him. He was already looking at me.

I said, "Take me to Cathedral's."

A slow smile came to him. He said, "You want to make amends. That right?"

I could lie to him, I knew, just agree to what he figured could be the only reason I'd want to see her. Or I could deal him the truth, hand him all I knew, which is what I decided to do.

I said, "I don't know why. But please do it."

He lost the smile, pulled away from me until his back touched his door. He said, "Oh," then turned in his seat. He reached a hand to the gearshift on the column, put it in gear. "Okay," he said, and we were gone, and as we pulled away I imagined behind us the face of a young girl, a girl I decided right then to name Brenda Kay, a big-bosomed girl whose momma wasn't home, a girl who watched us from an open window, behind her the voice of a boy, calling for her, giving out her name again, while she watched us disappear off the face of the earth.

Chapter 37

Nelson sat out front in a rocker not much different than the one that'd been thrown on a fire in a backyard in Purvis. Leston parked the car in front of the house, and Nelson stopped rocking, slowly stood while Leston climbed out the car.

Calling the place a house was giving it more credit than is due: it was a shanty on the right side of an ancient road, to my left a wide field of sweet potatoes, and suddenly all of it was too much like the shanty I'd stood in front of and'd spilled a story to a colored woman while Cleopatra Sinclair and Bessy Swansea stole her food. I got a cold shiver just then, the feeling an ugly surprise in all the heat.

Nelson seemed thinner, shorter, and wore thick glasses, though there wasn't any doubt it was him as he stepped off the small front porch, an old man with steps as ginger as Brenda Kay's had been out in the Gulf, each one measured and certain as he headed for the car. His head was down, and slowly he shook it back and forth. One hand was in his back pocket, the other to his forehead, a cigarette between his fingers. He talked to himself as he came toward us. Only when Leston saw he wasn't going to stop, was headed right up to the hood, did Leston finally close his door, slowly come round to meet him.

I watched all this from the front seat, Brenda Kay asleep

behind me; it'd taken almost forty-five minutes to find the place, neither Leston nor me remembering exactly where they lived. I'd been here only once before, couldn't remember why. I only remembered a huge live oak that'd grown halfway out into their road so that the road jogged out the way of it. When we finally stumbled onto that queer bend in the road, the tree grown even bigger, the branches hanging even lower to the road, I knew we were only a few minutes away, and I'd said, "Brenda Kay, we're going to see Cathedral," and turned in my seat to face her.

She'd nodded off, her head back and lolling side to side, mouth open, hair matted down on her head. The growth was so thick back here, so close to the road and the car, we weren't moving fast enough to cool things down.

Nelson stopped in front of the car. He was old, older than I could have imagined, his hair gone white, wrinkles at his throat, the glasses magnifying his eyes so that in the late afternoon light they were huge and wet.

"Mister Hilburn?" Nelson said, and brought the hand down from his forehead, the other out of his back pocket. He leaned back as though he couldn't bend his neck, and looked at my husband.

"Nelson," Leston said, and put out a hand.

A moment or two passed between them before Nelson looked down from Leston to his hand, then slowly put his own hand out, and the two shook. Three or four nails on Nelson's hand'd gone bad, the nails themselves white and crumbled and dead.

He said, "We heard you was here," and smiled, slowly shook Leston's hand. "We was wondering if you'd stop in."

Leston let go Nelson's hand, said, "How'd you know we were back?"

"Word," Nelson said, and nodded, satisfied at his answer.

He turned to me, sitting there in the front seat and taking all this in as though it were some performance, staged right off the front of the car just for me. Nelson nodded, said, "Miss Jewel," and put his hands in his back pockets.

I climbed out then, made careful not to close the door too hard for fear of waking Brenda Kay. I walked to the end of the fender, nodded. Though I felt I ought to put out my hand, let him shake it, I didn't. I only smiled, looked at Leston.

"Nelson," Leston started, rubbed the back of his neck. "We come by to say hello." He paused. "You looking good."

"No complaints," he said, and slowly shook his head, the move exaggerated for how slow it was. "Just growing old in the Lord," he said. He looked up at Leston, still smiling, and said, "How you doing youselves?"

"Fine," Leston said. "Fine. Just out looking around at the old haunts, old stomping grounds." He swatted at a mosquito on his arm, smiled.

Nelson turned to me, his whole body moving, even his feet, as if his back were a board, unable to bend. He faced me, said, "You bring along yo' beautiful daughter? Missy Brenda Kay."

I nodded, smiled at him. "Right here," I said, and turned, made for her window.

He followed me, and I wondered how old he really was. It seemed at some time I'd known he was five or six years older than Cathedral, who was a year or so older than me. Maybe sixty-five, sixty-six, I figured, then wondered what I'd look like, how I'd walk in that not so distant future.

He leaned over, peered in the window, watched her in silence a few moments. Then he stood straight, smiled at me, his eyes growing even larger with the smile. He said, "Bless her heart."

I was tired of the pleasantries then, tired of the slow movement all this was carrying with it. All of life here in Mississippi carried with it this small dance around the matters at hand rather than talk *on* the matters, and I smiled back at him, cut my eyes to Leston just behind him, gave a sharp nod he would know.

But before Leston could say or do anything, in only enough time for him to blink at my silent demand that he tell Nelson what it was we were really here for, Nelson said, "She be in the house. She waiting for you."

I looked at him, saw he'd lost the smile in just that moment. He turned, his feet moving in the slow way they had on his long march from the porch to the car, and now I was behind him, had no choice but to look at the black pants he had on, at how the cuffs were frayed through all the way round, the elastic in the suspenders stretched out and ragged so that they had nothing to do with holding up his pants. It was his old man's paunch that held them up, and as he walked in front of me, I thought of how this was the man who'd leaned into the light cast from my kitchen doorway to touch his wife's elbow, tell her it was time to go on home while she prophesied my life, gave me God's will whether I wanted to hear it or not. This was the man who'd led her on home after that, out into a moonless night, me left outside my kitchen with only the knowledge of what my life would hold: *the baby you be carrying be yo' hardship, yo' test in the world.*

I walked behind him, moved closer and closer to his porch and toward the woman I still wasn't certain I knew what to say to, what to ask. But she was the woman, I knew then, I'd been heading toward every day since we'd moved here, and maybe every day since I'd thrown her out of my house, forcing fault on her, blame for the fire that'd scarred my baby's legs. Scars that, in a twisted blessing all its own, had finally gotten us away from here, and to California, as much the Promised Land as any place could ever be.

We finally made it to the porch, and I looked up.

I do not know what I expected to see, did not know if I'd wanted her to be older than I remembered, or younger, heavier or thinner or grayer, stooped or standing tall. She'd worn an old quilt over her shoulders the night she prophesied my life, had on a shapeless cotton dress when she showed up at our back door toting food the morning after my daddy'd been killed, had on *my own* yellow sweater the day I'd slapped her in my own stab at delivering myself of the guilt I bore for being no more than the selfish granddaughter of a selfish grandmother, me a woman who Cathedral'd already known was forsaking the heart of her husband to further the good of my retarded daughter. She was the one to lead me, I finally saw, from life into life into life, had seen me move from the shack in the woods to my grandmother's house, had seen me carted away to the Mississippi Industrial School for Girls, had delivered my first five children into this world and'd warned me of the smile of God on the sixth. So many lives she'd marshaled me into, only to wind down to this, the porch of her own home.

She stood in the doorway of the shanty, a hand to one doorjamb, the other buried in the pocket of the brown plaid dress she had on. I couldn't see a single hair on her head for the blue kerchief she wore, so I couldn't say whether she'd gone gray or white or salt and pepper. She was still tall, still thin, still only and always the same woman, Cathedral.

But the piece of sorrow she'd worn in her eyes the morning I'd slapped her, the morning she'd taken that slap and then offered me her other cheek, was huge now, exploded in her eyes so that there seemed no touching on what misery she'd known. This seemed the only difference in her: her eyes, the whites of them brilliant and cold against her black skin, filled with a brilliant and cutting sorrow.

Cathedral said, "You come here looking for comfort, then go on home."

Nelson stopped, leaned back and saw his wife. He whispered, "Don't go to carrying on now. These Mr. Hilburn, Miss Jewel."

Cathedral didn't move, only let her eyes slice into mine, those same eyes that'd seen God once she'd surfaced from the Pearl River, baptized in the same river as I'd been. Her God was and always would be, I could see, some different face, some different voice and angle, one I'd never know.

I said, "Didn't come for comfort."

"Then you came for Hell," she shot back at me, though her face hadn't changed, the crisp wrinkles across her forehead and down her cheeks giving away nothing.

"Cathedral," Nelson whispered. He made it to the rocker, just touched one arm of it, then turned, slowly lowered himself down to the seat. He didn't start up the rocking again, only sat with both feet firm on the ground, hands on his knees. He was looking past us all, and for a moment I thought he might be looking at Leston, still just behind me. But then he blinked, lifted his chin a little higher, and I could see he was looking someplace altogether different, some place I hadn't yet been.

He said, "We lost a boy year and five month ago. It been hard on us." He paused, and I felt myself swallow, looked to Cathedral for her reaction to his words.

Her eyes were right on mine, and I had to break her gaze, look down at something, anything, and found I was staring at Nelson's knees, at those black pants again and how thin the material was, skin straining to break through, it seemed, though it was only an old man's knees, an old man's pair of pants.

"Sepulcher," he whispered, and the name hung there in the air like it was a ghost itself, taken on form and motion, life of its own.

"We got no comfort to give," Cathedral said out clear and simple.

I looked at her. I said, "I am sorry to hear this," and found I couldn't picture Sepulcher himself, only knew him to be one of the two boys who'd carried me downstairs, loaded me into Leston's pickup for the bumpy ride into town and the hospital. And he'd been the one to fiddle with the cars out to the repair shed.

She looked away from me, brought a hand up in front of her, looked at it instead. She said, "Dead in a ditch. Eyes open."

"Cathedral," Nelson whispered.

"No accident," she said.

The whole world was silent a moment, and then she looked at me. "You say you don't want no comfort," she said. "But I know the truth. You want me to give you the words of Jesus, give something to you like Luke nine sixty-nine: And Jesus said unto him, 'No man, having put his hand to the plough, and looking back, is fit for the kingdom of God.'" She stopped, looked to the hand again. Her face still told me nothing, only her words falling down to me here on the ground, this time her the one up on the porch.

"I am truly sorry," I said, swallowed again at the idea of a dead child, a grief I couldn't touch. "I am sorry," I said, and heard from behind me Leston's words: "Nelson, we're sorry."

I felt my husband's hand at my elbow, heard him say, "Come on now," and tried to remember if those weren't the same exact words Nelson'd used on his own wife, him coaxing her away from giving the truth to me.

"Prophesy ain't worth the widow's mite," she said. "Nor tongues. No God gifts worth anything but the grace of a child."

She still stared at the hand, looked at the palm. She turned it over, looked at the back as if it might speak.

She said, "You want me to give you words to help you make yo' way in this world, but I ain't here to give them." She paused. "But I give you words anyhow. Not the ones you come for, but words down from God all the same. Words more the truth than any prophesy of yo' life I ever give."

The sun was fast going down now, sat just above the tops of trees at the far end of the sweet potato field across the road, the gray porch and the gray clapboards and Nelson and Cathedral all going a pale red, all changing color before my eyes. She said, "I give unto you words from the Eighty-eight Psalm."

Finally, she shot her eyes at me, and I nearly flinched with the weight of them, the heat and storm there. She whispered, "The wicked are estranged from the womb: they go astray as soon they be born, speaking lies. Their poison is like the poison of a serpent: they is like the deaf adder that stoppeth her ear; which will not hearken to the voice of charmers, charming never so wisely." She paused, made a quick fist of her hand, eyes still on me. "Break their teeth, O God, in their mouth: break out the great teeth of the young lions, O Lord."

The color of all things went deeper red, the sky above us near scarlet now, the sun touching the trees. I backed away from the porch, backed away until I felt my shoulders touch Leston's chest, and stopped.

She let the hand drop to her side, made it disappear into her pocket again. She nodded, the sky's color gone to her eyes, so that the brilliant, cold white of them was now blood red, the color, I figured, of a sorrow I hadn't yet touched, the color of a place I'd never been.

"If they a prophesy here," she said, "it that yo' life going to end up this way some day. Will for all of us. We going to see death, and not know what to make of it. Even Jesus," she said, her voice going back to the whisper now, "even Jesus say upon the cross, 'My God, my God, why hast thou forsaken me?' Even Jesus not know what to make of it."

"Let's go now," Leston said, and I felt his arm move round my shoulder, felt him start to pull me back toward the car.

"Miss Jewel," Cathedral said, and I turned to her, stopped moving.

I looked at her there on the porch, the brown plaid dress soaking up blood from the sky. She smiled, said, "Don't a day go by I don't dream on slapping you with this hand of mine." She brought the hand from the pocket again, held it up firm and high in front of her, fingers spread. "Don't a day. Yo' children, all of them, they alive. I got one dead in a ditch, eyes open, killed for trying to teach burrhead niggers how to read in a town a hundred miles north of here don't want no niggers knowing how to read."

She nodded again, and I felt my heart lurch again, not in the way it had when that big-bosomed girl'd surprised me at the kitchen window, but in a way I knew I'd never recover from. I felt it shudder under a sudden and permanent weight, set there like a stone on my chest. "It *you* who taught *me*," she said. "That yo' legacy." She nodded again. "Even yo' baby daughter, yo' hardship and test in this world, she only asleep in a back seat of yo' shiny car. She only asleep."

I looked down, away from her eyes. I whispered, "I'm sorry," those two words too small and insignificant to mean anything.

I closed my eyes a moment, then opened them, looked up at her what I was certain would be the final time.

But she was already gone, disappeared into the black hole her front doorway'd become in the gathering dark.

There was only Nelson, slowly rocking in his chair, hands still on his knees, the creak the chair made the smallest sliver of sound. The coming dark'd erased all detail to him, though he sat not fifteen feet away, and I couldn't see if his eyes were open or closed behind those thick glasses. And with that loss of detail his black pants'd turned clean, brand-new, the suspenders down his chest taut and crisp against his fine white shirt.

"You take care now," his voice came to us.

Chapter 38

While I rinsed Brenda Kay in the tub, squeezed cool water over her back and shoulders and face, I heard Leston turn Toxie back, heard low talk out on the porch, then the sound his pickup made starting up, backing out. I took Brenda Kay's hand, helped her out the tub. Her eyes closed, me drying her off with the towel, she half-whispered, half-sang, "Ah ahh stop, love you."

Once I'd gotten her to bed—she'd slept all the way home—I went to the front room, saw Leston at the screen door staring out at nothing, a beer in one hand, the other in his pocket.

I said nothing, only went to the kitchen, then out the back door, down the steps to the yard. Treefrogs started up.

It was dark now, and I headed for the sheets on the line, knew that if I didn't get them in soon they'd be drenched in dew by tomorrow morning. Above me, above the bayou and the cypress and oak and pine, above everything, hung a half-moon, perched out over the water at the end of the dock like some lost and dying star, trying to find a place to rest.

I stopped in the yard, looked to the trees around me. To my left were the clotheslines, the two T-bars at either end, hanging between them rows of white sheets a bright gray out here. They hung straight down from the lines, no breeze anywhere, and I went to one end, touched the sheet. It was still damp, hadn't been out long enough to dry in the humid heat of the day.

I pulled back that sheet, ducked beneath the line so that I stood between the two rows. Slowly I moved down them from one end to the other, a hand out to either side, my fingertips trailing along each damp sheet, and for a moment I imagined I was surrounded by gentle ghosts, ghosts who meant nothing, who carried no weight of death or grief or sorrow, ghosts making no demands.

I reached the far end, and turned, planned to head back down the gray corridor, touch each sheet, send each empty ghost shivering one last time.

There at the opposite end stood Leston, him with no detail at all, just a huge and looming shadow. The tip of a cigarette glowed at his side. He lifted it up, and I saw the tip go bright red as he drew on it.

He said, "You asked me today if something happened out at the shed." He paused. "It did."

I let one hand touch the sheet next to me. I caught a corner of it, fingered it between my thumb and first finger, and remembered a moment on a porch when a man with wet and stringy black hair did the same with the corner of a black wool blanket he and three other men had carried my dead father in.

I let go the sheet, said, "What's that?"

He took in a breath, the cigarette still at his side. He said, "We was back to the shed, looking around, and Brenda Kay near stepped on a copperhead."

"What?" I said. My voice was too loud out here, carried across the water, shot up and into darkness. I started toward him, my hands suddenly at my chest, clutching each other, holding on. "She what?"

"She didn't step on it, just walked right over it," he said, and as I came near him I saw his head drop, saw he was looking at the ground.

I stopped in front of him, searched the shadow of him for more of what'd happened, more words about how she'd been safe after all.

He said to the ground, "She didn't even see it. And I wasn't paying attention." He paused, said, "I was looking up at the rafters, thinking on how fine she'd held up, the shed."

"And?" I said. Now my hands let go each other, and one went to him, touched a shoulder.

"I hear this shift in the leaves at my feet, and there he was, just slithering right between us." He paused again, brought up the cigarette, held it at his mouth, though the tip didn't brighten any. He just held it there.

"I didn't even grab for it, like I'd of done ten years ago," he said. "Ten years ago I'd of just bent down, picked him up by the tail and swung him, snapped him."

Finally he drew in, and I could see in the light from the ember just the barest face, the shine of his eyes, the bones beneath his cheeks.

He whispered, "I was scared."

I touched him with both hands now, and through his shirt—a yellow shirt only a shade of gray out here beneath that piecemeal moon—I could feel his arms, the bones of them, the thin flesh.

I said, "I'm scared, too."

"Of what?" he said. The cigarette had died down now, and I could only make out the shadow of his eyes, the idea of his mouth. But I knew he was looking at me, and I hoped he might find my answer in whatever of my eyes he could see in this darkness: Scared I was losing my baby daughter to the nothing this place had to give; scared of

Cathedral's words and the death of all of us I felt this night. Scared my own life was out of my hands.

But I said nothing, no words forming in me, and suddenly I heard waves again, felt fog on my skin, saw the bones of a pier.

I let go his arms, turned to the sheet nearest me, reached up and took off the first clothespin.

He didn't move, and out the corner of my eye I could see his own pale fog again, smoke breath easing out his lungs and into the night.

Then he was next to me, flicked the cigarette away, took from my hand the sheet corner I held. He ducked beneath the line, moved out into the yard as I took off the next pin, and the next, until I stood with the other end of the sheet, three clothespins in my apron pocket.

Without a word we moved away from the clotheslines, both of us with a sheet corner to a hand. Gently we popped the sheet, shook out any bugs may have been there.

Then we came toward each other, and when our hands touched, the sheet folded in half, he said, "Don't even put these back up tomorrow. Just go ahead, pack them up."

I nodded, took one end of the folded sheet, took a few steps back. I said, "I'll bleach them once we get home, get out any mildew."

We came toward each other again, and our hands touched again.

He said, "I didn't mean it to be this way, Sugar."

I stopped with the sheet, stared up at him. We were turned a different way now, the rising moon full in his face: a gray man looking down to his wife, him giving up.

I said, "What do you mean?" though I knew. I knew and knew.

He whispered, "I didn't mean for it to end like this, Sug."

I tried to smile up at him, hoped in the dark he'd think this smile came easy to me, came from down in me and needed no prompting at all. I said, "This isn't the end." I paused, swallowed. I said, "Sug, this isn't the end at all."

He looked at me a moment more, then broke his eyes from mine, nodded.

This time he took a step back from me, and we folded the sheet one last time. He took it from me, held it to his chest, then went for the stairs up to the kitchen.

I didn't move for the next sheet, the next clothespin. Instead I watched him go, and thought on his naming of me once again: *Sugar, Sug*, the last time him calling me that the night we'd ridden into Purvis, me about to bear Brenda Kay, our lives about to take the giant blind turn it had.

And I thought again on Cathedral's words, on blessed words come down from God, words right out of the Bible: *Break their teeth, O God, in their mouth: break out the great teeth of the young lions, O Lord.*

Whether she'd known it or not, Cathedral'd broken my teeth, broken them out in a way better than any slap to the cheek could have done. A son dead in a ditch, I thought. Eyes open because of me and what I'd taught his mother, and I thought of my Brenda Kay asleep in a bed in a bayou palace, a child unable at my own hands to make even the letter *R*.

Leston made it to the steps, but he didn't start up them, as I'd thought he would. No, he placed the folded sheet on the third or fourth step up, then turned, started back across the lawn, and as my husband came toward me I wondered how he felt, now I'd broken all his teeth, broken them once again with a prayer to God, a prayer he'd die enough to see what was best for us. Here was my answered prayer, my husband dead enough now, teeth broken.

He was walking easily, hands on his hips as he crossed the lawn, steps big and comfortable as he made it to the clothesline, started in on the next sheet. *I am your wife,* I thought. Leston's. Him all movement and peace.

1984

Epilogue

Four-fifteen, and she hasn't got home yet, and what I'm doing is what I do every other time this happens, though it doesn't happen enough for me to feel fine about it, feel a routine to it. Maybe once in three months or so she'll be late for one reason or another. And each time I do what I do now: watch the clock on the wall above the sofa, walk to the window every three minutes or so and pull back the curtains with a single finger, a finger just like every other of mine, so old, so brown and gnarled I can hardly recognize it as my own. I touch the white material, pull it back an inch or so to see the same empty street we moved to more than twenty years back, this house in Redondo Beach only a hair larger than the one in Manhattan Beach. But this house has a bigger front yard, a bigger back yard, and behind the row of oleanders at the rear of the yard is a chain link fence, behind the fence a raised platform of dirt, on top of that train tracks.

Trains come through three or four times a day, and for the first few months we'd lived here it'd been a strange thing to wake up in the middle of the night, heavy in my head the dream of Cleopatra Sinclair disappearing into thick green woods, her turning one last time and calling out to me, while around me the room shook, the bed trembling beneath me, the tumble and scrape of wheels on the rails there in the dark. But it wasn't long before all of us, including Brenda

Kay, got used to the sound. Not a month after we moved here, too, Leston and Burton'd taken out one of those oleanders, cleared a spot for Brenda Kay, who'd taken to making her way to the fence, her with enough courage to stand and wave at the trains passing by, especially at the red caboose, where sometimes a man would lean out, wave back to her.

The house was what we'd been able to afford. Wilman and Barbara and Billie Jean lived just down the freeway in Buena Park; living right over to Torrance was Annie and Gene and, back before they'd divorced, Burton and Sarah, my middle boy finding eleven years ago the same ugly territory his older sister'd discovered so many years before.

I looked out at that street, the gray asphalt of it, the cracked white cement sidewalk that crosses in front of my house, the green lawn, all of it a place where, once, my grandchildren, every one of them grown now, used to ride bikes, used to tussle and fuss and wrestle and laugh.

But this afternoon I don't see the yellow van, *Los Angeles County School District* printed in black letters across the side of it, pull up to the curb. I don't see any of Brenda Kay's friends, eyes straight ahead or out the window, none of them, it seems, ever blinking. I don't see Brenda Kay stand from her seat, Barbie lunchbox in hand, pink canvas knapsack in the other, don't see her slowly make her way out the door and step down to that sidewalk, her white shoes maybe scuffed a little. I don't see Lupe, the Mexican girl who's been driving for eight years now, don't see her single gold tooth in amidst all the perfect white teeth she shows when she smiles at me.

Nothing. That's what I see. Just that empty out there.

Early of a Saturday morning last month Wilman and Barbara came over, him in his nice new Oldsmobile company car, parking in the driveway right here next to the kitchen windows. I'd been up for an hour or so already, Brenda Kay and me dressed and ready, though it was only seven-thirty. Brenda Kay was in her recliner, the radio on next to her, and had a ruler and some crayons and a tablet of pastel papers. She was singing and singing, like always so far from any tune that it didn't matter. Just her voice, her attention on the crayon in her hand, her eyes on the paper. When I heard Wilman's car pull up I said, "They're here now, let's get a move on!"

She didn't look up.

We were headed to Saugus for the day, to visit a Mrs. Tindle, a woman I'd never met before, but who I'd been told about by the people over to the Gardena Human Services Department.

We were headed there for a reason, one I'd been putting off thinking on for the whole of my life, and on that morning a month ago I still wasn't ready for it.

We were headed there because it was a house where retarded girls lived, a house in the valley up there where this Mrs. Tindle and her husband cared for girls like my Brenda Kay.

For the past six or seven months, Wilman and Burton and James and Anne and Billie Jean had all talked to me about this eventuality, this looking for a place Brenda Kay could live some day, and of course what this said to me, the real words beneath the ones they kept giving to me, was that my own days left were lined up and waiting, the last of them not too far distant.

No news here, this realization lately come into my children's heads a notion that'd been bounding through my own since before I could remember.

Since before, certainly, the death of my Leston, him

unable to get back on at ECC when we moved back. He'd had to take on a job as a janitor, him dying of a heart attack in a grade-school hallway after pushing a mop for two years.

Or perhaps I'd even known my life was on its way to over even before Brenda Kay was born, when on an evenings in March James'd told us he was signing up for the Army, him the first of my children to leave, that old movement from inside my home out into the world the first sign in a world filled with signs that my own death was coming up. Nothing more than that: my term of days here on earth were already winding down even that far back.

That was what the trip meant, even though when Wilman came in I reached up and hugged him and kissed his neck like any other day he came to see me, then did the same to Barbara, who fussed over me, told me how fine my dress looked, though it was something I'd had for years, a shapeless blue thing I'd bought even before Brenda Kay'd started over to the high school. We were each of us acting like this was just any other Saturday morning visit.

Wilman went past me and on into the living room, said, "Billie Jean'd be here if she'd been able to get off at the hospital." He paused. "Burt, you know, he's off to Phoenix with that girlfriend of his. Anne and Gene are out to Lake Havasu."

"I know," I said.

Then Wilman hollered, "Brenda Kay, you fat!"

"Wimn!" she shouted, "you fat too!"

Barbara said, "We're going to have fun today. We'll go to breakfast at Spires first, then drive on up there. They're expecting us." She reached to the collar of my dress, straightened it out, though I'd taken a moment myself in the mirror before they came, knew my collar looked just so. Still, I smiled, said, "Sounds fine."

"Bill?" she said, looked past me to the living room. "Did you remember the pillow for the car?"

Bill, I thought, and for a moment I wondered who that was, who this woman could be calling out to, and then I remembered. *Bill*.

"Yep," Wilman answered, and I heard Brenda Kay laugh "Huh! Huh! Huh!" to something he said, I didn't know what. I only heard her laughter.

We drove north on the San Diego Freeway, me up front with Wilman. Barbara'd bought a sack full of *Tiger Beat* and *Teen* magazines and the like, Brenda Kay flipping through them and taking in all the pictures of boys with shirts ripped open to show pale hairless chests. "Who's that?" Barbara would ask, point to a photograph, and Brenda Kay would shoot back a name, give the television program the boy starred in, or simply say "Bandstand" or "Soul Train" if she'd seen him there. Barbara clapped with each answer, said, "That's right, Brenda Kay, that's right," then pointed to another photo, started all over again.

Though I loved Barbara and what she was doing, a piece of me wanted quiet, wanted to just sit there in the bright morning light of a Saturday freeway. Traffic was just as slow as any other day, cars and cars round us, more buildings and billboards and reflections off glass and bumpers and all else. More broken light and colors and cars than ever, this city grown too large from that place we'd entered like it was the new Jerusalem in 1952. Then there'd been only the one freeway, us stumbling blind into Bundy Mufflers and deliverance from our past lives, safe passage into the next.

And Burton's old words came to me, traffic stopped on the freeway, us not even out to the airport yet: *I hope that ain't just a dream of yours, Momma.* I saw his face as we leaned against the drainboard in the house his daddy'd built by hand, a face all the clean and soft angles of a boy just out of the woods after following his sister, the face of a boy not yet left from home, and then came my pitiful words back to him, me all knowledge and light and wise years even back then: *Once you let it turn into a dream, then it won't ever happen on you,* I'd said.

But it was a dream, all of it, a dream of how I might fix things for us: Brenda Kay'd never tested higher than a six-year-old, not even with the new programs and all the new research and innovations we were always being told about in the newsletters, Mr. White and his speeches and chair all long gone. Brenda Kay made no progress, even when there'd surfaced those new terms bestowed upon our children by the school: EMR, for Educable Mentally Retarded; TMR, for Trainable Mentally Retarded. And always, always she was a TMR, her programs at the Instruction Center geared that way. TMR children had the task of setting the right number of bolts on a cardboard template, then slipping those bolts into a plastic bag provided by the company paying for the service. One day they'd do the bolts, another day the nuts, then the bolts, then the nuts. Certainly there'd been joy in her accomplishing that much; she even brought home a paycheck once a month, always for some odd small amount, $7.31 or $6.96. On those afternoons she came home waving the check, we'd go right down to the bank, cash it, then go to dinner at a Denny's or Sizzler, where I'd let her pay for her meal herself, though money still meant nothing to her, only pieces of paper, chunks of metal handed over to a smiling waitress.

But then, the Tuesday before Wilman and Barbara'd come over, Brenda Kay'd brought home with her Barbie lunchbox and her pink canvas knapsack a note from the

Instruction Center teacher, a Mrs. Samuelson, telling me Brenda Kay would have to be removed from the TMR program for a few months: she couldn't seem to match up the right number of bolts to the template, Mrs. Samuelson informed me, and probably needed a break from the work. For "Refueling" was the word the woman'd used.

Refueling.

And there we were, on a freeway and headed for the moment when Brenda Kay and I would lay eyes on the real Jerusalem, a house in Saugus where retarded girls no different from my own would end up their own days, the world spinning round them, while Los Angeles and its cars and freeways and buildings and clean, shiny people lived and made love and money. It was a dream, I saw, Burton knowing more than I ever would even that far back.

My arms were crossed against the cool of the air conditioner, that air suddenly too cold, ice in me, and I shivered, turned to my son. I looked at him, there with his sunglasses on, and saw how the skin beneath his chin had started to sagging, saw the trace of blood vessels across his cheeks and how they'd started to break up here and there. I saw the sharp edge of wrinkles beside his mouth, him there in profile to me, and I saw my boy for what he was: a forty-eight-years-old man driving his ancient mother to a place called Saugus and a house were retarded girls lived once their mothers died, this the same man I'd seen watch a doctor change dressings on the dead flesh of Brenda Kay's burned legs. He was an orphan, I saw, one of the five I'd left here on earth, and I quick took my eyes from him, looked out the windshield, looked for some deliverance of my own out there.

Above the buildings and cars and billboards was a still

blue sky, and all of Los Angeles seemed suddenly far behind us. It was years behind us, the sky out there the same sky we'd followed like a star, escaping Mississippi and headed for here on a day when we'd passed from the desert and into green orchards, oranges not ready to pick, broccoli and strawberries and lettuce.

Then the stopped cars all swarmed up, swallowed that sky, and I knew the only thing I would do was to look back at my son, try and give him whatever it was I'd kept from him in order to take care of his sister.

Here was the boy, I saw in the man beside me, who I let stand all on his own in that doctor's office above the hardware store, the boy who'd been afraid to cry while he watched the horror of his baby sister's rotting legs and brown and oozing skin.

Cars all round us picked up speed, and I could feel my blood move more quickly in me as Wilman drove faster. I felt my arms prickling over in goose flesh, and knew it was because I saw the chance to make up to my son—at least to this one of my children—that moment I'd lost to him so long ago. I knew I could make it up to him here in the car before we found the end of my life and what would happen after I was gone, all of it played out in whatever this Mrs. Tindle's turned out to be. This was the moment I couldn't lose, and so I turned to him, my arms tight against my chest, and I smiled at him, smiled and smiled, and I spoke.

"Wilman," I said, and I paused.

"Yes, Momma," he said. He quick turned to me, then faced forward again, sunglasses still on. He said, "You cold?" He reached down with one hand, fiddled with the air conditioning.

"Wilman," I said again, "I want you to know I love you."

The cold air stopped, too quick in its place the sun through the windows, all beautiful and light, but hot all the same. I waited for him to say something.

"Momma," he said, and smiled, though I couldn't tell if his heart was in it, his eyes still hidden behind his sunglasses. Barbara'd gone quiet in the back seat, listening.

He said, "Don't be afraid," and turned to me. He was still smiling. "Us going up here only means you're planning for the future, planning for the day when you can take it easy, rest yourself after so long."

I turned from him, from the lie he and I both knew was a lie. I looked out my window, let a few seconds of Los Angeles and California disappear before I said to him, "You drank a date shake once and threw up behind a Texaco station." I was quiet a moment, then turned back to him. "You remember."

Now he had his sunglasses off, and he was looking at me. He was smiling, and I could see his heart in it, see all of him right there in his smile, and I saw, too, more of my Leston in him than I'd ever thought possible: the wrinkles beside his eyes, his high forehead and sure, easy smile, the freckles across his nose. But his eyes were brown, not Leston's deepwater green. His eyes were deep black-brown, my own eyes, and not just my own eyes, but my father's eyes as well, and the eyes of Jacob Chetauga, all of us still here every minute my son breathed.

He said, "I remember," and then he turned back to the freeway. He said, "I love you, Momma."

"What's this about?" Barbara said. She leaned forward, her hand just touching my shoulder. "Who threw up? Bill?"

Bill, I thought again.

"It wa a long time ago," I said, and I reached up, touched Barbara's fingers, patted them. "Too long," I said.

"Willie Ames!" Brenda Kay shouted then. " 'Eight Enough'! 'Eight Enough'!"

Barbara let go my shoulder, and I heard her clap behind me, say, "That's right, Brenda Kay."

Wilman slipped back on the sunglasses, put both hands to the wheel, drove us on.

We got there near eleven, the sun up high now as we drove along a thin strip of pavement, Mrs. Tindle's road. The town of Saugus itself had been pretty enough, something of a German village, or at least what someone thought a German village might look like settled out here on the edge of California desert: little houses with lots of gingerbread and shutters, picket fences, a Safeway and Von's market built to look more like chalets than grocery stores. Then we were out of town, Barbara calling out directions from a sheet of paper she held, Wilman nodding each time he found the right street.

To the left of us lay a row of brown hills, here and there a lone cottonwood, nothing more; at the base of the hill was a railroad line, empty and straight and heading off into the distance; to the right lay huge fields, flat and not yet plowed up for whatever it was they grew here.

My hands'd gone all sweaty, started to shaking a bit, too, with how close we were coming to this end, my end. My hands shook, and then I could feel the sweat on my back, even though I was sitting in this plush beige velour seat, seats almost the same color as those hills out there, seats more soft, more comfortable than any piece of furniture I'd ever had in my house.

And I smiled at that thought, at Wilman and his cars, at him driving us on into Los Angeles that first time, his hollering out to City Hall, Annie burying herself in the back seat, amazed and embarrassed and disgusted with her white trash brother.

"What, Momma?" Wilman said, and I turned to him, saw he was looking at me. "What's so funny?" he said.

Nothing," I said, still smiling. I rubbed my hands together. "Everything," I said. I looked at him, touched a hand to my forehead, felt how cold my skin was, clammy and wet.

"Momma?" he whispered.

"There it is!" Barbara said from the back seat, her arm shooting out between the two of us like she was some little girl herself, finally got to some place she'd ridden weeks to get to.

It was only a house: two storys with pale blue clapboard, no shutters, a chimney running up the near side. The house was on our right, a hundred yards or so set off from the road and out in the fields. The front of the house had two windows downstairs; the second floor in the front had three windows across it, and I wondered right off which of those windows might end up being the window of my Brenda Kay's room, wondered if she might be in a room that looked out on lonesome empty highway, past it that railroad track so that freight cars would rumble through of a night, shake the house. She would be used to that, I knew, maybe that shaking even comfort to her once I was gone, something to help her through. Or maybe she'd end up on the back end of the house, have a window that looked out onto all these fields.

Then we eased onto that drive, and suddenly the house seemed huge, and I couldn't move.

Wilman popped open his door, as did Barbara. But before either got out they stopped, and I could tell they were watching me watch this house.

I turned in my seat, made my eyes go straight to Brenda Kay. I wanted to see her reaction to this place, this house that could end up her home. I wanted to see on her face whatever it was this place registered in her, some face that might betray she knew what was going on here. I was looking for some fear in her, maybe some kind of dread in how her eyes took it in, in how she held her mouth.

But she was only looking at the magazine in her hand, her eyes going back and forth across it as though she might be able to read the small amount of words beneath the pictures there.

I felt tears well up in me, the hard knot at my throat like a cold fist, because this was the truth of me: I wanted to find in my child fear of the future, when all along, I saw, it was me who was afraid, Brenda Kay more equipped than any of us for my ending, because she could not know what loss was. "Miss Daddy," she'd sometimes call out to me in the kitchen of an evening, and I'd go in to the living room, a dishtowel in my hands as I dried them off, and I'd search her face for some sign of tears, of genuine grief, only to see her smile, point at a tall man in a Marlboro ad in a magazine.

"Let's go on in," Wilman whispered, and I felt his hand on my shoulder, felt him give a gentle squeeze there. Still I searched for something in Brenda Kay, some evidence, I knew and did not want to know, of me, of *me*.

I found nothing. Finally she only looked up, smiled at me, her heavy, wide face near as wrinkled, near as old and sagging and aged as my baby son's next to me. She was forty-one years old now, a baby the doctors said would never live past two, would never walk. Here, smiling at me.

And there were her eyes, her almond-shaped eyes beneath auburn eyebrows, her auburn hair cut short as always, bangs across her forehead like she was ten.

But it was her eyes I saw, and that green. Leston's eyes.

She pointed a finger at the page, said, "John Stamos, John Stamos! Hospital!"

"Yes," I said. "Yes," and I tried to smile, her image trembling for the tears I held in my eyes, tears I didn't want to let fall, not now. Those were Leston's eyes she had, and I could not cry at that.

She turned to her window, looked at the house then, lost the smile. She squinted one eye at the sun coming in on her, and looked.

I said, "What do you see, Brenda Kay?"

She paused a moment, lifted the hand from the magazine, held it up to block the sun as she looked.

"School?" she said. She looked at me, on her face the same look of puzzlement, eyebrows up, mouth open.

I said, "No," and swallowed. I reached over the seat to her, and she put her other hand in mine. I swallowed hard again, squeezed her hand, said, "Let's go see."

Mrs. Tindle opened the front door even before I could knock. She was a woman of Barbara's age, but thinner, her brown hair pulled back in a ponytail at the base of her neck, wrinkles beside her eyes, smaller ones beside her mouth. Her skin was dark and tan and clean. "Welcome, welcome," she said, and put out her hand to me, said, "Mrs. Hilburn, I'm Nancy Tindle."

I took her hand. She shook mine hard and strong and firm, and already I liked her just for that, and for the reason she seemed happy, smiled without putting too much in it. She seemed real, and when she let go my hand, she went right to Brenda Kay, held out a hand for her to take.

"You have to be Brenda Kay Hilburn," she said.

Brenda Kay took her hand, though she hadn't yet committed to smiling, only shot her eyes from me to this woman and back again.

"We've got lunch coming up soon as we can round up the girls," she said to my daughter, and she turned, still with Brenda Kay's hand in hers, and headed into the house. I saw then what she had on: a pair of jeans and a pink cotton blouse, an apron tied round the waist. She said, "You guys just follow me. Pardon whatever mess you find in here, too."

And we followed her.

The girls: Jenny, Adelaide, Margaret, Jo, Rachel, Patty, Karen, Sammy, Wendy, Olivia, Martha. Eleven of them, with room for twelve. Janine, number twelve, had died a month ago, Mrs. Tindle'd told me over the phone when I'd called her the first time to set all this up. She'd lingered a moment over the girl's name, letting the word *Janine* hang there on the line for a moment or two before she'd hooked to it the words *died last month*, and I wasn't certain if she was putting the words together that slowly for herself and what grief she had in her, or if it were for me, some sort of revealing of the obvious: our children die, every one of them, whether we are here or not.

So there were eleven of them, all with about the same degree of mental retardation, Brenda Kay right in the middle of them. "We don't want to bite off more than we can chew," Nancy Tindle told us while we ate lunch in the kitchen, her husband, Larry, a small man with quiet eyes and big hands, in the dining room supervising the girls. We leaned against the countertops in the kitchen, a room filled with light from the row of big windows that looked onto the back of the place. There was the barn, and a swimming pool out there, too, something I couldn't see when we'd driven in. "We want to give them the best care we can, and spread that care as even as we can. One girl needs more care than another, there's bound to be rifts open up, jealousies, that sort of stuff. We want each of them to be loved." She smiled, lifted onto a plate a grilled cheese sandwich. "Mrs. Hilburn, this is for you," she said, and handed it to me.

"Jewel," I said, and met her eyes with mine. "Thank you."

Visitors made some of the girls nervous sometimes, Nancy'd told us, and so we'd eat in here, have our sandwiches in the peace and quiet of this room, so we could talk. And we talked, and I felt myself laugh a couple times, a feeling in my chest I hadn't expected, a surprise, but a sorrowful one, too, because each time I came down from that laughter I came back to the purpose at hand: finding out about this place, this person, these girls.

Why I laughed: Larry'd built the swimming pool for the girls, Nancy'd explained, in order to help them get a different kind of exercise. So he'd built a cement, in-ground pool all the way out here in the desert, only to find that, though the girls'd said originally they'd like to go swimming, not a one of them would dare step foot in it once it was done.

"One of them, Sammy, I think it was, hollers out 'Fishing!'" Nancy said, holding out to me and Wilman and Barbara a plate of Oreo cookies, each of us taking one. "There they all are, twelve girls—this was back when Janine was still with us—all of them lined up in their swimsuits and standing at the edge, scared stiff of that water. They all look at Sammy, who gets this big smile on her face, then they all turn to Larry, and every one of them yells, 'Fishing!' at the top of their lungs—" She laughed then, one hand covering her mouth, and I couldn't help but laugh myself. Wilman took it up, too, and Barbara, who laughed the hardest of us all.

"And here's Larry," she said, still smiling. She shook her head, closed her eyes, and looked suddenly much younger for that smile, for the joy in how she could find the humor in all these girls. I smiled.

"Here's Larry," she said again, "here with a revolt on his hands, twelve girls ready to throw him into the water. So what does he do? He goes on out to the fishery in Ontario, the closest thing around, and by nightfall he's back here with a couple of books on the subject, and then the next day he starts prepping the pool, and by the next week he's got the pool stocked with these little rainbow trout, and then there's the girls, all of them, standing in a circle around the pool twice a day ever since, mornings and evenings. We never eat any of them—the girls threw a fit, especially Jo and Rachel and Margaret, crying and ranting and raving—the one time Larry tried to clean one of them. He didn't even have the thing half-scaled before he had to quit. So it's been just recreational fishing ever since then. And hell trying to get them to eat fish sticks, too."

Barbara burst out at that, and Wilman shook his head, snickered in his quiet way. And I laughed, too, said, "Her daddy, Leston, took her fishing, when we moved back to Mississippi for a while. All I can recall is the mosquitoes." I crossed my arms, pushed myself off the counter. For a moment I thought maybe the laughter, the lightness in me, would die with that memory, the two of them on the edge of the bayou, Leston swatting away at mosquitoes and cursing, Brenda Kay swatting all the same, but turning to me and just staring at me there in the kitchen window. But once I gave myself to that picture, twenty-two years old in my head, of Leston behind Brenda Kay, his hand letting out line, his mouth moving in words I'd never want Brenda Kay to hear, her just there and looking at me, I still found I was smiling.

"Oh, no need to worry about mosquitoes. This is the desert. Not many of them at all," she said.

"Fishing!" one of the girls in the dining room called out, and in came Larry, in his hands a stack of paper plates piled with breadcrusts, napkins and orange peels. He crossed the kitchen to the trash can at the end of the counter, smiled at us.

"They heard you," he said, and dropped the plates into the trash, dusted his hands. "Now you've done it," he said.

"Line up," Nancy called over her shoulder. She held a washrag under running water there in the sink, and suddenly here came the girls. We three stepped back as they came in, stood against one wall while the girls did exactly as Nancy Tindle asked: they lined up, the first one at the sink, the line going out the kitchen door and disappearing into the dining room. Nancy rung out the rag, handed it to the first girl, a girl a little shorter than Brenda Kay and with black hair that fell to her shoulders. She took the rag, wiped her hands with it, handed it back to Nancy. "Thank you for lunch, Nancy," she said, her voice different than Brenda Kay's, darker, deeper, but just as loud. Her eyes were right on Nancy's, and Nancy leaned over, gave her a hug, the first girl's arms reaching around Nancy's shoulders. Her hands patted Nancy's back a couple times, and then the two let go. Nancy said, "You're welcome, Rachel."

She turned, rinsed out the washrag under the hot water again, and the next girl stepped up, wiped herself down. She was about as tall as Nancy, thin with red hair, but with the same face and thick arms and hands as all the girls, each of them Down's Syndrome girls. She handed the rag back to Nancy, her face down, her eyes unable, it seemed, to meet Nancy's. "Thank you for lunch," she nearly whispered. She put up her arms, hugged Nancy in just the quickest way, her hands patting Nancy's back only once before she let go. But while she'd been hugging Nancy, I'd seen her eyes cut over to us, take us in in just a moment's time, then look back at the floor. Nancy smiled at her. "You're welcome, Olivia," she said, and Olivia turned, walked past her and out the back door.

I looked at Wilman, saw him standing with his arms crossed, his bottom lip between his teeth. He was watching it all, too. Then he saw me watching him, and he smiled, brought up a hand and touched his chin. He nodded, his eyes back to the girls.

Nancy did each girl this way, and we watched it all. Three girls didn't say anything to her—Wendy, Martha and Adelaide—but it didn't seem to matter to Nancy, who still gave each girl a hug and said, "You're welcome," no matter what. In a way it was funny to watch all this going on in the kitchen, eleven retarded girls all about the same age as Brenda Kay, give or take five years or so, parading through, most of them short and round, some, like Olivia, a little taller, thinner. But each of them looked happy in her own way, even if they weren't all loves and kisses when Nancy hugged them. They were just girls, each of them different, each of them dressed in clean clothes, whether sweatshirts and sweatpants or in shorts and blouses and tennis shoes. They were all happy, it seemed, and I knew one couldn't ask for anything more than that. Nothing more.

Then came the last girl from the dining room, my Brenda Kay, who stood behind a girl that could have been her sister, a girl it turned out was Sammy, the girl who'd started up the whole idea of fishing. She had hair near the same auburn as my daughter's, but longer, and had thicker eyebrows. She smiled and smiled at Nancy, her teeth ragged and brown in her mouth, but it didn't matter. She held Nancy the longest of any girl so far, held her and patted her back until Nancy said, "Now Sammy, I think Larry's out there baiting up the lines," and let her go. Sammy stood back from Nancy, then reached to her hands, took them. She said, "I love you, Nancy," and still smiled.

"I love you, too, Sammy," she said. She gave her hands a squeeze.

Sammy finally let go her hands, and came round Nancy, who turned back to the water. Then Sammy stopped in front of us. She smiled, held up a hand as though she were a traffic top stopping us.

"How!" she said, and Nancy turned quick to us.

"Oh, Sammy," Nancy said, smiling.

But I'd already put up my hand the same way, held it out in front of me just as Sammy did. "How!" I said.

Sammy dropped her hand, and laughed, her shoulders suddenly going up and down with it, eyes all squinted shut with the laughter. She turned, headed out the door.

Now Nancy held the rag out to Brenda Kay, who stood with her hands at her sides. She was looking at Nancy's eyes, her mouth open the way she does when she's not certain what to do.

I cleared my throat, said, "She's doesn't know—"

But Nancy put up a hand to me, held it out the same way Sammy'd done. Like a traffic top, ordering me to stop.

"Thank you for lunch," Brenda Kay whispered, her eyes still on Nancy's. Her hands were still at her sides.

Nancy nodded, said, "You're welcome, Brenda Kay." She reached to one of Brenda Kay's hands, took it in hers, gently wiped it with the warm washrag.

I stood there, and felt myself growing smaller, shrinking away from the world and everything I'd ever tried to do in it. She held my daughter's hand, and wiped it, turned it in her own and wiped it again. Then she let go that hand, took Brenda Kay's other hand in hers, and I felt myself disappearing into the air around me, a feeling I'd known would someday come, but which, now it was here, wasn't welcome at all.

Yet here we were, and I watched as Nancy put the rag in the sink, and bent down, put her arms round my daughter, my Brenda Kay, the child born out of twenty-two hours of labor and countless hours of pain. And suddenly the pain I'd known in giving her to this earth was a simple pinprick, a splinter in my finger compared to this feeling now, and how my daughter seemed to be swallowed up in the arms of this woman.

Nancy's arms were around my daughter, and I felt I'd already lost her, felt I might as well have been dead and gone already for those loving arms round my Brenda Kay.

But then I saw Brenda Kay's eyes look to me, those deepwater green eyes of Leston's. Her eyes were on mine, asking, I could see in them, still looking for me and what she ought to do.

And with those eyes on me, I finally knew the truth of why we were here in a house in Saugus: it wasn't the end of my life we were preparing for, but the beginning of the next life for Brenda Kay. My lives, the long string of them that started with the death of my daddy and went on from there, right up to and including this moment, that long string of lives wasn't over. My life would never be over, but would be carried on, I saw, in Wilman here at my side, and in James in Texas, in Burton in his big house in Palos Verdes and in Billie Jean in her mobile home in Buena Park, and in Annie in her house in Torrance, and in all the hordes of grand-children and great-grandchildren to follow after me.

My life would never end, I saw, not even in my own Brenda Kay, because of those eyes turned to me and asking what to do, the only true victory any mother could ever hope for: the looking of a child, whether retarded or not, to you for what wisdom you could give away before you left for whatever reckoning you had with the God who'd given you that wisdom in the first place.

And so because it seemed the only valuable thing I could give her, the sum total of my life wrapped up into this moment, I gave to her all I knew: my eyes on her own, meeting for what felt the last time, I nodded for her to go right ahead, for her to hold on to Mrs. Tindle. I nodded.

Her eyes hung on mine a moment more, then she closed them, and as if in proof to me she'd learned every-thing there in that moment, she slowly brought her arms up and placed them on this Nancy Tindle's shoulders, and she held her, patted Nancy's back once, twice, three times.

I closed my eyes.

There is still nothing out my window, still nothing, though the sun is fast on its way down out there, just beneath it and beyond the tops of houses the thick bank of gray fog just off the coast, ready to roll in and swallow us all.

And so it is settled: whenever I want, Brenda Kay has a home in Saugus. I don't need any more visits to any more homes for retarded girls, though I'm certain there's folly in this, in having no other place in mind for her. But what I took from that place is worth everything to me: the pic-ture, just after Brenda Kay'd left the kitchen for outside, of twelve girls standing round a swimming pool in the hot dry desert afternoon, Brenda Kay settled in between

Martha and Sammy, every girl with a cane pole in her hand, each waiting for a fish to bite; and the picture of Brenda Kay's eyes on me, waiting. That is everything.

But none of that matters, because she's not here now, and I picture again for the thousandth time a yellow van rolled on Sepulveda or some such street where cars drive too fast, and where it is easy to get killed any day of the week, any hour of a day, here in California.

I let the curtain fall from my fingers again, resolved now to call the school, though each time she's late they say the same thing: *You know traffic* and *Don't worry, she'll be home soon.*

But I call anyway, because there is no reason why I can't have an answer, however lame, as to why my daughter isn't yet here. I stand at the wall phone in the kitchen, the receiver in my hand, and lean as far as I can into the front room, my eyes trying to dig through those awful white curtains even a deeper orange now, almost scarlet for that sun, and I try to see, but see nothing.

Someone answers on the sixth ring, and my words spill out of me, a tangled chain of them that betray how old I am, how afraid I can be at the simple fact of a late van from the school, and once those words have left me, the woman at the other end says, *Torrance-Redondo Beach run?* and I nod and nod, finally say, *Yes, yes.*

New driver, she says. *You're not the only one to call. It's his first day,* she says, then pauses, says, *And you know traffic. Okay?* Her last word is tacked on as if I am to take this reason and wrap myself in the comfort of it, feel somehow safer, both for me and for my child, and suddenly, as I watch my hand place the receiver back in its cradle, my hand even smaller, even more wrinkled than twenty minutes ago, I see myself standing at the edge of a swimming

pool in Saugus. I see my own end there, Brenda Kay dead
and gone, nowhere for me to go but there. It's a funny
image, but one I cannot laugh at; too many times I've
thought on her dying before me, and wondered if I would
still wake up early of a morning after having laid out her
clothes the night before, and make her breakfast, then
lunch. I wonder, too, if I would tape over her lunchbox so
it won't pop open, only to turn from that task, call out her
name to the empty house, and hear nothing. Standing at
the pool seems a logical end now, where I ought to end up,
and I envy my child, envy her seeing Leston in Marlboro
ads, envy the feel of Mrs. Tindle's arms around her, envy
her having a friend who raises a hand to strangers, says
How! with all the authority one can need in this world.

It's almost five now, and already I can feel the slow tremble of the house, the train on its way. It'll be here in a minute
or so, and I wonder if anyone will be in that caboose to see
that Brenda Kay is not here, is not waving to him.

I stand at the kitchen window, waiting for the train to
come, for the tremendous heave and rumble that used to
wake my grandchildren when they spent nights, and that
used to wake me, too, my first months here, Leston warm
in bed next to me, Brenda Kay settled in her own room and
asleep. Those first nights I would sit up in bed and listen to
the huge and shambling sound the train made passing by, a
black animal high on the dirt platform above the bushes at
the back of the yard. How big that sound seemed then, how
important and lonely and dangerous there in the middle of
the night, those first days when all my children were grown
and gone, married, making children of their own.

I wonder at all these things, me standing at the window, and hear, finally, after what I only then realize is perhaps the second or third time, a horn honking in front of

my house, the sound of it nearly lost to me wallowing here
in my kitchen.

I make it to the door and down the steps. There are
things I want to say to this driver, words I don't yet know,
but words I want to utter nonetheless. Brenda Kay is already
stepping off the van and moving fast up the driveway. She
just brushes past me, her mouth closed tight, her eyes to the
ground as she moves quickly, her arms swinging away, in
one hand the lunchbox, the other her pink knapsack.

For a moment I turn to her, watch her moving away
from me, and I can see there, above the garage, the train
moving fast past us all, and I see how dark that eastern sky
really is, and how late in my life all of this is coming, all of
it. Brenda Kay is headed to the back yard, where she will
stand with her face pressed to the small space of chain link
fence Burton still keeps cleared for her. She'll stand there,
do as she has for more than twenty years now: peer up at
the train passing by, and wave.

I turn to the van, still a few yards off, and for a moment
I hesitate, not certain there is any call for my anger toward
a new driver. I think on when I was driving the station
wagon myself, the children hollering and crying and throwing up and the mothers coming out to you when you are
late only to damn you for having been stuck in that traffic.

So the only words I have forming in my throat, in my
head and heart, are the words *Thank you.* Brenda Kay is
home safe, standing at the back fence and waving while
round us the air is filled with the rhythm and scrape of the
train.

I make it to the van, place a hand on the rail up, and lean
in, only to see the driver, a man who looks Chinese to me.
He has on gold wire-frame glasses, and he is smiling, already
nodding, though he doesn't know what I am about to say.

Sorry, he says. *Sorry for late. New route.* He leans over in his seat toward me, puts out a hand, and says a word, what I take must be his name: *Nuyen* perhaps, and it occurs to me he is one of these Vietnamese people I have read of in the paper, and who I've seen at the market and at the pier and everywhere now, and suddenly I miss Lupe and her gold tooth, and then I miss Laqwanda, the colored girl disappeared back to upstate New York soon as the children were taken up by the school district, his mission here completed, and then I miss, finally, Cathedral, a name as strong and steady and clear as any I have ever known.

And, as with every day since he has died, maybe even every day since he'd helped me fold sheets on a night in Mississippi, I miss my husband, my Leston.

Okay? this Nuyen says, and I have to swallow, blink, nod my head. I glance back into the van, see Dennis there, him the only child left. He smiles at me soon as he sees I am looking at him, and pushes his glasses up higher on his nose. He's forty-eight or so now, an old man himself, his hair gone gray, **his** face gone to thick flesh. Yet still he smiles at me, remembers who I am.

I wave to him, say, *Hey, Dennis.*

He waves, then stands, points to the seat across the aisle from him. He says, *Brenda Kay sit over there,* and nods at me, sits back down.

I look at him a moment longer, smile at him. I say, *Dennis, you're a fine boy.*

He smiles, nods, pushes his glasses back up.

I turn back to this Nuyen, nod at him, step off the van onto the street. I say, *You better get a move on,* and I point down the street ahead of him. *Head out to Crenshaw and turn right,* I say, *then left at the third street, four houses down.*

That's the quickest way to Dennis'. I hear my voice in the street, hear how loud it is, the train long gone.

His face is all concentration, his eyebrows together, mouth pursed.

I swallow, slowly say, *Crenshaw right, tnird street left, four houses down.* I say, *Be careful.* I say, *Thank you.*

He nods again, this time a hard quick move, his face still working on my words, trying to record them as best he can. He pulls closed the van door, gives it the gas, and he is gone.

Brenda Kay is already at the kitchen table, back from waving at the train; she's turned on the kitchen lights, and is pulling out today's papers from her knapsack, the lunchbox already left in the sink.

Though I need to start dinner, need to get us ready for the night ahead of us, need to start thinking about running water for the bath, about laying out her clothes for tomorrow, and about what she'll bring for lunch tomorrow, too; though there is all of this to think about, the only thing I can see myself doing right then is sitting down at the table with her, and looking at her, taking her in. Not long from this moment she will be up from the table and in the living room, the television popped on to reruns of shows she's seen a hundred times already but which she'll laugh at all the same. She'll sit there in the recliner and slather her hands with hand lotion, then wipe them on the towels I've draped on the armrests for just that purpose. Not long from this moment I will be cooking up the box of macaroni and cheese, slicing up bits of ham to toss in with it, boiling up snap beans. Not long from this moment we will none of us be here.

She pulls from the knapsack a purple sheet of paper, a flyer from school. She holds it up, says: *Dance, Momma!*

and hands it to me, her face in its smile, her eyes alive with
the prospect of going to one of these events.

I take the paper, read it. Snoopy is on it, there in his
ranger hat and grinning. He holds a placard, on it typed

DANCE!
For those with Developmental Disabilities,
Their Friends, and Family.
When: Friday April 14
Where: GARDENA COMMUNITY CENTER
1600 W. 160th St.
TIME: 7:00–9:30 P.M.
COST $1.00

I look at her, expecting her to be watching me, but she
is only digging in her knapsack for something else, her
mind on the next thing she has to show me. She pulls it
out, smiling again, shouts, *Bingo!* and hands me the next
sheet. This one is yellow, the words on it set off in a square
border decorated with butterflies and flowers:

FAMILY BINGO
FOR PERSONS WITH
DEVELOPMENTAL DISABILITIES,
THEIR FRIENDS, AND FAMILY MEMBERS.

I quick read through it, see that this event, like all the
others, is at the Center, the Friday two weeks from now,
and that I have to call Jennie or Dawn to reserve a space.
At the bottom of the sheet, in big balloony letters and with
a smiling sun coming up behind it, are the words *Have a
Happy Day.*

And again I turn to Brenda Kay, expecting to see her

watching my face for whatever might come across it, evidence of whether or not we'll go to either of these events. They're at night, I am ready to say and I don't like driving all the way out there. I can offer that reason up to her, something I know she can understand, and I ready myself for what she might say, whether she'll cry or pout or push her knapsack off the table, and I start to smile, look up at her.

But she is still digging in her knapsack, and I say, How much more, Brenda Kay? and tilt my head to one side, ready and waiting to be annoyed at how the girls down to the Center organize too much for these children, too many events in lives already jammed and overflowing with the simple and giant tasks of making it through a day.

Then she pulls out the next sheet. Look, Momma! she shouts, and it seems her voice is louder than it has ever been, louder than me shouting into the school van, louder than my wailing in the delivery room, louder than the cries of my children at their father's funeral, or the sounds of treefrogs on a night in Mississippi. Louder than anything I have ever heard, her small words filling the world: Look, Momma!

She holds up only a sheet of paper, a thin sheet of lined newsprint paper torn from a tablet not much different than I'd had when I was a girl, when the world was ready and willing to be filled with all I could teach it; she holds up a sheet of paper torn from a tablet like those she's had all her own life, too, tablets she's been filling for more than thirty years now; she holds up a single sheet torn from a tablet like the one I'd taught Cathedral to write on, a woman who'd portended all this, who'd told me the truth all the way back then on an evening in Mississippi, the first day I'd known Brenda Kay was in me: this baby I've carried my entire life is my hardship in this world, my test. And the way God has smiled down on me, too.

She holds the sheet up for me to read, holds it in front of my face, a hand on either edge, those short fingers of hers gripping tight the paper, what is written on it everything that could ever matter to her here in this world:

Only letters, rows of them, the first letter of her name. She's written thousands of these before, filled tablet and tablet and tablet, but on this night, they are enough. More than enough, the sky now black outside the kitchen window, the train tracks gone quiet until sometime late tonight, when the house will shudder once again, and God might wake me from my sleep, bring me to the bedroom window to see the train moving outside, that black shadow moving forward on into the night and leading me away from here, from Brenda Kay alone and asleep in the next room, from the rest of my children, from the ghosts of the lives I've been blessed enough and cursed enough to have led.

Only letters, labored, indifferent, yet full as she can make them of herself. Letters, I finally hear, singing with all they have, scores of them swirling round me in voices I'll never understand, but beautiful all the same, God smiling and smiling and smiling.

POCKET BOOKS
PROUDLY PRESENTS

FATHERS, SONS, AND BROTHERS

Bret Lott

Coming soon in trade paperback from
Pocket Books

The following is a preview of
FATHERS, SONS, AND BROTHERS. . . .

In the Garage

This is the last room: the garage.

We've been in the new house more than a month already, each day thus far filled with putting away all we own, each day filled with trying to find order in chaos. This is our dream house, after all, the one for which we bought the lot, the one we helped design, the one we plan to see filled with our lives and our children's lives here in South Carolina, so putting things in their just and proper places once and for all seems only right.

We—Melanie, my wife, and our two boys, Zeb, age ten, and Jacob, age seven—live a five-minute walk from the tidal marsh along the Wando River, where these spring evenings we can stand and watch the sun set behind Daniel Island, the sky above us reflected on the river to form a wide and shimmering band of blue and red and magenta, and where we can watch slender stalks of yellowgrass and saw grass and salt-marsh hay sway with the movement of the tide. A ten-minute bike ride takes us to the clubhouse, perched on the edge of the Wando, and the swimming pool there, and the marina, where on a quiet morning you can hear the breeze off Charleston Harbor gently rattle the halyards on the sailboats, the rhythmic metal tap on the masts like some impatient dream of open seas, full sails billowing.

Already there are three forts in the surrounding woods to which the boys can retreat; already there is talk of signing them up for the club's swim team. At breakfast we've seen out the bay window everything from pileated woodpeckers to Carolina wrens; yesterday morning, when I took the dog out to get the paper, there stood a doe in the empty lot next door, only to dart, at the sight of our Lab, for the woods at the end of the street.

We're home.

But the garage. No matter how crisp and ordered the inside of the house, no matter how many empty and flattened boxes piled up outside the kitchen door, a house is not a home, at least in my mind, until the garage has been put together. It's only a rudderless ship set for sail, a freshly waxed and gleaming car up on blocks, a perfectly detailed map with no true North. That's what I think, anyway, though I know that if I were to tell this to my wife, she'd only shake her head, let out an exasperated sigh.

"Men," she'd say.

• • •

I sit on the bottom step of the stairs down into the garage and survey it all, this endless mass of material goods we've accrued: a two-car garage piled haphazardly with boxes, yard tools, Zeb and Jake's outside toys and sports equipment; and the camping equipment, recycling bins, bicycles, lawn mower, more boxes. A thousand items, all ready and waiting for me, and though I have no clue as to where to start, still my heart shines at the prospect of the job before me, as though by putting it all away I will become a better husband, a better father, a better *man*.

My father, I know, would have thrown as much of it out as he could. His garage was always a lean, pristine place, and it seems now, on this Friday I've cleared for the express mission of setting up the garage, that throwing things out is the way to begin. Separating the wheat from the chaff, as it were.

I stand, go to the mounds of our belongings on the left side of the garage, and pick up the first victim: an old and holey garden hose I've been meaning to repair for the last year or two. But now the truth rises in me, ugly and incriminating: I'd rather just buy a new one than seek out the pinhole leaks and replace the hardware at either end, and so I toss the hose out the side door, the one that leads off into the backyard. So begins, if in a heartless way, my association with my garage.

• • •

My father was a man of few words, and even fewer tools. What I remember of the first garage I ever knew was that it was a dark and windowless place: tar paper and bare studs, open rafters above. This was back in Buena Park, California, in a tiny stucco tract house where we lived from the time I was two until I was nine, and I can remember, too, the small Peg-Board above the workbench at the back of the garage. On it hung one hammer, one hand saw, and two screwdrivers, a Phillips-head and a flathead. That was it.

Sure, there must have been other stuff somewhere in there, but back then garage paraphernalia wasn't important to me. What was important was that after Saturday yard work, we three boys finally done pulling weeds along the fence in the backyard, my dad would hose out the entire garage, giving the concrete floor a slick sheen, a temptation too great for us. Brad, Tim, and I had no choice but to take turns running as fast as we could along the asphalt driveway, then jumping flat-footed onto that cement, blasting from pure California Saturday-morning sunlight into the black garage to slide barefooted as far as we could, arms out like surfers' for balance.

And of course my mother forbade our doing this, hollering from the front porch each Saturday about broken arms and concussions. But my father only shook his head at us, gave what we supposed was a smile, then set about sweeping out the water, his garage once more pristine, every item in its place, we boys sliding and laughing and falling and laughing again.

But when I was nine, my father was transferred, and we moved from Buena Park to Phoenix, a place so strange and alien it might have been another planet: saguaro cactus as decorative landscaping, snakes sunning themselves on warm driveways at daybreak, coyotes rooting through the garbage cans.

And nobody had garages.

Instead, we all had carports, open-air structures under which you simply parked your car. Gone overnight was the sense of mystery about the garage, the dark and cool of it, the bare studs and tar paper replaced with eight painted wooden posts holding up a roof.

Though there were still weeds to be pulled, there was no grass to be mowed; instead people had gravel yards, and my father had us out there every Saturday morning raking the gravel into careful, thin lines while he swept the driveway. Gone were the days of slick and wet concrete, the hose replaced by a push broom. This was the desert; hosing down the carport was a frivolous waste of water.

We lived there until I was sixteen, seven years that saw momentous changes in the life of our family: We three brothers entered our teen years and splintered up, Tim, the youngest, following in my dad's foot-prints, raking the gravel in a manner that would, later in my life, remind me of Japanese rock gardens; me, the middle boy, burrowing into books and band; and Brad, the oldest, falling in with the wrong crowd, turning rebel, finally dropping out of high school his senior year to join the navy.

I can't help but think that, somehow, this loss of a garage had something to do with it. Back in California, we three boys used the garage as a haven from Mom and Dad, built extravagant forts of blankets and chairs and the grille of our '62 Dodge once Dad got home, the engine warm and ticking beside us. In that garage we rode our bikes in endless figure eights all summer long, passed time in the cool dark; in that garage we gave each other practice swats with the Ping-Pong paddle, the three of us having put on two pairs of pants and three pairs of underwear apiece, all in antic-ipation of what was to come once Dad got home and Mom told him of how we'd raided the garage refriger-ator, had eaten every Kool-Pop and Fudgsicle and even the watermelon that afternoon.

It was in that garage that we became, it only occurs to me now, *brothers*.

There is no *there* there in a carport, no sense of place other than one to park the car in; instead of rid-ing bikes in the cool dark of a garage all summer long we stayed indoors, where it was air-conditioned, and watched *Gilligan's Island* reruns until we could guess the episode before the opening credits were over. We took our swats without the luxury of practices with the Ping-Pong paddle, forced to gauge solo how many layers to wear, Mom too nosy and poking her head into our bedrooms whenever we attempted mock tribunals. We tried building our forts in the living room, but the lack of the engine's tick and the absence of the dangerously sweet smell of gasoline revealed to us the sad truth of our improvised architecture: Here were only chairs, here were only blankets. No wonder, then, we each broke for our own lives.

By the time my father was transferred back to California when I was sixteen, we brothers were as good as strangers: Brad somewhere in the South Pacific on the first of his three SEAPAC cruises, Tim attending the new high school, Shadow Mountain, me the old one, Paradise Valley, this split a result of overdevelopment of the area and the opening of a new district. I was first tenor in the jazz ensemble, Timmy a hack tuba player. We three bore nothing in common, though I suppose, of course, it was inevitable, this splintering up; all of us, for better or worse, grow up and away.

Then, literally overnight, there we were, once again in a stucco tract home in Southern California, though this one was bigger, closer to the ocean. More importantly, we had a garage once again.

Saturday mornings we two remaining boys helped with the yard: Tim with a religious fervor that would later find its release in the opening of his own landscaping business, me with the begrudging attitude of the unjustly persecuted. I was a sixteen-year-old who only wanted to live back in Phoenix, where his friends were, no matter the carports or gravel yards. While my dad, oblivious as far as I could tell, only hosed out the garage.

I was a hayseed from Phoenix dropped square in the middle of the surf capital of America: Huntington Beach, California. Timmy was now at the same school with me, though I acted as though I didn't know him, a freshman. I still wore bib overalls and flannel shirts just like everyone else back at Paradise Valley, even when I was surrounded by longhaired blond surfers, male and female alike, wearing Hawaiian shirts turned inside-out, corduroy shorts, and thongs. Timmy took on that disguise with ease, shucking his overalls for colorful rayon hula girls and those shorts in a move that further distanced him, the traitor, from my peripheral vision. Finally band, my refuge back in Arizona once we boys had made our split, turned its back on me: I couldn't even make the band at Huntington Beach High because, the director quietly explained to me my first day there, their jazz ensemble was going on tour the next month, and everyone had had to sell cheese in order to go, and since I hadn't sold any cheese I couldn't truly expect to be included in the trip to Modesto, now could I?

So my days were spent inside a funk of the first degree, me silent save for the muted grunts around the dinner and breakfast tables, a shorthand of squelched anger at my parents, at my little brother, even at Brad. Nowhere to be seen, he was somehow nonetheless implicated in my getting shafted by the world.

Then one morning a month or so after we'd moved, my father of few words nudged me awake in the predawn dark of my bedroom, and I opened my eyes to see him above me, a silhouette against the light from the hallway, there, in his business suit, briefcase in hand, faceless for the dark. As every weekday morning of my entire life, he was dressed and ready to walk out the door before daylight, and I remember sitting up in my bed, rubbing my eyes, then looking up at him again, wondering what the heck had made him wake me.

"Read this," he said, and handed me an index card.

I took it, then reached with my other hand to the desk beside my bed, put on my glasses. I blinked a few times, held the card so that I could read it in the light from the hallway behind him. On the card was typed the words, "God grant me the serenity to accept the things I cannot change, the courage to change the things I can, and the wisdom to know the difference."

"Someone gave it to me at the office," he said. He

was quiet a moment, then said, "He heard me talking about you to one of the guys. Thought you'd appreciate that." He paused again, then turned, headed for the hall. He stopped once he was out there, and now I could see his face, could see his eyes on me, his middle son.

He was the man who'd looked at us three boys lined up on the living room couch in our protective layers of clothes that day we'd raided the garage refrigerator, only to pierce us each with his eyes and say in a voice so strong and solid we'd had no choice but to obey: "Boys. Don't do that again." He was the same man who parked the Dodge just so, one or another of us directing him into the garage like a ground-crewman for a DC-8, him setting the brake and smiling, shaking his head while he climbed out of the car, we three already setting up the chairs, unfolding the blankets.

He was the same man who, on Saturday mornings, worked the hose inside our garage, the man who seemed to smile while our mother hollered, we boys having no choice but to run for the cement, blast from pure California Saturday-morning sunlight into the black garage, then slide barefooted as far as we could.

I looked at the index card, then back at him. I said, "Thanks." I paused, shrugged, a little stunned at this moment of help offered by a man of so few words. "Thanks," I said again.

He gave again what I supposed was a smile, then headed down the hall to the stairs, turned out the light. I lay back in bed, heard a few moments later the slow groan of the garage door as my father pulled it open, a sound I almost never heard for the fact I was usually stone asleep this time each morning. I heard the car start, heard it back out. Then came the same slow groan, the cold twist and strain of metal springs, as he eased the garage door closed.

We have survived. Brad is a carpenter in Sequim, Washington, where he lives with his wife and their two daughters. Tim designs and sells wooden playground equipment, those huge structures you see in city parks all over the country, and lives with his wife and son and daughter not three miles from our parents' house in Huntington Beach. And I am a writer in South Carolina, a land so alien to Southern California and Phoenix, Arizona, it might as well be another planet. I'm still stunned at a deer in the yard next door, at woodpeckers and wrens out the breakfast-nook bay window, at yellowgrass and saw grass and the shimmering face of a river at sunset.

And now, at a little after two on a Friday afternoon, the garage is finished. It's a different garage from that one in Buena Park, the walls here Sheetrocked and painted, the two windows that look out on the front lawn filling the place with light, no tar paper, no bare studs. To the right I've stacked a box filled with bats and badminton rackets and the volleyball net, another packed with baseball gloves and various Nerf balls, Rollerblades, and radio-control cars. Above it all I've nailed a metal rack for yard tools: two shovels, two spring rakes, a push broom, and an edger.

To the left are the boxes of gardening paraphernalia, my wife's obsession: hand shovels and garden hose fixtures, sprinklers and sprayers, fertilizers and insecticides and empty terra-cotta pots, all waiting for her gentle hand. Next comes the electric blower, next to that my Weedwacker, next to that the lawn mower. There sits my toolbox, the small gray plastic one; inside it a couple of screwdrivers, a tape measure, a small socket set.

That's it for my tools. Like father, like son.

I'm planning on building a workbench in here, planning to hang a Peg-Board above it to give a home to those tools. Eventually I'll build shelves in here, too, and place these boxes on them so that on Saturday mornings, after the lawn is done, I can hose the place down and teach my boys the finer points of garage sliding. But not before I buy that new hose, the one to replace the holey one buried beneath the discard pile outside, a pile so high I know I've done my father proud.

It's time now for me to pick the boys up from school, Melanie having gone for groceries, and I step out of this pristine garage, this newly waxed hot rod finally off the blocks, this map of my life finally given its own true North. Time, too, to make some phone calls this evening: one to Washington to talk to a carpenter, one to a man who designs toys for kids like my own. And one to a man of few words, even fewer tools.

I stand back from my garage, hands on hips, to survey it all, then reach to the garage door above me, take hold the handle, and pull it closed.

Look for
Fathers, Sons, and Brothers
Wherever Books
Are Sold.
Coming Soon in Trade Paperback
from
Pocket Books.